Praise for Cheryl Williford and her novels

"A breath of fresh air."
—*RT Book Reviews* on *The Amish Midwife's Courtship*

"Well done and will have you rooting for a [happily-ever-after]."
—*RT Book Reviews* on *The Amish Widow's Secret*

Praise for Kit Wilkinson and her novels

"An engaging, well-paced tale."
—*RT Book Reviews* on *Lancaster County Target*

"Plenty of action, a heartwarming love story and a good mystery make this a compelling read."
—*RT Book Reviews* on *Protector's Honor*

"This excellent story builds an intriguing mystery around a developing romance in the fascinating world of competitive steeplechase."
—*RT Book Reviews* on *Sabotage*

Cheryl Williford and her veteran husband, Henry, live in South Texas, where they've raised three children and numerous foster children, alongside a menagerie of rescued cats, dogs and hamsters. Her love for writing began in a literature class, and now her characters keep her grabbing for paper and pen. She is a member of her local ACFW and CWA chapters, and is a seamstress, watercolorist and loving grandmother.

Kit Wilkinson lives in the heart of Central Virginia, where she works full-time as a French and English teacher and overtime as a mother of two. A graduate of the University of Virginia and the University of Tennessee, Kit loves to study, learn and read. She finds through writing she is able to do both with a purpose, while creating something new in the process. You can visit her website at www.kitwilkinson.com.

CHERYL WILLIFORD

Her Secret Amish Child

&

KIT WILKINSON

Lancaster County Reckoning

H **HARLEQUIN**® LOVE INSPIRED®
™

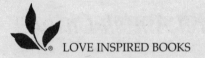

LOVE INSPIRED BOOKS

Recycling programs for this product may not exist in your area.

ISBN-13: 978-1-335-08021-9

Her Secret Amish Child and
Lancaster County Reckoning

Copyright © 2018 by Harlequin Books S.A.

The publisher acknowledges the copyright holders of the individual works as follows:

Her Secret Amish Child
Copyright © 2017 by Cheryl Williford

Lancaster County Reckoning
Copyright © 2017 by Kit Wilkinson

www.Harlequin.com

Printed in U.S.A.

CONTENTS

HER SECRET AMISH CHILD

Cheryl Williford

I dedicate this book to my husband, Henry,
who endures endless hours of backstory and plot. To
my two daughters, Barbara and Susan. You make me
want to succeed. And to God, who gave me writing
when I needed a clear and untroubled path.
God bless ACFW's Golden Girls critique group.
Nanci, Liz, Shannon and Jan…you dear,
talented ladies make my job so much easier.

Fear not, for I am with you; Be not dismayed,
for I am your God. I will strengthen you,
Yes, I will help you, I will uphold you
with My righteous right hand.
                —*Isaiah* 41:10

Chapter One

Pinecraft, Florida—a midsummer afternoon

Had she made yet another mistake?

"Don't touch that seat again," Lizbeth Mullet said, stretching across her son's extended legs to wedge their carry-on bag in front of his small brown shoes, hoping to block his incessant movement.

Three times in the past hour Benuel had slapped or kicked at her when she'd scolded him. Each time she hadn't known what to do, how to change the overactive four-year-old boy's behavior. She knew what she wanted to do, what felt like the right thing to do, but her built-in insecurities held her back, forced her to doubt her abilities as a single parent. A torturous night without sleep and little to eat added to her misery.

"Pinecraft, Florida," the bus driver announced. With the flick of his wrist he turned the bus's steering wheel and headed off the highway to his designated stop.

Several people milled around the parking lot of the Pinecraft Tourist Church, waiting for loved ones to arrive. With her father running late, no one would be waiting for her and the boy. They'd left Ohio in secret, telling no one except her father they were leaving or where they were going. There would be no going back. Her late husband's family could not hurt them now.

The Amish and Mennonite people scattered throughout the Pioneer Trails bus began to reach under seats for bags and wake up sleeping children.

Memories of the quaint little resort town she once called home beckoned. Pinecraft Park was on her right, and her father's prosperous chicken farm a few miles down the road, on the outskirts of the small town of Sarasota. She had grown up in this community of Old and New Order Amish people. This is where she belonged. *Gott* willing, she would heal and regain her strength here, around the people who knew her best and loved her.

Scrambling to gather up their belongings while trying to keep Benuel from climbing over her legs and escaping, Lizbeth tucked his bag of toys under her arm and scooped up their satchel from the floor.

"I want my car," he demanded, grabbing for the toy sack.

Standing, Lizbeth put out her hand and forced a smile she didn't feel. "Not now, *soh*. When your *Grossdaddi* comes for us I'll find it for you."

"I'm thirsty." Tall like her and lightly dotted with ginger freckles across his nose, he allowed her to take his hand after a moment of debate and shuffled by her side to the front of the bus. He touched each seat as he passed, counting aloud. "One, two, three."

"That's very good," Lizbeth encouraged. Early on Benuel had showed signs of being slow with numbers and letters. Perhaps his developmental delay had been caused by the long, painful labor she'd endured, but she noticed he'd come out of his shell some since her husband Jonah's death and was beginning to respond to her positive encouragement.

Taking the bus driver's extended hand, Lizbeth stepped down into the sultry heat of the cloudless summer day. She had missed the smell of the sea.

Benuel hopped down each step. His eyes darted around, the enthusiasm in them making her grin. He'd spent too many hours on the farm and was seldom with children his age. Seeing only her husband's family had left him shy and unsocial and sometimes angry, but today he looked different, ready to conquer the world.

"Do you have more bags on the bus, ma'am?"

Lizbeth nodded and let go of Benuel's hand as she dug through her purse for the silver ticket she'd been given when she'd relinquished their larger suitcase back in Ohio. Blond hairs escaping from her crushed prayer *kapp* blew around her face. "Yes. A small one, but I'd like to pick it up a bit later when my *daed* arrives, if that's all right. He warned me he'd be running late."

"Sure. You hold on to that ticket and come get it inside the church when you're ready." He tipped his head. "Thanks for riding Pioneer Trails."

She turned to make sure Benuel was at her side, found him gone and held back a groan. He was nowhere to be seen. Twisting back and forth, she searched the remaining cluster of people standing close by and then saw movement near a row of picturesque shops on her right. Her heart began to pound against her breastbone. It was Benuel, and he was running.

Forgetting to breathe, she chased after him, her black lace-up shoes slapping hard against the hot pavement.

Fear pushed her forward. She had to catch him before he made it to the street and oncoming traffic. He had no fear of roads. His experience with the small-town streets of Iris, Ohio, could be counted on one hand. Someone had always been holding on to him, directing his path. But not now.

"Benuel James, stop!"

Startled by her shout, a swarm of shiny black grackles took flight and made their way to treetops across the street.

She quickly crossed the shop's parking lot and pushed off the curb, fear building and twisting her stomach into knots. She couldn't lose Benuel, too.

Her son rushed on, laughing, his reddish-blond hair blowing in the breeze, blissfully unaware of the danger he was in.

Crossing the road, Benuel's body mere inches from her grasp, she glanced both ways as she sprinted close behind him.

Sunrays reflected off the silver scooter approaching. Her heart skipped a beat, uncertain she could reach Benuel before it was too late. She ignored the blast of the scooter's horn and lunged forward, desperate to reach her son before the speeding scooter. Bent forward, she stumbled, but managed to grasp the back of Benuel's shirt as she went down.

Dread grabbed her by the throat. Hot, sticky air filled her lungs as she gasped for breath.

Please, Gott, please. Don't let us be hit. She pulled his squirming body close to hers and rolled.

The whirr of the scooter's motor and the screeching of the tires braking caused Lizbeth's body to tense. She held tight to her son and squeezed her eyes closed.

The raw sounds of scraping metal enveloped them and then stopped.

The fast-paced beat of her heart hammered in her ears, her chest, ticking off the seconds.

Close by, birds squawked high in the trees lining the road, and then all was silent.

What had happened?

Afraid to look, she slowly opened her eyes.

Heat shimmered off the deserted two-lane road where they lay. She scrambled up and searched her son's body for injuries.

A startled expression widened Benuel's sky blue eyes. She hugged him close and whispered, "You're fine. Don't be frightened, *soh*." He seemed unharmed, with the exception of an insignificant graze on his left elbow, no doubt caused from being pulled down on the hot asphalt.

Her breath came fast. She had to force herself to calm down. The boy didn't need to see her fear. He'd had enough trauma in his young life. He was her only living child and so precious to her. What if *Gott* had snatched him away, too? How would she have lived?

She placed him on his feet and watched for signs of pain, but saw none. Relieved, she crushed him to her and cooed as if he were a baby. "My sweet boy. *Mamm* loves you."

"You're hurting me," Benuel squealed, the flat of his hands pushing her away.

Lizbeth sighed with relief. She was upset. Not her son. It had been an adventure to him. "I'm sorry, *liebling*. I didn't mean to squish you." She forced a smile, tried to look normal.

The midday sun beat down on them, penetrating her

starched white *kapp.* Sweat beaded on her upper lip. The wrecked scooter had to be somewhere close by.

She grabbed Benuel's wrist and urged him out of harm's way, to the side of the road where a ragged palm tree's fronds rustled in the breeze.

A few feet away, a row of blossoming bushes nestled against sturdy privacy fencing. She scanned under them, and then along the curb where several cars and adult tricycles were parked. The silver scooter had to be nearby. *I know what I heard.*

But there was nothing. No scooter. No rider.

"Look at that man, *Mamm,*" Benuel said. "He's sleeping on the ground."

Lizbeth glanced in the direction her son pointed. "Oh, no." Hidden behind a parked car, a ginger-haired man dressed in traditional Amish clothes and black boots lay sprawled across the sidewalk a few yards away. The silver scooter teetered on its side a foot from him, its back wheel still spinning.

Benuel's hand clasped firmly in hers, she hurried over, pausing long enough to instruct her son in a trembling voice, "You stay right here."

His bottom lip puckered. "But I want to see."

Releasing his hand, she said, "I know you do, but stay put, please." Dreading what she might see, she fell to her knees in front of the man's prostrate body and gave him a quick once-over, searching for twisted limbs and blood. He groaned and then stirred, his single status clearly stated by his clean-shaven chin that scraped the rough sidewalk as his head turned in her direction. Dirt and grit smudged his face and neck.

Why is there no one left on the street? I need help, Gott.

"Lie still. You may have broken something," she instructed.

His hand moved and then his arm. Blue eyes—so like her son's—opened to slits. He blinked at her. A shaggy brow arched in question. Full, well-shaped lips moved, but no words came out.

She leaned back in surprise. She knew this face as well as she knew her own. The man on the ground was Fredrik Lapp, her brother's childhood friend. The last man in Pinecraft she wanted to see. "Are you all right?" she asked, bending close.

His coloring looked normal enough, but she knew nothing about broken bones or head trauma. She looked down the length of his body. His clothes were dirty, but seemed intact.

The last time she'd seen him she'd been a skinny girl of nineteen, and he'd been a wiry young man of twenty-three, with shaggy auburn hair and blue eyes the color of a summer sky. Unbaptized and not yet a member of the church, he'd had an unruliness about him, a restlessness that kept his *mamm* and *daed* worried for his future, and the rumor mill turning with tales of his latest wild escapades.

Now he was a fully matured man, with a thick neck and neatly trimmed hair, cut in a traditional Amish style to his ears. A man who could rip her life apart if he learned about the secret she'd kept all these years.

She leaned in and eyed his clean-shaven chin. *Why is he still unwed and living in Pinecraft?* There were no significant scrapes on his face, with the exception of a small cut above his left eyebrow.

The sidewalk under him had to be uncomfortably hot. She jerked a length of attached quilt squares from her bag and squatted, carefully slipping the soft folds under his head.

He coughed several times and scowled as he drew in a deep breath.

"Do you hurt anywhere?" Lizbeth used her clean handkerchief to wipe away the blood slowly oozing from the small cut above his left eye.

"Ouch!" He twisted his head out of her reach.

She jerked her hand away and rose. "I thought the blood might blur your vision."

"Is the *kinner* all right?" Fredrik's voice sounded deeper and raspier than it had years ago. He coughed, and with a grunt braced himself with his arms and struggled into a sitting position.

Lizbeth glanced Benuel's way. He was looking at them, his young face pinched with concern. Her heart ached for the intense, worried child.

"*Ya*, he's fine," she assured him, and tried to hold Fredrik down as he started to move about. "Please don't get up. Let me get some help first. You might have really hurt yourself." He had no family left in the area. *Why had he come back?*

He ignored her direction and rose to his feet, dusting the long legs of his dark trousers down, and then bent to pick her fabric off the ground. He handed her the bundle after doing his best to refold the length of colorful cotton squares. "I got the wind knocked out of me, that's all." He laughed.

He peered at his bleeding arm, shrugged his broad shoulders and rotated his neck as she'd seen him do a hundred times as a boy.

"That was a foolish thing you did," he muttered, his brow arched.

"What was?" she asked, mesmerized by the way his muscles bulged along his freckled arm. It had to be wonderful to be strong and afraid of nothing.

He gestured toward the boy. "Letting your *soh* run wild like that? He could have been killed. Why didn't you hold his hand while you crossed the road?"

She took exception to Fredrik's sharp tone, the disapproving expression on his face. The knot in her stomach tightened and grew. She pushed the ribbon of her prayer *kapp* away and then wiped sweat from her top lip, her frustration growing. She may not know how to properly raise an energetic, belligerent boy, but she was learning and doing the best she could. How dare he chastise her like Jonah and his family had done so many times? "I know we could all have been killed."

Her face grew warm. If only she had been more careful, grabbed Benuel's hand as soon as she'd handed over the ticket to the bus driver. She knew what the boy was like lately. Acting out, not listening to anyone. She looked toward the curb. Benuel's head was turned away, no doubt watching the birds peck away at bugs in the short tufts of grass a few feet away.

With a grunt of frustration, she stuffed the bloodied handkerchief back into her apron pocket and dusted down her skirt. She hadn't been back in Pinecraft a full hour and already was involved in a situation with Fredrik. She had plans for the money she had on her, like paying for somewhere to live. If Fredrik blamed Benuel for the crash, repairing the scooter could leave her totally dependent on her father, and she could not allow that to happen.

"You'll need someone to come get you." She pointed at the crumpled machine on the ground. "It looks like that *Englischer* contraption of yours is ruined." Fredrik had always been a risk taker, never considering the cost to himself or those around him. She knew Benuel was equally to blame for the accident, but it would be just like Fredrik to blame someone else for his share of the mishap.

Fredrik's brows furrowed as he shoved his hand though his disheveled hair. He dropped his arm with a grimace. "That *Englischer* contraption, as you call it, was an expensive scooter. I saved for a year. Bought it less than an hour ago."

Lizbeth swallowed hard. She ran her hands down her arms, her nerves sending tremors through her body, no doubt her reaction to their near miss.

She twisted back toward the scooter. She knew all about men's "big boy" toys, thanks to her Amish *daed*, who prized all things with wheels and gears. This man was cut from similar cloth, but he lacked her father's love of *familye* and commitment to this small community. No doubt he had once again set aside his Amish beliefs to fulfill some foolhardy need for speed.

"I was on my way to the insurance company," he grunted. He turned his broad back on her.

She watched him glance down the empty road shimmering with watery mirages.

He spoke to the sultry air around him. "I thought… what can happen? The insurance office is only a few blocks down the road. What a *bensel* I am."

"It's not insured then?" She stepped back, waited for his reply while gulping down a knot the size of her fist.

He turned back to her, his brow furrowed. "*Nee*, not insured."

* * *

Fredrik Lapp didn't know whether to laugh or cry at his own stupidity, not that he wasn't used to making rash decisions that managed to put him in a bad light. He should have made a call from the bike shop, gotten the scooter insured before he left the showroom. But no, he didn't want to be late for work and disappoint Mose Fischer, his boss, who firmly believed in punctuality. *And look what a mess I'm in now.*

With a glance, he calculated the damage to the scooter. The front tire looked flat, the frame slightly bent, the fender folded back where it had hit the metal street pole. No telling what kind of scratches dug into the underside of the machine when it hit the ground.

He groaned aloud, but not from pain. The fancy front light he'd been so excited about, and special ordered, now hung suspended in the air by a single black wire. He'd be out hundreds of dollars for restoration and the scooter's odometer didn't read a mile.

He looked over at the ginger-haired boy with freckles across his button nose and instantly felt contrite, regretting his immature, self-centered thoughts. The boy looked to be young, maybe five or six. Fredrik's heart flip-flopped, the rhythm of the beat kicking up as he realized he might have killed the *kinner* with his carelessness. But the boy had been at fault, too. He should have been holding his mother's hand.

The boy's mother, a tall willowy woman dressed in mourning black, stood next to the child, her protective arm around her son's thin shoulders. *She's protecting him from me.* He silently asked *Gott* for forgiveness. He could have taken a life.

The woman's arched brow told him she didn't believe

she and her son had caused the accident, even though she hadn't uttered a single word of accusation toward him. She didn't have to. He knew he'd also made an error in judgment and driven too fast.

Instead of enjoying the exhilaration of speed, he should have been watching the traffic more closely, paying attention to what he was doing. This was no golf cart or three-wheeled bike. He had no experience on a scooter. No idea how to control the metal machine.

Perhaps this was *Gott*'s punishment for him buying such a fancy scooter in the first place. The idea of fast, dependable transportation had made all the sense in the world while looking at the showroom's catalog a year ago. "I'm sorry. I don't know your name," he said, glancing at the widow.

"Mullet. Lizbeth Mullet. And this is Benuel." She nodded briskly, her thin fingers nervously rubbing the side of her son's neck.

Her crooked *kapp* had bobbed on her blond head when she nodded. There were laugh lines etched in her cheeks, but no smile appeared today. He realized she looked slightly familiar, like someone he should know, but he couldn't place her. A lot of snowbirds and Plain people visited the tourist town of Pinecraft, even during the summer months, but she could easily be someone he'd been introduced to at church or met at work.

He glanced over at the fidgeting, serious-faced child and then back to the woman. Sweat curled the fine hairs at the nape of her neck.

Not sure what to do, he extended his hand to her. "My name's Fredrik Lapp. I hope I didn't scare you too much." At first he thought she would ignore his gesture, but then her hand was placed in his. It was soft and looked fragile, even though she wasn't a diminutive woman and stood nearly as tall as him. He felt the power of her grasp, the hidden strength in her, but she was trembling and he was to blame.

An arrow of pain shot through his shoulder and he winced. As she held his gaze, one perfectly arched brow lifted. She inspected his face with probing eyes the color of his *mamm*'s blue-violet periwinkles. A pretty woman, he realized. Someone who would fit fine on his list of women to step out with—if he seriously decided to look for a *fraa*.

Her frown deepened. "Are you certain-sure you're fine?" she asked. "You've gone all washed out. Perhaps you should go to the hospital, be checked by an *Englisch* doctor. I've heard a person can have brain damage and not know it until it's too late."

"*Nee*, it wasn't my head that hit," he said with a laugh and rubbed his shoulder like a child might. "The scooter's front bumper took the impact. I just got the wind knocked out of me when I landed."

"Even so, shouldn't the police be called? It was an accident, and they'll want you to make a report, or do whatever is required."

Fredrik considered her words. He probably should, even though calling would probably cost him a traffic ticket. "*Ya*, you're right. I'll call them now." He gestured toward a café's front door and motioned her forward. "Come in with me. It's too hot to be standing on the sidewalk. I don't know about you, but a glass of sweet tea sure sounds *gut* to me."

Chapter Two

Inside, the café pulsed with life. The lunch crowd of local Amish and Mennonite folks, with some summer tourists sprinkled in, blended into a loud, but happy, sea of faces.

Still shaking, Lizbeth followed a waitress in and ushered Benuel into the small booth upholstered in cheap red leather. Fredrik flopped down across from them a few moments later, making himself comfortable as he ordered a glass of tea and one of the cook's famous sweet rolls.

"What would you two like? Sweet tea, a Coke?"

"We'll have ice water, *danki*," she answered, watching Fredrik's face. She searched for and found the bump on his nose. She'd caused the break when she'd thrown a basketball at him years ago.

She relaxed. He still didn't seem to recognize her, but there was no reason he would. She'd been dishwater blond as a teen, and full of life. Nothing like the rake-thin, ordinary, mouse-blond woman she'd become, with her unremarkable face that drew no second glances.

"Can I have Coke?" Benuel blurted out.

She gave her son a warning look. He shouldn't be asking for treats. Not after running off. Unsure, she fought an inner battle, trying to decide whether to be hard on the troubled child and not knowing when to hold firm to her convictions. She hadn't been allowed to discipline Benuel in any way while her husband was alive. He or his mother always stepped in, took control of the boy. Punished him for her mistakes.

Benuel's hopeful expression vanished. His forehead took on a sulky frown. She reached to pull him closer, but he pushed away with a grunt of annoyance.

"My treat," Fredrik offered.

She looked across the table at Fredrik. His grin was easygoing, relaxed. "*Danki*, but *nee*. He has to learn to obey."

Fredrik made a face at the boy, his nose crinkling up in a comical way. Benuel giggled slightly and then ducked his head. Silence had been a firm rule enforced by Jonah and his parents back in Ohio. Children should be seen and seldom heard. Especially *her* child.

Lizbeth watched the all-too-familiar lift of Fredrik's brow, the way his lips curved as he laughed at Benuel's reaction to his teasing. His smile revealed a tiny chip on his front tooth. He'd fallen his last summer in Pinecraft. He'd chased her, trying to get his straw hat from her hand, and slipped on wet stones.

"How about some pancakes with strawberries? They're my favorite. Come on, *Mamm*. Let the boy enjoy life."

He had no idea the inner conflict she endured, the indecisiveness she fought regarding Benuel's discipline. Her reply came out harsher than she intended. "I *am* letting the boy enjoy life. Benuel's being disciplined for running away and can't have sweets right now. He'll be having plain food for the rest of the day as his punishment."

The bell over the café door rang. Lizbeth glanced over and then jumped up, rushing into her father's waiting arms.

"I've been looking all over for you, girl," John Schwarts scolded, but gave his daughter another tight hug that spoke of his love for her. "You should have waited at the church. I told you I'd be a bit late."

"I'm sorry, *Daed*. It got so hot. We came in for a quick cold drink of water." She looked at Fredrik over her father's shoulder and saw a glimmer of recognition in his eyes. He finally knew who she was. *Something to worry about later*, she thought, lowering her gaze.

Her cheek nuzzled against her father's barrowed chest as she listened to the sound of him breathing, the beat of his heart. It had been five long years since she'd left the safety of his arms. It was good to be home.

"It's no matter," he responded, as he slid in beside Fredrik. "So, what are you doing here? I thought Mose told me you were working early today."

Fredrik had the decency to look a little embarrassed. He glanced over at Lizbeth.

She gently shook her head, praying he wouldn't say anything about their near accident. She already had Fredrik thinking she was a bad *mamm*. She didn't need her *daed* thinking it, too.

"I was…ah…am working early today. I just thought I'd stop and get a cold glass of tea first," Fredrik stammered, pulling his summer hat off and setting it on his lap. "Lizbeth was kind enough to share a booth with me. It's pretty busy in here."

The waitress hurried over and interrupted the men's

chatter. Lizbeth took a deep, calming breath. Her *daed* looked good. His new wife, Ulla, must have been taking fine care of him.

John smiled his grandson's way. "So this is Benuel. How are you, *soh*?"

Benuel frowned and then looked away, all the while tapping his fingers on the table. "I'm not allowed to speak to strangers," he muttered.

Lizbeth patted her *daed*'s hand. "He'll warm up. It'll just take him a while."

"*Ya*, sure. I understand. You were always a bit stand-offish with strangers at his age. We'll get to know each other at the chicken farm, won't we, Benuel?"

Benuel ducked his head, his ginger-colored hair falling in his eyes as he nodded slightly.

Fredrik spoke up, ending the awkward moment. "You going to work at the church tomorrow, John?"

"Certain-sure, I am. That roof's leaking like a sieve when it rains."

Lizbeth took the glass of water handed to her by the waitress, slid Benuel's water to him and watched her father's face light up as he talked about future church repairs with Fredrik.

It was so good to be back home. Her *daed* had changed very little. Oh, he'd gotten some grayer, a bit more round at the middle, but he looked happy.

Benuel kicked her leg under the table. She flinched. "Drink your water, and keep your legs under you," she instructed, warning him with her eyes.

"He's as fidgety as those new roosters I bought." John laughed.

Lizbeth tried to act normal. Her father didn't understand, didn't know about Benuel's medical issues yet. She realized she'd have to tell him about the boy's ADHD issues, but now wasn't the time, not with Fredrik Lapp sitting there, listening to every word said. "He's a hyper young man, that's for sure," she said and pushed Benuel's water closer to him. She hoped she'd never have to tell her *daed* about the things she and the boy had seen and been through while in Ohio.

Benuel swished his hand across the table, knocking over the water glass. He smirked Lizbeth's way, rebellion written across his young face. "I'm sorry," he said, righting the glass as cold water and chips of ice streamed into her lap.

Fredrik watched Lizbeth's face redden, saw the way her hands shook as she grabbed napkins to sop up the spill. He still couldn't believe this woman was the Little Lizzy he'd grown up with. She'd changed. And here she was, back in town, with a rowdy little boy. Her son had knocked over the glass on purpose. Fredrik was sure of it, and he could tell John knew it, too. The older man's forehead was creased into an irritated scowl. Turning his head, he looked at the *kinner* closely. Benuel's expression had become calm again, almost serene. As if nothing had happened.

That boy needed a talking-to, but Fredrik could tell by the look on Lizbeth's face that she wasn't going to discipline him in front of his grandfather the first time they met. She'd leave it for another time. Poor woman looked exhausted and frazzled from her long trip home.

Fredrik grabbed the napkin under his water and helped Lizbeth clean up the mess. "Kids always seem to manage to spill their water," he reassured her with a smile.

"Ya," she muttered, picking up the last of the ice cubes scattered across the table. Her face still flushed with embarrassment. *"Danki*, Fredrik."

She looked at her father, her fingers twisting the wet napkin in her hand.

Fredrik watched the tiny blue vein in her neck pulse with tension.

"Benuel is often overactive, *Daed,"* she said, glancing at Benuel squirming in his seat. "But he's a *gut* boy."

"Ya, I know he is," John said, nodding. His smile was that of a patient grandfather who understood the ways of rambunctious boys.

Lizbeth visibly relaxed, her lips turning up at the ends. "I'm so glad to be home. Benuel needs a strong man like you in his life."

"Ya, well. You've got the whole town of Pinecraft at your disposal, *dochder.* We'll all pitch in. You're not alone."

Tears glistened in her eyes as she put her arm around her son and pulled him close. "I'm so glad, *Daed.* Change can be hard for Benuel. All he's ever known is the farm. Life's been difficult for him."

John smiled gently. His big calloused hand patted hers. "I'll go and grab your bag from the church. You can wait here until I get back." She handed a ticket to John and he nodded at Fredrik. "Don't be too late to work," he said with a smile.

Fredrik shook John's hand. "I'll see *you* tomorrow at the church. Make sure you wear your loose pants. The ladies are cooking for us."

John nodded. "I'll be there." And he walked to the door.

Fredrik turned back to Lizbeth and saw a slight smile on her face. "It's been years, and I know I've changed," she said, "but I'm assuming you've remembered me by now, Fredrik. I'm Little Lizzy, Saul's *schweschder.*"

Fredrik leaned toward her with a grin. "Of course I know who you are. I realized it as soon as you greeted your *daed.* Little Lizzy. I can't believe it. I'd heard you had married and had moved away while I was in Lancaster. Why didn't you tell me who you were as soon as we met?"

She shrugged her shoulders. "It didn't seem important. And I wanted to see how long it would take for you to remember. I knew it was you the minute I saw that ginger hair of yours and your broken nose."

He trailed his finger down the bridge, to the almost invisible bump, thinking of that day so many years ago. "*Ya*, and I remember who broke that nose. You had a mean pitching arm back then."

"I still do."

Fredrik glanced up and saw one of Sarasota's finest walk through the café door, the gun on his hip standing out in the crowd of Plain people and tourists. "The police officer is here. I've got to go. It was good to see you again, Lizbeth." He stood and pulled her to his side in a hug, his arm sliding around her slim waist.

Then he let her go and walked off, peeking over his shoulder at her one last time. She'd been the picture of calm since her father arrived. Her *daed* was what she needed. A strong man to lean on.

He walked toward the police officer, his heartbeat kicking up. He'd leave Lizbeth and the boy out of this situation. She had enough on her plate. Going by the shake of her head earlier, she wouldn't want to talk to the police right now anyway, not when her father could return at any moment. Could she have thought Benuel was at fault for the accident? If she did, she was mistaken. He knew he was to blame and would make sure the police knew it, too.

Chapter Three

The next morning, Ulla Schwarts glanced at the quilt top Lizbeth had been working on since sunrise, and smiled. "You've only been home a day and that top is almost finished." Bent at the waist, she swished a sudsy dishcloth across the big wooden farm table, reaching for and finding a spot of dried plum jelly that needed scrubbing. "You sew pretty fast."

"*Ya*, it came together quickly," Lizbeth agreed, looking up from her breakfast, over to her father and then his wife of one month. She smiled as the gray-haired woman wiped sweat from her forehead with the back of her hand, and then went back to cleaning the big wooden table positioned in the middle of her *mamm*'s well-loved kitchen.

Lizbeth already liked the spirited older Amish woman and found merit in her humor and work ethic. It would take some time to adjust to seeing another woman in her mother's *haus*, caring for her *daed*, even though years had passed since her *mamm*'s sudden passing.

"It's time I go check on the chickens," her father stated, then wiped egg off his mouth. His chair scraped the floor as he rose. He lightly kissed Lizbeth on the forehead. "I'm so glad you're back," he said for the hundredth time that morning.

Lizbeth smiled, joy warming her heart. "Me, too, *Daed*."

"You have any plans for today?" he asked.

"Nothing important," Lizbeth muttered, and grinned. She'd had a hard morning with Benuel and didn't have much energy left in her.

"I'm off then." John kissed his wife's cheek and whispered something in her ear that had her giggling as she swatted him out the back door with her dishcloth.

Still smiling, Ulla commented to Lizbeth, "There's a sewing circle that meets at the civic hall on Tuesday mornings if you have a mind to go." Ulla shoved a stubby water glass into the sea of dishwater and swished a cloth around in it.

Lizbeth gathered up her plate, coffee cup and the remains of her half-eaten bacon and eggs destined for the chickens' scrap bowl. "Does Berta King still go?"

Ulla shook her head and moved to clean the stove. "Not since the cancer took hold."

Lizbeth paused, her hand going to her heart. "I didn't know." The spry little woman had taught her to quilt and had been her mother's best friend and confidante for more years than she could remember. Berta had been there to wave her off when she'd quickly married and left Pinecraft five years before.

"*Nee*, you wouldn't, would you? Living so far away. I only see her when I take meals over on Tuesday and Friday nights. She looks bad. So thin and frail. Abram's not looking so good himself, poor man. Someone told me their daughter from Ohio is coming on the bus. She'll help out until her *mamm* passes, and then take her *daed* home with her."

"It's never *gut* to be alone." Lizbeth adjusted the work scarf on her head and then plunged her hands into the sink of hot soapy water. The water burned a small scrape caused by her fall in the street the day before.

She began scrubbing dried egg yolk off her plate. She had to find a way to make Benuel understand that roads were dangerous. Living in a busy tourist town held hazards he didn't understand at such a young age. It would take time and patience to guide him.

Perhaps she clung to him too tightly now that she had him all to herself. Benuel had always been easily distracted, but he had grown more willful of late, even cruel at times. She remembered the kick he'd given her under the booth the day before and sighed deeply. He needed a man's firm hand, but the thought of marrying again sent her pulse racing wild with fear. Not that any man in his right mind would want her as his *fraa* once he found out she was emotionally damaged.

And the last time she had married for her child's sake hadn't gone so well. What would she do if anyone discovered the truth about Benuel? It would ruin both of them.

There had to be another way to help him grow into a strong man without a father in his life. Perhaps settling down near her *daed* and the kind people of Pinecraft *would* bring about the stability he needed, as her father had suggested. At least she prayed that it would.

Ulla plugged in a portable electric fan and positioned it on the long wooden counter nearest her. "You'll need this if you're going to wash those breakfast dishes. The humidity is high. We must be expecting a storm."

"Danki," Lizbeth muttered and plunged in another yolk-covered plate.

Ulla hummed as she shuffled across the room, a stack of folded towels in her arms.

A glance out the kitchen window revealed threatening gray clouds. A gust of wind twisted two small palm trees to the ground.

The old German clock in the living room ticked away the remaining minutes of the morning. She rinsed her hands and rehung the dish towel on its wooden peg next to the window and then pressed her hands into the small of her back. A long, busy day stretched out in front of her and she had no energy left.

She had to talk to Benuel about his behavior at the breakfast table, and was dreading it. He'd poured milk on Ulla's clean tablecloth. He'd done it on purpose, even though her father claimed it had been an accident. All she seemed to do was scold the child, when all she wanted was to pull him onto her lap and hold him until his anger went away.

"So, you have nothing planned for your day?" Ulla came back into the room with a load of sheets ready to be washed. Her tone and smile were friendly and inviting, unlike the daily dramatic scenes that played out back in Ohio with her mother-in-law. She could never please the woman, no matter how hard she tried. And she had tried.

Lizbeth took in a deep, cleansing breath, her memories of Ohio pushed to the darkest recesses of her mind once more. She smiled. "I've got the usual. Keeping Benuel entertained and getting that quilt top finished after I make our beds."

Ulla paused under the kitchen's arched door. She

braced a wicker basket, fluffy with unfolded sheets, against her stomach. "We have church service tomorrow. I make it a practice to help with the cooking of the communal meal. You can join me if you like. It would give you a chance to get reacquainted with some of the ladies of the community."

Preparing the communal meal had been one of Lizbeth's mother's favorite chores. Being one of the volunteer church cooks was something Lizbeth could embrace now that she was back, not that she was a very good cook. Going along with Ulla would give Benuel a chance to play with children his own age. But doubt stalled her. "I don't know. He's such a handful today."

"*Ach*, don't let his acting up stop you from doing a good deed. You haven't met Beatrice, my oldest *kinskind* yet." Ulla laughed, her smile animating her wrinkled face with a glow. "Now that child is a certain-sure handful. She and her sister Mercy will be there." The woman's tone became serious. "Benuel needs the company of other *kinner*, Lizbeth."

Lizbeth's face flushed. He needed so much more than she seemed able to give him, but she would learn. "*Ya*, maybe I will come after all."

"*Gut*. I'll get this load of sheets folded and then we'll make a list for our trip to the store. I thought I'd make chicken and dumplings and a peanut butter shoofly pie. Is there anything special you'd like to make?"

Benuel had smashed his fist into the center of the last cake she'd baked, sending chunks of chocolate cake all over her mother-in-law's kitchen floor. "Maybe I'll make chocolate cupcakes for the *kinner*. Chocolate is Benuel's favorite."

Ulla laughed. "Beatrice and I have an understanding

when it comes to cupcakes of any flavor. She behaves and does what I tell her, or I get to eat hers. You might try that on Benuel. Missing a few cupcakes might bring about a bit of good behavior from the boy."

Lizbeth found herself smiling. "*Ya*, I might try that. *Danki*." Her smile grew. "You've been so kind to us since we arrived, Ulla. I want to thank you for opening your home, taking us in."

"Nonsense. This is your home, too. John and I are happy you moved back to Pinecraft, sudden or not." Ulla set the basket on the floor. "Having you here has been a blessing. But what's this John tells me about you already looking for a home of your own?"

"*Ya*, I am looking, not that you both haven't made us feel so very *willkumm*. It's just that Benuel needs to settle into a routine before school begins." Still so unsure of her parenting skills, she wasn't positive she would be putting him in school. She had to decide soon, but not today.

Ulla grinned as she flipped out a square tablecloth and shoved it into the washer. "I own an empty house that's up for sale and begging for a family to bring it back to life. It's simple and *Amisch* Plain, but not too far from here and close to the Christian school. If the local man who asked about it doesn't buy it, you're welcome to rent it until you marry again. We have a busy weekend, but John can show it to you on Monday."

"That would be *wunderbaar*. A simple house would be an answer to prayer," Lizbeth said, ignoring Ulla's comment about a new marriage. She had no intention of marrying again. It would be just her and Benuel from now on.

Surely the money she had squirreled away would be

enough to make rent payments until she could find a part-time job and someone safe to leave Benuel with. Maybe there would be enough left over for a few pieces of secondhand furniture. When they had left Ohio, she had taken nothing but their clothes and a few of Benuel's favorite toys. She pushed away her reasons for leaving the farm, unwilling to bring back the harsh memories that haunted her unguarded sleep each night.

Gott's will be done. He had brought them back to Pinecraft, to the Plain people she'd grown up with, and she was grateful to be home.

At noon on Monday, Fredrik leaned his old bike against an orange tree and turned on his heel, ready to begin his search for a wife in the crowd of Amish women standing around, chatting.

After seeing Lizbeth Mullet wearing a pretty blue dress at church the day before, and hearing two pastors preach on the joys of married life, he'd lost sleep that night, tossing and turning, but managed to make a firm decision. It *was* time to forget Bette, who had accepted his proposal and then run off and wed his best friend in Lancaster County, where Fredrik was completing his apprenticeship. He would buy Ulla's house and settle down. It shouldn't be too hard to find someone to marry him. Perhaps Lizbeth Mullet would consider him and if not her, someone else just as comely. Whoever he chose, though, would have to understand that theirs would be only a friendly partnership. An attempt at showing the community—and himself—that he could grow and become responsible. He'd never give another woman his heart after the way Bette had stomped on it.

The woman he married would have to be patient, accept him as he was. He wasn't exactly sure how much he could change his youthful ways, but almost killing a child had affected him deeply. It was past time he stopped behaving like a *youngie* and got on with his life.

He ambled across the dry park grass, over to the food tables and joined his boss, Mose. The square-shouldered Amish man greeted him with a nod of his head and then filled one side of his sturdy paper plate with fried chicken. He inched his way forward, toward a bowl of hot potato salad decorated with perfect slices of boiled eggs and olives.

"You're late. You almost missed out on my Sarah's specialty," Mose said, adding an extra helping of the creamy potatoes to his too-full plate. "It's almost gone."

"I see that," Fredrik smiled and took the last of the potato salad with a half-moon of boiled egg buried on top.

"You oversleep?"

Fredrik cleared his throat before speaking. "No, I had to pay a traffic ticket. No insurance."

Glancing back, Mose said, "Is this one of your yarns?"

Fredrik glanced up. "*Nee*, I'm not joking."

"Then what do you mean? The police don't give tickets for bike riding."

Fredrik lumbered close behind Mose, both men still circling around the table laden with food. "I wasn't exactly riding a bike." He reached across the table for three meaty ribs shining with barbecue sauce. He added a forkful of pickles as an afterthought and then speared a meaty chicken leg covered in crispy fried batter.

Together they headed for the drinks table, and stood in a line with community leaders and hardworking Plain men waiting for a cold glass of sweet tea. The big oak tree draped with moss spared them the bright overhead sun.

Fredrik had hoped to speak privately with Mose, but the park grounds were already packed with people supporting the lunch that would bring in enough money to pay for the new roof on the church.

Fredrik frowned, not liking the idea of someone from the congregation overhearing what a fool he'd been. In Pinecraft, simple situations were known to grow into full-blown gossip sessions, innocent words passed on from family to family until the truth could barely be recognized.

Balancing his tall glass of tea and a few napkins against his chest, Fredrik followed close behind Mose.

"What were you riding, a golf cart?"

"No, a scooter." He waited for the critical remark he knew was coming. Acting as his mentor and older brother, Mose had warned him about leaning too close to *Englischer* ways, but Fredrik had prayed about buying the scooter and *Gott* had remained silent. Fredrik had taken His silence as approval, and he'd been wrong.

"Were you speeding?" Mose's brow arched as he placed his glass of tea on a cloth-covered picnic table and slid his plate in front of it.

Fredrik joined him at the table and smiled at Sarah, Mose's *fraa*, as she kissed her husband fondly on the forehead, then hurried off, pushing a twin stroller of chubby *kinner*. A curly-haired toddler followed her, tugging at the back of her skirt. "Sarah's looking well rested. The twins must be sleeping through the night at last."

The big blond-haired man wasn't smiling. "Don't change the subject. You'll have to tell me sometime. Are you hiding a secret about this scooter you borrowed?"

"I didn't borrow the scooter. It's mine. I picked it up

the other day. That's why I was late to work." Fredrik took a gulp of tea and sat the sweating glass back on the table.

"*Ya*, well. You said you were buying one with your savings, but didn't you know you'd need insurance for the thing?"

Fredrik nodded. "I did know, but I got ticketed before I could get the insurance." He paused to pray silently over his food and then shoveled in a mouthful of potato salad and chewed as he thought back to the day of the accident. An image of the pretty widow came back to haunt him. If only he could get her and her son off his mind. He pictured them round-eyed with worried looks. Were they still traumatized by his stupidity? He hoped not.

"Well, it makes me to wonder if you should have prayed more about this magnificent piece of machinery of yours," Mose said after he'd prayed. "Perhaps *Gott* isn't pleased with your purchase and is letting you tie a rope around your neck." Mose flashed a sardonic smile that showed a piece of mustard green stuck to the front of his tooth. The man bent forward and went back to attacking his food.

"*Ya*, you might be right." Fredrik nodded. "Nothing *gut* has come from the purchase." The other side of their picnic table was still empty. Now was as good a time as any to speak to Mose. He blurted out the lines he had practiced. "You think there's any chance I could get a church loan for a down payment on Ulla's house?"

Mose laid down his fork. "*Ya*, sure. We have money set aside for such as this. Ulla's house would make a fine house for a young man like yourself. There's plenty of room for a *fraa* and *kinner*." He smiled, probably expecting his words to unsettle the unmarried man. "I'm sure she'll sell it to you. She has no use for it now. Let's walk over by the river and talk for a moment."

Throwing his paper plate into the trash for the flies to buzz around, Fredrik ambled alongside Mose, his mind racing.

Houses in Pinecraft seldom came up for sale since they were usually passed on from family member to family member. When they were put on the market, they were too dear for most young people. Perhaps Mose could convince Ulla to sell the house to him at a reasonable price.

"So, you're finally ready to marry," Mose said, stopping to sit at an old picnic table close to the river.

Fredrik followed his lead and sat. *"Ya."* He'd never experienced being tongue-tied in his life, but it seemed he couldn't get his words to untangle on his tongue to form a complete sentence. "I…" he said and hiccupped from a nervous stomach. He groaned silently and then plunged on, forcing the words out. "Before we talk about the loan, I need to tell you I had an accident on the scooter the first day it was mine." There! The words were out.

"My *daed* used to talk to me about his *bruder*, Thomas. Seems all his life my *onkel* liked all things fast. The *Englisch* ways appealed to him more than *Gott* and the church." Mose waved at his small blond son running past on short, dimpled knees.

Fredrik watched clusters of Amish and Mennonite people eating their meal. A cooling breeze blew across the park. Tablecloth edges flapped in the breeze like white sails at sea. A gull's sharp cry rang out overhead, perhaps predicting doom and gloom for Fredrik's project.

He got a quick glimpse of Lizbeth Mullet and Benuel

sitting with a crowd of women one table over. Today she was smiling and talking to her son in an animated way, the wind blowing lengths of her fine blond hair around the simple neckline of her yellow dress. Regret tightened his stomach once again.

"Church and *Gott* mean a lot to me. More than that scooter," Fredrik said, and swallowed hard. "I'll be thirty soon. It's time I settle down and get married."

"Have you found anyone suitable?"

"I've made a list of available women in the area." He laughed and glanced back at Lizbeth, wishing she was someone he could mention as a prospective *fraa.* "Ulla's sister is a matchmaker, and coming for a visit soon. If I can't decide on someone, I hope she'll help me find a woman from the surrounding communities while she's here."

"Have you considered Lizbeth Mullet? She's widowed now and could use a husband to help raise her *soh.*"

Fredrik wanted to admit he was considering her, but he had a feeling she'd never agree to stepping out with him. She just thought of him as her big brother's annoying friend. "Not really, but I will add her name to my list. Nothing ventured, nothing gained," he said with a smile. "Who knows? *Gott* might speak to her about me." A home and wife was what he needed, but could he find the right bride without allowing his heart to be broken again? He hoped so.

Chapter Four

Later that afternoon, Lizbeth hoisted the heavy green garbage bag out of the industrial-size plastic container and hastily placed it on the church's tiled kitchen floor. It was heavier than she'd anticipated, and made bulky by several plastic milk jugs she'd added to the jumble after making chocolate pudding. She tied the bag off, and with a grunt of determination, gathered her strength, lifted the burden and wrestled it to the back door.

Twisting, she turned the knob and hip bumped the sticking door open. Sunlight and a cool breeze poured into the sweltering kitchen.

Five narrow steps and a four-foot drop greeted her. *Great! Just what I need. More obstacles in my path.*

She glanced around and found a row of enormous black trash cans lined along the church. They were at least six feet away.

Six feet or six inches, she was going to get the trash into one of those cans if it took her the rest of the afternoon. Stubbornness fed her resolve. *I can do this.*

Positioned on the second step, her back to the yard,

she heaved the plastic bag up and then dropped it on the top stair.

"You need help with that?" a masculine voice asked from somewhere behind her. She recognized it was Fredrik.

"*Nee*, but *danki*." She shot a glance over her shoulder. Fredrik was bareheaded and wiping sweat from his brow with a colorful bandana.

"You sure?"

Doubt rang in his words and spurred her on. As a girl she'd had no defenses against his teasing, but infatuation didn't rob her of her voice now. "*Ya*, I'm sure. Go about your business, Fredrik. I can manage." Somewhere in her mind she knew she probably should accept the man's offer of help, but she shut out the voice of reason. She'd been controlled too many years, her choices taken away from her. This was her project. She had something to prove to herself. She'd get the bag of trash into one of the cans if it was the last thing she did.

With another grunt, she stepped down, lifted the oversize green bag and repositioned it on the second step. She heard Fredrik's muffled snicker and tensed. Her shoulders came back and her backbone went rigid. With trembling fingers, she straightened her work scarf, took a deep breath and prepared for the next step. She might not be as strong as the muscular man standing behind her, but she had determination that would carry her through to the end.

She grabbed hold of the bag, stepped down, her foot finding the edge of the narrow step.

Her stomach tightened into a knot as she swayed, fought to regain her balance and repositioned her foot. With another grunt, she jerked the bag up. It caught on the edge of the step and puckered. She tugged carefully. The slit formed and then grew. The bottom of the bag gave way with a rush.

There was no time to jerk her feet away. Trash covered her legs and the toes of her black shoes with a goopy mixture of tomato sauce and coffee grinds. Potato peels and an assortment of empty plastic containers fell through the stairs onto the dirt.

Lizbeth glared down between the stair's wooden slats to the growing heap of trash. Her *mamm*'s gentle words of reprimand echoed through her mind. *Pride is a sin, child. It will only bring you misery.*

"Here, let me help you with that." Fredrik came into view.

She noticed the ends of his ginger hair curled attractively around his light blue shirt collar. He was covered in sawdust and small wood chips. A smudge of roof tar told her he'd been working with the roofing crew she and the other ladies cooked for.

He reached for the bag, his hand covering the gash at the bottom as he eased it away from her.

She released her hold, not wanting his touch, and watched the muscles in his forearm bulge as he raised her burden as if it were weightless. She slipped him the fresh bag she had tucked in her apron pocket and watched as he lifted the trash can lid and chucked the bag in, wiping his hands down the front legs of his pants as he gave her a satisfied grin.

She stamped her feet against the wooden step, dislodging most of the coffee grounds from her shoe, but red sauce splotched her legs.

Heat suffused her face as she looked up and noticed the last of the kitchen staff standing in the open doorway, all smiles and giggles, watching her exchange with Fredrik with great interest.

Lizbeth cringed. Every time she turned around she was causing herself some kind of embarrassment, and somehow Fredrik always managed to be involved. "*Danki*. I appreciate your help, but I can clean the rest myself," she assured him.

One of the ladies tossed him a new trash bag. He squatted and began to work on the pile of trash under the steps. "This is my fault," he said, glancing up and grinning at her in the goofy way he had when he was a boy. The memory made her heart skip a beat.

"But I made the mess." She picked up a half-eaten apple off the step and tossed it into the bag.

Fredrik's grin spread into a full-blown smile. "*Ya*, but I was supposed to fix that raised nail this morning before it could cause someone trouble."

The past fell away and she was a girl of seventeen again, looking into the sparkling blue eyes of the young Fredrik Lapp. He continued to hold her gaze. She pulled her eyes away. The man was having too much fun at her expense. She didn't have a clue what to do about it or the ripple of emotions churning in her stomach. But she knew she couldn't let herself grow too close to him. Not this time. Too much was at stake.

An hour later Fredrik and six other men sat at the square table in the corner of the kitchen. Lizbeth refilled each man's glass with cold milk, accepted their thanks and then busied herself with the last of the pots and pans.

She listened to the deep hum of their conversation, not to eavesdrop, but to enjoy the sound of men talking in a friendly manner. She'd spent too much time alone on the farm in Ohio. And the only conversations she'd heard when her husband and his family were around had been harsh and ugly. She'd used the time to gather her thoughts and make life-changing decisions. Jonah's sudden death allowed her to act on her choices.

Memories of Jonah filled her mind. Lean, with plain, unremarkable features, he had been the only man she'd stepped out with after Fredrik had left Pinecraft without a word of goodbye. Always kind and gentle, Jonah's love for her had been evident in the way he'd talked to her and showed her respect at the start. And he'd been one of the few who knew the truth, knew of her sin. She'd thought he'd be willing to treat Benuel as his own son. But she'd been wrong. About everything.

In Ohio, where his family farmed, she'd found herself embedded in a hostile community of rigid Old Order Amish rules. The people lived bitter lives. The painful memories of Benuel's birth followed quickly by news of her mother's sudden death had put a fresh sting of unshed tears in her eyes.

After his birth, Benuel was taken from her and given to Jonah's mother, who'd just lost her youngest boy in a farming accident. Jonah had longed for sons of his own, children who would work the family farm with him in his later years.

And when Lizbeth got pregnant again, she'd thought he'd get his wish. But the babies died a few moments after their birth, born too early to survive. Jonah grew impatient with her as the years passed. She could still feel the sting of his words after their deaths. *Where are my sohs? You carry them in your stomach, but they die, gasping for air. What have I done to earn this punish-*

ment? You have brought sin into my home. Their deaths are your fault.

Deep inside, she knew Jonah was at fault for the loss of her twin sons. When he drank, his physical abuse had cost her much too much.

Lizbeth shoved a chocolate chip cookie loaded with walnuts into her mouth, eating out of taut nerves and not pleasure. She had to remind herself Jonah would never hurt her or Benuel again.

She submerged an oversize saucepan into the hot dishwater and began to scrub. Once again she relived the sound of the accident that took her husband's life. The terrible screech of tires, the scream of their horse.

Visions of the overturned buggy, the *Englischers'* car mangled and burning next to it. Her breath grew ragged. The terrible sights and sounds of that night were seared deeply into her memory. Jonah had been badly burned, his chest crushed by the weight of their dead horse. She could still see the sterile white hospital room where he later died, his suffering finally over. She'd disappointed him in every way imaginable.

The police later confirmed her suspicions. Her husband had been driving drunk the night of the accident, and their old mare, Rosie, was out of control and running wild when the *Englischers'* car hit the buggy.

She'd been too ashamed to admit she knew he had taken to drink to dull the pain of his lost sons. Jonah had lashed out at her earlier that dreadful night at the supper table. He'd screamed at her, told her she was useless. But she knew it had been the drink talking and she had forgiven him everything he'd said. Who could blame a man whose *fraa* could not give him more sons? Benuel had been a witness to the wreck, to her moments of insanity.

She glanced down at her trembling hands, at her little finger, once broken and now permanently twisted out of shape. A reminder of Jonah's fits of rage when her tiny boys were laid to rest in the cold ground. Dark memories surrounded her like a heavy shawl. She pushed the memories away and went back to work, her thoughts on Benuel. He mattered now. No one else.

The final pan scrubbed and rinsed, she placed it on a dish towel and leaned against the stainless steel sink, her eyes closed, pushing away all the misery, the memories of her past life with Jonah.

Her son had paid the highest price of all. He had no *daed* to follow around, no man to emulate, to show him how to grow strong. And it was her fault. She knew she had to do something. He needed a father, but she didn't want another husband, someone she would disappoint. No Amish man in his right mind would want a traumatized woman with the built-in ability to fail. Gott*'s will be done in Benuel's life.*

The scrape of a chair behind her caused her to turn. Fredrik moved toward the commercial-size refrigerator, his empty glass in hand. The other server had left the room moments before, leaving her alone with the last shift of workers. She jerked a square of paper towel from the roll and dried her hands. "Can I get you something?"

He stopped, turned toward her with a warm smile. "You're busy. I can pour my own milk."

"Would you like some ice in it?"

He quietly observed her. "Little Lizzy, I can't believe you remember I like ice in my milk."

"I'm the one who introduced you to it." She narrowed her eyes at him. "And I'm not so little anymore. Neither one of us is, Freddie."

"I still see your *bruder* as often as I can. I'm sure *he* still thinks of you as little."

Lizbeth found herself smiling at the mention of her older brother. "*Ya.* His two boys look just like him, ain't so?"

Fredrik nodded. "Remember those childish fights we used to get into? You were always such a pesky kid, hanging around, bothering us. Back then, Saul and I were convinced you were only born to annoy us."

He laughed again and Lizbeth felt her face and neck flush pink with warmth. When she was little, both boys had made it clear they didn't want her tagging along. Her young life had been full of merciless teasing. "*Mamm* made Saul take me along. I didn't want to go." Her mother's image impressed itself on her mind. The beloved woman had been tall and always too lean. She'd worn simple dresses of cotton made by her own hands. Lizbeth could almost hear her *mamm*'s words floating in the air around her. *Ya, Saul. You will take Lizbeth with you, or you won't go yourself.*

She gently edged her memories of her mother away, along with the pain of her loss. "*Mamm* always wanted me out from under her feet so she could clean or quilt with the ladies." She wiped at the side of the big fridge and opened the door, her thoughts back to her youth as she wiped down the rack where milk had been spilled. Her childhood feelings for the man standing next to her flushed her face warm again. She felt eleven years old again, longing for Fredrik to take notice of her. Embarrassment had her chatting again. "You boys teased me terrible when you took me fishing. You threatened to use me as bait."

"*Ya*, because you didn't know how to shut up." He

softened his words with a lopsided grin. "You were so skinny back then. I was always afraid you'd fall in the river and we'd have to fish you out."

She stood tall, almost eye to eye with him. With a mind of its own, her finger poked at his broad chest. "*Ya*, well. I never fell in and you didn't have to save me once." She snickered. This was one of the few times her above-average height served her well.

"*Nee.*" He stepped back and removed his hand from her arm. "I never did have to save you, but you ran off lots of fish."

She took the glass from his hand, splashed in frothy milk from a cold metal pitcher and then dropped two ice cubes into the milky swirl. "Two enough?" she asked, looking up at him.

He had a strange expression on his face and was smiling like someone who had just been given a special Christmas gift. "*Ya*. Sure. Two is perfect," he said and turned away with the glass of milk in hand, but not before winking at her with one bright blue eye lined with rusty brown lashes.

She turned on her heel and left the room, but not before turning back and giving the man one last look. He sat down at the kitchen table circled with men and went back to eating like nothing had happened.

She hurried away from the kitchen, leaving the men to fend for themselves. She'd left Benuel alone with the other children a long time. It was best she checked up on him and made sure he was behaving himself. Left to his own devices, there was no telling what he'd get up to.

She forced her thoughts to Benuel and off Fredrik. What foolishness. The man had never been drawn to her.

Chapter Five

Lizbeth leaned her borrowed bike next to her father's big-seated tricycle and followed him up the steps of the porch. She was encouraged the two of them had finally found spare time to look at the empty house together.

The street was quiet, the homes well kept. The front lawn was neatly cut and edged. Made of white clapboard, with a brown tiled roof, Ulla's house looked exactly like every other home in the small Amish community. Plain and nondescript as it had been described to her. The dwelling had a big wraparound porch, graced by two oversize cushioned rockers. They made the home more inviting, an added bonus she hadn't expected but was thrilled to see.

Her foot on the last step, she glanced back at the neighborhood, trying to take it all in at once. She turned back to the white house and admired the tidy beds of fragrant pink rosebushes nestled along each side of the porch. The wood fence surrounding the backyard had a pleasant gray patina and looked strong enough to hold her son behind its sturdy walls.

She smiled as she went up the steps, picturing Benuel

climbing trees and running around in the privacy of his own yard, where he'd be safe from the dangers of the road. This house would suit them to perfection if the inside was as nice as the outside.

Her *daed* turned the key and stepped back so Lizbeth could precede him. "*Ya*, well. Like I told you. There's a few repairs to be done. The roof needs a shingle or two, but all that will be fixed before you move in."

The entry hall was clean and spacious, the hardwood floors shining from a fresh coat of beeswax. He led the way to the great room filled with comfortable-looking furniture. Solid navy drapes were pulled back at each side of the big windows. "You'll get the morning sun in here."

"Gut," Lizbeth said, hoping to find a brick fireplace and then realizing she wouldn't need one in Florida. There'd be no more snow or icy roads to contend with. No more shivering in buggies, carting wood and milking cows. She smiled and continued to follow her father.

Across the entry hall he led her into a big square kitchen. The walls were lined with wooden cabinets painted a glossy white. A large *Englischer* stove and refrigerator sat across from each other. The sunny kitchen window, framed with pale blue checkered curtains, crowned the deep country sink in front of her.

"Ulla kept a small table and chairs placed by the door, but her daughter wanted them since her *daed* had made them. I'm sure you can get a set for a fair price at one of the auctions coming up."

Lizbeth imagined a round table with four chairs in the empty floor space and grinned. "Perhaps I can get Mose Fischer to make me one."

"Ya, he could make it fit perfectly in here. He's known

for the quality of his work." Her father ran his hand down the length of the kitchen's work-top counter and smiled. "I'm sure Ulla and her daughters had many good times here, baking and making memories."

"Perhaps renting the house to me isn't a good idea. It could be difficult for her."

"*Ya*, well, not that hard. She said she took her memories with her when we married. She seemed happy to move in to my home. This phase of her life is over. Her new life has begun, just like yours will when you marry again. Now, let's go look at the bedrooms at the back and see if you think Benuel would be happy in one of them."

"Will she be leaving all the furniture?" Lizbeth ignored her father's comment about her getting married again and ambled toward a beautiful hall table made of oak wood and polished to a high shine. A real beauty. She held her breath as she waited for an answer.

"That's up to the renter." Her *daed* chuckled. "Houses are hard to come by in Pinecraft and most renters want their homes to be furnished, especially if they're snow-birds from up north and only staying a short while each year."

"If I decide to rent the house, I'd want the furniture to remain," Lizbeth assured him and then hurried into the first bedroom off the hall, her excitement building as she examined the good-size room with a double bed and wooden dresser that matched. "I left the farmhouse in Ohio as is and walked away with nothing but our clothes." She could have said more, but didn't. She hadn't told anyone about her life in Ohio. Why share the misery? Speaking out would change nothing in her past and erase none of the damage done to her soul. Her one regret was walking away from the graveyard that held the bodies of her babies.

She would always grieve the two tiny souls. She'd asked *Gott* to protect them from Jonah's bruising blows. But *Gott* chose a different path for them. Both had died in her arms. It had been *Gott*'s will, but she would never understand. She'd left a part of her heart there in that cold Ohio soil. She would never forget her boys.

Fredrik moved fast through the spacious apartment behind the house on Ulla's property—*his* property— noting the discolored walls begged for a lick of paint. He frowned as he walked into the kitchen and viewed the table. Once sturdy, it now made do on three legs and threatened to fall. It would have to be thrown out and a new one built. Someday he would be building furniture for his home, maybe even a cradle for his firstborn son.

He rubbed his hands together as he visualized the new eating area. He would build the replacement table a bit bigger than this tiny one.

He opened a door at the back of the kitchen. Narrow shelves lined the shallow pantry walls, ready for jars of homemade jams and spices.

He turned on his heel and looked back into the kitchen. He could picture someone in the galley-shaped work space, cooking their simple meals. He took in a long, satisfying breath of air. Whiffs of gasoline and machine oil wiped the smile off his face. To keep its musky smell from seeping into the apartment, he'd need to seal the walls of the storage shed built against the outer partition of the room.

He glanced out the window to the big white house down the driveway. His spirits rose. He had finally found the home he had been looking for. Ulla's house was certain-sure good enough to bring a *fraa* home to, and he'd been surprised when she'd lowered the price down to a manageable amount for him this morning. He'd start to search for his bride from amongst the church ladies. He'd missed a lot of church services the past three months, his mind busy with work and not on spiritual growth.

He was a little hesitant when conjuring up faces of the eligible women he knew. What if he decided on someone and they turned him down? Without a doubt, he knew Lizbeth Mullet would reject him.

The color of Lizbeth's hair caught his attention, drawing him away from his thoughts. He couldn't settle on her just yet. He would have to grow spiritually, find a way to make himself the kind of man she'd want for a husband, and then see.

Thoughts of marriage were on his mind all the time, filling every moment of the day now that he'd made his decision to wed.

For years the idea of courtship with anyone set alarm bells ringing. Unrequited love had sent him running back to Pinecraft and the comfort of a small, lonely apartment in Sarasota. He'd finally healed, but he hadn't been ready for this step of faith. Until now.

He didn't know what had changed, but something was building in him, an excitement, some emotion he didn't completely understand. Perhaps it came because of the loneliness he endured, or the way his body ached when he worked extrahard for nothing more than his own benefit. Both were reminders that he wasn't a boy anymore. At twenty-nine he wasn't exactly long in the tooth, but time was passing and he wanted to find someone to share his life with. Maybe even start a family now that he had a family home to raise *kinner* in.

He heard voices and made his way to the open apartment door. Chicken John stood on the side steps of the house Fredrik had just purchased, his back to him, talking to someone inside.

"There's a work shed outside, not that you'll need one. But the backyard is perfect for Benuel." Chicken John stepped down onto the driveway.

From inside the house a feminine voice called out, "*Gut.* I'll be right out."

Fredrik walked into the bright sunshine, leaving the apartment door ajar.

Chicken John placed a hand against his brow, shielding his eyes from the bright sunlight. A smile of welcome lifted the corners of his mouth. "You scared the life out of me, Fredrik. I thought we were the only ones on the property. Weren't you supposed to come by yesterday?"

Fredrik returned his smile. "I was, but I got busy at work and ran out of daylight. I hope you don't mind me coming by today."

"*Nee.* Today is *gut.* You know you're always welcome, but I think you might have left it a bit too late if you were interested in buying this house." He leaned toward Fredrik and whispered, "Lizbeth needs a rental house. If she likes what she sees she'll snatch this place away from you."

Nerves gripped his stomach. He'd have to be the one to break the news about the sale of the house to Lizbeth and her father. He hated the idea of slipping the house from her grasp, but he needed it as much as she did. She could always stay at her father's if she didn't find a place to rent. His need was more urgent. He wanted to marry. If he could talk Lizbeth into courting him, she would have this house as her own, and he'd have a wife he might eventually learn to love. If he could find a way to trust her with his heart.

The screen door squealed for oil as Lizbeth appeared and stepped onto the porch. She turned in his direction, her brow furrowing from the bright noontime sun. She wore the same navy dress and shoes she'd worn to church on Sunday. Again today her expression was relaxed and friendly.

"Fredrik," she said and nodded.

He tipped his straw hat in her direction and grinned back, noticing her smile reached her warm blue eyes. "Lizbeth."

"You two have made friends?" Chicken John said, his tone inquisitive.

Fredrik spoke first. "A long time ago—"

"*Ya*, well. Remember, Benuel and I just happened to meet Fredrik at the café and became friends," Lizbeth interjected, cutting off his words. Something in her gaze told Fredrik she still didn't want her *daed* to remember they knew each other as children. "And speaking of Benuel, we really should be on our way. Ulla offered to watch him for a few hours. Not the whole day."

"*Ya*, you're right. We've taken too long," her father agreed. He reached around, locked the doorknob from the inside and then shut the side door behind him. "Good seeing you, Fredrik. I'll call you about the house repairs later today."

"*Ya*. Later today is perfect. I'll be at the shop. It's *gut* seeing you again, Lizbeth. Tell Benuel I said hello."

She dipped her head in acknowledgment. "I'll tell

him. You have a pleasant night," she said and hurried away, the sun reflecting strands of gold in her hair.

His heart racing at the sight of her, Fredrik pushed his straw hat down on his head and followed behind them as they crunched down the pea gravel driveway. He was ashamed he hadn't found the nerve to tell Lizbeth he'd bought the house she wanted as her own, but his dreams of working in the leaning shed blossomed. Became bigger than life.

He observed Lizbeth as she gathered up the skirt of her plain blue cotton dress and climbed onto her bike. He liked the way she held her head high, as if nothing could touch her.

Both turned and waved as they pedaled off. He wondered about the widow wearing a different colored dress now. Did that mean she was over her time of mourning? When she'd arrived in Pinecraft she'd still dressed in black.

He knew grief could make a woman distant and unfriendly, but Lizbeth seemed friendlier now. Perhaps he'd done the right thing putting her name on his list of potential women to step out with. The fact she had a boy didn't bother him one bit. It just made his odds better, since she might be looking for a prospective husband to help raise her son. And she might not expect a potential husband to immediately surrender his heart.

He looked back at the simple wood house and lifted his shoulders as he took in a long, contented breath. He or Ulla would tell John he'd bought the house. No doubt the man could find another house for Lizbeth, but until Fredrik found a suitable wife, he was in no hurry. The widow could rent from him and live in the house if she wanted. He didn't mind sharing, but she'd have to move once he married. He truly believed *Gott* would help him find his bride soon.

Fredrik made his way back to the apartment door, his gaze wandering to the backyard shaded by a big oak draped full of hanging moss. Lizbeth's son seemed full of energy. This yard would have been the perfect place for a boy like him to play. It still could be.

Pushing those thoughts aside, he opened the solid wooden apartment door he'd left ajar and stepped back inside, his eyes quickly adjusting to the dim light. The picture window at the side of the big room had a set of closed, wide wooden blinds that blotted out the daylight. He tugged on their dangling cord and stepped back as dust floated on the sunlight flooding the room. The walls had once been a bright white, but now looked yellow with age. Just as he'd thought, they would need to be washed down and painted.

A slow walk back around the apartment's galley kitchen and bathroom told him there were a lot of small jobs to be done, but the bones of the place were sound enough and well worth the price of a few repairs. This place could bring in a good bit of profit if he could get it finished by tourist time.

He opened the only bedroom door and was surprised at how large it was. He could see a full-size bed fitting in the room, and a big dresser. A comfortable chair placed over by the window would be perfect for reading.

The closet door almost fell off its hinges as he opened it wide. Inside, space was limited, but Plain people didn't need lots of space for clothes and shoes. He propped up the closet door and began to tap his pencil against his chin as he wandered back through the rooms, pondering the price of the work needing done in the bathroom as he passed. It might take a while to get a new wall of tiles up, but it would be well worth the effort.

Concentrating on the task at hand, he walked back into the kitchen and pulled out a chair. He'd make a to-do list and hope he'd get the opportunity to restore the apartment back to its original beauty before winter when places rented for a premium. If it came out as good as he thought it would, he may want to increase the amount of rent he'd had in mind.

Living in Pinecraft, instead of his apartment in Sarasota, would bring him closer to work, give him extra time to find the perfect wife. If Lizbeth moved in for a time, he could live in the apartment and keep an eye on her and the boy. A woman living alone with a *kinner* would always need looking out for and he was just the man to do it. A smile creased his face as he wrote down his supply list. That idea of living close to Lizbeth Mullet appealed to him. In fact, the idea of marriage to her appealed even more.

Chapter Six

At dusk the next day, Fredrik lumbered up the house's front steps, the leather soles of his boots squeaking as he made his way across the wooden porch left wet by a sudden summer storm.

Too full from a hot meal at the café, and tired from a long day at the furniture shop, his shoulders sagged as he lugged his heavy toolbox by his side. He longed to go back to his apartment and kick up his feet, but he'd made a promise to himself he'd start the work in the newly acquired house and wasn't backing out. He'd get busy with the list of jobs needing done inside, finish inspecting and making additional plans on the separate apartment at the back of the property, and relax later tonight.

He stumbled over a can of paint and nudged it out of his way, weaving in and out of several other cans he'd left scattered too close to the front door. His thoughts touched on the attractive Amish waitress who'd served him at the local café during his dinner. She was new to Pinecraft and full of questions.

Marriage fresh on his mind, he'd enjoyed her chatter, but Lizbeth Mullet was the only woman he could imagine on his arm. And that had to change. He had no idea what she thought of him, or if she'd even be agreeable to starting a courtship.

He wiped sweat from his forehead with the back of his hand, unlocked the front door and nudged it open with his shoulder.

Inside, the house was quiet. The warm air smelled musty from weeks of being shut tight. He'd need to work fast if he hoped to get through the foot-long list of jobs that needed doing inside the house. Chicken John had spoken with Lizbeth about the sale of the house, and she'd agreed to be Fredrik's tenant for as long as he needed one. She wanted to move in the next day so he knew he must hurry.

He set the toolbox down, opened the windows in the living room and then went back to eyeballing the entry hall's wood trim and walls. He had seen several dings on the outside of the wooden front door that would need seeing to. The dents looked like they'd been there for years, but he saw no good reason to just overlook them. His father had taught him if a job was worth doing, it was worth doing well.

His fingers scrubbed at the fine stubble on his chin as he made a mental note to add wood dap and fine-grit sandpaper to his list of supplies that needed to be picked up.

Fredrik meandered from room to room. He opened doors and looked in all the usual places that received wear and tear.

He made a mental note that the worn linoleum in the front bathroom would need to be switched out. New tiles would spruce the small room up, but would probably take more time than he had. Lizbeth wouldn't want him underfoot once she moved in with her son, but she may have to put up with him being around from time to time. It would be a *gut* opportunity for him to get to know her and the boy.

The bathroom doorknob wiggled in his grasp. One more job on his list. Might as well get to it now. Fredrik made an adjustment and tightened down a few screws and then wiggled the knob again. Done.

He ran the faucets in the sink and tub. All were in good working order.

His mind always raced ahead of the projects at hand. He wondered about the gallons of white paint he had brought with him. The house was smaller than he remembered. He'd probably bought too much, not that he couldn't use the leftovers when he began the apartment remodel at the back of the property. He was in a hurry to finish both projects. He'd decided he would live in the apartment for a few months when his lease ran out at the end of the month, or maybe rent it now, and lease it out during the Christmas holidays, when rentals went for top dollar. Hopefully he'd have enough time to work on his projects on his days off.

He flushed the toilet and waited for the tank to fill. The sound of a crash came from the direction of the kitchen.

He froze midstep, listening.

Posters had been put up at the post office warning that several houses had been broken into recently, ransacked by thieves and then left for the local family to find.

He tiptoed past the toolbox. Soundlessly, he eased out a heavy wrench and moved toward the closed kitchen door. A nonviolent man by belief and custom, he still couldn't stand by and let someone break into the home without trying to stop them.

He raised the wrench high and leaned against the kitchen door while silently twisting the old-fashioned glass doorknob.

On high alert, he peered into the well-lit kitchen. Everything seemed in order.

A cardboard box lay on its side on the floor. The contents, a plastic bottle of bleach and a tight bundle of dust cloths and cleaning brushes, lay scattered around.

The hair on his neck rose. Ulla had said she and Molly would clean the house after he finished with the repairs in a day or two.

Fredrik stepped into the room. His heart skipped a beat as a feminine voice ordered, "Stop, or I'll shoot."

Lizbeth had no weapon, with the exception of the long scrub brush she brandished across her arm like a shotgun. What was she to do? She'd never struck a person, but the brush seemed to have a mind of its own and lifted, poised to strike. Didn't she have a right to defend herself? Would it be so wrong?

She pressed the long-handled brush against her heaving chest. A labyrinth of emotions surged through her as a dark boot and trouser-covered leg stepped into the room.

She'd been warned by Ulla to be cautious when she'd left the house that afternoon. Thieves had been targeting the vacant homes of hardworking Amish families who spent the hot summer months in the north. She should have had her father come with her to check the house.

She whispered a brief prayer and waited for the right moment to strike. With all her might she shoved at the opening door, cringed as she heard it hit something solid and then watched as the booted foot disappeared. Metal clanked against the floor on the other side of the door.

She gulped in air and raced for the back door, only to find she'd blocked her own getaway with the new kitchen table and chairs.

She whirled around, her teeth clenched as she struggled to face the intruder. Her only way out was past the man sprawled on the hallway floor, his head in his hands.

Her heart beat loudly in her ears as she inched closer. There was something familiar about the ginger hair protruding through the man's fingers as he massaged his head. Concern replaced fear. "Fredrik! What are you doing here?" She straightened, her arms thrown open wide in disbelief. "I could have hurt you."

"I'd say you did hurt me." Fredrik raked his hair out of his eyes and frowned up at her as he rubbed his forehead.

"I'm so sorry. I thought you were a burglar. Here, let me help you up." She offered him her hand, but he ignored it.

He winced and rubbed his head again. "I heard a noise and came to check it out. I see no reason for you to clobber me with the door." He rose with a stagger and used the doorjamb to brace himself. Ginger curls dangled across his flushed forehead.

Guilt-ridden, she grabbed a kitchen chair and shoved it toward him. "Here, please sit." She motioned toward the chair. "I thought you were someone up to no good." She tugged at the prayer *kapp* ribbon dangling against her neck.

He dropped onto the wooden seat of the chair. *"Danki,"* he muttered, his tone none too friendly.

In the past they would have made a joke about all this,

laughed and poked fun at each other for being afraid in an empty house. But they weren't children anymore, or misbehaving teens. They were adults. Strangers really. She wasn't sure how he'd react to being pushed to the ground by a swinging door in his own house. "You didn't answer my question. What are you doing here?"

"I told your *daed* I'd be doing some of the repairs in the *haus* this afternoon."

She wiped sweat off her top lip. "Why didn't he tell me? I'd hoped to make preparations for our move tomorrow."

"Your guess is as *gut* as mine. Maybe he thought you'd be finished by now. It is gone seven." He looked toward the kitchen curtains blowing in the wind. "Most *mamms* would be at home, feeding their *kinner* and getting them ready for bed." He glanced around, scowling. "Where is Benuel?"

Was his comment a rebuke? Probably not. She was just being touchy. Benuel was with her father and Ulla, well fed and bathed by now, and waiting for his bedtime story. She owed Fredrik no explanation, but she gave him one anyway. "He's with my *daed*, probably eating the chocolate cupcakes I made earlier and no doubt staying up till all hours while I behave wickedly with my broom and dustrag."

"I didn't mean to imply—"

Out of past frustrations she'd reacted too harshly. "No, I know you didn't. Forgive me. I guess I'm tired." Lizbeth picked up the spilled cleaning utensils scattered across the floor. She glanced back at Fredrik, her grip tightening on the handle of the scrub brush. Feeling threatened moments before, she would have used it on him. The thought disturbed her. Poor man was only doing what he'd promised to do. Getting the house ready for his first tenant.

Lizbeth put away the brush and sat the box of supplies back on the counter. She gave Fredrik a long glance and found he looked remarkably young, his hair tossed from his fall, the freckles on his nose more pronounced under the indoor lighting. But then she noticed the slight bags under his eyes, signs of exhaustion around his mouth. Her mood softened even more.

No doubt the man had worked all day and now was here to work on the house. Had he had time to eat his evening meal? The least she could do was offer him a cold bottle of refreshment. She reached for her carry-all and pulled out a sweating bottle of cold apple juice. "Why don't you drink this and then get back to your projects."

He reached for the bottle and downed half with one long pull. *"Danki,"* he said and wiped his mouth with the back of his hand as he rose. He moved to leave the room, but paused just inside the door. "I'm sorry I scared you." His gaze held hers for a long moment, but then he vanished, leaving her alone with her thoughts, though the woodsy fragrance of his soap stayed with her.

Lizbeth busied herself for a few minutes, spraying vinegar on the already-clean windowpanes and wiping them. She scrubbed with all her might and then paused as she heard footsteps coming back toward the front of the house. She waited for Fredrik to reenter the kitchen.

His boots shuffled as he crossed the entry hall and made his way back to the bedrooms. Without even trying, Fredrik had a way of pulling out memories, making her think of how things used to be when they were young.

She heard a window in the back bedroom open and then close. He was probably checking the caulking. She'd seen slight cracks around several of the windows from the constant Florida heat. No doubt he'd patch where it looked like the rain could get in.

Silence surrounded her. The last of the sunlight coming in through the opened kitchen window waned and disappeared. As she locked the small window over the sink, an outdoor light came on in the neighbor's house, chasing away the beginnings of night shadows and flooding the backyard with a golden hue.

She glanced around the unfamiliar kitchen that was to become hers to use. She compared this warm, welcoming space to the drafty, uninviting farmhouse she'd shared with Jonah, and sighed. One day *Gott* would allow her a measure of peace.

With the cleaning box in her arms, she left the kitchen and made her way into the great room. Two side-by-side windows had been left open. A brisk breeze blew in, fluttering the long drapes hanging at each side of the twin windows. The fragrances of damp foliage and the sea intertwined.

A feeling of melancholy settled over her. She wished she was sharing this house with a man, a husband who would love her and her *soh*. But she knew that was not to be. She'd make do with Benuel's love. He would be enough. Later, after she'd gotten over the painful memories of her first marriage, maybe *Gott* would send someone her way. Someone she could deeply love. Someone who wouldn't judge her for her past mistakes. Once emotionally healed, she'd welcome a kind and gentle husband into her lonely life. But now was too soon. She had things to forget, things that still troubled her dreams.

She pulled the chocolate whoopie pie out of her starched apron and walked slowly down the hall. Squatting in front of the electric socket on the wall, Fredrik used a yellow screwdriver to twist in a screw. She paused, watching him, interested in the way his muscles rippled beneath his shirt and then went taut across his back when he stretched.

She cleared her throat and he shot to his feet. She held out the whoopie pie. "I thought you might have missed your dinner. This might help."

"Danki," he said, reaching out and taking it.

He looked at her in a way that made her stomach clench. His blue eyes had always fascinated her. "I made it myself," she muttered. "I hope you like it."

"I'm certain-sure I will," he said, touching her hand as he reached out.

She couldn't ignore the tingle coursing through her fingers. "I'll be going now. Benuel will want his stories read to him."

"Okay, see you later," he said, pocketing the treat.

She held his gaze. "Don't work too late. You look tired."

"I'll be going soon." As an afterthought, he added, "Would you like me to walk you home? It's getting dark."

"Nee, there's no need. I have my bike. *Daed* told you I'll be moving in tomorrow morning, right? I gave him the rent to give you," she asked, watching him, taking in the way the shine from the bedroom's overhead light reflected on his ginger hair, the way his generous smile pressed grooves around his mouth.

"Ya, he gave me the money and told me you were eager to get settled. I hope you have a good night," Fredrik said, shoving his hand through his hair and pushing the curls off his forehead.

"Danki," Lizbeth whispered and left the room. She walked briskly out the door and down the walk to her bike, her thoughts on Fredrik Lapp and the man he had become. The thought came to her. Would he make a good husband now? Could he love her? What kind of father would he be? She pushed such foolish thoughts aside and pedaled with all her might toward her father's chicken farm. She'd entertained those thoughts about Fredrik once before. But he'd left, and she'd moved on. What did it matter to her now if he'd make a good partner? She wasn't looking for a husband.

Was she?

Chapter Seven

"Look out! The cat—"

Before Fredrik could react, a streak of gray fur jumped over his booted foot, skittered on the entryway's shiny floor and scampered off toward the back bedrooms.

"Oh, no! Look what you've done now!"

His friendly mood waned. Did she think he purposely let the cat into the house? "I didn't mean—"

"I know. I'm sorry, Fredrik. Forgive me," Lizbeth said, her expression apologetic. "Perhaps you should come back another time, when I'm not so tired and out of sorts."

He witnessed her inward struggle to be civil, saw a nerve tick in her jaw. She smiled, but she didn't look like any ray of sunshine.

Had moving day been that hard on her? All the furniture was in the house and he'd seen Otto, Chicken John and several sweaty community leaders milling around outside with glasses of sweet tea in their hands. She had plenty of help. And from the tower of boxes lining the entryway, he could see there were lots of donations coming in, everything she'd need to set up the rented house.

Lizbeth was different since returning to Pinecraft. More intense. As a kid she'd been a mild-mannered pest, with more energy than he and her *bruder* could keep up with. She'd kept him laughing with her silly antics. Perhaps marriage hadn't agreed with her, or she had poor health. What had happened to her while she was away in Ohio? None of it was his business, but he still wondered.

Ulla's head poked out of the kitchen door, her face red and sweaty, a frizzy riot of gray curls circling her round face. The edges of her mouth lifted in a slight grin and then she disappeared with a wave.

He rubbed the back of his neck. "Your note on the door said—"

"I know, but you let that cat in and it took me hours to get her out the last time she got in." She cut him a frustrated glance as she raked a dangling curl out of her eyes and shoved it up under her cleaning scarf.

He was frustrated, too. Mornings off were hard to come by. The shop was usually too busy, or a furniture order had to go out. Mose had called and asked him to deliver a box of linens to Lizbeth's on his way out of work yesterday and he'd forgotten until this morning. Sarah, Mose's wife, was busy with sick children. He'd agreed to tote the box over, even though it was an inconvenience and meant he'd miss an hour of fishing while it was still cool. He'd agreed because he enjoyed Lizbeth's company, liked being around her a lot more than made him comfortable. He could have just as easily claimed to be too busy and let someone else bring the box to her. He slid a guarded look at the overtired widow.

Dark shadows bruised the tender skin under her eyes. He regretted his uncharitable thoughts. This poor woman needed cheering up and he was just the man to do it.

He hid a grin as he noticed a cluster of spiderwebs clinging to the edge of Lizbeth's left eyebrow. It danced around as her frown deepened. As a child she'd hated spiders. If she knew one's web dangled off her face, she'd panic. And he wasn't going to tell her. It would be too much fun to see her reaction when she noticed on her own.

Always ready for a good prank, he cleared his throat. He held back the full-blown laugh that begged to come out.

She frowned at him, her brows low. "*Ya*, well, I still have to catch that cat again."

He stepped through the threshold with his burden. The perfectly folded stack of sheets and pillowcases smelled of homemade lavender soap and fresh air. "Sarah Fischer sent these yesterday," he said, and presented the box to her. "I forgot to bring them to you."

"*Danki*. Put them there." Lizbeth jabbed her finger toward the floor and then adjusted the cleaning scarf on her head. She unknowingly knocked the dangling cobweb off her brow and onto her wrist. "How am I going to catch that cat? It took me half my tuna sandwich and the patience of Job to run her out last time." She hurried away down the hallway, muttering to herself, "I have no sandwiches left. What am I going to do?"

"Let me help you. It's the least I can do," he offered. He couldn't help himself. He wanted to be around when she found the spider's web and went running through the house, screaming.

She stopped in her tracks and turned, hands back on her hips. "You've done so much already."

"I only—"

"*Ya*, let the animal in." Her shoulders drooped as soon

as her words were out. "Oh, don't listen to me. I'm just not dealing with all this very well." She smiled weakly.

"Look," he said, pointing to the flash of gray that told him the cat was on the move.

They both rushed down the hall. Lizbeth ran into the room and crouched down, searching under an unmade bed. Her headscarf almost fell off in her rush and she positioned it back in place with a pin.

Fredrik joined her on the floor, looked under the bed. Two bright green eyes glowed back at him. "What a pretty kitty," he crooned. "Come close and I'll pet you."

Lizbeth lifted her head, an incredulous expression lingering on her features. Her brow rose. "Don't get friendly—"

"Shush," he hissed, the edge of his mouth lifting in a grin as he shoved his hand under the bed. "Come here, pretty baby. Let me pet you."

"I can't believe—"

"Shush," he repeated. "I know what I'm doing. If you'll just be quiet for a moment, woman, I can solve your problem."

The cat hissed and slapped at him, but its claws weren't extended.

"*Ya*, I can see you're making great strides," Lizbeth said, her mood lightening as she tried to hide a giggle behind her hand. She glanced back under the bed. "Perhaps a broom will encourage her out?"

Fredrik sat and reached low, his hand slipping closer to the cat. "Come on, kitty. You remember me. I gave you a good scratching yesterday."

Her head bobbed back up. Her smile failed her. She scowled. "You encouraged that cat to hang around?" There was an edge to Lizbeth's whisper.

He ignored her for the moment, which was hard to do. She looked beautiful today, her cheeks rosy, her eyes spitting fire from a morning of frustrations. "Come on, kitty. Let me touch you." He bent lower, moving his fingers carefully as the cat whipped its tail back and forth in agitation.

"I'm getting the broom. I don't have time for this," Lizbeth groused and rose to her feet.

He glanced up. The cobweb had moved from her hand to her cleaning scarf. It was just a matter of time now till she found the web. "*Ya*, you get the broom," he said and went back to coaxing the cat out.

The room grew quiet. As soon as Lizbeth was gone, the cat came out of hiding and sauntered toward him, surrendering to the temptation of a neck rub. Fredrik scooped up the ball of fur and scratched it under one ginger-and-gray ear. Content, it purred. He smiled as Lizbeth hollered in the kitchen. He could hear Ulla's attempt to calm her, but she was having none of it. He chuckled to the cat. "She must have found the cobweb, Purr-Baby. Our work here is done. Time to go fishing."

Lizbeth carried the broom back to the bedroom, her thoughts on Fredrik. She was grateful he'd brought the box of linens. She really was, but why didn't he just go? She had so much to do before nightfall. She had no time for his silly pranks. He had to have seen the spiderweb on her scarf. Ulla saw it quickly enough.

Fredrik knew she'd had a strong aversion to spiders and their webs as a teen. And how dare he shush her like a child? This was *her* home for now. He may be the owner, but she'd paid her rent. He was just there to deliver a box, nothing more. It was time for him to go.

She had more than enough to stress over this morning with her concerns about moving in to the big house. Plus, Benuel had woken in rare form and started the morning off on the wrong foot. She'd never lived alone, and as the local break-ins continued, they fed her feelings of insecurity. She sighed.

It wasn't that she didn't like cats. She did. She just didn't have time to bother with one right now.

Determination in her every step, she hurried to the back of the house and entered the bedroom, only to stop in amazement. Fredrik stood next to the bed, the cat cozied up in his arms. "Poor little kitty," he said as he glanced at her and then back to the cat, his expression innocent.

"That cat's been nothing but trouble and I want it gone." Lizbeth lowered the broom to the floor.

"This little darling is looking for a place to have her babies, that's all. She doesn't mean to be a bother." Fredrik lounged back against the wall.

Lizbeth's heart dropped. "Babies?" Her eyes widened. "That pregnant cat is not staying here. I have enough to do, plus I have to find a job once we're settled." A frown creased her forehead.

Fredrik beamed across the room at her. "You might want to reconsider your decision about keeping it around. I saw evidence of mouse droppings in the shed. You're going to need a cat if you don't want the mice coming inside the house."

A shiver of revulsion slithered up her spine. She'd been chased by Fredrik holding a live mouse more than once. She'd been scared of them ever since. Defeat left a bitter taste in her mouth, but he was right. The cat would stay and earn its keep. "It can stay, but I'm not keeping the kittens."

The cat yawned.

Fredrik looked miffed, his brow lifting. "*Ya*, sure." He didn't sound confident at all, but he wasn't backing down. "Ulla and John are always in need of a good barn cat. I'll find them all homes."

"Do you have any grand ideas where we should put her for the night?" She looked up and found Fredrik watching her.

"What?" she asked. Why was he looking at her like that?

He smiled at her. Really smiled. Not just the grin of a friendly man, but a man who might see her as acceptable. A smile that reached all the way up to his eyes.

She grew flustered, her face warming. She had work to do. He could take that cat out to the shed, make it a bed and go.

She knew how to get rid of him. "Rumor has it you're looking for a wife. That so?"

"*Ya*," he muttered, his expression becoming serious. "Why do you ask?" He went back to stroking the cat, his intense, blue-eyed gaze remaining on her.

"No reason. I was just wondering, is all."

"You planning on applying for the job?"

"Me? *Nee*. I'm a new widow with a child to raise and now kittens to look after, thanks to you."

Fredrik straightened himself and headed for the door, his boots making noise against the hardwood floors as he shuffled past her. "I think kitty and I will be out in the shed if you need us."

Lizbeth picked up a box of crumpled newspapers left

over from the unpacked dishes. "You can take this with you, if you don't mind," she said.

He grabbed the edge of the box. "You're different now, you know." His gaze wandered over her face.

"You're still the same. A jokester, always pulling pranks at everyone else's expense."

Fredrik stepped into the hall, but looked back. "I'm sure I am, but it makes me wonder what made you so bitter and out of sorts."

She wiped her hand down her apron, her remorse lowering her head. "It's just been a long day…a long week."

"*Ya*, it has. Perhaps a day at the fair would put you in a better mood," he said with a smile that made her legs grow weak. "I'm going tomorrow after work. Would you and Benuel like to come with me?"

"*Nee*, but *danki*, Fredrik. I already promised Ulla I'd go with her and the sewing ladies."

"Perhaps another time. There's always the Christmas auction," he suggested, patting his hat in place.

Her heart skipped a beat. "*Ya*, that sounds *gut*."

"*Ya*, it does. Well, good night," he said with a fresh smile and turned to go.

"Good night," she murmured, listening to the sound of his footfalls as he ambled through the house and out the front door.

She hung her head. *Gott* had to be disappointed in her. Just because she was bone tired didn't mean she could behave in such a way with Fredrik. He was only trying to be a help to her. She shuffled back toward the kitchen. It seemed the man wanted nothing more than to be her friend. He had no real interest in her as a prospective bride. Which was exactly what she wanted. So why was it so disappointing?

Chapter Eight

"Who'll give me sixteen fifty?" the auctioneer called out.

Several hands flew up. The crowd of auction-goers formed a tight knot, their placards waving, hoping to be seen.

He waited, his left hand shading his eyes from the bright Florida sun overhead. "Do I hear seventeen fifty, now eighteen?" A warm summer afternoon sweat dampened the man's shirt a darker blue around his neck and ringed his armpits.

He squinted, scanning the swarm of Amish, Mennonite and *Englischers* milling around the front of his improvised auction stand. He appeared content to wait a few moments longer to see if the price would advance.

Fredrik lifted his number high. "Twenty-five dollars," he shouted over the hum of the generator vibrating behind him. The shelf would fit perfectly over the toilet in the apartment and add much-needed storage to the tiny bathroom space he was remodeling. He hoped to find some spare time to work on the place, if work at the furniture store slowed down.

The auctioneer's long gray beard touched the front of his pale blue shirt as he nodded his silver head in approval and pointed in Fredrik's direction. "Fair warning... and it's gone, gone, gone at twenty-five dollars and not a penny more."

Motioned forward, Fredrik wove his way toward the front of the crowd. An Amish teenager of fifteen or sixteen, with a bad complexion and a full head of dark hair, handed over the shelf. "Pay my *mamm* over there," the boy muttered and pointed to a tiny woman sitting at a table under a moss-covered shade tree.

"*Ya*, sure," Fredrik agreed and strode away, only to step into the path of a running child.

To keep from knocking the boy down, he had to grab hold of the child's black suspenders. He was surprised to see he had young Benuel Mullet, Lizbeth's son, in tow.

"What are you doing running around all by yourself?" he asked. The boy's sweaty face scrunched up, his bottom lip quivering as he prepared to cry. Fredrik skimmed the faces around them. Lizbeth had to be somewhere close by. "Where's your *mamm*?"

"Let me be," Benuel wailed in *Deitch* as he twisted and kicked at Fredrik's shin.

"Not till you tell me where your *mamm* is, young man. I have a feeling she hasn't a clue where you are."

"*Ya*, she does," he declared. A tear glistened in his eye as he pointed to a fenced-in children's pool filled with water and crowded with fluffy yellow ducklings. "She promised I could see the baby ducks my *grossdaddi* is selling."

The boy nervously glanced over his shoulder and peered into the crowd of shoppers behind them. Lizbeth, wearing a dress of pale blue cotton, surged from a group of local women in their customary *kapps* and aprons and rushed forward. Her long legs ate up the distance between them. Normally pale cheeked, her face glowed from her exertion in the hot afternoon sun. A vexed expression creased her forehead into deep lines, indicating to Fredrik that she might have been searching for the boy awhile.

"Thank you for catching him," she said.

He released Benuel's narrow suspenders and stepped back.

Benuel's small body stilled. He wiped away the dampness from his eyes and watched his mother advance. "*Grossdaddi* said I could see the ducks," he called to her.

Lizbeth scooped up the small boy. "You scared the life from me. Do you know that?" She kissed the boy's cheeks and then his hair and pulled him close. "I thought you'd been taken." She sent a look of appreciation Fredrik's way.

Benuel wiggled in her arms. "I just wanted—"

"*Ya*, I know. You want to see those silly ducks swim." She hugged him close, even though he pushed at her with his small hands. "Didn't your *grossdaddi* promise to take you later, after we ate? Always stay with me, Benuel. Never wander off alone." She looked into his eyes. "We're not on the farm now. There are hidden dangers in Pinecraft from cars on the streets and crowds of strangers."

The boy's eyes widened.

Fredrik took in a deep breath. The boy needed the firm hand of a father, not the scary tales about danger his mother was telling him. He had been a boy much like Benuel. Always running off, giving his mother reason to worry. Lizbeth needed help raising the boy. That much was certain-sure.

Preoccupied with thoughts of Benuel, Fredrik waved goodbye to Lizbeth and strolled away, merging into the crowd around him. He stood under the shade of an ancient oak tree watching mother and son from a distance. Was he the man to help raise the boy? Lizbeth was a fine woman. A devoted *mamm*. He'd be proud to call her his *fraa*. He longed to help teach the boy how to behave and grow into a *gut* man. Something unexplainable drew him to Lizbeth and her son.

In frustration, he kicked at a stone on the path and sent it flying into the gnarled trunk of a palm tree at the edge of the largest auction tent. Was Lizbeth the woman for him? She was available, but a grieving widow. Perhaps he should step back awhile and wait on *Gott*'s direction.

He cast her a veiled glance and headed back under the large tent where another auction was about to start. He contemplated his odd behavior of late. When had Lizbeth Mullet gotten so deeply under his skin? Was he falling in love with the widow?

By late afternoon the auctions under the big tent were in full swing. Lizbeth watched people mill around, their chatter sounding like the constant hum of a bee's nest. The blue tarp, stretched taut by ropes, provided shade for the local sewing ladies all dressed in varying shades of pale lavender, blue and yellow. The covering danced and flapped overhead as a gust of wind swirled across the park and deposited dead leaves at their feet.

Lizbeth plunged her short quilting needle into the soft layers of cotton for safekeeping and then stomped her old black lace-up shoes, sending leaves flying. She went back to making tiny stitches on the beautiful double-wedding-ring quilt the sewing group was finishing for Bertha Zook's December wedding.

Thankfully she hadn't forgotten everything she knew about quilting while she'd been in Ohio. Her mother-in-law had never allowed her to sit in with the local sewing group. She was seldom allowed to go into town for groceries or fabric for clothes, and when she did, Jonah was always with her. The ladies of the community came routinely to the farm to sew, but Lizbeth was always banished to her bedroom, as if she were an embarrassment to the family. It had been another way to humiliate her, which seemed to bring pleasure to the mean-spirited older woman.

"You ready to move in to your new home, Lizbeth?" Kitty Troyer asked, her brown-eyed gaze darting toward Lizbeth and then back to the row of minute stitches she was making on her end of the quilt. As habit would have it, a tiny wedge of her pink tongue stuck out as she concentrated on what she was doing with her needle.

"Benuel and I should finish moving in soon," Lizbeth answered. But was she ready to move in to the big house with a *kinner* and live alone for the first time in her life? Most of her belongings, meager as they were, already hung in the generous closets, sat on the newly papered shelves. Benuel's shirts and britches were folded in the old, but well-preserved, dresser in the smaller room next to hers.

She'd managed to delay the actual move-in date, but she'd run out of time. Most of the house repairs had been made by Fredrik and her *daed*, with the exception of a short list, including new tile floors that were to be laid some time next week.

It was move in or admit she wasn't ready to be a single parent to Benuel. Did she have the parenting skills needed to keep such an overactive child contained? She doubted she did, but she was learning fast and would soon have them. The night before it had taken the joined efforts of her *daed*, Ulla and herself to get Benuel to bed. He'd been placed back in his cot over and over, threatened with punishment by her father, but still he'd resisted. Later, he had snuck into her bed late in the night, while everyone was asleep.

Beyond exhausted, she'd allowed him to sleep with her for a few additional minutes and then carried him back to his bed, only to find him snuggled under her quilt when the sunshine came streaming into her bedroom window this morning.

She couldn't keep allowing him to sleep in her bed. He was getting too big. He needed to catch up with other boys his age.

She'd struggled to teach him to tie his own shoes before breakfast, promising him the treat of his favorite pancakes if he'd just listen to her instructions and try for himself. His mind didn't seem able to settle on what she'd been telling him. For mere seconds he'd paid attention and then was off to watch a ladybug crawl on the screen door. She'd ended up tying his shoes for him and sending him off to brush his teeth.

The doctor she'd taken him to just after Jonah's death had diagnosed him with ADHD. She'd been given a pamphlet. The doctor's comments clarified why Benuel had such a hard time learning new skills and why he was never able to sit still long enough to listen to words of instruction. But knowing the name of the problem didn't make him any easier to teach.

The doctor had spoken of medication that could be used when he was older and in school. The pamphlets she'd read and placed on the table had turned up missing, no doubt thrown out by her father-in-law, who swore there was nothing wrong with the boy that a good whipping wouldn't cure. It was that man's answer for everything.

Lost in her own world, Lizbeth didn't hear her name being called until Ulla touched her arm.

Lizbeth glanced up, acknowledging Ulla with a glance and then noticed all the women around the quilting hoop looking her way. She'd known some of the older women most of her life. A few were strangers to her, but they all accepted her in a way that told her she was welcomed to the sewing circle. She scrambled to remember what the topic of conversation had been a moment before. She felt her face warm. "I'm sorry. Was someone speaking to me?"

At the far end of the large square hoop, Theda Fischer, the bishop's wife, leaned forward and spoke, a tiny dimple appearing as she smiled sweetly Lizbeth's way. The day's humidity had the older woman's crisp *kapp* floating atop a mass of frazzled reddish-gray hair. "*Ya*, it was me, Lizzy. I was wondering if you'd be starting Benuel at the Mennonite school. There'll be two openings now that Henry Schrock took his twins back to live with his *mamm*."

Benuel's birthday was in a few days. He'd turn five and be old enough to attend. But she hadn't considered putting him in school since his behavior had become so volatile of late. She'd decided to wait a bit, at least until he turned six.

If he *were* an average boy of five, she thought, she'd consider sending him. But sadly, he wasn't. He was a handful, even for her *daed*, who had managed to keep her rambunctious brother in line until he'd been baptized and married at twenty-four. "He seems so young to be cooped up in a classroom all those hours. Perhaps it's best…" Lizbeth let her words float away on the breeze, not sure what else to add.

After threading another needle, Theda glanced back at her. "Mark my words. It's the best thing that could happen to a young man with his level of intelligence and energy."

So others in the small community *had* noticed Benuel's inability to contain himself. Lizbeth thrust her needle in the fabric and pricked herself. Careful not to get the droplet of blood on the quilt, she jerked her handkerchief from her apron and wrapped it around her finger. "Time will tell," she offered and went back to sewing.

Around the hoop several ladies murmured their opinions. Lizbeth glanced over at Ulla and watched as her father's new wife smoothed the quilt out in front of her and tightened her edge of the hoop. She affectionately shared a smile with Lizbeth.

A moment later Lizbeth glanced back up as Ulla murmured to no one in particular, "It makes me to wonder if all this talk of Benuel's behavior and the merits of school isn't stressing Lizbeth. We must remember she *is* a new widow, with enough on her plate for now. She's dealing with the loss of her beloved husband, and moving in to a new home. Instead of us concerning ourselves with the pros and cons of school, let's sing some songs and lighten her spirits."

A nervous giggle came from Pearly, the community's favorite soloist at their local New Order Amish church. Ulla nodded her way and the sweet words of "I'll Meet You in The Morning" began in the woman's high, clear voice, leaving Lizbeth time to gather her troubled thoughts.

As she sang along, she contemplated her and Benuel's future. The choices she'd make in the next few weeks could change the little boy's life. She wanted what was best for him, wanted him to grow into a fine, strong man, with or without a father around to guide him. Benuel would have her *daed* as a guiding light and he would have to be enough. He was a far cry better than Benuel's last stand-in father.

Sunlight filtering through the trees revealed Fredrik walking past their little canvas-topped island. He was with a man Lizbeth recognized as Lon Yoder, one of their classmates back in school. He and Fredrik pulled at the rims of their straw hats and nodded in her direction as they silently passed.

She was careful to take in a slow breath and not let anyone see how thrilled she really was to be near Fredrik again. She'd had a crush on him as a girl, and she'd thought it could turn into more. But then he'd walked out of her life without so much as a wave goodbye. Someday he might make a good husband, but not yet. Besides, she wasn't sure she'd ever be ready to marry. Would she be able to trust a man again? To love again? She hoped so.

A cooling breeze ruffled her hair and brought her back to her surroundings. She looped a strand of hair behind her ear and picked up her needle. Fredrik was out of sight, lost in the sea of people mingling around. She tried to quiet her thoughts, but her heart kept beating loudly in her ears.

She glanced around the quilting hoop. The singing had ended and several of the ladies where chatting amongst themselves, sharing stories about new grandbabies or the friendly *Englischer* who'd taken their pictures when they'd met on the street and then offered them a dollar in payment. Lizbeth resumed her work on the quilt, determined in her heart to do her best for Benuel as he grew into a man of faith.

Chapter Nine

The wind caught the farmhouse door and slammed it shut with a bang behind Lizbeth's father and Fredrik Lapp.

Seeing them walk in, Lizbeth lowered her eyes and steadied her hand as she placed a steaming bowl of homegrown string beans on the table. "Is Fredrik eating with us tonight?" Her heart skipped a beat, reminding her of her growing attraction to the man. She smoothed out wrinkles from the simple white tablecloth covering the table before heading back toward the kitchen for the pot roast, new potatoes and carrots platter.

Ulla's eyes darted toward the front of the house. A corner of her mouth lifted. "*Ya.* He's ready to start work on the apartment behind the house and needs John's advice on some of the projects. Your *daed* told me he'd invited Fredrik to stay for dinner a while ago. I just forgot to tell you."

Lizbeth's brows lifted. She tried hard not to smile and show the joy she felt. She was acting like a silly teen and knew it. "That's fine with me."

Ulla slipped Lizbeth a curious glance and then went

back to stirring tiny lumps out of John's favorite brown gravy bubbling in the iron skillet. "You don't have any feelings for Fredrik, do you?"

Lizbeth brushed away a ringlet of hair from her forehead and then reached overhead for the gravy boat her mother had always used for special occasions such as this. It was Benuel's fifth birthday, a reason to celebrate. "*Nee.* Not a bit."

She felt her face warm because of her lie. She'd have to repent during bedtime prayers. "I was just wondering, is all," she added and placed the bowl in front of Ulla, watching as the thick mixture of browned flour, chicken broth, thick cream, and salt and pepper was poured into the fragile, spouted container. When it was full to overflowing, Lizbeth wiped the sides of the old dish and carried it over to the condiments tray. She waited for Ulla to lead the way back to the table being readied for their meal.

Ulla carried in a covered basket of piping hot rolls and positioned them next to the steaming meat platter. Her face was flushed from working over a hot stove. She favored the right knee she'd injured stepping on one of Benuel's small cars left on the floor. The hobbling woman whispered over her shoulder, "The man's always seemed nice to me. Maybe you should show him some interest. I hear he's looking for a *fraa*." She smiled and looked hopeful. "He'd make a *gut* father for Benuel."

Lizbeth faked a smile. The last thing she needed was to fall for Fredrik Lapp again, or let Benuel get too attached to him, and have him chose another woman for his *fraa*.

John strode into the dining room with Fredrik trailing close behind. Her father grinned over at Ulla and then dipped his head in a friendly manner at Lizbeth as he removed his sweaty hat. His gray hair was trimmed shorter than usual, exposing the generous ears *Gott* had blessed him with. He hitched up his overlong trouser legs by pulling on his drooping black suspenders and headed for his usual chair at the big wooden table.

"I see Ulla finally caught you unawares with scissors in hand," Lizbeth teased, causing her father to laugh in a robust manner.

"She did, indeed," he admitted and impatiently beckoned for the younger man to sit next to him. "Sit there, Fredrik. Next to Lizbeth and me."

Hat in hand, Fredrik pulled out a chair and lowered himself, his gaze shifting to Lizbeth, who stood across the table from him.

She smiled his way and felt her stomach tighten.

He smiled back, his eyes sparkling.

She tried not to show how thrilled she was. Her affection toward the man was getting out of hand. She'd have to control her emotions.

"I'm sure you ladies have prepared enough food," Fredrik said. He licked his lips, flashed a nervous smile.

Ulla threw her head back and chuckled. "Have you ever known me to cook small meals, Fredrik? Every night I cook enough food for five hearty men." She grabbed the back of the chair closest to John, pulled it out and lowered herself with a groan.

"I'll…ah…just go get Benuel and *daed*'s hound," Lizbeth stammered. "He and that dog should be tired of feeding those chickens by now." She found her hand nervously patting her loose bun, her fingers toying with the hairs curling around her neck as she marched to the back door. Did she look a mess? It seemed the man always caught her in her worst moments.

As soon as she realized what she was doing she mentally scolded herself, her face flaming as she stepped onto the back porch. What foolishness. So what if her hair was flying around her face in a haphazard way. She secured her wayward curls with pins and shoved her *kapp* down on the back of her head.

"Supper time. Come get your hands washed," she called out. She saw the boy and dog rush to the barn to put away the bag of cracked corn he was dragging along the ground behind him.

"*Ya*, I'm coming," he called out with a wave.

This was Benuel's special day. It wasn't every day a boy turned five. "Quick. Come," she said in old *Deitch* and beckoned him up the steps.

Fredrik cut into the tender pot roast and stifled a groan of delight as he chewed the delicious morsel. John and Ulla had always made him feel welcome at their table, but it was Lizbeth's smile that warmed him—and made him a bit uncomfortable.

Benuel's short legs kicked back and forth as he played with his food, less than a mouthful eaten the whole time he'd been sitting in his chair. "Can I have cake now?" he asked, his words directed to his mother across from him.

"Once you finish your food," she said and speared a wedge of carrot off her plate.

"But I don't like—"

Fredrik interrupted, "When I was your age I ate all my vegetables and my *bruder*'s, too. My *mamm* said they built big muscles." He flexed his arm and showed off a well-rounded biceps to the boy. "See."

Benuel's eyes grew round with wonder. "Is so?" he asked his *mamm*, his look skeptical.

"*Ya*, is so." She bobbed her head. She had seemed impressed with the flex of his muscles, too.

Hesitant, Benuel broke off the tiniest sliver of potato and thrust it in his mouth. "I don't like how they taste," he said, and laid down his fork.

"Never mind," Fredrik muttered and shoveled in a mound of potatoes slathered in melted butter. "I'll eat your share. I need to keep up my strength for the shuffleboard game tomorrow."

"I've never played shuffleboard," Benuel informed him. "My *mamm* says I'm too little."

Fredrik smacked the bottom of the ketchup bottle and drowned his perfectly cooked beef in a sea of red sauce. "It makes me to wonder if you're too little because you leave your vegetables on your plate and not in your stomach."

Benuel pressed his lips together and kicked at the chair leg under him. "*Ya*, well. I don't want to play shuffleboard anyway. The game looks dumb." He impatiently brushed away a curl falling down on his forehead, his gaze on the offending vegetables.

"Don't kick your chair at the table," Lizbeth reminded the boy as she laid down her fork and knife next to her plate. She cocked her head and smiled. "Why don't you eat the last of your dinner? I'm sure everyone's wanting to have some chocolate birthday cake." Her tone was light and affectionate.

Ulla smiled her encouragement to Benuel and took a bite of her own vegetables.

John ate the last bite of the thick slab of beef that had been on his plate and rubbed his protruding stomach in satisfaction. "Some say that sauce makes anything green taste better." He gestured toward the ketchup bottle and relocated it close to Benuel.

The young boy looked at his grandfather and nibbled on his bottom lip, contemplating the advice while he looked at the bottle.

John shoved his empty plate forward. "It matters not to me whether you get cake. I'm having mine with ice cream and sprinkles."

Benuel gave a shrug of defeat and grabbed the bottle of sauce. Three insignificant drops fell on the single slice of carrot on his plate. He shoved his hair away from his face again and then drove his fork into the glazed wedge.

Fredrik found himself holding his breath. Silence filled the room, all eyes on the child who had disrupted the entire meal with his complaints.

The boy gingerly put the bite in his mouth and chewed. He lifted his chin and eyed his grandfather with new respect. "*Ya*, it is *gut*," he said and covered his potatoes in a circle of red.

Fredrik watched as the tension drained from Lizbeth's face. She brightened, her eyes sparkling from the overhead light.

"I'll go get the cake now." She slid a guarded look at Benuel and then hurried away.

Fredrik cleared his throat, surprised at the level of emotion he felt for the young boy. It had to be hard losing his father and moving to a new place, seeing all new faces around him. "John, why don't you come to the shuffleboard game with us tomorrow? I hear there's going to be a competition between the boys and the men. You could bring Benuel with you." He put his hands on the table and turned to Benuel. "You're sure to win eating all those vegetables," he told the boy with a grin.

"*Ya*, that sounds *gut*," John said and they both looked toward the doorway.

Lizbeth stood in the door's arch, listening to their chatter, the simple cake in her hands. A silly grin played on her lips.

Lizbeth sat the cake on the middle of the table. "Who wants a slice?" she asked. Her breath was ragged from rushing, but she rose to the occasion and began to sing the birthday song to her son in their native tongue. She cut thick wedges for everyone but herself.

Benuel received his cake first and then her father, who nodded his approval. Ulla was next. When she handed Fredrik his plate, she made sure her fingers were well away from his reach, and then cut the thinnest sliver for herself and sat. She watched as Benuel dug into the rich chocolate cake and poked a huge bite into his mouth. He smiled her way, his top lip circled in the thick chocolate icing she'd made this morning.

"It's certain-sure *gut*," he said, licking his lips with his tongue.

Lizbeth continued to watch the child, the love she felt for him brightening her mood. He was growing up too fast. He would be her only child. She was determined to enjoy his younger years while she could.

A fleeting moment of remorse cut through her. If by some twist of fate, she and Fredrik did marry, would she be able to give him a half-dozen sons? The doctor had never said for sure she could carry another *boppli* to term. She frowned, her disappointment weighing her down. She couldn't continue to encourage the man. He deserved more children than just Benuel. She thrust away her regrets and enjoyed the smile on Benuel's face. Today she'd concentrate on him. Tomorrow she'd figure out a way to keep Fredrik out of her life, even if the thought broke her heart.

Chapter Ten

Fredrik skidded to a stop and fell to the ground, his legs imprisoned by a laughing Mennonite boy of ten or twelve. Minor pain in his left elbow told him he wasn't completely over the fall he'd taken when he'd almost run over Lizbeth and Benuel.

He kept his smile pasted to his face, but the memory of almost killing them was still too fresh in his mind. He snatched his straw hat off the ground and pushed his hair out of his eyes before placing it back on his head. He knew *Gott* had forgiven him, but he hung on to his remorse as a humbling lesson. One day he'd forgive himself, but not today.

Mennonite and Amish men and their sons wandered across the field and started another free-for-all football game. He wished young Benuel had been allowed to come to the park with his grandfather. The boy would have enjoyed the opportunity to run wild and not be watched so closely by his *mamm*. The child was hyperactive, prone to getting into mischief, just as he'd been as a boy. He understood the need for speed and the urge to talk too much.

Fredrik accepted the hand that reached out to help him up and scrambled to his feet. A chuckle escaped him. He, and everyone around him, found his clumsiness amusing. Head down, he dusted the dirt off his shirt-sleeve, and then congratulated the boy who'd brought him down. "You've got great tackling skills," he said, with a firm pat on the back. "*Gut* job." He watched the boy run across the field to join his friends. "I think I'm getting too old for this game," he remarked.

"*Ya*, could be," Mose Fischer commented from behind him and laughed when Fredrik turned and made a face.

"I noticed you took a few spills yourself this afternoon, elder Fischer," Fredrik shot back and snickered at his boss's counterfeit wounded expression.

"That I did," Mose admitted and pointed to a tear in his pants. "Sarah will be grievously offended by my abuse to the new trousers she stitched this week."

Someone snatched up the football and kicked it high in the air. The game was on again, but Fredrik and Mose lagged behind, letting the younger boys keep the games going. "I'm ready for some cold lemonade."

"*Ya*, me too." Fredrik nodded, and then paused just long enough to brush grass off his green-stained trouser leg. "Are Sarah and the *kinner* with you today?"

"*Nee*. She and Ulla took the *kinner* to see how Lizbeth is faring at the house. I hear she's got her hands full with that young boy of hers. Beatrice tells me he's a real stinker."

Fredrik's mouth twitched in a lopsided grin. "That he is."

Mose glanced his way. "Lizbeth's about your age. Were you scholars together?"

"We were. I used to run around with her *bruder* as a

boy and her *mamm* would send Lizbeth along for good measure." He chortled. "She used to drive us crazy." He tugged at his straw hat, his memories of a younger, skinnier version of Lizbeth causing him to smile broadly. "She talked too much and was always into mischief."

"Like Benuel?" Mose asked, wiping sweat from his glistening forehead.

"*Nee*, not like him. Lizbeth got into innocent mischief, but Benuel's behavior is different." He laughed at his own ridiculous thought. "He's more like I was as a boy. Easily distracted. Always into trouble or getting paddled for doing something stupid."

"If he's hyper like you, then I'd say poor kid and poor Lizbeth." Mose laughed. "I was older than you, but I remember you tearing around the playground full tilt, knocking down girls and making them cry."

Fredrik dropped his head and faked remorse. "*Ya.* My *mamm* used to say she held her breath until I went to bed each night."

"Beatrice took a liking to Benuel right off," Mose said, "but then swore he hit her. She's not so enamored with the boy now."

They both laughed at the thought of Mose's outspoken eldest daughter, Beatrice, and Benuel in the same room together. "I'm sure she'll change her mind about him when they get a bit older," Fredrik said, and couldn't resist adding, "One day you might find her married to Chicken John's grandson."

Mose stopped, squeezed his eyes shut for a second and then looked up into the sky. "Don't wish that on me. Can you imagine what my grandchildren would be like?"

Fredrik thought about an older Mose holding grandchildren in his arms. He could see it, but couldn't see himself with children yet, much less grandchildren. If he didn't start stepping out soon he wouldn't have a wife to share grandchildren with. Lizbeth's face came to his mind, her butter-blond hair blowing around it. The widow interested him deeply, but was she ready for marriage? Would she consider him good husband material? She knew him too well, so probably not.

The next day Lizbeth couldn't believe her eyes. Hands high on her hips, she bellowed, "Benuel James Mullet! Put down that nasty frog and come into the house right now. Wash your hands. Do you want to get warts?"

She gasped as she watched Benuel kiss the slimy frog on the head again. With all the tenderness of a mother, he placed the speckled critter back on the ground and encouraged it along with the wave of his small hands.

"I'll come find you later and we'll play," he said loud enough for his mother to hear. He shot her an accusing glance as the frog seemed to understand his words and worked its way under the root of an old moss-covered tree.

"You will not find him later. You'll leave that nasty frog alone and any other wild critters you find in this backyard." She wiped her hands on her clean work apron as if she felt the slime on them, and laughed. She knew what frogs felt like thanks to her brother's and Fredrik Lapp's practical jokes back in school. At least once a week she would find one in her lunch bag or stuck down in one of her shoes. She fought the urge to cringe. She knew boys loved their lizards and toads, but she was determined not to find one in her *soh*'s trouser pockets come wash day.

Benuel stomped past her, his lips pouted. "He was

my only friend and now he's gone." His head dropped as he rounded the corner of the house and made a hasty retreat for the kitchen door.

Maybe she'd been too harsh on the child. She was repulsed by frogs, but he wasn't. She had to let him be himself. Like what he liked. He was growing up, would want to discover the wonders of the world for himself.

A glance at his retreating back told her his clothes were getting too small, the hems of his trousers exposing his bony ankles. She'd have to get out her *mamm*'s old sewing machine and stitch up two pairs of trousers and a new shirt for church. Sewing men's clothes had never been one of her strong suits, but Sarah Fischer had offered to give her a refresher class with a few other women from the community.

The back door banged shut. She hurried along. There was lunch to prepare, laundry to wash and she needed to buy a bag of food for the cat out in the shed. This morning she'd found evidence the cat's midnight hunts were paying off. The little mother-to-be was earning her keep. She'd had to throw a long, skinny rat tail away before Benuel found it and kept it as a souvenir.

Lizbeth heard the water splashing in the front bathroom. A moment later, Benuel came into the kitchen, his hands dripping water all over her freshly mopped kitchen floor. "Did you dry your hands?"

He looked down at his still-moist hands and nodded. "I think so."

She tossed him a kitchen towel and suggested, "Perhaps not as well as you could have."

His casual shrug told her how worried he was to have damp hands. He pulled out a chair and plopped himself down, his legs still going at a fast clip. Back and forth. Back and forth.

Lizbeth took in a deep breath and turned back to the beef patties she was forming. How did it feel, this ADHD? It couldn't be easy dealing with the constant urge to be in motion, your mind racing before you could complete a thought. "Would you like cheese on your burger?"

"No. Just ketchup," he said, his fingers tapping out a tune only he heard.

Two extra bottles of red sauce waited in the kitchen closet. Since her father had suggested vegetables tasted better with sauce on them, the boy ate everything with a good dousing. There was no way hot oatmeal could taste better with butter, maple syrup and ketchup, but Benuel had gobbled it down this morning. She wasn't going to complain. No fussing over food was fine with her.

"Why is that man in our back garden?"

Lizbeth pulled back the curtain and peered out the kitchen window. "What man?"

He wrote his name in the salt he'd sprinkled on the table.

"Don't waste the salt and make a mess." She watched a dark form become the shape of a man and realized it was Fredrik working on the back apartment. Banging began. "That's Fredrik, our landlord. How long has he been out there?" The sun was shining, and it was warm out, but Fredrik had no hat covering his ginger hair.

"I don't know. He was there when I went out."

The hammering stopped. Fredrik moved out of sight. Lizbeth, who was tall for a woman, stretched to see where he had gone. Her sight was encumbered by a row of leafy trees lining the back fence. "Was he friendly?"

"*Ya*. He said he likes kids and frogs."

Sizzling fat popped out of the frying pan and hit her on the arm. She flipped over the burgers and put a bun on the gas burner to toast. "You're not to bother him while he works, do you hear?"

"I'm hungry. Is the meat cooked yet?" he said, ignoring her comment. With a flourish, he added pepper to the mess he was making on the tablecloth and squiggled his name in it. He sneezed twice and then used his hand to remove the mess he'd made.

"I asked you a question. Did you bother him while he was working?" She turned the gas off under the toasted bun and used a fork to place it on the plate, and then added the burger before she turned around.

Benuel ran his hands through his hair, dislodging a leaf and tree bark and placing them where the salt and pepper had been. "I don't remember." His expression looked sincere.

Lizbeth sat the boy's food in front of him and placed the ketchup next to his plate. "Was he working hard?"

He grinned and grabbed the red bottle in front of him. "*Ya*. He's nailing in new wood around the door." He dumped a circle of red on his plate. "Stuff like that."

The banging began again. She glanced toward the window, watched the breeze flip the curtain in a swirl. Fredrik's back came into view, his blue shirtsleeve stretching taut as he lifted his arm and swung the hammer in his hand. It seemed he was everywhere she went, or was she just noticing him because she liked being around him? This foolish attraction to the man had to stop. He needed a wife to give him children and there was no guarantee she could do that, even if she was interested in finding a new husband.

"*Nee!* Don't do that," she scolded as she turned back toward her son, but it was too late. Benuel had already dunked his burger in a pool of ketchup. He smiled in satisfaction as he chewed, and took another big bite of hamburger slathered in red sauce. He ignored her comment.

Lizbeth shrugged her shoulders and went back to washing dishes. At least he was eating now. Maybe she'd try some lettuce and tomato on his bun the next time. Eating this hardy, he just might put some weight on at last, and she had Fredrik and her father to thank for it.

Fredrik had already fixed the broken gutter over the apartment door, but the damage had allowed wood rot to form at the base of the door. He yanked on the crumbling wood with a crowbar, cleaned out the leaves and dirt and then replaced the length of wood with a fresh board. Content, he hummed as he nailed the wood into place. He'd paint the strip later, while he sanded and painted the peeling front door. The small concrete porch was intact and the sidewalk to the wire gate seemed fit enough, even though there was a slight crack in one section.

Lizbeth's kitchen window was open. Perhaps her cooking was the source of the delicious aroma floating on the late-afternoon breeze. His stomach grumbled. It had been a long time since lunch.

Two days a week he worked half days at Mose's furniture barn. Being off today gave him the opportunity to do a few jobs on the apartment and some of the handyman jobs he had lined up around Pinecraft and Sarasota, but they sure messed with his eating schedule.

He checked his pocket watch and snapped it shut, surprised to see it was already six, an hour past his usual dinner meal. He would stop soon and grab a bite to eat at the café, but he still had a lot of work to do. He wanted to rent the apartment before the month ended since he had decided to sublet it for profit.

Sweat beaded his forehead. He swiped at it, and then banged another nail into the wood.

He slipped the hammer into his waist belt, heard the sound of a child giggling and turned to see Benuel running out the side door of the white house.

"Come back and let me wipe your face," Lizbeth shouted, hot on her son's heels. The gate slammed behind the boy. His mother managed to seize his arm before he could climb into the swing hanging from the old oak tree covered in moss.

Memories of his childhood and his *mamm* having to haul him back into the house for a good face scrubbing flashed in his mind. *Boys will be boys*, his *daed* used to tell her when she complained about his lack of table manners at the supper table.

Boys needed a man in their lives, someone to show them how to behave and still have fun. He was glad to be around to see Benuel at his best, when he was relaxed and growing more secure in his new home.

Too hungry to wait to eat, he packed up his tools, locked the apartment door and then glanced back to Lizbeth. He watched as she scrubbed at Benuel's face with a cloth. The boy squirmed and kicked just like Fredrik used to fight his *mamm* at that age. Lizbeth looked like she'd been busy, her hair wild under her *kapp* in the fading light of day. Her cheeks were rosy from the heat of the kitchen. Smudges of something she'd been cooking were wiped down the front of her apron, making her look adorable. He wanted a wife like her. Someone who took care of her family and loved them.

He couldn't help but laugh when Benuel got away. The memory of the thrill of the chase was still so alive in Fredrik's mind that he took in a deep breath of excitement. He let loose a guffaw as mother and son ran around the yard, her skirts swirling, the boy's long legs making fast work of the distance between him and the swing.

Benuel pumped himself high into the air. Lizbeth stood a yard away, her hands dangling at her sides. Frustration etched lines across her forehead. "You have to come off that swing sometime, young man. And when you do, your face is mine."

"A little dirt won't hurt him," Fredrik supposed out loud.

Lizbeth turned just her head in his direction. She smiled her welcome. "No. A bit of dirt won't hurt him, but him not listening to me might. I'm trying to teach him to obey."

Fredrik did his best to sober his expression, but knew he'd failed miserably. He nodded his head. "*Ya*, you're certain-sure right. *Mamms* always are." He glanced back at Benuel. The child was ignoring them both, the wind blowing his ginger hair into spikes, his boyish voice singing a simple children's worship song Fredrik had sung himself at the boy's age.

A smile lifted one side of Lizbeth's mouth as she listened to Benuel sing.

"He has a good, strong voice," Fredrik commented, but continued to walk toward his bike resting at the side of the shed.

"*Ya*, he does. Like my *daed*," she muttered, more to herself than to him.

He walked his bike to the gate, considering the lonely mood that had come over him. He was tired of being alone. He would have rather gone into Lizbeth's kitchen and settled himself in one of her chairs than go to the café and eat alone. Sharing a meal with her and the boy would have been a treat.

When had he begun to think this way…begun to seriously long for a family of his own? This family? "Have a good night," he called, waving as he threw his leg over the bike.

She turned and waved back, her expression friendly and relaxed. "And you, Fredrik Lapp."

He headed north and minutes later turned into the graveled parking lot across from the café. He'd have to seriously begin his search for a wife. It was past time to settle, begin a family of his own, but first he'd have to see if Lizbeth would have him. He just had to find the nerve to ask her. If she wasn't interested, he needed to pull back and put some distance between them. Fredrik wasn't willing to risk his heart once more.

Benuel's voice still sounded in his subconscious, putting a smile on Fredrik's face. He lifted his head, looked at the darkening sky. What a shame Lizbeth seemed so uneasy about sharing her life again.

From the way she distanced herself from all men, perhaps he knew he didn't have a chance with her now, but he wouldn't give up easily. She was a fine woman, a woman who needed a father for her son. He thought of the soft curve of her cheek, the way her eyes sparkled when she was happy. Perhaps he *was* the man meant to put a smile back on her face and she just didn't realize it yet.

He walked into the café humming the childish song Benuel had been singing about letting his light shine for Jesus. Would Fredrik continue to hide his light under a bucket? *Nee*, he didn't think so.

Chapter Eleven

The first two weeks in the rental house had gone smoother than Lizbeth had expected. Fredrik was often underfoot with this project or that, but she'd grown comfortable with his sudden appearances. When he used Benuel as his helper, it freed her up to cook special meals they could share together. Was it so wrong to feel as if they were becoming a family of sorts?

She tossed in her bed. The nights were hard on her. She heard every groan and moan the old house made, knew when Benuel turned in his small bed.

Unable to sleep, she'd let the young mama cat in for company and found herself petting her as she prepared to put another load of colored clothes in the washing machine. She was grateful Fredrik had left it for his renters to use.

As they walked into the kitchen, the cat indicated she'd like to go out. Lizbeth opened the side door a crack and watched the cat's belly sway from side to side as she rushed away into the darkness. There should be a litter of kittens coming soon. She was surprised to find herself looking forward to the big event as much as Benuel and Fredrik were.

Once the door was locked tight again, she decided a hot cup of chocolate would help her sleep and got busy pouring milk into a pan. On impulse she grabbed one of her son's favorite oatmeal cookies before settling into the overstuffed chair in the living room with her steaming cup.

Content to read the Bible, she leafed through until she found her marker at Romans 8:28.

And we know that all things work together for good to them that love God, to them who are the called according to his purpose.

She would have to wait for *Gott* to show her His path for her and Benuel's life. She continued to read.

For whom he did foreknow, he also did predestinate to be conformed to the image of his Son, that he might be the firstborn among many brethren.

Her eyes growing tired, she closed the Bible and meditated on the lines she'd read. All things *had* seemed to work together for good since they'd returned to Pinecraft. She just hadn't gotten used to the idea of being alone yet.

As the last bite of her cookie was shoved in her mouth, she slipped off her house shoes, pulled her legs up under her gown and robe and burrowed deep into the soft cushions of the chair.

Long sips of the hot chocolate soothed her. She set the cup down as her eyes began to feel heavy. Sleep wasn't far off. If she wasn't careful she'd fall asleep where she was.

The sound of Benuel crying roused her from her light slumber.

"*Nee*, get away," he yelled.

Heart pounding, her bare feet smacked against the wood floors as she raced to him and scooped him into her arms.

He fought her. *"Nee, nee,"* he shouted, pushing at her.

She turned on his lamp and spoke to him in *Deitch*. "It's me, Benuel. Wake up. *Mamm* has you. It was only a dream."

He blinked up at her, his eyes glistening with unshed tears. *"Daed* was shouting." He used his hand to swipe at a tear threatening to run down his face. "I saw him hit you and you cried out."

"*Nee*, it was only a dream, Benuel. You see? I'm wonderful-*gut*."

"Ya, but I saw—"

"What you saw was a dream. I'm fine, look." She laid him back against his pillow and smiled down at him as she ruffled his tangled hair. "We are safe now. I promise you. We must never worry again. *Gott* is protecting us from all harm. Jonah will never hurt us again."

"Ya?" he questioned, glancing around his room, his eyes wide and round.

She soothed him, her hand gently touching his face. "We are safe. Now, close your eyes. I'll sing your favorite song."

She trembled as she quietly sang the "Father Abraham" hymn he'd come to love.

His lids closed, but she felt the shuddering breath he took just before he dropped off. Sobs broke from her.

No child should have witnessed what Benuel had seen in his short life. She should have taken him and fled long before her husband died. The child paid for her mistakes. Others didn't understand, but she knew why she kept the boy close to her. She knew the horrors the small child had experienced. If only she could tell him that the man who terrified him wasn't his true father. But if anyone ever found out, she could be ruined. And so could Fredrik.

She rose from Benuel's bed, leaving the light on and the door open.

In her room she threw herself across her rumpled bed and wept for her fatherless boy who had lived through so much, for her tiny babies left behind on the hill and for herself. Would she ever find peace? Perhaps if she prayed with all her might at church tomorrow, *Gott* would erase these memories from both their minds.

Fredrik found it hard to sit through three hours of church without stirring. He surveyed the group of smaller boys in the row in front of him. Their hair all neatly combed in place, most sat quietly, waiting to be called forward.

Someone sneezed and he recognized Benuel Mullet as the boy turned toward the noise. The corners of Fredrik's mouth lifted. He remembered how it was to be a boy and long for the service to be over.

Fredrik heard Lizbeth clear her throat as a warning. The child had better behave or his *mamm* was going to do something about it as soon as church was over. The *kinner* turned back toward the front, but squirmed until he found a comfortable spot on the bench and settled.

Isaac Graber, owner of the bike shop in town, and

his new wife, Molly, sang the last stanza of "Amazing Grace." He clapped his hands with the rest of the church, appreciating the good job they had done.

A hand gestured and he observed someone in a blue dress motioning the small boys forward. All eight of them, including Benuel, popped up and shuffled to the front of the church in a jagged line. They wormed their way across the elevated platform, sidestepping until they were a few inches away from each other. The lady in blue ticked off the beat of the hymn and on three they began to sing "Deep and Wide" and make motions with their hands.

Benuel Mullet's voice rang out over the other boys', his motions exaggerated, feet tapping. Two rows over, he heard Lizbeth groan her disapproval.

Fredrik's foot tapped, too. Awe transformed his face into a wide smile. The boy could really sing, his voice revealing a hidden talent much like Fredrik's own.

He remembered singing with the other boys in the community when he was Benuel's age. What an exciting time it had been, singing on the stage with everyone looking at him. Too quick, the song was over and the boys returned to their places on the front bench. Benuel's eyes twinkled as he spotted his mother in the crowd and gave a quick wave. He plopped down, causing the boy next to him to yelp. Fredrik couldn't help but grin. The boy was a handful, but talented and full of life.

Mose Fischer ended the service with a silent prayer and people began to file out of the church. Caught in the crush of people and *kinner*, Fredrik stepped behind Ulla and her husband, Chicken John, and followed them out.

"You coming to the potluck dinner in the park?" Ulla asked a moment later. "We're trying to raise money for a new family who's moved here from Beeville, Texas." Her eyes grew wide as she spoke. "A tornado blew everything they owned away. *Gott* was with them. Their neighbors didn't make it out."

He'd thought about going straight to the café to eat and then taking a nap, but the idea of doing a good deed and eating food Pinecraft's best cooks prepared changed his mind. His spirits lifted. "*Ya*, sure. I'll see you there." His bike was parked at the back of the church. He passed Lizbeth and Benuel and tugged at the brim of his Sunday best black wool hat. "Someday that boy's going to make you a very proud *mamm*."

She nodded and smiled. "*Danki*, Fredrik. He already makes me a proud *mamm*." She walked toward him. "You going to the meal at the park?" she asked, holding tight to her son's hand.

"*Ya*, I am."

She walked past him. "*Gut*. See you there."

His eyes followed her as she walked to her three-wheel bike and rode off with Benuel in the wire basket. He wished he was riding beside them, but he would see them there. Lizbeth may have put away her black dresses, but she was still distant and wore the look of a widow in mourning. He had to be patient and bide his time. Or move on and find someone else willing to become his wife. That might be the safer option.

With the exception of a strong wind blowing, the day was perfect for a meal in the park. Fredrik looked around for a couple of his friends and found nothing but families sitting together. He made his way to the long tables covered in plastic bowls, roasting pans and heated chafing dishes. The food line was already lengthy. He stepped behind one of his favorite elders and shuffled along. The man's wife and six children were in line ahead of him. It seemed everyone had a *fraa*. Was he the last bachelor in Pinecraft?

He looked over and saw Mose, Sarah and their children at a long table. If he hurried, he might be able to find room to eat with them.

A big glass jar on the first table held the receipts for the moneymaker. He drew out a crisp twenty-dollar bill and dropped it in, thought better of it and added another twenty to the jar. If it were his family who'd lost everything… But it wasn't his family. He didn't have one.

Sometimes it seemed *Gott*'s will for his life was to live alone and lonely. Or that he had missed *Gott*'s plan by letting Bette slip past. Her decision to drop him for his best friend still stung and grieved his heart. If he'd fought for her, he'd have children by now, a home. But if Bette had been the one for him, *Gott* would have made a way. No, the problem was in him. He'd dated a lot in his youth, but hadn't settled down. He'd have to keep looking, find that perfect someone made just for him, if he hadn't found her already.

Hungry after the long service, he chose a thick slice of slightly pink pot roast and plump potatoes, glazed carrots and onions to go with it. Someone bumped into him from behind and said with a laugh, *"Dummle sich,"* encouraging him to hurry along.

Fredrik balanced his plate as he glanced back and smiled with good-natured amusement. Isaac Graber, with Molly at his side, trailed behind him. "You and the missus sang a fine song this morning," he said and speared a slice of bread.

"*Danki*. We do our best," Isaac said. "Your bike should be ready to pick up by tomorrow."

Fredrik laughed. "*Gut*, I was hoping you'd say that. Mose said if I keep driving in on that scooter he's going to fire me. I keep falling off since I got it back from the shop last week." Fredrik laughed as he scooped a couple of pickled beets onto his filled plate, and saw there was no more room for bread-and-butter pickles.

Isaac nodded. "I was delayed a day by Molly. She had an ultrasound appointment. Seems we're having a *boppli* come early spring."

"Congratulations!" Fredrik exclaimed, stepping away from the table so others could help themselves to food.

Molly Graber beamed with excitement as they walked toward an empty table with him. "I think my *mamm*'s more excited than we are. You'd think this was her first grandchild to hear her talk."

Isaac grinned at his wife. "My *mamm* will be coming down in December with a couple of my sisters. We'll have plenty of help when the *boppli* arrives."

"This is wonderful-*gut* news. You are truly blessed, Isaac Graber," Fredrik said, placing his plate down on the table.

"*Ya*, sure. That we are." He motioned toward a group of tables under the trees. "Come. You are *willkumm* to join us at the long tables. There is no need for you to eat alone just because you're unwed."

Fredrik hesitated when he saw Lizbeth at the end of the mixed families table, her son sitting close to her hip. "Perhaps I should—"

"Don't be a *bensel*. Join us."

"You can meet my *aenti* Hilda. She's a matchmaker,

and come to visit, but I'm sure she'll have time to find you a *fraa* while she's here," Molly said.

He picked up his plate, but his steps slowed. Ulla had told him her matchmaker sister was coming soon and could help him in his search for a *fraa*, but now that she was here a funny feeling went over him. He looked toward Lizbeth. Had he already found the woman he wanted as his *fraa*?

He muttered, *"Danki,"* but his eye caught Lizbeth looking back at him. She glanced away after a few seconds, but he'd caught the content expression on her face. She didn't need him in her life. She was happy the way things were. As long as she was mourning, she and her son were off-limits to him and the thought ate at him. Perhaps he should meet with the matchmaker.

Chapter Twelve

Fredrik slipped onto the bench. Two people down, Lizbeth watched him scoot in. She began to eat as if his joining them at their table was of no importance to her. He tipped the edge of his straw hat in her direction a moment later. She did her best to conceal the thrill tugging at her heart.

She was glad he sat so near. She might get a chance to talk to him, tell him how silly Benuel had acted when she brought home a glass house for his beloved frog. She tussled with her feelings for the handsome man a few feet away. Frustration brought a frown to her face. She knew she could be a good *fraa* for Fredrik, but what if the doctor had been wrong about her miscarriage? Was it her body's fault her *bopplis* died within minutes of being born as Jonah suggested? And what would Fredrik think if she told him the truth about Benuel?

She pushed her food around her plate, making no effort to eavesdrop on his conversation with Isaac, but his deep voice carried. He mentioned his work at the furniture barn and the fact he'd been working on the apartment behind her home.

Gracie Troyer, slim and pretty and one of Pinecraft's new widows, made it a point to stop by the table and say hello to Sarah. She asked what time the next youth quilting class began. Her eyes stayed on Fredrik as the women chatted.

Her daughter of ten or eleven flushed pink when her mother suggested Fredrik should come by and fix a few things that needed to be repaired around their house. No doubt her mother was more taken with the man than the girl, whose father had died a few months earlier.

Lizbeth knew her thoughts were uncharitable. The widow might have a genuine need of Fredrik's skills. But then the widow put her small hand on the back of Fredrik's fold up chair. Lizbeth took notice of the subtle way the woman's fingers brushed his shoulder blade and drew his attention back to her.

Ya, there was more than just home repairs on the widow's mind. This forwardness was not the way Amish women behaved in Pinecraft. As girls, mothers taught their daughters to be respected for their virtue, and Gracie seemed to have forgotten some of her training.

Lizbeth dropped her head in shame, her eyes glued to her uneaten food. She had no right to think so critically about Gracie. *Gott* would not be pleased. Fredrik had been very clear with his intentions. He was looking for a *fraa*, and if she put up a hedge around herself, it was her own fault he was looking at Gracie with an interested eye.

Mose collected Benuel for a game of tug-of-war with the younger *kinner*. She waved the small boy off with a smile and reminded Mose to keep a close eye on him. Benuel was learning, but he still had a fondness for running off, forgetting to stay close in crowds.

"I'm told you've rented the *haus* my *schweschder* used to own."

Wrapped in her own thoughts, Lizbeth jerked around, unaware she'd drawn Hilda Albrecht's attention. "*Ya*, the *haus* is perfect for the boy and me. We've found contentment there." Lizbeth replied in *Deitch*, the language the woman was fluently speaking.

Hilda had been introduced to Lizbeth at lunch. She was visiting her older sister, Ulla, and staying at the chicken farm for the next two weeks. The older woman looked young for the seventy years she claimed. Hilda was nothing like Ulla, who was average height, a bit on the stout side, with an unkempt look about her, thanks to her unruly gray hair.

Hilda was no more than four foot ten, if that, and thin as a reed. Every hair on Hilda's brown head was neatly in place, her heart-shaped *kapp* starched stiff and pressed. Dressed in a navy church dress and black apron, she seldom spoke anything but Pennsylvania *Deitch*, with a sprinkling of High German added with authority.

Rumor had it she had been the local matchmaker in the Shipshewana district of Lancaster County for the past sixty years. She was said to be looked upon as a mentor for the young women in her community. Since her beloved husband's death, she'd taken up travel and often arranged marriages between the Old and New Order communities in Ohio and Indiana. Her visit here was to see Ulla, but it was evident she planned on using her skills of matchmaking on some of Pinecraft's single and widowed folk.

The corners of Hilda's eyes crinkled, her suntanned face a craggy road map of present and past smiles and frowns. Her eyes flashed with energy and a love of life.

The smiling little woman carried a small leather-bound notebook everywhere she went, and was prepared to jot down a prospective couple's names as she saw similarities and possible connections. Lizbeth's pupils flared as she observed the little woman squinting at Fredrik and Gracie, scrawling something down in her book and then shutting it with a satisfied twitch around her mouth.

"Surely you must be planning on living but a short while in the house." Hilda turned back to Lizbeth and put a hand on her arm. "I assume you'll remarry soon. Benuel could use the firm hand of a father."

Heat stained Lizbeth's neck and cheeks and warmed her face. Surely this wasn't the place to bring up the subject of a future marriage for her. Not with Fredrik and Gracie sitting close enough to hear every word they were saying.

There had been a time, many years ago, when her quick marriage to Jonah caused local tongues to waggle. Since then she'd become a closed-off person, unwilling to discuss her past or present with anyone, even her *daed*.

She gave Fredrik a fleeting glance. Sunrays glinted off the deeper red tones in his hair. Shoveling food into his mouth, he continued to nod as Gracie drew up chairs for herself and her daughter and spoke to him in muted tones. He seemed interested in what she had to say.

Pen in hand, Hilda scribbled another notation in her book, her eyes glinting with something akin to mischief. "You've known Fredrik Lapp a long time?"

Lizbeth's eyes darted Fredrik's way again. Surely Hilda didn't consider them a possible match? But hadn't she thought the same herself a dozen times? "*Ya*, we've known each other since we were *kinner*. Why?"

The diminutive woman laid down her journal and accepted a slice of cake from one of the girls passing out sweets from a large tray. "This looks good. Did you make it?" She turned to Lizbeth.

"*Nee*, not me. I believe it was Molly who brought the cake."

"*Ach*...yes. Molly." She took a bit of cake and looked around, surveying the people around her. "My niece already has a fine husband, with a *boppli* on the way."

"I'm sure—"

"Oh, yes. There will be many children for Molly and Isaac. And perhaps more for you, too." A line of chocolate icing was quickly licked from the older woman's top lip.

Lizbeth blinked. "I don't—"

"Oh, you will, my dear. It's only a matter of time until *Gott* moves the obstacles out of the way and shows you His will for your life." She sipped at her sweating glass of sweet tea. A smile danced on her lips. "You want more children. Don't you?"

She answered, speaking the truth. "*Ya*, I want more." She cleared her throat. "I'd *willkumm* more children if it were in *Gott*'s plan."

"*Gut*. Then that is settled."

"Settled?" Lizbeth nibbled on her bottom lip.

"*Ya*, it's certain-sure settled. It's only a matter of time."

"For what?" Lizbeth's voice sounded strained to her own ears. She laid down her fork.

"For a new husband, of course. I have several prosperous men in mind for you. All you have to do is pick one." Hilda swallowed her last bit of cake and smiled, her eyes even brighter.

Lizbeth struggled to moisten her lips, which had suddenly gone desert dry. From the corner of her eye she watched as Fredrik rose with Gracie in tow, her arm tucked in his elbow as they walked toward the grassy baseball field. The widow's daughter and two sons trailed behind them. They looked like a family and Lizbeth didn't like it one bit.

Hilda seemed to scrutinize her reaction to the pair leaving and sent Lizbeth a consoling smile. Fredrik passed and smiled. "See you in the morning," he commented, and then shuffled along, his head turned, looking down into Gracie's upturned face.

Fredrik stilled his hammer. "*Gut mariye*, Benuel. What are you doing with that stick?"

Inside the backyard fence, the boy's head swiveled around, the stick he'd been poking into the ground covered in mud. He hesitated and then muttered, "*Rutsching* round."

"Fooling around or causing problems for something in that mud? Did you find something interesting?"

"*Ach, ya.*" The boy shook his head, dislodging a clump of caked mud from his ear. "Another *frosch*."

Holding back a smile, Fredrik tried to remain as serious as the boy who had turned back to his task. "A frog, huh? I collected them when I was a boy. Is it a tree frog or ground frog?"

Benuel's hand came up. "*Is fattgange.*"

Fredrik put down the board he'd been holding and walked toward the fence. "You know it's not polite to tell adults to go way, don't you? It makes me to wonder if you're supposed to be staying out of the water. I'm sure your *mamm* won't like that mud on your trousers."

Benuel gave him a frosty look. "*Mei mamm*'s in the *haus*."

"Can I see your friend?"

"*Ya*, but he's *mein*. You can't take him."

The old gate creaked as it opened and then snapped closed behind Fredrik as he stepped into the yard. He took two more steps forward and paused. "I wouldn't dream of taking your frog." He stepped closer. Lizbeth would throw a fit when she saw the muddy condition the boy was in. "I promise to only look."

"*Dummle sich.*" Benuel motioned for him to hurry with his hand. "He wants to jump out of the hole."

"Then you must let him."

Benuel shook his head in determination, his arms crossed against his chest in a defiant pose. "*Nee*, he's one of *meine freundins*."

Fredrik stood over the hole the boy had been digging around in. Lizbeth wouldn't like Benuel having another frog, no matter how much the boy hollered. He'd heard her say one was enough. "It's lunchtime. He could be hungry for a fat fly. Let's see if we can catch him later."

"I gave him a piece of *mein* sandwich. I want to play with him *now*." Bending at the knee, the boy used the stick to poke the muddy ground, searching for the frog.

Not sure what to do, Fredrik rubbed his hands together. The child was young. He didn't know he could hurt the frog with the stick. Waiting for the critter to move was the best way to see where it had gone in the mire. "Wait, don't poke at him, Benuel. You could hurt him." He grabbed the child's arm, prepared to move him away. "If we stand here and watch, we'll see the frog's movement and be able to catch him and have a good look."

Benuel's expression hardened. "*Nee*, let me go. I want to see him."

Lizbeth had only been in the house a few minutes, but she still hurried and almost took a tumble down the steps in her haste. She knew she couldn't leave her son alone for more than a few minutes without some kind of situation taking place. Last time she'd turned her back on him to make his bed, he'd gotten into a jar of pickles and eaten most of the sour treats.

He'd been sick later that night and there was no doubt in her mind it had been the pickles. She'd gone to bed convinced she still had much to learn as a *mamm*. She had to be more diligent, set down stronger boundaries. One day he'd learn her rules were for his own good.

The wicker basket she carried through the gate was heavy with Benuel's damp trousers and dark shirts. She repositioned her burden, glanced up and then stopped in her tracks.

What was Fredrik doing holding her son's arm?

"*Was tut Si hier?*"

Benuel reached down, grabbed something out of the dirt and stuck it in his trouser pocket before he looked her way.

"Nothing's going on." Fredrik took his straw hat off, stepped away from the child and then raked his fingers through his sweaty hair. "I'm working on the apartment."

"The apartment is over there." Her brow raised, she pointed behind the shed toward the small structure showing through the hedges. "Perhaps you should explain to me what you were doing holding my *soh*'s arm in that manner?"

"*Ya*, sure. The boy was playing with a frog and I thought—"

"He might hurt it?"

"*Ya*. I didn't want Benuel to harm the poor creature and thought it best to pull him away." He massaged the back of his neck. "*Kinner* should be taught how to treat *Gott*'s small creatures when they are young."

"He hasn't had much training around small critters," Lizbeth acknowledged, setting the basket of clothes down and tucking a curl of hair behind her ear. Benuel had grown tired of their conversation and ran for the rope swing dangling from the old oak tree. "*Danki* for explaining it to him."

Fredrik's chin lifted and he smiled broadly. "I was glad to help."

He put his hat back on and walked toward the gate. "I'd better get back to work. I'm eager to finish the apartment by the end of the month. Northerners will be coming soon and I may want to rent the apartment when it's ready."

She watched him go through the gate and down the drive, her eyes misting. This kind of training was what a father was supposed to give his *soh*. She should have known Fredrik had no intention of hurting Benuel when he'd grabbed his arm. He'd been nothing but kind and considerate to both of them.

Her shoulders slumped as she turned away and bent to grab a pair of wet trousers from the basket. With a snap, she flipped the wrinkles out of the garment before pegging it on the clothesline. Her stomach churned. If only she could encourage Fredrik, like Gracie had done at the park the day before. But there were so many things left unsaid, so much that needed mentioning. She had to concentrate more on finding work instead of mooning over Fredrik Lapp, she thought, flipping out another pair of Benuel's trousers. She was in no rush to remarry.

Chapter Thirteen

The help-wanted sign in the bakery window was still there, giving Lizbeth renewed hope.

Careful that her hair was tidy and her *kapp* on straight, Lizbeth smoothed down her crisp apron over the soft blue dress Sarah Fischer had helped her make. She entered the bakery, a fake smile plastered on. She was nervous. More nervous than she wanted to admit.

She'd put on a good front when she'd left Benuel with Ulla, and hoped to continued her ruse of confidence until the job interview was over and she had the job. She needed an income. The independent streak in her insisted she find a way to support her son without her father, or the community's financial help. She'd do whatever it took to make a good impression on Lila Zook, the owner of the established bakery.

The fragrance of freshly cooked bread and sweet rolls assailed her, making her mouth water. She'd been too anxious to eat breakfast when she'd fed Benuel earlier.

She glanced around and found Lila, one of Pinecraft's finest cake decorators, waiting on a customer at the side counter. The busy little woman gave her a friendly wave and pointed to a chair against the wall, close to the door.

Lizbeth sat. A glance at the big round wall clock in front of her told her she was more than ten minutes late for her interview.

Benuel had thrown a fit when he'd discovered she was leaving him. It had taken far too long to calm him down and redirect his attention to a red bird in the back garden. With the promise of a cupcake if he behaved, she'd rushed out the door and down the street. Being late didn't paint a very good picture of her ability to be punctual.

"Lizbeth, come join me in the back for a cup of tea." Lila motioned to her from behind the counter.

Lizbeth nodded at Lila's youngest daughter, who was a year or so younger than herself. She made her way through the curtained door to a square table and chairs tucked at the back of the large kitchen.

"I'm sorry I'm so late. I had a—"

Lila poured two cups of strong tea and encouraged Lizbeth to join her at the table. "Not to worry. *Komm*, join me for a cup of tea and eat yourself full of doughnut holes." Lila laughed as she held up a plate of the sugary treats. "I felt too ambitious this morning and thought the whole town of Pinecraft was as hungry for doughnuts as me."

"Danki," Lizbeth said, taking a sugary doughnut hole and placing it on the small plate handed to her.

After a long pull of her steaming tea, Lila grinned. "You've come about the opening?"

The strong black tea was warm and refreshing against Lizbeth's dry throat. *"Ya.* I saw the sign and spoke to your *soh* about an interview."

"Gut, gut. I can always use a strong back to lift flour

sacks and such. My own back gave out on me years ago."
Lila studied her. "You're certain-sure you can lift fifty
pounds, Lizbeth? You're awfully scrawny."

Lizbeth placed her teacup on the old table and sighed.
"I thought the sign said you needed a day-shift worker,
someone to ice cakes and make doughnuts."

"*Ya*, I did, but that job was snatched up by Rosy Hess
yesterday morning. Luke should have told you." Lila
gave an apologetic half smile as she patted white pow-
der off her sizable chest. "But I still have that night shift
position open if you're interested," she said and ate another doughnut hole.

Minutes later, disappointment weighed Lizbeth down
as she walked out of the shop and down the street. She
couldn't take the job Lila offered. The hours were
wrong, and the job required someone who knew the
ins and outs of a busy kitchen. She baked a good cake
and her cookies were always a hit, but she knew nothing
about making huge batches of bread and rolls.

Catching the glint of a sign in the window of Yoder's
Pizza, she stepped down into the street and crossed to
the other side, hope rising in her. She knew good day
jobs were hard to find in Pinecraft, especially during the
long summer months when things were slow and tourists
few. Most owners used their *kinner* or *familye* to fill in
when staff was needed, but there had to be something
she could do to earn her way.

What her *daed* had said was true. She *wasn't* prepared for working, but she had no choice. She had to
support her family.

Her nerves roiling her stomach into knots, she managed to order a slice of pizza and force down the cheesy

triangle, nibble by nibble, as she worked up the nerve to inquire about the job opening.

Laughter coming from the back of the tiny restaurant drew Lizbeth's interest. Gracie and two of her young children sat on a bench, her youngest son's gaze glued to Fredrik's face as he punctuated his tale of Daniel and the lion's den with roars and gyrations.

The story was one of Benuel's favorites. Her *daed* told it to him often. The boy would roar to his heart's content as he listened, just like Gracie's son, Isaiah, was doing now.

A tear escaped the corner of her eye. It was her fault Benuel didn't have Fredrik to tell him tales from the Bible. Everything was her fault. A burst of jealousy clawed at her gut. Gracie had done nothing wrong, didn't deserved the harsh feelings Lizbeth had against her.

The woman was enjoying her time with an eligible bachelor, like any woman who needed a respectable husband to help raise her children would do. Lizbeth had no right to care who Fredrik ate with, whose child he told Bible stories to. She'd given up that right long ago.

She threw down her napkin and walked to the front of the store, determination in every step. If her fear of commitment kept Benuel without a father, the least she could do was find a job and provide for her boy all that she could. Even if it meant making pizzas all day alongside teenagers. She wanted to be a *gut mamm*, be someone Benuel would grow to be proud of, and she would. But what if no one would hire her? What would she do then?

Fredrik walked up behind Lizbeth and watched Ralf Yoder's expression soften as he spoke to her from behind the counter. "Lizbeth, if I had known you were

looking for work, I would have saved that shift for you."
He grinned. "I might have something later in the week,
though, when the young scholars go back to school.
Check back with me if you're still looking for hours."

She nibbled at her bottom lip as she turned to leave
and bumped into Fredrik's arm. "*Ach*, I'm sorry," she
said and then saw who it was. She slipped him a guarded
look.

"Hello, Lizbeth." He tipped his head in greeting, taking in her blanched face. The woman had to need a job
pretty badly if she was willing to work at a busy pizza
café.

Her expression softened. "Hi, Fredrik," she murmured in greeting and walked away, through the door
and out into the afternoon heat.

"Wait," he called out, rushing down the sidewalk to
catch up with her. "You're looking for work?"

She nodded. "We must all work if we are to eat."

Fredrik took her elbow and moved her to the side
of the sidewalk. "I would have thought your husband's
family would have—"

Sadness clouded her features. "*Ya*, sure. One would
think that, but life isn't always black-and-white." She
hurried down the sidewalk, her long dress swinging with
her quick steps as she hurried away.

"Wait! Mose Fischer is looking for a bookkeeper, if
you're interested in the job."

She stopped. Turned back toward him. "Are you
sure?"

"*Ya*, as sure as my name is Fredrik. He told me he
was going to start looking for someone today." He offered her a grin.

A smile of relief spread across her face. "Tell him I

will be in early tomorrow morning if you would please."
She turned on her heel and strolled away, her back a bit
straighter than it had been.

Fredrik watched the woman walk the length of the
block and then disappear into a crowd of tourists. He
wondered about what she had said about her husband's
family. Had they shut her out when Jonah died? Could
that be what was making her so sad at times?

He went back into the pizza café and sat down beside
Gracie and her children. He surveyed the woman's happy
countenance, her children's carefree manner.

"I thought you'd run out on us." Gracie's eyebrows
waggled in good humor.

"*Nee*, never that. I had a good deed to do, is all. Now
I've got to get back to work before Mose puts out the
alarm that I'm missing."

"Sure, you go," Gracie said, her eyes smiling across
at him good-naturedly. "The *kinner* and I hope you'll
come by for a meal."

"Maybe soon," Fredrik said, and paused, taking a
long sip of water from his frosty glass. He would be
disappointing the widow, but he had made up his mind.
She wasn't the one for him, no matter how friendly and
kind she was. He wanted to find her attractive, someone
he couldn't do without, but the sight of Lizbeth fighting
so hard for employment dispelled all his doubts, brought
clarity to his mind. She was the one for him and somehow he had to convince her or die of a broken heart.

Gracie gathered her *kinner* around her like a mother
hen and made her way out of the restaurant, her smile
gone. Was he so transparent? Did she realize he wouldn't
be coming around anymore? Fredrik ran his hands
through his hair and then placed his hat back on his

head. As he watched her march along, she turned to wave goodbye, her eyes squinting in the noonday sun. "*Gott* bless you, Fredrik Lapp," she said and hurried her children across the street while the path was clear.

He sought out Mose the moment he was back at the furniture barn. "I think I've found you a bookkeeper."

Sandpapering down a leg for an *Englischer* order, Mose paused. "*Gut*, I had no interest in searching. Everyone I know is as bad with numbers as I am, yourself included." He laughed when Fredrik frowned. "I remember hearing about you cheating at school and still getting the answer wrong when you were in the eighth grade."

"*Ya*, well. Lizbeth Mullet won't get the answers wrong. When I cheated off her pages I always got good marks," he said, teasing. He hung up his hat on the office nail and headed toward the back with Mose. "She said to tell you she'd be in to see you first thing in the morning."

"I thought your lunch was with Gracie," Mose questioned, his brows raised.

"It was, but Lizbeth happened to come in."

Mose nodded. "You think Lizbeth would mind doing some dusting while she's here? This place looks like we had a sandstorm, not a downpour yesterday." Writing his name in the dust on one of the newly finished dining room tables as he passed, he tutted in disgust and then opened the noisy building room.

"I think Lizbeth's prepared to do just about anything to keep from marrying again. She's independent and determined."

Mose looked at the day's schedule, grabbed a thick apron made of linen and wrapped it around his waist, his eyes watching Fredrik. "But you're not giving up, are you? I've seen the way you look at her."

Fredrik selected an order to fill and grabbed a matching apron from the hook. "We're just friends, but I wouldn't be brokenhearted if it turned into something more," he admitted with a playful smile.

"You'll have to be patient as you approach, Fredrik. I've seen the look in her eyes around men. That husband of hers did something bad, abused her in some way. She used to be strong spirited, ready to take on the world. Now she's as skittish as a colt not yet broke in."

Fredrik nodded. "I've seen it, too. I'm willing to wait, as long as I see there is hope."

"You may have a long wait," Mose told him, flipping on the noisy sander and going to work on forming a table leg.

Busy working with his hands, Fredrik's mind went back to the first day Lizbeth and Benuel came back to Pinecraft. Perhaps it wasn't just the near wreck that had her hands shaking when she'd rolled him over in the street. Perhaps she'd already been scared by something or someone. Had her husband's family made threats? She said they'd given her nothing to start out fresh. He'd heard rumors about some of the Old Order Amish in Ohio. Strict Ordnung rules didn't begin to describe the rigid way they lived.

Anger pushed at him, bunching up his muscles, making his heart hammer. She'd had a haunted look on her face that day. The boy had seemed on edge, too, and had jumped at every noise. If *Gott* gave him an opportunity, he'd ask her about her life in Ohio. It was time her heartache ended. He'd make sure no one abused her and Benuel again. If only she'd let him rescue her...

Chapter Fourteen

The next morning the furniture store door shut behind Lizbeth, the bell over the door announcing her arrival. The barn-shaped building with a connecting shop was large, but cool inside. It smelled of freshly cut wood and furniture polish.

Lizbeth struggled to pull her shoulders back and forced a smile. She wanted to exude confidence, but all she felt was dread. What would she do if Mose Fischer didn't find her qualifications acceptable and refused her work? She wrapped her arms around herself, saw an unfamiliar man approaching and adjusted herself. Her mouth went dry. She licked her lips, waiting.

"*Willkumm!* My name's Leroy King. How can I help you today?" The man strolling toward her was young and tall and unbelievably lean in black trousers, suspenders and a bright white shirt. His traditionally cut hair was ragged around his oversize ears. The tuft of straggly blond hair on his chin announced he was newly married.

With a nod of her head, she acknowledged him and then glanced nervously around. She knew Fredrik worked somewhere in the big barn, doing exactly what she had no idea, but she was glad it wasn't his job to greet customers. The last thing her already stretched nerves needed was a conversation with the man. "I have an appointment with Mose Fischer. At eleven."

"Hmm. He didn't mention anything to me. Perhaps you could come back in…say an hour, and perhaps he'll be in by then."

"He called and warned me he might be a bit late coming in, and asked me to wait for him in his office."

"*Ya*, sure. That sounds *gut* to me." He turned on his heel, headed toward the side of the huge room and then unlocked a small office door and flipped on the overhead lights. Fluorescent bulbs flickered and then exploded into a brilliant glow.

A cluttered old desk, computer chair on wheels and single straight-back wooden chair filled most of the room to overflowing. Several accounting books and a weathered box of crayons were scooped up by the salesman, allowing Lizbeth to sit down while she waited.

"May I get you a bottle of water, or some refreshment?"

"*Nee,*" she answered too quickly and swallowed hard. She would have loved a drink of something cool after walking seven blocks in the midday heat. "I'm fine." She nodded, her throat so dry she almost choked on her own lie.

She wasn't fine. She was thirsty, nervous and more than a little afraid she was about to make a fool out of herself again. Who was she trying to kid? She was no bookkeeper. The closest thing she'd done to bookkeeping was help her *mamm* add up the proceeds from a quilt sale and divvy up the cash. She'd given the wrong amount of change back on her first try. But she needed the job and would do whatever it took to figure out the numbers with *Gott*'s help.

Working a half day after volunteering as morning cook for the local firehouse, Fredrik breezed through the open back door, his thoughts on the bride's chest he'd designed the day before. Today he'd build the model, line it with cedar and stain it a dark mahogany before showing it to Mose for his approval. He'd need to add some kind of short legs to the case. He made his way to his workstation and then leafed through the latch fixture catalog. He may have to order something special for a wedding box like this. New brides were particular about what they brought into their new homes. They'd want the best. Hinges that would last a lifetime, like their marriages.

He whistled as he worked, his mind at last at rest. He'd had a hard time getting Lizbeth Mullet off his mind the night before. He hadn't missed the embarrassed look on her face when she'd hurried out of the pizza shop. She'd needed that job. She may not like him enough to marry him, but he felt more than a little interest in her. Lizbeth's situation reminded him of his sister, Ada. She'd had a difficult marriage and then was widowed early on. It hadn't been easy for her, either. He felt like he knew what the young widow was going through. He ambled into the showroom and saw one of their newest salesmen heading his way.

"Hey, Levi. Did a woman come in this morning looking for Mose?"

Leroy put down his dust cloth and glanced toward

the front. "She did. I put her in his office to wait. I hope that's certain-fine with you."

"*Ya*, sure it is. I'll just go keep her company for a few minutes, until Mose can get here." He grabbed two cold water bottles from the ice chest and meandered through the showroom, admiring Mose's craftsmanship, as well as his own, as he made his way to the front of the store through a sea of fine furniture.

Through the glass window at the front he could see Lizbeth seated in the straight-back wooden chair, her legs crossed primly at her ankles, her hands nervously twisting in her lap. He slowed. Sadness clouded her features, made her look older than her years. Perhaps lack of money was her issue and this bookkeeping job would take away some of her depression. He'd talk to Mose before the man could make his decision on who to hire. Putting in a good word for her was the least Fredrik could do for Lizbeth.

When the door opened she looked up, hopeful. But then the color drained out of her face as she realized it was only him entering. Not the reaction he was hoping for, but the one he usually got.

Lizbeth looked pretty, even though her complexion was pale. He watched her try to act natural, smile normally, but she failed miserably. At times he suspected there was something about him that set the woman's teeth on edge, and he didn't have a clue what it was. Perhaps she just didn't like his hyperactive personality and easy laugh.

She couldn't still be holding on to her childhood frustration with him, could she? When they were younger, he'd kept his interest in her a secret as much as he could. And by the time she was old enough to step out with him, her *bruder* said she was interested in Jonah, who worked in the lumberyard, robbing Fredrik of all his hope. He still found her appealing, and would do whatever it took to convince her he was the one to marry when the time came.

"Waiting to talk to Mose about the bookkeeping job?" he asked as he placed the drawings for the cedar chest on the center of the desk.

She lifted her chin. "*Ya*. As I said yesterday. I have to work."

He stepped back toward the door. "You always were good with numbers in school. I won't be surprised if he gives you the job."

She toyed with a wispy lock of her own hair and tucked it behind her ear. Her fingers went to the ribbons dangling from her *kapp*. "*Danki.*"

He stopped in front of her chair. "I could talk to him for you, if you'd like."

Her face reddened. "*Nee*, please. I don't need you to plead my case. I either get the job or I don't."

"*Ya*. Sure. I understand. You want to get the position on your own merit."

He watched as her hands squeezed into fists, her knuckles turning white. She was stressed about interviewing for the job. He handed her a bottle of water and kept one for himself. "I best be getting back to work now. I'll pray you get the job."

He thought he heard her mutter that she needed all the prayers she could get, but when he glanced back at her she was relaxed against the chair and leafing through a furniture magazine as if she didn't have a care in the world.

* * *

The next morning Lizbeth poured hot water over the last of the breakfast dishes and threw a kitchen towel over the tub until she could get around to washing them later. Benuel was in rare form this morning, getting into everything, crying over the least little thing. She needed to spend time with him, calm him down so she could finish her housework. Today *would* have to be Thursday, one of her busiest days of the week now that she'd accepted work from Mose Fischer.

She had the first set of furniture barn's books to work on, but that would have to wait until later this evening, when Benuel was in bed for the night. There was wash to do. She sighed. Wash day had never been her favorite day of the week, but Benuel's swelling clothes basket needed her attention and she'd just heard on the radio that a line of thundershowers was approaching from the Gulf of Mexico and bringing torrential rains with it.

A knock came on the front door. In a rush, she glanced in on Benuel. He sat at the coffee table, scribbling his name onto a piece of drawing paper. Stretched out in front of him, his restless feet rocked back and forth as he concentrated on forming each letter of his name with precision. She frowned at the thought of his pensive expression as she hurried to the door. She peeked out the sheer curtain.

Fredrik stood at the front door as he did many mornings, his head turned toward the pink rosebushes at the side of the porch.

She bit her lip and stepped out of sight. What should she do? Open the door and have to deal with another one of his repair projects, or pretend to be out?

Consternation crossed her face. She wished she could

ignore his knock. Being around him made her like him more, put him in her thoughts the whole day and into the night.

Without giving herself a moment to consider what she was doing, she jerked open the front door and greeted him. "*Gut mariye*, Fredrik. How are you this fine day?" she asked, holding his gaze. Her hand nervously tidied up the loose tendrils of hair cascading around her right ear.

She must look a mess. She'd been busy all morning, stripping beds and remaking them, cleaning walls where Benuel had expressed his artistic flare while she was distracted. A glance at her apron reinforced her dread. Grape jelly and a clump of peanut butter toast stuck to her bust. Her shoulders slumped.

"*Gut mariye*. I came by in the off chance I could install that new tile in the front bathroom."

He must have noticed her frown, because he quickly amended, "I could come back later if the time's not right."

She might have a day full of chores ahead of her, but she would be even busier the next few days preparing baked goods for the family dinner. Better to get the project done today and out of the way than dread it all weekend long. "*Ya*, sure. Today is fine." She opened the door wide and stepped back, allowing the big man through.

"*Danki*," he said and stepped in. His work belt clanged as he strode toward the bathroom. No longer the tall, slim boy he'd been at eighteen, he'd filled out and walked with a certainty that spoke of self-control and confidence.

She hurried past him into the kitchen, and got busy with her chores. Her mind lingered on Fredrik for a few moments and then her thoughts moved to Benuel in the living room. He was being far too quiet, which was never a good thing with an ADHD child. With a sense of urgency in her steps, she hurried through the entry hall and into the front room of the house. Benuel stood on a stool on one foot, his thin body plastered flat against the corner wall.

"Was isht?"

"Fredrik is here," he said in a whisper.

"*Ya*, he is, but you have nothing to be afraid of." She took him by the hand and encouraged him off the stool. "He's putting in new tiles for the bathroom. Isn't that nice?"

"He tried to take my other frog." He looked up at her, his eyes troubled.

"He explained. You could have hurt the frog and he wanted to spare it pain."

"I was trying to save it." The boy's eyes glowed with indignation.

She smiled down at him and ruffled his ginger hair. "*Ya*, well, silly *schnickelfritz*, he didn't know that, did he?"

"*Nee*, but he could have asked," Benuel said, one corner of his mouth hiking up in a grimace. "Can I have a cookie now? You said if I played quietly I could have one."

"Sure, I think that sounds fair." She looked around the room scattered with toys. "You tidy up in here and I'll have a treat waiting for you in the kitchen. *Yea?*"

"But what about him?" he asked and pointed toward the bathroom door. He ducked as Lizbeth tried to slide her fingers through his ruffled hair.

"You will be brave and walk right past him, or I'll eat your treat. *Komm schell*, or all the cookies will be gone."

Her skirt twirled around her calves as she walked out the living room door and then slowed her march. She could see Fredrik down on his hands and knees, unscrewing the doorjamb stripping. He looked so much like the young Fredrik she remembered, his knees always on the ground, flicking a glass marble through the dirt or digging a hole.

She smiled at the unexpected memory. Fredrik chose that moment to lift his head and glance her way. Everything around her slipped away. She was a young girl again, no more than sixteen. Old memories returned, stirred her heart. Long-dead feelings poured in, strong emotions held at bay. In that moment he was still her Fredrik, her secret love. Her affection for him had grown over the span of their childhood and had never died. But he'd walked away without even a goodbye.

She put her hands on her cheeks to hide the rush of blood suffusing her face. Nothing had changed and yet everything had changed. There was a tiny chance he might grow to love her, but once he heard it was possible she would never have more children, he would walk away and find someone else.

"Is something wrong?" he asked, pausing in his work, one eyebrow arched.

"*Nee*, nothing. I was just remembering."

"You looked so sad. What did you remember?" He braced himself up on his hands, waiting for her reply.

"I remembered you in the dirt, on your hands and knees."

He smiled. "If I was in the dirt, you were probably right there with me."

She shrugged. "*Ya*. You're probably right."

"I thought you might have forgotten all the good times we had," he said, his smile widening.

"*Nee*, I'm not one to forget."

Benuel rushed up and pushed her from behind, propelling her toward the kitchen and breaking the moment. "You promised me cookies. Remember?"

"*Ya, ya*. Your cookies are waiting," she said, her heart still beating fast against her ribs.

"When you're finished with your snack come help me work, Benuel. I need a good helper," Fredrik called out.

"*Mamm?*" Benuel asked, his eyes glowing with something akin to anticipation. The child was finally coming out of himself, daring to reach out to others.

"*Ya*, sure. You can help, but only if you do as you are told."

"Hurray!" Benuel shouted and hurried to the kitchen.

She shrugged and gave Fredrik a glance, her lips turned up in a wide grin. "I hope you know what you're getting into."

He grinned back and inspected her face. "*Ya*, sure I do, or I wouldn't have asked."

Lizbeth made her way to the kitchen and grabbed the full pitcher of orange juice from Benuel's hand just as he attempted to pour it into a tiny glass. Another mess averted. She smiled broadly. The man may have thought he knew what he'd bargained for, inviting Benuel to help, but he didn't.

The house felt different when Fredrik was in it. Like a home. She turned to wash the dishes. If Fredrik picked a woman to court, Lizbeth's heart would be broken—again. Unless it was her. But there wasn't much chance in that.

Chapter Fifteen

"Go back up there and wait for me," Fredrik said to Benuel, his finger pointing to the top step. A grin spread across Fredrik's damp, ruddy face. He lifted his straw hat and wiped sweat from his forehead with the sleeve of his shirt.

The boy stopped his fast-paced trek down the steps and froze in his ankle-high boots. "But you said I could help you."

"You are helping me by staying a safe distance away from these sharp broken tiles. We'll go back inside in a moment and lay the missing edge by the door."

His head dropping, Benuel pivoted and scuffed up the steps, then paced at the top like a caged lion, turning his puppy-dog look toward Fredrik. "Okay, but you won't forget to let me help. Will you?"

Satisfied the boy was staying put, Fredrik scored another tile on his pencil line and snapped the stone. "*Nee*, I won't forget my promise. You're my helper." He turned back to Benuel and winked. "I couldn't have done the room without your expert help. Your *mamm*'s going to be proud of you."

A smile transformed his young face and crinkled the corners of his eyes. "She thinks I'm a *boppli* and can't do anything right."

Snapping another tile, Fredrik glanced Benuel's way. "Did she tell you that?"

"*Nee*, but she thinks it. I can tell." Benuel sat on the top step and stretched out his legs, his fingers tapping impatiently at his sides. "She's always telling me to slow down or stop having fun." The sides of the *kinner*'s mouth dropped once again.

"I was the same when I was a young." He gave a mirthless laugh. Being an overactive child had always gotten him into trouble. "If my *mamm* wasn't yelling at me, she was smacking my bottom for breaking something of my *daed*'s." He gathered up the pile of tiles he'd cut and started up the stairs. Lizbeth appeared in the window beside the door and then darted away as she realized she'd been caught watching them. Did the woman ever take a moment away from worrying about the boy?

Benuel threaded a hand through his damp hair, paused, but then rose and declared, "My *daed* is dead."

Fredrik paused, his boot inches from the boy's smaller foot. He patted Benuel's head. "*Ya*, I know. You must miss him a lot."

His face lost all expression. "*Nee*, I don't miss him. Can I open the door for you?"

"*Ya*, sure. You get the door and I'll carry the tiles." Fredrik observed the return of emotion to the child's face. Perhaps Benuel's comment explained why Lizbeth was so different now. Had her husband been a difficult man, a poor example of a father? Why else would a young, impressionable boy say he didn't miss his newly buried *daed*? "You see? We make a good team, you and I."

Benuel shouldered the door open and skipped inside. The smells and sounds of frying chicken made the kitchen once more a home.

Lizbeth continued washing dishes at the sink. The flush on her face and the clatter she was making washing the cutlery told him she'd heard the mention of her husband's death and was distraught.

The sun streaming in past fluttering curtains at the kitchen window made Lizbeth's butterscotch-colored hair look almost white blond, like it had been when she was a child. Recollections of a younger, happier Lizbeth flooded his mind. She cleared her throat and asked without turning, "Is he behaving for you?"

Benuel's arms dangled at his sides, waiting for the man's answer.

Fredrik knew the feeling of longing for someone to say something good about him. He'd always been so active he seldom slowed down long enough to draw much more than negative attention. He put his hand on Benuel's shoulder and squeezed gently. "Certain-sure, he is. Your *soh*'s a hard worker. I'm impressed how *gut* he follows directions."

Surprise spread across the boy's face, brightening his eyes, causing one brow to lift. "We're almost done, *Mamm*. Fredrik said I could help him mend the fence later, if that's all right."

Lizbeth turned on her heel and faced them.

"*Ya*, well. Maybe another time. Lunch will be ready in a few minutes and you'd best hurry and get cleaned up. I have errands to run later this afternoon. I hope that bathroom's finished by then." She touched the grout on her son's shirt collar. Her brow knitted as she glanced at Fredrik. Then she looked back to Benuel with a smile.

"Yeah!" Benuel clamored. "Fredrik can eat with us again, right, *Mamm*?"

Lizbeth's lips parted as her smile widened. "*Ya*, sure. I made plenty."

"I'll stay, but you have to promise to eat all your food or the deal's off."

Benuel scratched his arm, his eyes on his mother. "Even if there's no red sauce?"

Fredrik blotted his forehead with his handkerchief, the corner of his mouth lifting. "Even if there's no sauce."

The boy shuffled his feet, scrutinized his mother and then nodded. "Even if there's no sauce."

Scrubbing the last pan, Lizbeth glanced out the back window. The two of them were cleaning up the mess from the tile cutting, the sun glinting off both ginger heads. Fredrik called out directions and Benuel followed them to the letter.

Thrilled that Benuel was learning, she wanted to shout hallelujah, dance for joy. He was doing what he was told without grumbling.

She was making headway with the boy, but in a lesser way than Fredrik. Her mother's words came back to haunt her. *It often takes a community to raise a kinner.*

Her *mamm* used the words when Lizbeth was a teen and complaining about some old *aenti* telling her to be still or put her *kapp* back on while they were fishing or running through the ocean surf.

Ya. She'd prayed for *Gott* to send someone who was able to reach her boy, and that someone had been Fredrik. She shrugged, knowing she still lacked some parenting skills, but she was learning as she went, picking up on what made Benuel more agreeable, easier to deal with. She no longer felt so overwhelmed or troubled.

But aren't you considering your own needs over Benuel's?

Her thought came from out of the blue and penetrated her head like a lightning bolt. She braced herself against the kitchen sink and bowed her head, tears rolling down her cheeks.

Seeing Benuel with Fredrik today spoke loud and clear. She covered her ears with her hands, trying to keep out the truth.

It was time to tell Fredrik he had a *kinner.* Benuel needed to know the truth about Fredrik's connection to him. But what if she lost them both? Somehow, she could live without Fredrik in her life, but what about Benuel? Could Fredrik keep Benuel away to punish her for her secret?

What about Benuel's needs?

The thought vibrated in her head until she could no longer stand it. She had kept her secret too long. She would tell Fredrik the truth, but first she'd ask for her father's wisdom. She had to tell them both about that night in the barn.

She had prayed for *Gott*'s forgiveness and guidance all those years ago, but now was the time for the truth.

After Fredrik left, Lizbeth directed her son. "Please shut the door behind me, Benuel."

The heat from the deep roasting pan of beef was burning through the dish towels she used as pot holders.

"Benuel?" She braced the pan against the back porch's wooden handrail, looked around her and then down the driveway. Where could the boy have gone? He couldn't be far. He'd been in front of her when she'd walked out the kitchen door just seconds ago.

"Benuel, please answer me." Her voice went up an octave. She resorted to the Old Amish language he was so familiar with. *"Wo bist du?"*

Making sounds like a buzzing bee, he dashed up the steps, and then began to swarm around her, circling closer and closer. *"Komm. Schell, Mamm,"* he said. "I don't like to wait. It's a special *familye* day."

Placing the hot pan on the porch behind her, she took him by the arms and forced him to stand still. "Why didn't you answer me when I called?"

His brow went up and he looked genuinely surprised. "I didn't hear you call my name."

"Then how did you know to come?" she inquired.

A smile danced on his lips. "I got scared and came back for you."

"You must stay close to me."

"Ya, sure. I was just *rutsching* round by the front porch. I heard a frog." He gave a half smile, the deep dimple in his cheek spoiling her moment of discipline. Fredrik had the same dimple, but his had almost vanished with maturity. Shame. She'd found that dimple fascinating as a child. Pulling herself back into the moment, she shrugged and gave a deep sigh. "You are enough to test the patience of *Gott* Himself."

"Is *Gott* mad at me?" he asked, not looking the least bit concerned.

She slapped a hand over her mouth so he wouldn't see her wide smile. *"Nee, Gott's* not mad at you and neither am I, but you must follow directions. What did I tell you just now as I opened the door?"

He glanced up at the sky, several of his fingers going into his mouth. "I can't remember," he finally said. "I think you said I could have a dog if I behaved at *Grossmammi*'s."

She took in the sight of him standing on the porch. Her only living child. For now, she would think only of Benuel. Soon Fredrik had to be told and she needed her father's insight on the matter of Benuel's real father.

Lengths of ginger hair protruded out from under the straw hat sitting at an angle on Benuel's head. He hadn't changed out of his dusty dark trousers, and she noticed he had only one side of his suspenders up over his arm. The other hung limp at his waistline. "Do you know how much I love you?"

He lifted his head, gave her a lopsided smile. "*Grossdaddi* said he knows a man with puppies in his barn. Can we go see them tonight, after we eat?"

"*Nee*, but I'll make sure your *grossdaddi* takes you to see them soon." She relaxed, smiled again. "Now shut that door behind me so we can be on our way. We can't have the *familye* thinking we're not coming to dinner." She snatched up the roasting pan and led the way.

He bounced down the steps and then grabbed the handle of his wagon as she placed the cooling food amongst the toys cluttering the bottom of the wagon bed.

"Is Fredrik a *schreiner*?" His question came out of nowhere.

"*Ya*, he's a carpenter. Why do you ask?"

Sunlight shone in Benuel's blue eyes. "I want to be a *schreiner* when I grow up."

"That's nice." Lizbeth made no additional comment. She was too stunned. "Let's get to your *grossmammi*'s house before dark falls.

An hour later she left Benuel with a plate of warm cookies Ulla had just pulled from the oven and walked out to the old farmhouse door, heading toward the chicken pens.

She opened the first gate into the large, noisy chicken coop and called out, *"Daed!"*

Others complained about the ammonia smell and noise of the farm, but they had never been a problem to Lizbeth. She had wonderful memories of cuddling down-covered chicks and laughing as she chased after her *grossmammi*'s pet hens who ran wild in the yard.

She'd been told her *grossdaddi* had started the farm back in the fifties, some years after Pinecraft's conception. Her *daed* had taken over the running of the farm when the leathered old man passed on to be with the Lord. What stayed with her now was the look of *Grossdaadi*'s weathered face and his winning smile that reappeared in her *daed*'s aged appearance.

Both old men were stubborn when it came to their dedication to this farm, but they had vibrant affection for their families that couldn't be faulted.

The muscles in Lizbeth's chest restricted. Her father wouldn't live forever, just like her *grossdaddi* hadn't. *"Daed?"*

Short and squat, but full of energy and a love of life, Chicken John dumped the overflowing basket of leafy kitchen greens and breakfast scraps and turned toward her. *"Ya,* I'm here."

She'd been indoors most of the day supervising Benuel as he helped Fredrik lay the tiles, but knew the day had started out warm and then an unexpected morning shower had left the afternoon miserably humid. Her father's face looked flushed, his lip beaded with sweat.

He was getting too old for such vigorous work, but no one could tell him anything, not even the local doctor, who'd declared him arthritic and insisted he slow down. He'd probably never retire from his beloved chicken farm, unless Ulla could convince the headstrong old man he needed to turn the farm over to Lizbeth's *bruder*, Saul.

Her father took a colorful handkerchief from his pant pocket and rubbed his brow and face and then stuck the damp cloth back in his pocket with little regard.

"I need to talk with you, if you have time to spare," Lizbeth said.

His head bobbed. "*Ya*, sure." He motioned her back through the gate and latched it behind them.

"Let me wash up first and then we'll sit under your *mamm*'s apple trees for a spell."

Under the spindly branches of the adult trees, Lizbeth settled herself on the wooden bench her *grossdaddi* had made before she was born and tried to organize her thoughts.

She watched as the outdoor faucet sloshed water on her *daed*'s boots and then half smiled as he hollered when he splashed his face and neck with cold water.

Not sure what all needed saying, she didn't have a clue how to start this conversation, or exactly how much to reveal.

Moments later, his face still damp and shining, her father shuffled over and lowered himself to the bench with a familiar groan. He observed her for a moment and then spoke. "*Was ist letz?* You have important words to speak to me, *dochder*?"

Did he look older or was it the dread filling her that made him look too fragile to handle her news?

She spoke in a rush for fear she'd snatch the words back before she could get them out. "Fredrik Lapp is Benuel's natural father." She looked up, saw his pale eyes widen and then glisten with unshed tears.

His jaw tightened. "I had no idea he was the one. You never said." He raked his fingers through his damp hair and then scrutinized her face. "Why are you telling me now, *liebling*?"

She took in the sight of her father's set mouth, the way his jaw ticked with fury. Benuel's conception was her fault, not Fredrik's. "Fredrik never knew he was the father of my child."

His pupils dilated. "*Nee*, it is not possible. He would remember."

"Not if he had been too drunk to stand up, he wouldn't."

John rose, towering over her. "He took advantage of you?"

Lizbeth's lashes fluttered, heavy with tears. "*Nee*, I was the one who took advantage."

"You?" He kneeled in front of her, taking her hands in his. "How is it possible, Lizbeth? You were little more than a child."

Her lower lip quivered. "I was at the singing frolic. Fredrik and Saul were on *rumspringa* and still sowing their wild oats. I knew Fredrik was drunk when he offered to walk me home. He had a flask of something that smelled strong of spirits." Her voice shook as she continued. "In the moonlight he kissed me." Her voice broke as she continued. "I led him into the barn." She lowered her head, her shame turning her voice into little more than a whisper. A tear escaped her eye. "The next day he didn't remember any of it. Nothing! I was still just Saul's little *schweschder*, someone to be tolerated."

"But—"

"*Nee*, let me finish." She squeezed her father's hand, saw the strain of her words on his craggy face and felt heartache like never before. "Fredrik left for his training before he and Saul were baptized. He was completely unaware he'd been with me, that we'd made a child together." She clutched her father's rough hands. "How can I tell him, *Daed*? He will hate me."

"Oh, *mein kinner*."

She wept openly, her voice cracking. "He remembers nothing, but shows an interest in Benuel's welfare now." She pushed back a wisp of hair from her face. "Once he finds out Benuel is his *soh*, that it's my fault he's missed out on the boy's life, he'll hate me, take Benuel away. Yet I feel *Gott* leading me to tell him. What am I to do?"

"There is nothing more to be done. You must follow *Gott*'s plan. Fredrik has a right to know. It must be you who tells him." Her father's face blanched. The look he gave her touched her breaking heart.

"I will tell him, but in my time." She would tell him. If she could find the courage.

Chapter Sixteen

Fredrik had eaten many meals at Chicken John and Ulla Schwarts's house, but he'd never felt more uncomfortable than he did this time. His affection for Lizbeth was growing and he knew she wanted no part of a new marriage. Not while she was still grieving the loss of her husband. He lumbered into the large dining room, shuffled his way around Ulla's feisty, diminutive sister, Hilda, and then stuffed his freshly washed hands deep in his trouser pockets.

As expected, Lizbeth smiled at him over the bowl she was carrying and hurried away.

He rubbed his chin as he watched her scurry between Ulla and Hilda. He couldn't blame her for not wanting him always hanging around. Had he been too obvious with his affection?

He'd told Chicken John he had things to do after spending his morning at Lizbeth's laying tile and then working on the chicken coops in the afternoon, but the old church deacon was stubborn and wasn't having any of it. His habit had always been to feed those who worked on his chicken farm, and they had both labored in the hot sun that afternoon.

He smiled as Ulla passed him. The sunburn on his face made his skin feel tight and painful. He'd meant to put sunscreen on this afternoon, but a call from his *bruder* had broken his routine and left him scorched at the end of the long day.

Chicken John came bustling in, took his seat at the head of the big wooden table laden with plates, platters and bowls of food, and pointed to a chair on his right. "Sit yourself there, Fredrik. Across from Lizbeth and Hilda."

Lizbeth grabbed the back of the chair farther down the table. "I'll sit here, *Daed*. Close to Benuel."

Benuel scrambled out of the chair he'd climbed into, crawled under the table to a chair next to Fredrik. "I want to sit near Fredrik," he declared to no one in particular. "He's my friend."

Lizbeth nodded her approval.

John's bushy brows lifted as he glanced at the child and then over to his daughter. "Lizbeth. Your chair is there, where you've sat all your life. There's been enough musical chairs tonight. Two men are hungry at this table. We've both had a long day of work. Sit."

She nodded, her face an empty canvas. "But first I have to help finish putting the meal on the table," she said and took a step back, promptly bumping into Ulla, who carried a steaming bowl of mashed potatoes in her hand. "I'm sorry. Excuse me," she muttered and hurried off into the kitchen, her hands adjusting her *kapp*, pulling at her ribbon.

A smile tugged at Ulla's mouth. "Leave her alone,

John. She's a grown woman with a child. Let the girl sit where she likes."

"*Ya*, sure. I'm certain-sure you're right." John leaned toward Fredrik and laughed. "Whatever it takes to get a meal in my belly." He rubbed the rotund stomach straining at his shirt.

"*Ya*," Fredrik said and glanced toward the kitchen. Lizbeth entered the room, with Hilda following close behind her. He redirected his gaze.

In the past he would have wiggled his eyebrows at Lizbeth and teased her about obeying her *daed*'s rules, but those days were gone.

The silent prayer, proceeded by Chicken John's clearing of his throat, came and went. Forks tinkling against plates covered Benuel's muffled comments about the evil of all things green.

Fredrik poked a slice of roast beef into his mouth. He winced as he rolled his sore shoulders. He'd need a hot shower when he got home. Laying the tiles in Lizbeth's bathroom had pulled at a few muscles and stretching chicken wire an hour ago hadn't helped any. He had the grouting to do early the next morning and then he'd be working the late shift at the furniture barn. He'd be busy all day again.

He dipped his fork into perfectly mashed potatoes and rich, creamy dark gravy and swirled a chunk of beef in it. It was time to speak to Lizbeth about marriage. Time was slipping past. Mose kept reminding him he wasn't getting any younger. He shoved a forkful of green beans in his mouth and tasted bacon. He'd grown tired of hamburgers and chili fries. He craved home cooking, clean sheets and someone to share his long, lonely evenings. Someone like Lizbeth.

"This beef is wonderful-*gut*," he remarked to Ulla across the table.

She hooked her thumb in Lizbeth's direction. "Give the praise to Lizbeth. She cooked the brisket."

"It's certain-sure tender," he told Lizbeth and quickly looked away.

He'd caught her staring at him, her countenance almost dreamy, a silly smile playing on her face, the same look she'd given him when she'd turned fifteen and tried to kiss him on the small bridge connecting his parents' property and hers. Confused, he glanced back at her. She had turned a brilliant shade of cranberry red and was frowning now. What had changed?

He saw Ulla nudge Hilda with her elbow. The tiny woman redirected her attention from her plate to Lizbeth.

"You thought any more about me finding you a suitable husband?"

Lizbeth swallowed the water she'd been sipping. Her eyes glistened with tears from almost choking. She didn't turn her head, but replied with a firm shake of her head. "*Nee*. My life is complicated enough."

Hilda plucked a green bean off her plate and stuck it in her mouth. She chewed and then spoke. "*Ya*, but a husband would bring you stability and take over some of the burdens of raising a *kinner* alone."

"Pinecraft is a small tourist town. Even if I had an interest in a *mann* and wanted to get married," she said with a glint to her eye, "who would I choose at the end of summer months?" She smirked. "Elder King?" She tucked a stray hair behind her ear. "He's old enough to be my *daed*."

"Your *grossdaddi*," Chicken John corrected with a

smile, then went back to eating as if an argument wasn't going on around him.

"You see? He's old and there's no one else who's single." She dabbed at her mouth with her napkin and placed it back on her lap, seemingly satisfied she'd won the battle.

All eyes turned to Fredrik, with the exception of Benuel, who was making a mess with his red sauce and potatoes.

Fredrik looked up, saw everyone's heads turned in his direction and sputtered, "Oh…wait now. It's true. I am looking for a *fraa*, and stepping out with a few ladies of the community from time to time, but placing Lizbeth and I on a marriage list won't work." His forehead puckered. "*Nee*, you see. Lizbeth is still in mourning…" His voice trailed off to a whisper.

"Oh, *ya*? You think so?" Hilda's eyebrows rose. She licked her lips and took her notebook out of her apron pocket, ready to scribble. "Tell me. When did this romance begin? Perhaps we can find a way to work through any problems and settle on a wedding date."

Lizbeth set her glass down too hard, her eyes beseeching her father to say something, end this fiasco. "I don't think this is the time or the place to be—"

Chicken John rose to his full height and dropped his napkin in his plate. "Enough talk about marriage and such at my dinner table. This conversation will continue another day," he boomed and then directed his gaze at Ulla. "I want my pineapple upside-down cake in the living room. I'm sitting in my favorite chair for a spell."

Fredrik put down his fork and shoved back in his chair. He cast Lizbeth a veiled glance, but her chair was empty. She'd left the dining room without him knowing it and taken Benuel with her.

Lizbeth hadn't slept well the night before, after Hilda's outburst about marriage to Fredrik. "Stand still, Benuel. You'll be late for your first day of school." Lizbeth caught the boy's wiggling foot, and then brushed at the tip of his scuffed black boot.

"I don't want to go to school!" He balled up his fists, his anger growing.

"There will be lots of *kinner* to play with and Beatrice will eat lunch with you." She'd prayed he'd be excited about his first day at school, not cross and uncooperative.

His eyes woefully sad, he sniffed. "You might forget to come pick me up when school is over."

"I would never do that. You know I'll be outside, waiting." She smiled. "Perhaps Beatrice can walk with us to school. Would you like to drop by and pick her up?" She scrutinized him, saw his anger building.

He dropped his head and scuffed his boot against the hardwood floor. "*Nee*, she's mean-spirited. If she says I'm a crybaby again, I'm going to hit her." His lips pursed.

Lizbeth's heart skipped a beat. He'd witnessed too much. "It's wrong to hit, Benuel."

"My *daed* used to hit you."

"*Ya*, but he was wrong for doing it."

His thin arms went around her legs and he hugged her close in a loving embrace. "I didn't like it when he hit you," he murmured into the folds of her skirt.

"I didn't like it, either. We must promise each other to never hit, never cause others pain. *Ya?*" An ache that never left tore at her heart.

"I want to stay here with you. Fredrik might come and he'll need my help."

"He's busy today. Don't you remember he said he'd be back in a day or so to grout the tiles?"

"But he might come and need my help." He scrubbed at his eye, making it red.

"*Nee*, not this time," she said, smiling down at him and running her fingers through his uncombed hair. He had Fredrik's hair. The color and texture was exactly the same. "We've got to hurry. Eat your breakfast and then comb your hair." She held him by his arms and looked down at him. "Will you promise to be good and do your best?"

He pursed his lips and then they spread into a big grin. "Okay, *mamm*."

As he hurried off, she felt dread building. Would his best be good enough for his teacher? The young woman in charge of the youngest children seemed too young and innocent to understand his difficulties. Had she even heard of ADHD, or learned what behavior the condition brought about?

She had to say something to the teacher about Benuel's anger, to give him a fair chance in school. "Hurry, Benuel," she called out, holding her hand to her roiling stomach. "Time's flying past."

Late-summer orders had slowed down to a trickle, leaving Fredrik with a half day's work at the furniture barn. He'd gotten off at noon, eaten a meal and headed to the apartment behind Lizbeth's house. He had plenty of time to apply a fresh coat of paint to the bedroom's walls and finish up the last of the small jobs that needed doing.

He revved the motor of his little scooter and pulled

into the driveway, watching out for the mama cat who often slept in a pile of leaves shaded from the sunshine by the eaves of the house.

Movement drew his attention toward the kitchen's side door. Lizbeth's actions were quick as she locked the side door and moved down the steps, her hair coming loose from her bun and flying around her face. "Is everything all right?" he shouted, his legs still straddling the bike.

She glanced his way, paused, and for a moment Fredrik thought she'd burst out crying.

"*Nee*. The school sent a runner to tell me I'm needed there." She hurried down the driveway, her long legs eating up the pavement.

"Is Benuel sick?"

She stopped and turned around, tucking hair up into her bun under her *kapp*. "They didn't say. Just that I should get to the school right away."

"Let me take you," he offered, patting the small seat behind his larger one.

He watched her battle good common sense for a moment before finally declaring, "I couldn't ride on that thing."

"They said quick, Lizbeth. Hop on. I can get you there in less than five minutes."

Still, she hesitated. "*Nee*, but *danki*." She turned and hurried away.

"Stubborn woman," he muttered to himself and turned the scooter's motor back on. Driving slowly, he caught up with her and growled, "What's important here? You getting to the school for Benuel or saving face by walking all the way and keeping him waiting for you? He could be hurt."

Her eyes flooded with tears and she began to weep, deep racking sobs. "I don't know what to do. I'm so scared for him."

Fredrik pulled his handkerchief out of his back pocket and thrust it at her, longing to hold her as she cried. He waited for her tears to slow and then said, "Wipe your tears and climb on."

She took the cloth, dabbed at her eyes and gave a bitter laugh. "What choice do I have? Benuel needs me."

Bunching her skirt up, she threw her leg over the scooter and moved up close behind Fredrik, her arms wrapping around his waist.

"Hold on tight." He tore off down the road toward the school. The woman would need a shoulder to cry on if something had happened to the boy. She needed a helpmate more than he did.

Reaching the school, he stopped, letting her jump off the back of the scooter. Should he come inside with her, help her deal with whatever had happened? But she ran into the school, forgetting he existed and leaving him to worry about the little boy he'd grown so attached to.

Chapter Seventeen

The next day was sunny and warm. Fredrik worked a half day at the furniture shop, grabbed a bite of lunch, and then headed over to the apartment to find out what happened at the school the day before and to finish a small project that needed doing before he could put the place up for rent for the tourist season. Feeling a little nervous a half hour later, he knocked on Lizbeth's front door. He continued to ask *Gott* for an opportunity to talk to her about starting a relationship, but realized the conversation may not happen with an inquisitive little boy running around.

"You're early. I didn't expect you until later this afternoon." Lizbeth grinned and allowed him inside.

"I only worked part-time today. Business is slow," he said, noticing how attractive she looked in the pink dress and crisp white apron she wore.

Her mood seemed easygoing, her smile flashing his way as he stepped over the threshold. Was this a good time to bring up the incident at school the day before? Wouldn't she have already told him if Benuel had gotten hurt? Still, he was aware she didn't want him hanging around her home any more than he had to. She was a busy mother with a hard-to-handle boy that kept her busy.

He spoke out of concern for the boy, his words hurried. "You seemed so worried about Benuel yesterday. Did everything work out okay?"

"*Ya*, it did, but Benuel was still upset when he went to bed. He and a boy had gotten into an argument and punches were thrown."

Fredrik nodded his head, understanding Benuel's need to fight. He'd fought the need to get physical many times as a boy, but his temper had often won out. "I'm glad he wasn't hurt."

"*Nee*, not a bit, but he got a good lecture from me this morning."

Minutes later, Fredrik thought about Lizbeth's comments about Benuel's fight as he mixed up a batch of grout the consistency of toothpaste.

Going back to concentrating on his work, Fredrik smiled to himself. Grouting had never been one of his favorite things to do, but sponging the glaze off the shiny new bathroom tiles relaxed him today.

Benuel sat on a small stool just outside the bathroom door, watching Fredrik's efforts. The smile on the child's grout-smeared face said he was enjoying his view of the new tiles and his day of suspension from school for fighting.

The boy leaned forward, his hands placed on his knees. Light tan grout dried between his fingers and dripped on his boots. "Can I help again?"

"*Nee*." Fredrik said the word too loud.

Benuel recoiled and shoved back his stool, his eyes wide.

"I'm sorry." Fredrik hung his head down and groaned.

He knew any kind of uproar undid the boy's calm moments. The child seemed afraid of loud noises, sudden movements. After yesterday's incident at the school, Fredrik knew he had to mind his attitude with Benuel. Keep things calm and easygoing.

He scooted the large bucket of murky water outside the bathroom door and stretched out his back. "Look. Why don't you just watch me for a minute and then you can help me clean up my tools. That would be a big help."

"Okay, but you won't forget?" Benuel scrunched up his nose and scratched the side of it, knocking a dried clump of grout the size of a dime onto his mother's clean floor.

Someone had disappointed this child over and over again. He took in the boy's condition. What a sight. Benuel had more grout on him than Fredrik did. He smiled broadly, hoping to show the boy all was well. "*Nee.* I won't forget. Now you'll need to back up a bit. I have to come out and get the cleanup started."

Like on a spring, Benuel popped off the stool, wiped his hands down the sides of his dark trousers, leaving two light-colored chalk streaks. "You want me to carry the bucket?"

"Benuel James Mullet. What have you done to yourself?" Lizbeth stood drying her hands in the kitchen doorway, her eyes taking in the two of them and her floor. She glanced down at Fredrik, the look in her eyes accusing him of causing mayhem, much like Benuel had the day before by hitting a boy on the playground. "I can't believe you let him get in this condition."

She advanced and then took a step back. "*Nee*, I won't clean him. You do it. You're the one who allowed him to get dirty." She pointed her finger toward the back door. "Outside! The both of you need a good hosing down."

Benuel's gritty hand in his, Fredrik smiled as he heard Lizbeth's laughter begin behind him. At times like this he felt like a father to Benuel, and he loved the feeling.

Lizbeth sat at the kitchen table for a moment, enjoying her cold glass of water and listening to Benuel shriek with glee as Fredrik hosed him down with water. A smile played on her lips. She tucked a strand of hair behind her ear and pondered the afternoon's goings-on. Benuel had been muddy before, even covered in pig trough goo when he was four, but an eyebrow and head full of dried grout topped anything she could remember.

The two of them deserved each other, she decided with a grin, and sat back with a sigh of contentment. It had been a long morning. A long week in fact, but having Fredrik around somehow brought order to Benuel's particular type of chaos, and for that she was grateful.

Fredrik yelled out in surprise. His muffled shout sounding something like "I'll get you for that, you *schnickelfritz*." There was no holding back the laughter bubbling inside her. As she laughed, a feeling of peace prevailed, soothing the inner turmoil she'd packed down until she'd been ready to scream.

Somehow she and Fredrik had become friends. Well, not exactly friends, but he was good for the boy and making a difference when no one else seemed able to.

Her hand bent under her chin as she contemplated the future. There would come a time she would have to tell Fredrik the truth. But not today. Was it possible he wouldn't take Benuel away? Would he understand her motives and forgive her?

She dropped her hand. Her eyebrows furrowed. Were thoughts of Fredrik's forgiveness pure foolishness? Somehow the truth would have to come out, and when it did… *Nee*, she didn't want to think about it.

She jerked as the doorbell rang and then rang again. Uncrossing her ankles, she rose and made her way to the front door. The shadow of a man showed through the foggy glass at the sides of the wooden door. Her *daed*, no doubt. It would be like him to check on her midweek.

With a grin on her face, she opened the door, and the friendly words she'd planned on saying wedged in her throat. With a powerful force of fury, she moved to slam shut the door, only to have it forced open against her.

"You don't seem happy to see me, Lizbeth," Ishmael Mullet said in his heavy Ohio Amish dialect. His hand held the door open. He stepped into the house and looked around. His clean-shaven face was moist with sweat from the hot summer day. "What a fine house you live in with your wayward *soh*."

Lizbeth avoided her brother-in-law's glance. He looked so much like Jonah. Memories faded in and out until she thought she would pass out. She couldn't make herself look back at him. Why was he here? It wasn't like him to leave his beloved farm during his busiest time of the year.

The palms of her hands dampened. She rubbed them down her arms and then intertwined her fingers behind her back to keep her hands from trembling.

Like a scene playing out in her mind, she remembered the man's parting threat the night before she and Benuel left Ohio. *You will be my* fraa *now.* His words had robbed her of breath. She knew what he wanted. Had he come to force her back to Ohio? A quaking spread to the core of her being. "Why are you here?"

He stepped toward her.

She stepped back and held her breath.

He moved past her, his long-sleeved shirt brushing against her. She cringed away as he strode into the living room. His presence brought a malevolence into the house that turned her stomach, sickened her. "I came to speak to you." He glanced back at her. "To extend a proposition that would benefit us both." He removed his straw hat, turned on his heel. "Where is Benuel?"

"He's busy…" She fought for the right words. She had to get him out of the house before Benuel saw him. "He and a friend—"

"Yes. I saw his friend in the back garden. He's a little old for Benuel to play with, don't you think?"

"You have no right—"

His breath was hot on her face as he jerked her close, his hand tangling in the wispy hair at her nape of her neck. "I have every right, woman. You were my brother's wife. The bishop said I could have you as my bride, if I wanted you. You and the boy are coming back with me." His eyes narrowed to slits. His voice rose. "My brother was too easy on you. There will be no mouthing off from you or that boy once you're mine." He moved his hand to her cheek and caressed the curve of her neck as he spoke softly, his mouth twisting in a smirk. "You'll like being my wife."

"I'd rather die," she assured him and turned her face away.

He reared back, his arm ready to strike her across the face. Lizbeth's vision blurred, anticipating the impact to be cruel.

The blue color of Fredrik's work shirt suddenly appeared and then the tall, muscular man stepped behind Ishmael and pulled back the man's arm.

Her brother-in-law's face contorted with pain. As he was moved toward the door, a moan slipped from his pinched lips. Lizbeth watched as Fredrik held on to the man's wrist and thumb, his face calm, almost docile.

For an instant, Ishmael hesitated. Fredrik jerked up. A deep groan sounded. Fredrik had the man's thumb twisted at an abnormal angle.

Together the men marched to the door. "You will never come to this house again, to this town again. Do I make myself clear?"

Ishmael spoke softly, words Lizbeth couldn't hear, but she saw Fredrik react to them.

"I wouldn't if I were you. If you do, you'll live to regret it," Fredrik replied. "This community has a way of dealing with men who abuse women and helpless children." Fredrik shoved the man out the door and onto the porch. His baritone voice came out like thunder. "Make your way back to Ohio. You're not *willkummed* here in Pinecraft."

Lizbeth's teeth chattered; her body shook. She closed her eyes in defeat, frozen with fear. The violence she'd experienced for years had followed her to Pinecraft, her sanctuary. A sound behind her alerted her. Benuel had come into the house. Had he seen it all? He stood shivering, his face pale, tears running down his cheeks. Fredrik hurried back in from the front porch and swept the weeping child into his arms.

"*Nee*, don't cry, Benuel," he crooned. "The man is gone now and won't return. Your *mamm* is fine," he promised as he patted the weeping child on the back.

But she wasn't fine. She was defeated. She'd thought she'd done the right thing coming back home, but all she'd done was draw the evil here, to her *familye*. "Bring him to me," she said, not trusting her trembling arms to hold Benuel as she stumbled into the living room. She sat on the edge of the couch and held her arms out for her son.

Fredrik released Benuel into her waiting arms and then sat across from her. "This man was your husband's *bruder*?"

Through tear-dampened lashes, she looked up, so grateful Fredrik had been here to deal with Ishmael. "*Ya*, but he is not a *gut mann*, Fredrik. He always gets his way. His father is an elder and a powerful man in their valley." She lowered her head, her hands holding Benuel tight.

"You have no interest in Ishmael as a husband and father for Benuel?"

She shook her head emphatically. "*Nee*. He came un-invited. He'd threatened he would find me if I ever left." Now was the time she should tell him about Jonah, how cruel he was, like his *bruder*, but she would not speak ill of the dead, not in front of Benuel. Perhaps someday.

Fredrik's lips thinned into a fine line. "I promise you, he won't bother you again. I'll call Otto later and meet with some of the elders. They'll make sure he faces pun-ishment for his actions if he doesn't leave."

She reached out a hand to the strong man across from her. His touch was warm and reassuring. For a moment she felt safe from Ishmael, from his threats. "*Danki*, Fredrik. You have been so kind to us."

A corner of his mouth lifted. He squeezed her fin-gers, his thumb rubbing the back of her knuckles. "I'll be around when you need me. You can count on it." Affection glowed in his eyes.

She took in the sight of him as she spoke softly to Benuel. "You see, Benuel? Fredrik will see that Ishmael never comes back." But even as she uttered the words, she wondered. Would Ishmael give up? Would Otto and the elders of Pinecraft be able to control the angry man? A tremor shook her. She prayed what Fredrik said was true. That Ishmael would go back to Ohio and never return.

Fredrik patted her hand. "Don't fret. I'll keep watch in the apartment out back. If you need me, all you have to do is yell and I'll come running."

Lizbeth nodded. "*Danki*. I appreciate your kindness to me and my *soh*."

His eyes became bright. "I'm not being kind, Lizbeth. I care about you both."

She knew that he did, but she also knew she wasn't ready for a romance of the heart. If Fredrik wanted more than just friendship, he'd have to wait a long time.

Trying to keep life on a normal footing, Lizbeth took Benuel to school the next day, and then took herself to work. The bookkeeping finished, she moved mechanically through the big barn, skimming her dust cloth on every surface she could reach. She stretched to finish wiping the top of a tall chest of drawers and felt strained muscles along her right arm, where Ishmael had grabbed her.

The night before, her father assured her that Ishmael had been put on a bus headed for Ohio, but not before the angry man had spread rumors about her virtue to all who would listen. How dare he say she had promised to marry him? She bent to pick up a piece of paper off the floor.

Nothing Ishmael did surprised her. Nothing. From the day she had met him, he'd made attempts to inappropriately touch her when no one was looking. Finally, she'd tried to tell Jonah, but he'd laughed at her, called her names. Said she deserved what she got.

She began to hum Benuel's favorite hymn, the one she'd hummed the night before to lull the troubled child to sleep. Thankfully Fredrik had offered to sleep in the apartment and be close at hand if they needed him. She thought about his reaction to Ishmael, how he'd set aside his gentle ways to rescue them. She'd never seen him hurt a fly before this.

Tears welled up as she pictured Benuel in her mind. He'd still had a haunted look in his eyes this morning, even after she and Fredrik assured him they'd seen the last of Ishmael Mullet the night before.

She shouldn't allow herself to think of that evil man again, but had no idea how to accomplish such a feat.

She dusted off a beautiful maple bed and smoothed the display quilt out. What a blessing the Fischer family had been to her. Mose's offer of additional work hours to clean at the big furniture barn was a blessing. Sarah teaching her to sew Benuel's clothing and her income from the store would help her afford all the additional costs she'd have now that Benuel had started school.

Her brows drew together and she sighed. Had she made the right choice enrolling him in school? Ulla and her father seemed to think so, and she'd counseled with Sarah before making a commitment and filling out the papers that would allow him to attend the Mennonite Christian school.

Beatrice had been going almost a semester now and Sarah said she already saw a marked improvement in her behavior. But Benuel had been suspended his first day, sent home to think about what he'd done when he'd hit another child.

Why had he hit the other boy? Benuel had kept quiet about the incident, refused to tell her what had led up to the slap. He remained belligerent, but promised he'd never hit another again. Ishmael showing up at their door hadn't done anything but flare Benuel's troubled mood. Would he behave today or would there be another call?

Passing Joe, an older man who had recently been hired by Mose to work short shifts when the need arose, Lizbeth nodded her head and made her way to the back of the store. A quiet man with a rotund belly and short legs, Joe reminded her of the *Englischers'* Santa Claus. He tugged at his long, fluffy white beard and nodded back to her.

The front bell dinged. She stilled her hand and glanced over. Her fingers tugged at her prayer *kapp* as Mose and Fredrik paraded in, both men drinking from cups with straws. Fredrik's eyes sought her out. He grinned her way as both men moved toward the workshop at the back of the building. His gaze lingered. Could he tell she was still reeling from the night before, her stomach still quaking? She smiled to reassure him she was fine and went back to dusting.

He'd spoken softly to Benuel before he'd left for the night and walked to the back of the property. His words were meant to reassure the quiet, troubled child. Had Benuel believed him? She didn't know, but the child had slept erratically next to her in the bed and cried out in his sleep more than once. He'd refused breakfast this morning, and when she'd left him at school later, he hadn't said much, just waved goodbye and walked into the building with his head low.

Her conversation with his teacher had given her a ray of hope that all would be well today. The smiling young teacher assured her she would be able to manage Benuel's ADHD issues now that she knew what was motivating his behavior. She would give him special consideration.

Lizbeth knew his attention problems would be an ongoing battle, but as he aged, his moods would mellow, his attention span lengthen. As a child, Fredrik had always been overactive and prone to silly moods, but his attitude had relaxed and changed for the better. He seemed able to cope with life's demands without a problem now. Like Fredrik, Benuel would never be a patient man, never be able to sit still for long, but he had *Gott* in his corner and her father around to help smooth out the rough spots.

Prayer brought her comfort after the day she'd had, but her nerves were still stretched taut.

When a man of Ishmael's coloring and stature entered the store a few minutes later, Lizbeth fought down the urge to run. Would she ever feel safe? If he came back she would have to take her *soh* and leave Pinecraft. And if she did, where would they go? *Nee*, she had to tell Fredrik the truth about Benuel soon. He would help keep the boy safe.

Her son's slumped shoulders and sad expression from this morning still troubled her. Maybe she should have taken him to Ulla's today. Like Lizbeth, his mind had to be on Ishmael's sudden visit.

She watched Fredrik move toward the back of the

store. He was whistling and seemed happy with life. She longed for that feeling of contentment. Would *Gott* grant her the wish in her heart? Would Fredrik forgive her for keeping Benuel a secret? Would the man ever grow to love her as she did him? Her common sense told her probably not.

Chapter Eighteen

⌒⌐

All caught up on his work at the furniture barn, Fredrik looked forward to the friendly camaraderie and distraction of his biweekly volunteer job with the fire department. Not fully trained yet, he often spent his late afternoons cooking at the local firehouse instead of fighting fires.

As it was located just blocks from his job, he had plenty of time to grab a quick bite of lunch and then ride over to Ringling Street. He parked between Les Cooley's big four-wheel-drive truck and the chain-link fence that surrounded the single-story fire station.

Glad to be out of the heat, he made his way through the side door and enjoyed the frigid air that surrounded him. Quieter than usual, Gabriel Torres sat manning the phone behind his cluttered desk. The dog-eared paperback the *Englischer* was reading showed a gory picture on the front, with the mystery's title written across a bloody body on the ground.

Fredrik lifted his hand and waved. "Afternoon, Gabe. How's life treating you?"

Overweight, with the personality of a comic and

the sensitivity of a mule, Gabriel Torres lowered his book and nodded. His smile was warm and welcoming. "Good. You?"

Fredrik laughed as he shrugged. "Can't complain. You guys been busy?"

"Not really. Just a small fire out by a couple of homes. You training today?"

"*Nee*, cooking. Anything special you want me to fix?" He was familiar with the man's ferocious appetite, knew most of his likes and dislikes. It would be chicken and dumplings or meatballs and noodles.

The big man licked his lips and grinned. "I wouldn't mind a plate of those Amish meatballs and cheesy noodles you make."

"You got it," Fredrik replied and then jerked open the swinging door on his left.

The kitchen was empty, the well-equipped galley cluttered with glasses filled with melting ice or half-drunk tea and cola cans. He was sure he had all the ingredients needed to prepare the simple, but filling, dish Gabriel asked for. There'd be at least a dozen volunteers and first responders coming in and out as the day shift ended and the night shift began.

The clean apron he pulled from the supply closet wrapped twice around his slim waist. He turned to face the long kitchen butcher-block island and picked up the small eraser board left by the day crew. His finger ran down the list of chores he'd need to cover before his shift was over. The meal needed to be cooked by five, but Tony, the kitchen manager, had noted that the pantry needed to be restocked by the day-shift workers as soon as possible.

To help out, he wrote a list of groceries needed for

the busy firemen and left it on the counter for them to find. He welcomed any additional work. The tasks would help him forget about Lizbeth for a while.

Since she'd returned to Pinecraft, his thoughts had somehow become focused on her little family. Lizbeth still mystified him with her grace and beauty, but she'd changed.

He'd enjoyed teasing her as a teen, but his once-casual feelings for her had developed into something more intense of late. If she showed even the least bit of serious interest in him, he would ask her to marry him. He liked it when they spent time together. He already knew they were compatible. They could make a good marriage, if she'd just give him half a chance.

He smiled to himself, enjoying the idea of them as a family. He'd have a fine son in Benuel. Maybe they'd have children of their own, too. He knew he was ready to settle down. There wasn't a doubt in his mind.

Not patient, especially about something so important, he sighed with frustration. He had a suspicion Lizbeth might never be interested in him. Not in the way he wanted. Why hadn't lively, good-spirited Gracie been enough for him? The young widow seemed to enjoy spending time with him. He found her comely and respectable, but their courtship hadn't gone anywhere and that was his fault. The widow had a winning personality, several great kids, but there had been something lacking between them. Something vital to him. He had to love the woman he married and he didn't love her, hard as he tried. He wanted a *fraa*, a *familye*, but was it too much to want love, too? Even if it meant risking another rejection?

He took his straw hat off and then raked his hands

through his hair. *May* Gott*'s will be done*, he prayed and washed his hands again before filling the dishwasher with glasses. Ishmael's threats had made a serious impact on Lizbeth and the boy the day before. He'd never seen a woman or child so terrified. If Ishmael was an example of what she'd dealt with in Ohio, no wonder she wanted no part of having a man in her life.

The mystery behind her years in Ohio intrigued him. Was abuse the cause of her change in personality? It would explain why Benuel was so stressed. He was just a little boy, someone who should be enjoying his young life to the fullest. But instead the child tensed at every noise, seemed unable to fit into the Plain life around him.

Several men with smutty faces and dressed in lightweight gear ambled into the kitchen, all complaining they were parched and looking for cold drinks, something to snack on. They'd been fighting a grass fire just inside Sarasota County and needed to cool down quick.

"Looks like you had a hot afternoon," Fredrik commented as he poured the fresh lemonade he'd prepared earlier. He added ice to tall plastic glasses and cracked open a new bag of chocolate chip cookies. The men gathered around as he dumped the whole bag onto a plate.

Five dirty hands reached out and grabbed handfuls of cookies. "The fire wasn't the problem. It's the humidity," Will said, pulling out a chair and straddling it. He stuffed two cookies into his mouth and smiled as he chewed, his cheeks bulging. New at the station and still not used to working outside in Florida's harsh summer heat, the *Englischer*'s face was red and sweaty.

Caught up in preparing the meal, Fredrik half listened to the men's friendly banter. The hamburger sizzled as he dropped the breaded meatballs loaded with onions, bell peppers and minced garlic cloves into the hot skillet and waited for them to start browning.

He was putting water in a big pan for noodles when he heard Benuel's name mentioned in conversation.

Fredrik set down the pan and turned on his heel. "What did you say about Benuel Mullet?"

Abraham, a grizzled old Amish volunteer Fredrik had known most of his life, answered, "I don't know all the facts, but he went missing this afternoon. They're checking all the usual places. If he's not found soon we're forming a search party over at the Mennonite school."

Fredrik quickly wiped at his hands as he asked, "Where was he last seen?"

"I heard he was on the school playground. His poor *mamm* sure is torn up. My *fraa* called on my work cell and said she couldn't get the woman to stop crying."

The shrill screech of the fire alarm went off, sending first responders scurrying for their protective gear.

Fredrik turned the flame off under the pans and flew through the swinging kitchen door and into the heart of the building. Gabriel shouted the address and description of the building to the lead firefighter as he hurried out the front of the building.

"Isn't that the old Murphy building located a few blocks from the Mennonite school?" Fredrik asked.

The big man's chair protested as he swiveled and faced Fredrik. "It sure is. Why?"

A cold chill sliced through him. His breath became fast and shallow. "A five-year-old boy is missing and his school's a few blocks away. You think there's any chance—"

"There's always a chance. Let's get over there and make sure that building is empty."

Fredrik's hands shook as he suited up. He wasn't fully trained, but he wasn't about to wait around to hear if Benuel had gone in that building's direction. His brow furrowed as he tugged on high boots and ran alongside Gabriel.

He'd grown more attached to Lizbeth's little boy than he'd realized. His heart pumped hard and fast as he jumped onto the fire truck and they sped away. *Please,* Gott. *Don't let Benuel be anywhere near that fire. Keep him safe for Lizbeth. And for me.*

The crowd of people gathered around the old building grew, their bodies pushing in on Lizbeth from every side. She fought to keep her place at the front of the police barricades and yellow tape.

"Please, my boy may be in there," she moaned, brushing hair out of her damp eyes. Ulla appeared out of nowhere and slipped her arm around Lizbeth's waist.

"We don't know that, Lizbeth."

Lizbeth nodded. "*Ya*, we don't know for sure." Her voice broke. But he could be in the burning building. Bile rose in her throat. Someone had seen him on the property less than an hour before. The *Englischer* had said the boy had paused and looked at the building, but the man had become distracted and didn't know if the child had gone into the building or not.

She rubbed her hands up and down her arms, freezing cold and trembling in the summer heat. Why had Benuel run away? Had he gotten into trouble again at school or had Ishmael's return upset him more than he'd let on?

People were whispering around her. Pointing her way. What were they saying? Did they think her *soh* was hurt and unable to make his way out of the fire? The thought agonized her. Another shudder racked her body. *Benuel, where are you?* Her eyes fixed on the double doors of the construction building.

Otto Fischer made his way to her and took her hand, speaking encouraging words. The strength of the old man's firm hold bolstered her. *Gott* was with her. *His will be done*, she repeated over and over in her head until she thought she would lose her mind.

She glanced up at the sky, looking for some sign that all would be well, but saw nothing but black smoke and the worried faces all around her. Would Benuel end up in a grave like her other *sohs*? Would she lose him, too? Was this *Gott*'s punishment for her keeping her secret from Fredrik? Her legs buckled and Otto and Ulla held her up, their arms locked around her waist. Gott*'s will be done*. Gott*'s will be done.*

Three firemen rushed from the building, their flame-retardant suits bulky on their bodies. Plumes of billowing black smoke shifted with the wind, licking at the ground around them. "Did *Daed* check the yard around the apartment again? He might have found a way into the house," she stammered, coughing from the acrid smoke burning her throat.

"*Ya*, he and the men are looking everywhere." Ulla's eyes pleaded with her. "Won't you please come with me? We'll check the roads leading up to the park. He likes to play there. I have your father's work phone. The police are certain-sure to call us when they find him."

"*Nee*, I've got to stay here. Benuel will need me if he's hurt."

"But you can't be sure he's in there, Lizbeth. He could be anywhere, safe and sound. Think positive. *Gott* is with him."

The building groaned. Lizbeth shuffled on the balls of her feet, trying hard not to fall as the crowd moved back. Two firemen rushed out of the building, one carrying a small bundle wrapped in a silver blanket. A stretcher was placed on the ground and the blanket unrolled. The blue shirt and dark trousers her son had worn to school covered the body of the small boy on the ground.

Lizbeth's heart skipped a beat, and she felt unable to breathe. She couldn't seem to swallow as she pushed forward and rushed toward the crowd of first responders. With a breaking heart she cried out, "*Gott* have mercy on my boy. Benuel!"

Fredrik stumbled forward, dense smoke swirling in the sunlight directing him toward the big doors. Joy filled his heart. They'd found Benuel on the second floor, curled up and crying, but he was all right. Thank *Gott* he was all right and they'd gotten him out of this furnace.

A board fell, and then two. Just behind him, Gabriel called out, "Make a run for it! The ceiling's coming down."

An explosion rocked the ground. Concrete and wood shook. The walls screamed, metal tearing metal. The darkness around him became alive with flames and falling rubble. Gabriel grabbed his arm, pulled him forward. The two men ran as one, stumbling over fallen debris. Something solid hit Fredrik and he went down. Unbelievable heat covered him. Pain pierced the side of his head. His world went silent and black.

Chapter Nineteen

A nurse in a white smock covered in yellow smiley faces pushed out a door down the hall. Her rubber-soled shoes squeaked as she walked with purpose, her gait long. The vibrant black color of her hair sparked under the fluorescent light overhead as she glanced at the chart in her hand and then surveyed the pensive faces in the cold waiting room.

Lizbeth half rose, her hands still grasping the arms of the uncomfortable hospital chair upholstered in cold, slick leatherette. Her mind was numb with fear and dread. She compressed her lips together and waited.

Tall and lean, the nurse made her way over and stopped in front of Lizbeth's chair. "Lizbeth Mullet?" she asked, her voice soft and inquiring.

"*Ya.* You have news? Is my boy…?" She stood to her feet and swayed.

"Calm down, Mama." The nurse smiled, urging Lizbeth back into the chair with her hand. "We don't want you passing out on us." Her pale brown eyes warmed with compassion as she patted Lizbeth's hand and said, "Your little boy's going to be just fine."

"The doctors are sure? He's breathing easy now?" She raked her hand through her tangled hair and tried to bring back a semblance of order to the falling bun at the base of her neck. Her *kapp* lay crumpled on the floor, forgotten.

The nurse chuckled, her easygoing demeanor calming Lizbeth. "He's breathing like a champ and calling for his mama. You can come see for yourself if you promise not to faint on me."

Lizbeth rose, but instantly saw an array of colorful stars swirling around her and slumped back down. She gave a mirthless laugh, annoyed at her own show of weakness. "I guess I'm a little shakier than I realized."

Taking the empty seat beside Lizbeth, the nurse sat a handful of files on her knees and looked Lizbeth over. "Did you inhale any of the smoke?"

"Some, but not a lot." She cleared her dry throat.

"Let me get you a cool glass of water and then we'll make our way slow and easy to the pediatric ward. I'll have one of the doctors check you over after you've had a word with your son."

Lizbeth nodded and then looked up, her hand clutching her throat. Her concern for Benuel was replaced by her fear for the firemen who'd been trapped in the building. "Do you know… Did all the firemen make it out alive?"

The nurse scooped up the files on her lap and stood. "I haven't heard anything, but I'm sure someone on the floor can find out for you. Why don't I find a wheelchair for you and get you to him?"

Lizbeth rubbed her temples. "*Ya*, I need to see my boy, make sure he's all right."

A moment later Lizbeth gasped as she was pushed

into her Benuel's room and saw him. He appeared small and frail in the twin-size hospital bed made up with glistening white sheets. A thin plastic tube came from around the side of the bed and supplied oxygen through a cannula positioned under his small nose.

"Benuel," she said and reached for his cold, limp hand.

The stench of smoke still clung to him. Someone had made an effort to clean Benuel's pale face, but gritty soot still lined his hair and brows.

His blue eyes blinked open and shut again. A cough racked his body.

Lizbeth twisted around. "Is he supposed—"

"Yes, he'll have a rattle and a cough for a while, but he's getting plenty of oxygen. The doctor must have given him something to make him sleep. He was a pretty sick boy when he came in."

Lizbeth shoved the loose hair out of her face and kissed Benuel's cheek. "And you're sure he's going to be fine?"

The nurse attached the file to the foot of the bed and turned to leave. "I'll ask the doctor to come in and see you," she said and opened the door. "You just make sure you're in his line of sight when he wakes up. That young man wants his mama." She chuckled and left the room, leaving Lizbeth with the sounds of Benuel's labored breathing and the steady beat of his heart registering on the monitors above his head.

Fredrik became conscious of a bright light shining in his eyes and tried to move. Pain fractured the light into a million shards inside his head. Someone close by groaned.

"Don't move, Mr. Lapp," a male voice said from a distance, but the words were muffled, distorted.

The dreadful groaning continued. Why didn't someone help the man suffering? Fredrik tried to voice his concerns, but the labored effort forced him into silence. Where was he? Who was crying out?

Unfamiliar sounds encircled him. Voices became clearer, filled his mind. Words that made no sense sent him back into the tumultuous maelstrom of fear. The sensation of falling jerked him down into a vortex of sensations. Light became pain.

Something cool and comforting covered him. Somewhere a clock ticked the minutes away. *Tick-tock.* The suffering man became silent. Had he died?

Consciousness returned, layer by layer. Fredrik's eyelashes fluttered. He strained to clear his throat.

The man groaned again.

A surge of excitement filled him. The suffering man was in pain, but alive. He struggled to open his eyes.

"Mr. Lapp. Wake up, Mr. Lapp."

My name is Fredrik. He tried to correct the man speaking to him. He'd seldom been called Mr. Lapp. It sounded foreign to him…inappropriate. *I'm plain Fredrik*, he insisted. He heard no sound, just the all-encompassing groaning filling the air around him.

The darkness slowly faded and the light around him brightened, compelling him to open his eyes. He struggled to sort out the black-and-white squiggles that became colored and then merged into the features of a man.

"Lie still, Mr. Lapp."

He was firmly held down. He began to struggle, hysteria building in his mind. *Why can't I move? What's wrong with me?* He sunk into the black emptiness coming for him.

* * *

Lizbeth spent two days in the hospital with Benuel, her bed the reclining chair in the corner of the small two-bed room in the pediatric ward. She hadn't gotten used to the antiseptic smell of bleach or the bad *Englischer* food, but she couldn't fault the brilliant care her cantankerous boy was receiving. His cough was much better, and the doctor promised he could go home in the morning if today's X-ray showed additional improvement to his lungs.

Ulla glanced at the clock on the wall. She knitted rhythmically on the navy sweater being made for Benuel. Her needles clicked as they created stitch after stitch. "Shouldn't Benuel be back from the X-ray by now?"

Lizbeth's leg was asleep and tingling under her, so she straightened it out and flexed her toes. She shoved her foot in her shoe and grimaced as the tingling turned to intense pain. "The nurse said they'd be doing a blood panel, too. Maybe they took him to the lab," she whispered and pointed to the closed curtain around the other small bed, "instead of jabbing him here. Last time he raised a real fuss and scared the other little boy."

Her knitting forgotten, Ulla placed the needles and yarn in her lap. "Have you asked Benuel why he ran away yet?"

Lizbeth rolled her shoulders and pulled them back, stiff from all the sitting. "*Nee*, not yet, but I will soon. I don't want to upset him, but I think it was because of the fight he'd had with the boy at school. He was still upset the next day and then Ishmael came and scared the life out of him." She bowed her head. She should have noticed how stressed he was. She looked up. "I did ask him about the fire, though, and he promised he hadn't started it. He said he saw smoke and went to see what was burning and saw flames coming from the wall. I'm guessing it was bad wiring in the old building." She paced the room, wishing she could have gone downstairs with him. The nurses were friendly, but waking to find his bed empty had shaken her this morning. Would he run again? She prayed not.

"John suggested you take Benuel out of school until he's a year older, more settled." Ulla picked up the knitting, checked her progress and plunged the needle in the last stitch dropped. She began to work on the sweater again.

"*Ya*, it makes me to wonder if that's not what's best for now." She was ashamed to tell the older woman she didn't know exactly what to do, but she would figure it out.

She wrapped her arms around her middle. If her *daed* thought school was too much for Benuel, perhaps she would keep him home with her awhile longer. His behavior had always been unpredictable, but she'd thought he'd been doing better than he was. She wanted to trust her own judgment but wasn't a mind reader.

Benuel's ADHD made changes hard on the boy. The trip to Pinecraft, new faces, new experiences, had shaken him, and then Ishmael had come and terrified him. She no longer trusted his teacher or the school to keep track of him. Not since the fire.

Fear gripped her as a new possibility squeezed her heart, made it skip a beat. Would there be a police investigation? Would they believe Benuel hadn't started the fire? She clenched her hands into fists at her sides. She had to pull herself together, not take on problems. She had enough issues to deal with. It would do no good to imagine situations that could change Benuel's life forever.

The door squeaked as it opened and her brother's face appeared, a brilliant smile lighting up his dark blue eyes as he asked, "Is it safe to come in?"

"Saul!" Lizbeth ran to him, threw herself into his open arms. "It's so *gut* to see you," she said, completely relaxing for the first time in days.

"And you." He pulled her away, surveyed her up and down. "Just look at you, little *schweschder*. It's *ser gut* to see you." His smile became mischievous, his eyes glittering as he lifted his hand in greeting to Ulla and then turned back to Lizbeth. "You've gotten taller, but not an ounce plumper," he said and dodged as she reached for his head, prepared to muss his light-colored hair as she always had as a child. "Still all bones and attitude, I see."

"No more than you." She threw her head back and laughed at his wounded expression. "When did you get in?"

"I drove the whole day and made it just in time to watch you sleeping in that chair last night."

"You were here? Why didn't you wake me, let me know?" Lizbeth tucked herself under his arm as she'd done a million times as a child. She was safe and content.

He brushed back the hair from her forehead and kissed it softly before he answered. "I didn't want to disturb you. The nurse said you hadn't slept in two nights, but thanks be to our merciful *Gott*, your boy is alive."

"*Ya*, they tell me he'll be fine and I can breathe again."

"They're still not sure about Fredrik," Saul said, tugging at his light-colored beard.

"What do you mean? Is Fredrik ill?" She touched her hand to her heart as she sat on the edge of the bed.

Saul eyed her. "Didn't anyone tell you? Fredrik ran into the building to find Benuel. The ceiling gave way and fell in on him and another firefighter. They're both in intensive care."

Her lower lip quivered as she asked, "What was he doing fighting a fire?"

"Someone said he volunteers a couple of times a week. You didn't know?"

"*Nee.* He never said anything to me about fighting fires." Shame engulfed her. She'd been so concerned for Benuel, she hadn't given much more than a passing thought to the firemen who fought the blaze and carried her son out to safety. *Fredrik is hurt!* Heat suffused her face. "Do they know what's wrong with him? Is he going to be all right?"

He took her hand and patted it. "They aren't saying. All I could find out is that the burning ceiling fell on Fredrik. Something must have hit him on the head, because he has a concussion." His face grew pensive. "He hasn't woken up yet."

A ripple of anxiety coursed through her. If Fredrik died he'd never know he had a son. She would have cheated him of that joy. Her body shook as she held tight to her brother and looked into his eyes. Somehow she had to tell Fredrik before it was too late. "I have to see Fredrik, Saul. It's important. I need to tell him."

"I know you want to thank him for saving Benuel, but the man's in no condition—"

Frustrated, she shook Saul's hand, beseeched him with her eyes. "You don't understand. I must see him. I never told him… Benuel is his *soh.*"

Chapter Twenty

"No one from the fire department told me Mr. Lapp had a wife. His papers show him as single."

"What?" Lizbeth's head turned, her brows raised, as she tried very hard to look surprised. The lie her brother had come up with weighed heavy on her conscience, but she had to see Fredrik and tell him about Benuel before it was too late.

She plastered a half smile on her face, felt her lips quiver with nerves. "Oh, yes. Fredrik and I married recently. I was out of town and just got word of his accident." Shame burned in her, flushed her face. She hated to lie, but what could she do? Fredrik deserved to know the truth and only family was allowed into the intensive care unit. She did what she had to. *Forgive me,* Gott.

The nurse observed her suspiciously for a moment, shrugged her shoulders, opened the wide, swinging hospital door marked ICU and turned toward a door. "He should be in here…"

Lizbeth nodded, her body trembling as she slipped on the protective gown the nurse handed her and walked through the door and into a bright hallway lined with single-occupancy rooms.

She scurried along behind the stout gray-haired nurse dressed in a cheerful smock and matching pants, all the while praying in earnest. *Let Fredrik live. Please,* Gott. *Let him live.*

The nurse stopped at the last room and peeked in. "Here he is." She yanked a heavy green drape open enough for her and Lizbeth to step in. Dim, the room seemed like a shrouded cocoon of beeping machines and wires. There was a single bed. Lizbeth halted in shock.

Her glance first went to Fredrik's ashen face, then to the blood-soaked bandage wrapped around his head. She tried to stifle her gasp, but failed miserably. The pallor of his skin shocked her. "He's so pale." She'd never seen Fredrik vulnerable before. Her eyes shimmered with unshed tears.

"Most head-trauma patients are," the nurse said and reached for his chart. "Have you spoken with any of his doctors yet?"

"*Nee*, not yet," she said, her voice wavering. She broke down, her shoulders shuddering as she cried.

The nurse pushed a narrow table away and assisted her to a gray metal chair next to the bed.

Lizbeth fell into the armchair, her head in her hands, sobbing. She hadn't told Fredrik about Benuel, and now it may be too late. Memories engulfed her, flashed through her mind. She and Fredrik as children, then their teenage years, when she'd hung on to his every word like it was gospel. Marrying Jonah out of desperation had wounded her heart, but the past five years had stolen all her joy, made her a miserable woman.

She'd sat in a chair just like this one before, watched

the life of her tiny *sohs* slowly ebb away until there was no hope, their immature lungs failing them. The *kinners'* deaths had been *Gott*'s will, but not hers. She'd wanted to see them grow into men of strong faith. But Jonah's abuse had robbed her yet again. The doctors had said their early births hadn't been her fault, and implied the beatings she'd taken had brought on her labor, but how could she be sure?

Her fists clenched. Would Fredrik die this time? Surely *Gott* wouldn't take him from her, too. This couldn't be His will for Benuel's life, to not have a father. She needed a second chance. *Please,* Gott. *Give me a second chance to do it right this time.*

The nurse patted her on her shoulder. "Don't let yourself get too upset, Mrs. Lapp. Your husband's young and strong. Looks pretty tough to me. I'm sure he'll be just fine."

Lizbeth lifted her head and looked into the nurse's eyes, desperately wanting her words to be true. She saw concern and resignation there, but no clear hope. *"Danki,"* she murmured, knowing the woman had been trained to say whatever she thought a wife might want to hear.

"I'll give you a moment alone with your husband," the nurse said softly and left the room.

Lizbeth remained silent. *Please, Father. Don't let him die, too. I love him.*

Fredrik's lashes fluttered as he sluggishly awoke from the black fog surrounding him. He became conscious of incessant pain hammering in his head and then the weight of something heavy on his left arm.

He moved, the effort costing him more pain than he

was willing to pay. He stilled. Instead he focused on his breathing, on the things he could see without moving, the sounds he heard. Close by a high-pitched beep matched the rhythmic beating of his heart.

Clarity came gradually. It was obvious he was in a hospital bed, his head without a pillow under it. A cylinder of oxygen hissed under his nose. Bright lights overhead caused him to wince. He momentarily blinked his eyes. He shifted his gaze and tried to refocus, but only managed to exhaust himself.

Questions bombarded his mind, made his head hurt worse, but he pushed for answers. Why was he in the hospital? How long had he been lying there? Was he badly injured? How did it all happen?

He calmed himself by gazing at the pale green curtain hanging from metal rings that ran along a silver railing. The curtains were so close he could almost reach out and touch them.

He heard the footfalls of someone walking, their shoes squeaking like basketball sneakers on a wooden court. He tried to call out, but his throat was dry. It hurt to swallow, to breathe. He coughed and then groaned. What had happened to him? Why didn't someone come to see about him?

"Fredrik."

He cast his eyes down toward the foot of the bed. Lizbeth's face appeared. Her *kapp* was off, her hair in disarray. He could see that she'd been crying. She nibbled on her bottom lip like she had as a young girl, when she was in trouble and needed his help. "Lizbeth." He tried to say her name, but it came out garbled. He lifted his hand toward her. It felt unusually heavy and he let it drop.

Relief suffused her features, but concern quickly took

its place. "*Nee*, don't move," she urged, touching his arm. Her fingers were cold against his skin. "You must remain still. You've been badly injured. Your head—"

"It hurts," he whispered and swallowed hard. *If only I had a drink of water.*

Sadness clouded her features. "I know it hurts. Please don't try to talk. Just listen." Her face contorted and then went blank. "I have to tell you now. Forgive me if I've waited too long, but I have to tell you in case—" A tear rolled down her cheek, and then another.

Fredrik knew it took a lot to make Lizbeth cry. Was he badly hurt? Fear gripped his insides. Was he dying? He closed his eyes and took in a deep breath. A spasm of pain gripped his chest, forced him to cough until his lungs seemed on fire.

Lizbeth came closer, bending over him. "Do you remember the night I turned nineteen? We celebrated by going to a singing frolic." She swallowed hard, drawing in a long breath. "You and Saul were on *rumspringa*. I don't know why, but you both came to the singing drunk."

He blinked his eyes. What was she talking about, this singing frolic? Had he and Saul been drunk? They had done a lot of crazy things on *rumspringa*. He sighed. Why couldn't he remember? Why was this particular event so important to her now? They went to a lot of singings when they were young. Dark circles of black clouded his mind, tried to draw him away from her voice.

"You took me home that night," she said.

He struggled to listen, to make sense of what she was saying.

"You offered me a drink from your flask." She paused, looking down at him with sadness shadowing her features. She sighed and went on. "Later we went into the barn."

"*Nee.*" He forced the word out, hoarse and rough. He would have never taken her into the barn. *Nee*, he would have never done such a thing. He looked at her, their gazes meeting. A deep flush crept up her face. Had he? He searched her face again, saw the truth in her words.

"Benuel was conceived that night," she whispered, her expression turning somber. She turned her head away.

"Benuel?" The name came out loud and clear.

"*Ya*, he is your *soh*, Fredrik. I had to tell you before…"

But the black swirls beckoned to him, tugging and churning and then pulling him away.

Lizbeth observed the young *Englischer* couple rambling along ahead of her. Both dark-haired and casually dressed in jeans and knit shirts, they looked the picture of health and contentment. They were young and in love. She could tell by the way he grasped the girl's hand, the way she snuggled under his arm as they walked. Both were smiling contently.

They didn't seem to have a care in the world and she envied their joy, even though she knew *Gott* wouldn't approve of her jealousy. The Ordnung was clear, the scriptures taught to her at her father's knee concise and unbending. Wanting what others had would bring forth sin and death. She'd made enough mistakes. Took too many wrong roads. She had to learn to be content with her life and make do.

She tried to shrug off her self-pity. Today was a *gut* day. She should be happy. Smile even. Benuel had been officially exonerated from any blame for the fire and a homeless man charged. Fredrik's condition had improved enough for him to be in a regular room and Benuel was finally coming home after three long days in the hospital.

The night before, Benuel had finally talked to her and Saul about why he'd run away, how terrified he'd been that Ishmael would steal him away from her and take him back to Ohio, to the farm. He'd been ashamed of himself for hitting the boy in school, afraid he'd become cruel like Ishmael.

Her shoulders straightened with resolve. She had to set aside the past five years of her life, reignite her joy of living and push forward. But there was so much left undone. So much uncertainty in her and Benuel's lives. Her strength would be tested, but with *Gott*'s help she could do anything. He'd proved Himself a faithful friend and had been with her through her most difficult times while married to Jonah.

She picked up her pace and hurried along, hoping if she walked fast enough all the foolish mistakes she'd made would somehow be left behind her.

The halls of the hospital's children's wing were painted in bright and cheerful colors, the walls plastered with posters of friendly faces of smiling rabbits, but the smell of chemical disinfectant hung heavy in the air.

She paused two feet away from Benuel's door when she heard the sound of laughter coming from the room. She approached slowly. Her brother's deep laugh joined in with Benuel's high-pitched shriek of joy. Her steps quickened to the door. "Well, someone certainly feels better today," she said with a smile and did her best not to cry at the sight of Saul holding Benuel in his arms. "It seems you two have become good friends."

"Mamm!" Benuel wailed, his arms going out to her. "The nurse said I could go home today. Is it true?"

He coughed, but the sound disturbed her far less than it had when he'd first entered this place of healing. She was grateful for all the good care he'd received. *"Ya,* it's true."

Saul passed her son's warm body to her and smiled. "He's a handful, this one. I know only one other person who fidgets as much."

Their eyes connected for a brief moment and she saw his approval of Benuel, but recognized his comment was to remind her they still needed to talk about Fredrik and the role he would play in this child's life.

"I remember you being just as squirmy," she threw back with a smile, but knew Saul was right. Benuel was a carbon copy of Fredrik, down to his radish-like toes.

Saul grinned as the boy wiggled out of his mother's arms and grabbed the carryall from her hand. "Is this my clothes?" he asked, dumping the contents on the bed before Lizbeth could react. He stripped off his hospital pajamas. With all his might he pushed his leg into the pressed pair of trousers, lost balance and ended up a giggling pile on the floor.

"Perhaps if you slow down a bit you might be able to accomplish your goal, young *soh*," she admonished, but couldn't hold back the laughter bubbling up. Benuel had made it through the fire, his lungs healing so quickly even the nurses were amazed at his progress. "Here, let me help you this one time."

"Nee, I'm a big boy. I can do it." He so naturally slipped into Pennsylvania *Deitch*, his accent as heavy as Jonah's had been.

Lizbeth lifted her head and looked over at Saul. Tears

shimmered in the tall, handsome man's blue eyes. "He is a handful," she admitted, "but we are working on the value of self-control and doing what is requested of us." She laughed when Saul chuckled at her words. "We are trying."

"Let me do that, old *soh*," Saul said to Benuel and lifted the boy off the floor and onto the bed. "You shove your leg in and I'll hold your pants."

"*Nee*, I can do it," Benuel repeated and pulled away from his uncle's reach. He struggled until he managed to get both legs in where they belonged. "I am five now."

"This little *mann* has a mind of his own and I have a feeling it will be many years of struggle before you reach your goal. But you're not alone. You have family and…others willing to invest their lives into Benuel."

Again a reference to Fredrik. She nodded. Saul was right. It would take a great deal of work and patience to deal with an ADHD child. She'd need all the help she could get. Especially Fredrik's.

As she watched Benuel's arms shove into the sleeves of his long-sleeved shirt, her thoughts stayed on Fredrik. She knew he was getting better day by day. Saul spent most of his days with the injured man and shared with her what he had seen and heard each night at the dinner table.

She'd almost stopped by Fredrik's room today, but dread had stopped her. She was probably the last person he'd want to see after what she'd done to his life. Being robbed of his *soh*'s childhood couldn't sit well with him. There could still be a high price to pay.

"I have a message for you."

"*Ya?*" she said and glanced over at Saul, expecting him to speak freely.

"Let's get one of the nurses to help this young man finish up with his hair combing and tooth brushing."

Her brow raised. "Someone?"

Saul nodded, his lips pursed. "I told Fredrik we'd be down in a bit."

Fredrik wanted to see her? She bit her lip. She wasn't prepared, but would she ever be? What he had to say could ruin her life. "Perhaps you should have spoken to me first before you agreed."

"I think you owe him at least a conversation."

She winced. "*Ya*, you are right," she admitted, her heart thumping hard at the thought of answering Fredrik's questions, listening to his accusations.

Occupied with trying to tie his own shoes, Benuel didn't seem to notice when she and Saul left the room a moment later. Lizbeth marched past the nurse's station, her mind overwhelmed with the next step in her life. She had to let Fredrik in. She had no choice, but why did she suddenly feel so relieved? Was it because Benuel would finally have Fredrik as his father?

Hadn't she wanted this for a long time? For Fredrik to be there every time she looked up? Had she been fighting her love for Fredrik all this time, lying to herself? Was he the man *Gott* had created for her? She hoped so.

Chapter Twenty-One

The red-faced nurse flounced out of the room, leaving behind her simply put words. "Either you eat your breakfast of bacon and eggs, Mr. Lapp, or there will be nothing until lunch, and that's a good four hours away."

"Powdered eggs and rubbery bacon don't appeal to me today," he called to the slowly closing door at the foot of the bed. He suffered a fit of coughing for his rebellious words.

She thrust the door open a crack and shoved her head back in. Her eyes sparkled with determination. "And Nurse O'Brian will not be sneaking in vending machine doughnuts or Snickers bars today. No more Cokes. Not on my watch."

He grinned at her, feeling good about something for the first time in days. Getting a rise out of the old girl confirmed what he'd suspected. He was getting better, stronger, maybe even ready to go home.

Her face softened, becoming almost motherly. "Good food is what you need, Fredrik. Not garbage."

"I'd eat *gut* food, if you brought me some." His thumb jerked toward the uneaten breakfast tray. "I wouldn't feed this swill to a pig," he said and grinned mischievously around a cough. He added for good measure, "If I owned one. But *danki* for being so concerned about me."

Her lips set in a firm line. "It's my job," she declared and shut the door behind her.

His lips drew back in a full smile, his thoughts instantly going to Benuel. His *soh*. "My *soh*." The words sounded natural coming out of his mouth. Joy flooded his spirit every time he said it. He was a father, the child's real father.

He'd felt an affinity to the boy since he'd watched the hyperactive child try to function in a world moving far too slowly for him. He knew the frustrations the boy faced. He'd dealt with racing thoughts, the inability to sit still for longer than a millisecond. Starting now, he would become a constant in his son's life. He would make sure the world made more sense to Benuel. He would make a difference, with *Gott*'s help.

Thoughts of Lizbeth cascaded in and were pushed away, confined to the dark recesses of his mind until he could figure out how he felt about what she had done. He didn't understand, but he would in a matter of minutes, as soon as Saul brought her to his room. He knew Lizbeth better than most. He would reserve judgment until he heard her reasons for withholding Benuel. He owed the mother of his son that much.

Fredrik shoved the tray on wheels away from the bed, threw back the sheet, then stopped. He eyed the hard cast on his arm, the bandage on his left thigh. He thought of the smaller bandage taped over the cut on the side of his shaved head.

He wanted to splash his face and comb what little hair hadn't burned off his head. Brushing his teeth with his left arm had proved difficult the night before, but it had been a hallelujah moment when he'd accomplished the task. He was glad he had the strength to get out of bed alone, to wait on himself for a change.

He hurt in places he couldn't see or touch, but he continued to make his way to the bathroom, flipped on the light with his cast and whistled as he accomplished his ablutions.

With his left hand, he combed through the dirty hair at the base of his neck and turned toward the mirror to see if he'd accomplished his goal. Not impressed with what he saw, he wiggled a singed brow at his own reflection and accepted his limitations. Using his cane, he ambled over to the comfortable-looking padded chair in the corner.

As he sat, his stomach rumbled. He rubbed it, leaned back and closed his eyes, picturing his mother's fluffy pumpkin pancakes. He turned toward the food tray, opened an eye and sighed. Perhaps he would try the pretend eggs, but only if he got desperate. For now, he was content to sit and wait for Lizbeth to arrive. Eyes closing, he laced his fingers across his sunken stomach and relaxed, his mind going back to Benuel. His *soh*.

Lizbeth felt her brother's hand on her back, his quicker steps urging her on down the empty hall. "*Ach*, there is no rush. We will get there when we get there."

"The man has waited six years to hear the truth from your lips. Don't you think you could speed up your crawl just a bit?"

She stopped and turned and was almost knocked over by her brother's bulk. "I know he deserves the truth. That's why I told him when I thought he was—"

"*Ya*. You told him, but not until you thought he was dying."

A couple strolled by and gave them a curious glance. Lizbeth allowed Saul to tug her by the arm over to the wall. "This is hard for me, *bruder*. All of this," she said, her lips quivering. "You've heard the truth. Every miserable mistake I've made. Do you think talking about this, especially with Fredrik, will come easy? He doesn't remember!" Lizbeth pulled away, her temper flaring. Too many sleepless nights of tossing and turning had made her short-tempered. She just wanted to take her boy and go home. Be at peace for a while before she had to explain everything to everyone, especially Fredrik.

Her brother pulled her into his arms, patted her back as he'd done a million times before. "I'm sorry. I truly am." With a look of concern, he explained, "I know you dread this moment, but think of what could come from it."

"*Ya*, that's all I think about, Saul. Fredrik could be so angry he'll take Benuel away from me. You know how hard it's been for me. The mistakes I've made since I've had the boy on my own. I can't expect Fredrik to say he's fine with everything and go on his merry way, making up his mind whether or not he wants to be in Benuel's life." A tear rolled from her eye. "I wasn't much of a mother when I came back to Pinecraft, but I've learned and grown. I haven't had the time to learn how to make the best of my boy's ADHD problems, but I will."

"Jonah is to blame for that. Not you. He kept you from the boy, allowed his mother to take over."

"*Ya*, but I should have protested more. Made a stronger effort to—"

"And been knocked back in your place? *Nee*, I think

you did what all Amish women do. They obey their husbands, kind or cruel. Not so?"

"*Ya*, but—"

"There are no *but*s," he said, cutting her off. "You will go into that room with your head held high, tell your story, and Fredrik Lapp better give you the benefit of the doubt. I believe in you because you're my little *schweschder*, and I love you."

Saul hugged her close, and then pushed her along. "We will both be sobbing in the hall if this conversation continues." His smile was infectious. "Move, you silly *bensel*. We have much to do and Benuel is waiting to go home."

Placing one foot in front of the other, Lizbeth hurried along beside her brother, her hands hanging by her side. *Gott* would bring about an outcome and it would be His will for her life. She had to learn to trust and smile again.

Fredrik woke to the sound of his hospital door closing behind someone. He opened his eyes and saw Saul standing with his back to the door. Lizbeth stood in front of Fredrik's chair.

Pale and gaunt, she appeared as troubled as he felt and more than a little unsure of herself. He could only imagine what she thought of how he looked, with his bandaged body and blood-splatted hair standing up at all angles around the bandage wrapped round his head.

It was painful to sit up, but he managed it with as little fanfare as possible. "Hello," he said in a voice he didn't recognize. He coughed. His lungs were still healing from the smoke he'd taken in, but he could breathe now without wanting to cry out in pain. That was an improvement.

"You look better," Lizbeth said and looked down, their gazes not meeting.

"*Ya*, better," he said, not sure how to start this conversation without her help.

Saul opened the door and slipped out quietly.

Fredrik turned back to Lizbeth, saw her eyes opened wide. Was she afraid of him? Did she think him a monster, void of feeling? She'd lied to him, kept secrets best said, but he'd never hurt or abuse her. She was the mother of his *soh*.

In that moment he knew she was the woman he loved with all his heart. He'd known his boyhood interest in her was still alive and well, but when had it turned into such a deep devotion? He didn't know, and he didn't care. All he knew was he had to listen to her explain and then tell her what was in his heart.

"Saul said you wanted to see me." She lowered herself to the straight-back chair next to the bed and sat, her shoulders back, ankles crossed. Both her hands clutched the fabric of her dress.

"I do." He paused as he coughed, and then wiped his mouth with the back of his hand. "I'm sorry. The smoke—"

She sat forward. "Don't apologize."

"*Nee,*" he said and prayed for *Gott* to put the right words into his mouth. "I have been thinking…about what you said. How Benuel is *mein soh*?"

"I had to tell you." She worried the fabric of her collar with her hand and squirmed uncomfortably in the chair. "If you had died, you would never have known. Every father deserves to know he has a child."

He caught her gaze, saw the pain she was going

through. "I'm glad you told me when you did. It made my will to live stronger."

He watched her relax, saw her hands unclench.

"I'm glad," she said.

"I'm sorry I took advantage of you that day. Sorry you had to deal with the reality of our *kinner* alone," Fredrik said.

She rose and slowly moved toward him, her hand outstretched. "But I was glad to be carrying your child. Didn't you know that I…I loved you? Since I was a young girl I clung to your every word, sought out ways to be around you." She knelt by his chair, her hand on his knee.

Fredrik shook his head, not believing the words she was saying. "Then why did you seem so distant when you came back to Pinecraft? You acted like the sight of me made you nervous."

The corner of her mouth angled up into a radiant smile. "You did make me nervous. You reminded me of how foolish I'd been. The mistakes I'd made." She dropped her gaze. "Every time I saw you with Benuel I thought of what could have been, what should have been."

He reached for her hand, rubbed his thumb across her knuckles. "Why didn't you find me, tell me about Benuel? We could have married. There'd have been no need for you to marry Jonah," he said and then added, "Unless you loved him."

She blanched. "*Nee*, I didn't love him. Not for a moment. At first he was kind to me."

"Go on," Fredrik urged, bitterly angry with himself for taking advantage of Lizbeth. She'd been so young when he'd left for training in Ohio. Only nineteen. He'd joined the church there, been baptized, courted Bette. His mind had been on his own life, not the life growing inside her body. Why had he forgotten such an important moment? He must have been very drunk. What a *bensel* he was. Why had she protected him like that? She should have sent her father to deal with him.

"I tried to find you on my own, but my father kept asking me who the *boppli*'s father was. Pressuring me. I didn't want you in trouble with the bishop, the elders of the church. You were finally getting your life in order, courting a girl." Her chin touched her chest. "Finally, my father paid Jonah to marry me." She blinked away the tears. "*Daed* did what he thought best for me, for the *kinner*. Jonah accepted the money after the marriage, promised he forgave the past and said he would be a real father to *our child*. I believed him for a time, but after we arrived in Ohio everything changed."

"What happened?" A terrible rage built in his gut, tearing at him.

"Jonah became abusive with his words and his hands." She turned her head toward the wall, her eyes staring.

"Why didn't you contact your father?" Fredrik demanded.

"I tried, but Jonah found out. I was punished, kept in a room, my arm chained to the bed like a dog. When my time came, Jonah's mother delivered our *kinner*. Benuel was taken from me at birth, only brought to me to nurse."

She turned back to Fredrik, her wide gaze showing her need for understanding. "I was seldom allowed to see him that first year. He lived on Jonah's parents' farm, miles away. I was only allowed to be around the child if I behaved. Obeyed Jonah's every word.

"But then Jonah died and I was suddenly freed. One of the women helped me get away with Benuel in tow.

She understood what I'd been going through, what most of the women in that community go through. That day you almost hit Benuel was my first day home. I was still in shock."

"And I almost ran you both down." Fredrik felt a shiver go through him.

"*Ya*, you did."

"I must have been a thorn in your flesh."

"Not a thorn for certain-sure."

"Why did you protect me, Lizbeth? You should have—"

"*Nee*, you can't say what I should have done. You didn't love me. Our love was one-sided. That night happened because I wanted it to. You have no blame in this. You didn't even remember."

"You have to know that fact doesn't make me feel any better. I had strong feelings for you. I should have realized something like this could happen. But you were still so young. I thought if I waited…"

"You said you loved me that night," she said, her eyes damp with tears. She studied his face.

Fredrik drew her to him, with his good arm wrapping around her waist. "I did love you, silly woman. Can't you see it in my eyes?"

Lizbeth's lips lifted in a perfect bow, her joy shining in her blue eyes. "I do see the love, Fredrik. For the first time I see true love and it is almost more than I can manage. I want so badly for you to kiss me."

Fredrik lowered his head, his lips touching her, pressing down until he could no longer breathe and had to pull away. "You take my breath away, Lizbeth."

"I think the smoke did that," she purred, snuggling close.

"*Nee*, it was you, my love."

Epilogue

A Christmas wedding was more than Lizbeth had dared hope for, but for the past few months Fredrik had seemed set on making her every dream come true.

He wore his best blue shirt and trousers, his hair trimmed expertly around his ears. The shade of his blue eyes darkened as he held her gaze and spoke his vows of unwavering love to her. "You are my one true love. I will be devoted to you and Benuel till my last breath."

A smile played on her lips as they were announced man and wife. *Thank You,* Gott. They were finally a *familye*.

"*Ya*, this is the part of the wedding I like best," Otto Fischer said and chortled as he wedged himself between Fredrik and Lizbeth on the church platform. "Congregation… I take great pleasure in introducing to you… Fredrik and Lizbeth Lapp. May *Gott*'s blessings rest upon them and, in His benevolent mercy, allow all their problems to be little ones. Now let's eat! A man grows hungry after such a long service."

Benuel bounded from the bench at the side of the

church and shouted to his mother, "Is he finally my *daed* now?"

Lizbeth's tears of joy rolled down her cheeks as Fredrik picked the small boy up in his arms and carried him out the church door, declaring emphatically, "*Ya*, I am your *daed*, Benuel. We have much to talk about, you and I."

Lizbeth hurried along after her two favorite men and sat on the same wooden bench well hidden under the old oak tree draped with moss at the side of the church.

Benuel glanced at his mother's face, saw her glistening tears and frowned, his rusty brows lowering. "Are you sad, *Mamm*? I thought you wanted to marry Fredrik?"

"I did. I do." She chuckled, brushing away her tears. "These are tears of joy. I love being married to your father."

"My friend Joseph said Fredrik's not really my *daed*," Benuel said, scratching at the stiff collar of his blue church shirt. "You are my *daed*, right?" he asked, looking at Fredrik for confirmation.

"I am, and have always been, Benuel. For a time, Jonah took care of you as a substitute *daed*, but I have always been your real father. I'm sorry I couldn't always be with you to protect and love you."

"You were my *daed* when I was a baby?" Benuel asked, his eyes growing round with wonder.

Lizbeth held her breath, her eyes seeking Fredrik's face. She smiled tenderly, looking into his blue-eyed gaze and thanking him for loving her enough to make this transition easier for Benuel. The boy was still too young to completely understand, but given time and patience, he would recognize life wasn't always cut-and-dried, didn't always go the way it should.

Fredrik sat the child on his lap, hugged him close. "I was your *daed* when you were born, but your mother couldn't find me. I had gone far away and she was alone and needed someone. Jonah promised to take care of you and your mother until she found me."

Benuel looked up, his eyes misty, the edges of his small mouth turned down. "Jonah was mean to my *mamm*. He made her cry."

Lizbeth thought her heart would break as a tear rolled down Benuel's cheek and then another. "But Jonah is gone now and Ishmael will come no more," she assured him in a firm voice. She smiled toward Fredrik, taking in the glint of red in his hair, his sweet smile. "Your *daed* will make sure of that. You need never think about Ohio again."

The child leaned back against Fredrik and sighed, as if the weight of the world had been lifted off his chest. "It's *gut, ya, mamm*? I have a real father."

A peace came over her unlike any she'd ever felt before. "*Ich ish gut,* Benuel. We are a family at last."

Benuel moved his leg back and forth, his face relaxed into a hopeful smile. "Can I have a *bruder* now that I have a real father? I've always wanted a *bruder* to play with."

Fredrik looked Lizbeth's way, his eyes searching. She'd told him about her *sohs* who had died, their lives cut short by the abuse she'd endured from Jonah. Could she have more children? Only *Gott* knew that answer, but Fredrik had said he was fine with one child or many. "If it is *Gott*'s will, you will have a *bruder* and maybe a *schweschder*, too."

"I'd like a *bruder* more," Benuel admitted with a smile and then squirmed down off his father's legs and ran around the churchyard, his energy suppressed far too long.

"He took the news well," Fredrik said and hugged her close, his lips coming down on hers in a warm kiss. "Now let's get something to eat before my belly has a say in all that matters. The hour grows late."

Arm in arm the newlyweds walked back into the church, their son at their side. Life often took many sharp twists and turns, but *Gott*'s will was finally done.

* * * * *

If you enjoyed HER SECRET AMISH CHILD,
look for these other Love Inspired titles
by Cheryl Williford.

THE AMISH WIDOW'S SECRET
THE AMISH MIDWIFE'S COURTSHIP

Find more great reads at www.LoveInspired.com

LANCASTER COUNTY RECKONING

Kit Wilkinson

To Dad, thanks for sharing your love, most especially your love for story and books. I miss you. And to my sister, Elizabeth, my biggest fan and most dear to my heart, the Lord shines through you still.

Behold, I stand at the door and knock.
If anyone hears my voice and opens the door,
I will come in to him and dine with him
and he with me.

—*Revelations* 3:20

Chapter One

Thomas Nolt spotted the bright red car the second he entered the clearing. It made for such an odd sight on his neighbor's land, in the middle of their Amish community, that he pulled up on the reins of his gelding. The sudden stop of the horse threw the weight of the satchel his grandmother Ruth had loaded up with baked goods and preserves for his "Uncle Jesse" against his back.

Not really an uncle but his close neighbor of twenty years and considered part of the Nolt family, Jesse Troyer had asked Thomas to come take a look at his well at lunch. So it seemed a bit odd that someone else was visiting at the same time. Not that it was unusual for Jesse to have any visitors, but most of his acquaintances drove the typical Amish horse and buggy—not cars. And certainly not a fancy, brightly colored automobile like this one.

To be sure, Jesse had not always been Amish. Thomas had been just a child when Jesse had joined their community twenty years earlier, but he remembered how hard the man had worked to embrace the plain life and leave his *Englisch* ways behind. Ever since, Jesse pretty much stuck to his friends in the Ordnung. He had never mentioned keeping in touch with anyone in the *Englisch* world.

Thomas wanted to tell himself that it was nothing to worry about. In all likelihood, the red car's driver was a tourist who had gotten lost and had stopped at Jesse's home for directions. Christmas was approaching and tourists seemed oddly fascinated by the simple, minimal decorations with which the Amish commemorated the holy season. Yes, there was surely nothing ominous about the appearance of the red car at all. And yet Thomas could not deny that he felt strangely unsettled.

His eyes moved over Jesse's house, and he finally realized what seemed off. It was a cold December day with a biting wind…and yet no smoke rose from Jesse's chimney. The old man was home. Jesse's little bay-colored Morgan horse was enclosed in her paddock and his buggy was parked, as always, next to the house. So why hadn't he lit a fire? An emotion washed over Thomas. It was a feeling deep in his gut—a feeling that something was wrong.

He nudged King into a gallop over the open field, only slowing when they'd reached the back of the house. Thomas dismounted with one smooth swing of his leg and rushed around to the front porch, where he came to a full, screeching halt.

"Who are ye?" The words flew out of his mouth before his brain could rephrase them into something more courteous. He took a slow step back as if he'd encountered a rattlesnake. It might as well have been seeing as what stood in front of him rattled his brain. It was a young woman. A young *Englisch* woman with modern clothes and styled hair and a face painted to a glossy fashion magazine's idea of perfection. She was petite but looked agile and adept.

"Who are *you*?" she countered in a flat tone. She looked down at the bench and snatched up a fancy little handbag, which she stuck under her arm as if to keep it safe.

This was no tourist. If she was simply passing by, she would have assumed Thomas was the home's owner, and would have launched into her explanation of where she was trying to go and how she'd gotten turned around. Her expression made it clear that she knew this wasn't Thomas's house. And that meant she was looking for Jesse specifically. But why? She looked at him with equal reservation. Tension exploded between them.

At least he belonged there. Thomas crossed his arms over his chest.

From the top of her coiffed head to the bottom of her designer boots, she looked as out of place as a chicken swimming in the river. "Are you lost, ma'am?" he asked, hoping he'd read her wrong. "I can tell you how to get back to the highway."

"I'm not lost," she retorted.

Thomas scratched his head. "Well, then, if you don't mind me asking, what are you doing here?"

"I don't see what concern that is of yours." Her voice was edgy.

His eyes locked on hers. "Well, I'm a neighbor of the folk that live here and I've never seen you before. I am just looking out for my neighbor."

Thomas noticed that the front door had been cracked open. "Have you been inside, ma'am?"

"No. Of course not."

"Then why is the door opened?" Thomas didn't mean to accuse her, but Jesse was a responsible man—he wouldn't have left his door open like that. He *would*, however, have left his door unlocked. Doors were rarely bolted in their close-knit community and Jesse in particular was known to keep his home accessible. He was unbothered by visitors at any hour who wanted his help or to borrow a tool or simply to sit and share a cup of tea. If this woman had wanted to let herself in, she could have easily done so.

"The door was opened when I got here, which was about a minute before you did. I didn't touch it. I didn't even look in. I was just..." She stopped and pressed her glossed lips together. She shook her head and glanced at her watch. "I was just waiting for Jesse. We had an appointment. You don't happen to know where Mr. Troyer is, do you?"

"Jesse was expecting you?" Thomas could feel the muscles in his face tightening. *Why?* Why would Jesse have a meeting with an *Englisch* woman? He wanted to ask but held that thought at bay. "I assume he is inside. Did you knock?"

"Of course I knocked." She backed out of the way as he moved toward the front door. "Since the door was already opened, I thought maybe he stepped around back or something. I was going to go check when you arrived."

"Jesse?" Thomas called.

He pushed the door open wide and stepped inside the small cottage. She followed him in as if she feared to be left by herself on the porch. Although what he found inside might have been worse. It was chaos. Everything inside had been turned upside down. Furniture toppled. Drawers emptied. Jesse's belongings had been scattered from one end of the home to the other. Behind him, the tiny woman gasped and threw a hand over her gaping mouth.

"Ach! Had ye seen this?" he asked.

"No. I told you I didn't go inside." Her gray eyes were wide with alarm.

"And you're alone? You came here alone?" he asked her.

"Yes," she said. Her voice was breathy and low. "Like I said, I just got here. I was supposed to meet Jesse at noon. I—I was a few minutes late. I knocked on the door and called inside. No one came, and then you were here."

Thomas didn't know whether or not to believe a word she was saying but the astonishment in her voice sounded genuine. "And you haven't seen anyone coming or going?"

"Just you." Her gaze flowed from one end of the room to the other, surveying the damage. "Whoever you are. You never told me your name."

"You never told me yours." Thomas unloaded the sack of food on his back. It landed with a clunk in the center of Jesse's kitchen table. He looked back into the woman's dark gray eyes. "I'm Thomas. Thomas Nolt. I live next door."

She seemed to take that in for a long moment, avoiding eye contact. But that was typical. Being Amish, Thomas was used to *Englisch* people either staring for too long, or just the opposite—not wanting to make any eye contact.

He frowned at the scattered mess. Of course, break-ins did happen, even in Amish communities from time to time. But they were rare, and usually there were teen-agers involved. Jesse was a sixty-year-old widower with no children. Not exactly a typical target for a teenage prank. And as for robbery as a motive, he had no elec-tronics, no money, no jewelry.

The strange woman bit her upper lip nervously as she moved around some of the clutter and farther into the house. "Who do you think did this?"

"I was just wondering that my—"

A faint moaning sounded overhead from the loft.

There was someone else in the cottage. Thomas looked at the woman. "Stay here."

Thomas raced up the back stairs. "Jesse? Is that you?"

The *Englisch* woman didn't listen to him. She was on his heels, on the narrow staircase to the loft.

At the top of the stairs, Thomas paused. More chaos. The loft looked much like the downstairs. Completely trashed. He took a few wide steps over the debris and made his way to an odd-looking lump in the corner, from where he estimated the sound had originated. *Jesse!*

The old man lay in a heap on the floor. His face was swollen. His lips bloodied and bruised. Jesse had been beaten. And from the looks of it, nearly to death.

His wounds looked fresh and in some places were bleeding out. And worse, Jesse wasn't moving. Thomas dropped down to his hands and knees and grabbed the old man's hand. Thomas had seen men after fights a few times. He'd never seen anyone roughed up like this, as if the people who'd attacked him hadn't cared whether he survived or not.

"It's okay, Jesse. It's Thomas. I've got you. Just rest. You're going to be fine."

The woman had slowly edged her way around the loft. She let out a horrible squeal as she saw Jesse on the ground. "Oh, no, no, no. Jesse. No."

She dropped to the floor to get closer to the wounded man. Her body moved in waves of silent sobs.

"He's not dead," Thomas said, although he could barely detect the old man's pulse. "Hang on, Jesse. Hang on. Help is here." He looked to the woman. "You have a phone in that fancy bag of yours?"

Still crying, she scrambled through the little bag, plucking out a shiny smartphone. Her hands were shaking so badly that she had to try three times to enter her pass code to unlock the phone. For efficiency's sake, Thomas grabbed it from her and called 911. He gave thorough directions to the dispatcher. He also asked him to notify the local clinic, which was even closer than the fire department and the EMS. He hoped they would make it in time.

As he spoke, the *Englisch* woman placed a small pillow under Jesse's head and a blanket over his torso. She touched Jesse's hand and whispered something low into his ear. *Who was she?*

He held the phone out for her to retrieve. Thomas's own hands were trembling, too. It was all he could do to control his emotions. He was filled with a mixture of horror and anger. What had happened? Who would do such a thing to a kind man like Jesse? And why?

He looked at the woman, wondering if her sudden and strange appearance had anything to do with the beating Jesse had taken. Thomas sighed aloud. He had to refocus his thoughts.

He had to remind himself that God was in control. His anger would solve nothing and it certainly wouldn't save Jesse, which should be his only concern at the moment.

The woman took the smartphone from his hand. "How long will it take someone to get here? Maybe you should carry him to my car? I can get to a hospital faster than waiting for an ambulance. Right?"

"Wrong."

"What?" She looked back at him with surprise. "Of course that would be faster."

"Maybe faster but not better. He may have broken bones that need to be stabilized before he can be moved. I don't want to cause any more damage than has already happened. I'm not moving him."

"Right. Right. You're right. I'm sorry." She stood back and put her hand to her forehead. She was trembling like a leaf. "But what can we do? We have to help him."

We? Thomas took off his hat and put it back on his head. It was something he did when his thoughts or emotions were getting away with him. A little trick his father had told him about when he was very young that reminded him to take a deep breath and pull himself together.

"For starters," he said, "why don't you tell me who you are."

The woman wiped her tears and swept her bangs carefully away from her face. At first, Thomas thought she hadn't heard him or was once again avoiding an answer. But then she looked him dead in the eye and sighed. "I'm…well, I'm Darcy Simmons and I'm—I'm Jesse's daughter."

Daughter? What? Jesse didn't have any kin that Thomas had ever heard of. Yes, he'd been married. But that had been years ago. In fact, his wife had died before Jesse had moved to Willow Trace. Jesse had always been all alone...

The woman—Darcy—had hardly gotten the words out when her fancy smartphone rang out a series of loud beeps that was apparently her ringtone.

She looked at the phone and frowned. "I don't know that number."

Still, she touched the screen to accept the call and lifted the phone to her ear. She was so close that Thomas could hear every crazy word of the call. The oddly distorted voice filled the room.

"Oh, Darcy, honey, you're just as lovely as your mother, but you do have your daddy's eyes... And you also have something of mine. I'll be coming around soon to get it back. You can either cooperate when I see you, or you can end up like your dear old dad. Either way, I get what's mine. See you soon."

The phone slipped from the woman's hand. Her head dropped back and her eyes fluttered as her legs collapsed under her and she fell toward the floor.

Chapter Two

The giant Amish man caught Darcy under the arms just before she hit the floor.

"I'm okay. I'm okay." She still felt light-headed and shaky, but she was able to straighten her legs and stand on her own…mostly.

Thomas backed away quickly, as if touching her had stung his hands. "What was that about? That phone call?"

"I have no idea. I told you I don't know that number." Darcy's head swirled. "I have no idea who that was or what he was talking about. The voice didn't even sound real. It was more like he was using some kind of distorter."

Thomas frowned down at her, his face darkening with suspicion. "But you *are* Jesse's daughter?"

She nodded. "But no one knows that. I only just found out myself."

The Amish man shook his head up and down as if he understood her words, but Darcy felt like he didn't believe her. She could hardly blame her. She had trouble believing it herself. After years of being told her father was dead, it had been a shock to have Jesse contact her.

"Okay. Let's just concentrate on Uncle Jesse," he said.

"He's your uncle?" Did that mean this man was her cousin?

"No, but lots of people call him that around here. When I was a kid, he didn't like us calling him Mister."

"Oh." Darcy tried to slow down her breathing. It was hard to imagine this massive, intimidating man had ever been a child.

She'd rarely seen such an imposing figure, so tall and strong, dressed in black trousers and a green button-down. Dark curls spilled out from under his hat and his beard—if you could call it one—was made of thin, sparse stubble, shaved clean to the edges of his broad face. No mustache—which she had heard was the Amish way. His wide brown eyes had golden flecks around the pupils, which seemed to pulse as he stared down at her. He was a Goliath of a man, one continuous string of muscle. If he had been around earlier, whenever the attack had taken place, she doubted anyone would have touched Jesse.

Poor Jesse. She knelt beside him and held his hand. Thomas sat opposite, his eyes closed. She guessed that he was praying as she saw his lips move in silent speech from time to time. She was thankful he asked her no more questions.

And he'd been right. It wasn't long before help arrived. The EMS workers quickly strapped Jesse on a gurney and started him on fluids. She and Thomas followed the gurney to the ambulance, and watched as it was loaded inside.

On the one hand, she was thankful for Thomas's pres-

ence and his ability to answer questions she couldn't—
about any medical conditions Jesse had and whether he
was allergic to any medications. But on the other hand,
she couldn't help resenting him just a little for knowing her own father so much better than she did herself.

When the ambulance was ready to drive away, she
and Thomas looked at each other.

"I'm going to follow. You want a ride with me?"
she asked.

"Are you sure?" he said hesitantly.

Was he kidding? After that phone call, she wasn't
exactly keen on being alone. She nodded.

Soon, they were at the hospital. The hours blurred
together as they waited for news on Jesse's condition.

Small groups of Amish men and women came through
the waiting area. They would talk quietly with Thomas,
glance her way once or twice then leave. Thomas stayed
on one side of the room. She chose to sit at the other side.
She didn't want to talk or meet more Amish people. She
didn't want to explain who she was or why she was there.

And certainly she didn't want to talk about the phone
call. She didn't even want to *think* about it. That hard
robotic voice and the person who, unaccountably, knew
her. Knew who she was. And knew her connection to
Jesse. Someone who, if they really were connected to
the attack against Jesse as they'd implied, had almost
killed her father. The thought of it sent a shiver down
her spine.

She shook away the terrifying thoughts. Right now
she just wanted some news about her father. Was he
going to live? Was she going to find out why everyone
had lied to her for so many years? Or was Jesse going

to leave her almost as quickly as he had come back into her life?

"I'm going to get a coffee. Could I get you one?" Thomas stood over her. His long dark curls, freed from his black felt hat, which he twisted nervously in his hands, sprung around his tanned face.

"Sure." Darcy reached in her bag for money.

"No. It's on me," he said. "But why don't you come down to the cafeteria with me? It will be good to sit in a different seat for a few minutes."

He hadn't seemed interested in talking to her in the hours up to now. Why the change? Realization struck as she recalled watching him speak quietly to a doctor at the end of the hall a few minutes earlier.

"You've had news?" Darcy stood so quickly her head felt light.

Instead of answering, Thomas nodded toward the elevator bank. She followed him out of the waiting area, into the elevator, then down the hall to the cafeteria. She wanted news of Jesse. Even if it meant talking to this stranger.

"Thank you for the ride to the hospital," he said, handing her a hot cup.

"Of course," she said. "Thanks for the coffee."

They sat opposite each other at one of the cafeteria tables. Darcy stared into the black liquid, watching steam swirl up from the cup. She took a drink. It was bitter and stale, and as it hit her stomach, she was reminded that she'd skipped breakfast and hadn't had a chance to eat lunch.

"So, how is he?" she asked at last. She had a feeling that the news wasn't going to be good or he would have already told her.

"They are operating on him." Thomas's voice was quiet and strained with emotion. "But…apparently there's some internal bleeding and they are having a hard time stopping it."

"So what does that mean?"

"They are going to try another procedure. If it works, it will stabilize his condition."

"And if not?"

"If it doesn't work…then they don't expect him to live through the night."

"What?" Darcy had not expected good news but she hadn't expected anything as bad as this. "That can't be. There must be something we can do. Maybe we need a second opinion?"

She pushed away from the table, fighting tears of rage and fear. Thomas grabbed her gently by the wrist. His hand felt strong and warm as he pulled her back to her seat.

"Dr. Jamison is one of the best ER doctors in the Northeast. He and his team are doing all they can. It's in God's hands."

Seemed more like Jesse was in this doctor's hands, not God's. And she wondered why one of the best doctors would be working all the way out here. But she couldn't muster the energy to ask.

Darcy slumped back into the chair. She felt so out of place and helpless. And confused. It wasn't like her at all. "It's just that… I don't know how to deal with all of this. I just found out my father has actually been alive all this time and now he's…well, beaten almost to death. I just wish there was something I could do to help. And yet, I don't even know if it's my place to help or if Jesse would even want me to."

"It's okay. It will all get sorted out. These things take time. The doctors are doing everything they can to save him. Plus, I know Jesse pretty well and I can tell you for sure and certain that he is a very strong man."

"I just hate doing nothing. Just sitting here and waiting."

"Well, there is something you can do. Something we all can do."

"What's that?" She lifted her head.

"We can pray."

"Oh." Pray? Really? Darcy looked away and tried to keep her facial expression neutral. It wasn't that she thought praying was stupid. It just wasn't for her. "Of course… I guess I was thinking of doing something more active and practical, maybe, like finding who did this to him."

"*Ja*, well, one thing at a time. Plus, I'm sure the police have been notified about the beating. They will look for whoever is responsible. There is no need for us to go anywhere until Jesse's condition is stable." There was a lovely lilt to his voice. He had a faint accent that she hadn't noticed before. "If Jesse were awake, he would be praying. That I am sure of. But you would know that, of course, since you're his daughter, *ja*?"

Darcy swallowed hard. She put her elbows on the table and surrounded the warm cup of coffee with her hands. "I only met Jesse a few weeks ago. And we mostly talked about me." She regretted that now.

"But you are his daughter?" He stared out at her from under a wisp of dark curls. He tilted his head, focusing hard on her face. "Truly Jesse Troyer's daughter?"

Strange emotions flowed through her. "I'm afraid so. And I understand your surprise."

He grinned, revealing a beautiful set of white teeth. "*Ja*, it is a surprise. But truly, if I hadn't known Jesse for the past twenty years, I would not question ye so many times. You have his eyes, for certain."

In spite of herself, Darcy smiled a little, remembering meeting Jesse for the first time and feeling that shock of recognition when faced with those unusual dark gray eyes she'd seen in the mirror every day of her life.

"But it is just that, well…he never mentioned you," Thomas said.

"No one ever mentioned him to me, either." Darcy rubbed her temples, thinking back to when she'd first met Jesse at the coffeehouse just a few weeks ago. "I grew up with my grandparents—my mother's parents—in northern Virginia. I was told my parents had both died in a car accident right after I was born. There were newspaper articles and everything, showing the crash. Turns out half of it was a lie. The crash did kill my mother…but my father was alive all along.

"I mean, I don't have any legal documents to show you as proof of paternity. Jesse talked about getting them if I wanted him to. But at this point I wasn't really sure where this whole thing was going. And anyway, he had proof enough for me—pictures of me as a baby. And pictures of my mother. Pictures of the three of us together. And he had this locket. My mother's locket. She always wore it. It's around her neck in almost every picture I've ever seen of her."

Darcy lifted the beautiful silver necklace off her collarbone to show him. Thomas looked at the locket then turned away. It was impossible to tell what he was thinking. Whether he believed her or not. His stoic face hid his emotions. Calm strength was all he allowed her to see. But she didn't really care what he thought of the situation. Thomas was just a neighbor. She was Jesse's daughter, his own flesh and blood.

After a long moment of silence, Thomas looked back at her with faraway eyes that were hazy with sadness. "Jesse did talk about your mother. He spoke of her often to me."

"Yes, my grandparents talked about her all the time. She was amazing," Darcy said, thinking of all the comparisons they'd made when raising her. Comparisons she'd never lived up to.

Thomas sighed. "So how did you find out? How did you and Jesse meet?"

"Jesse wrote to me." She smiled. "An old-fashioned letter. He told me who he was and he sent some pictures. One of them was a picture I had seen before in my mother's things."

"That must have been strange."

"Yes, at first. But then I became curious. I asked my grandparents about it. About him." A sharp pain stabbed at her heart. "But they wouldn't tell me anything, except that my mother was dead and that it was his fault. They told me if I wanted to go down that road of getting to know my father, that I would have to do it alone."

"I am truly sorry." Thomas's eyebrows pressed together, his brown eyes examining her carefully. "Family... Well, we should always be able to count on family."

"It's okay. My grandparents have always been a little...different." *Cold.* "But actually what they said only confirmed to me that Jesse was telling the truth. So I met with him. And when I saw him, I knew. Jesse is definitely my father. I just wish..." *I'd known about him...*

Tears started to well in her eyes. Thomas reached across the table and patted her hand.

"Hey, now, I am certain that he had a reason for not getting in touch with you sooner. And if I know Jesse, and I think I do, then he had a very, very *gut* reason." He gave her hand a quick squeeze, then slid his hand back to his side of the table. "Jesse—your father—is a *gut* man. A man of God. And he is strong. I am praying that God will let him stay with us a bit longer. We cannot change the past, but you can still have a future together as father and daughter."

The tears started to spill over. Darcy tried to hold them back. She didn't want to cry in front of this stranger. She covered her face with her hands.

Thomas stood. "We should go back now. The police will probably be here soon."

Darcy felt the blood drain from her face. She did not want to talk to the police. She couldn't imagine that she knew anything which would be helpful. And what if no one believed that she was Jesse's daughter? "Oh…but I don't know what to say to them…like I told you I don't have any real proof that he's my father."

"It is going to be okay, Darcy. Just tell them what you told me."

"Do they know about the phone call?"

"I haven't spoken with them yet. But I hope you plan to tell them. It may help them find out who did this. Isn't that what you want?"

"Of course it's what I want. But how can I explain what the man said to me? Not to mention, no one really knows I'm Jesse's daughter. What if Jesse doesn't want anyone to know?"

"I don't think you can keep being Jesse's daughter a

secret any longer." He smiled. "You have nothing to fear from Jesse's friends. I know that much. Which makes me wonder why—"

"Why he kept it a secret?" she said, finishing the question for him. "I don't know. It's not a topic you just jump right into the first time you meet your father."

And now he might die and she would never know.

Darcy closed her eyes. Thomas was right. There was no escaping her identity any longer. She was the daughter of a man who had been attacked for hiding something. And the man who had committed—or commissioned— the attack was now after her, unless she turned over something she knew nothing about. It was all so cryptic and horrifying. She didn't know what they wanted and if Jesse didn't wake up and give it to them then…

What did they have planned for her?

Chapter Three

"Chief McClendon." Thomas shook hands with the Lancaster head of police. They had met before during another stressful time in Thomas's life, when his own niece had been murdered. And while most Amish didn't have much to do with government or law enforcement agencies of any sort, Thomas had a healthy respect for the chief. McClendon had always kept his family's confidences and respected their boundaries. Right now, Thomas had a sense that the chief would be helping him again through whatever was going on with Jesse and Jesse's long-lost daughter.

"This is Darcy Simmons." Thomas moved his eyes quickly between her and McClendon. "And she is… well, she is Jesse Troyer's daughter."

"Oh." McClendon turned to Darcy, taking in her fancy clothes. "I guess you left the fold."

Darcy looked taken aback.

"She was not born or raised Amish," Thomas answered for her. "Jesse came to the Ordnung later in life."

"Oh, I see." McClendon frowned. "So I understand Mr. Troyer was badly beaten?"

"We hope he will pull through, but it's too early to know his status for certain," Thomas replied quickly, wanting to keep Darcy focused on the positive.

She looked well past the point of exhaustion. Her hands shook. Her eyes were swollen. She seemed so horribly...alone.

"I'll need to ask you a few questions about your... well, about Jesse," McClendon said to Darcy. "And about what happened earlier today."

She nodded.

"You add in anything in that might be helpful," Mc-Clendon said to Thomas. "I understand you were both there?"

"I arrived first," Darcy said, explaining how she and Jesse had planned for her to come at noon. "When I got there no one answered at the door, and I noticed it was cracked open. Then Thomas came. We went in together and found that someone had torn the place apart. Then we discovered Jesse upstairs on the floor. Thomas called 911. And then—then I got this strange phone call."

Thomas exhaled a sigh of relief, pleased that she'd overcome her hesitation and decided to share the truth with the police chief.

"How do you mean, *strange*?" McClendon asked.

Darcy quoted the caller verbatim. McClendon scratched his head. "And you have no idea who would have sent you a threatening message?"

"No." She shook her head.

"You didn't recognize the voice?"

"It was modified. Computerized. It didn't sound natural."

"Did either of you see anyone coming or going from the area around the house?"

They both shook their heads.

"Did you see anything unusual or missing?"

"It was impossible to tell. The place was wrecked."

"Right. We sent a team over to Mr. Troyer's place to investigate. But they won't know what or if anything is missing. Then again, based on this phone call you're telling me about, it seems likely that the caller didn't find what he wanted at Jesse's home."

Thomas nodded. That made sense. Whatever the man from the phone call was after, he'd probably tried to get Jesse to reveal where it was first. When that hadn't worked, he'd tried searching the house for it himself. When that failed, he'd threatened Darcy. But how had he known about Darcy? That was still a puzzle.

"So, you're from Philadelphia?" McClendon asked her.

"Originally, I'm from Virginia. But I've lived in the Philadelphia area since college. I work as a buyer for Winnefords department store."

"You live alone?"

She nodded. "I have a small town house in the suburbs."

"You work in the city?"

"Mostly. I travel to New York a lot."

McClendon flipped through his notes. "Now, what was your relationship with your father?"

"We…didn't have a relationship until recently."

The chief looked up at that. "None at all? Was it a custody issue?"

"No, it was… To be honest, I'm not really sure what it was. I was raised by my mother's parents. They blamed

Jesse for my mother's death, so maybe that's why they told me my father had died when I was a baby. They didn't want anything to do with him."

"And when did you find out the truth?"

"About a month ago. Jesse sent me a letter, and we met for the first time a week later."

"Did you tell anyone that you were coming to Willow Trace today? Did anyone of your acquaintance know about Jesse and your recent discovery that he is your father?"

"No. No one knew I was coming. Only Jesse. And I hadn't told anyone about him contacting me, other than my grandparents. But they didn't want to discuss it."

McClendon looked to Thomas, who hoped the questions were nearly over. Darcy looked ready to collapse.

"She's told you everything as it happened," Thomas said, hoping to head off any more questions.

"Has she?" the chief asked. "So you can confirm what she's said about the letter and meeting with Jesse? He told you about his daughter?"

Thomas flushed. "Well…no, actually, today was the first I heard of it."

"Do you consider yourself close to Mr. Troyer?"

"*Ja*, of course. We have been neighbors for twenty years."

"And he never mentioned a daughter? Not even in the past few weeks?"

"No," Thomas admitted. "He has spoken of his wife and I knew she had died, but there was never mention of a daughter." Thomas couldn't deny that the situation was strange. There were so many things that didn't make sense. And the only people with answers were the threatening man from the phone call and Jesse, who might never wake up again.

But Thomas believed that Darcy was being honest with them. Her shock and horror at Jesse's attack had been real. And so was her fear at the phone call.

"It must be related—the beating and the phone call," Thomas said. "Don't you think? It was almost like the caller was watching us. Like he knew exactly when to call."

"So what's your theory on why anyone would want to beat up a nice Amish man and threaten his daughter?" McClendon asked.

Thomas shook his head slightly. For that he had no answer. "I cannot even imagine who would want to hurt Jesse. He's just a sweet old Amish fellow who minds his own business."

"You said he's been your neighbor for twenty years. Where did he live before?"

Thomas took off his hat and scratched his head. "I don't recall. That would be a question for the bishop."

Could all this be tied to Jesse's past? Jesse's life before he came to Willow Trace? But that was so long ago. Even if he had enemies from decades in the past, why would they come to trouble him now?

Thomas shifted his weight and kept one eye on the door. He was on the lookout for his friend Elijah. Earlier he had asked the ER staff to notify not only the bishop and leader of the Ordnung about the beating, but also his friend, who had spent many years in the *Englisch* world working as a police detective before returning to his Amish roots. Thomas hoped Elijah's experience with police investigations could help them.

McClendon continued questioning Darcy. "Do you

give the police permission to track your incoming phone calls? In the case this happens again?"

"Of course. You can *have* my phone if that helps you find whoever did this to Jesse," she said, handing over her phone.

Thomas saw Elijah Miller enter through the waiting room doors and walked over to greet him. He met his good friend with a hearty handshake. "Are you a sight for sore eyes. Here. Come. McClendon is speaking to her."

"Chief," Elijah said as they joined Darcy and McClendon. "And you must be Miss Simmons. The whole Ordnung is praying for Jesse. And I'm here to help in any way I can."

Darcy seemed confused as she looked over Elijah and took in his Amish dress but somewhat *Englisch* mannerisms and speech, which Thomas had learned that his friend could turn on and off depending on what the situation might call for.

"Eli is a former detective," Thomas explained.

"Well, I'm just a farmer now, Miss Simmons. But I worked for ten years on the force in Philly, before coming back home," he said.

Darcy nodded.

"I just came from the cottage," Elijah said. "There was a team of investigators. So far, they seem to have no leads on who attacked Jesse. Jesse lived plain. Very plain. There was nothing in his home that anyone would want to steal. But there was a business card with Miss Simmons's personal information and number. We found that on the floor with a few papers and some old pictures."

"Well, that could be how they got your number,"

McClendon said, turning to Darcy. "But that doesn't explain how they would know you're Jesse's daughter."

"There was a letter there from Darcy," Elijah said. "I didn't read it. I think it was marked into evidence with the photos."

"Photos?" Thomas repeated. "I can't imagine Jesse having photos. It's verboten."

"Forbidden," Elijah said, translating. "But if they were his only tie to his daughter for all these years maybe he kept them anyway. Or maybe he just got them recently."

Still, pictures? Thomas's head spun with doubts and confusion. This did not sound like the Jesse that he knew.

"In the morning," Elijah continued, "a few of us are planning to meet up at Jesse's and help put the place back together. It's quite a mess."

"I'll be there." Thomas shook Elijah's hand.

"Miss Simmons—" Elijah tipped his hat "—I hope you hear some good news very soon."

"Thank you." Darcy nodded and finished up answering a few more questions from the chief.

Thomas walked Elijah from the waiting area.

"Thank you for coming." He shook his friend's hand. "It is *gut* to have someone who can help us make sense of these things. Not that I can see any sense in the harm that was done to Jesse. He was really beat up. And you heard about the phone call to Darcy?"

"No." Eli looked grim. "What phone call?"

Thomas filled Elijah in on every detail. "If only Jesse could tell us what this is all about."

"I think Darcy should take that threat seriously after

what happened to Jesse. But what could Jesse have that would be worth nearly killing him over?"

"That is what I keep asking myself over and over," Thomas said. "Do you remember when Jesse moved here? You and I wanted to go to his cottage every day after chores and play baseball or lawn croquet."

"I remember." Elijah laughed then stopped abruptly.

"Do you remember if he ever said where he came from?"

"No. I don't guess I ever really thought about it too much. He always just fit in. Like he'd been here forever."

"But he wasn't," Thomas said. "And he's got a full-grown *Englisch* daughter to prove it."

"Maybe the Elders know. They must know something about his past from when they accepted him in to the Ordnung. I could ask my father."

"Would you? But would he even be able to tell you anything?" Thomas wondered if that was the right thing to do. "I mean it's one thing for us to know he has a daughter. It's another for us to know the whole story behind their past and their separation."

"I'm sure if Jesse thought that his daughter was in danger, he'd want us to help, no?" Elijah patted him on the back. "And we can help a lot more if we know more."

"But if we interfere then are we leaving it up to God?"

"God will work through all of us. We will either get the answers or we won't."

"Okay. I'll see you at the cottage at noon tomorrow." Elijah smiled. "All will be well."

All will be well. In God's time.

Thomas returned to the waiting room. McClendon

had gone. Darcy had reseated herself on the other side of the room and did not look as if she wanted company. He could respect that. She had gone through a lot in one day. He imagined Darcy was barely holding it together.

Thomas slumped down into a seat that he decided looked the least uncomfortable. He lowered his hat over his eyes and let his chin rest on his chest.

Secret daughter? Jesse attacked and left for dead? Threats that he has something that belonged to someone else? Thomas just couldn't wrap his head around it. It was as if the Jesse he'd always known was someone else entirely. Images of Jesse swam in Thomas's head as he drifted off to sleep…

"Hey, man, wake up."

Thomas sat up fast. There was a horrible pain in his back and neck. Dr. Blake Jamison of the ER stood over him, looking like he hadn't slept in days. Thomas checked the clock on the wall.

"Seven thirty?" He stood and rubbed his neck. "Last I saw, it was midnight. I guess I fell asleep."

"Glad somebody did." Blake glanced over toward Darcy. "Is that Jesse's daughter? I have news."

"*Ja.* Come." Thomas shook the ache from his stiff bones and led his doctor friend across the large waiting area. He hoped and prayed that Blake had good news.

"Darcy, this is Dr. Jamison." Thomas cleared the sleep from his voice. "Blake is the head of the ER here. He's been with Jesse."

A brief smile brushed over Darcy's lips. The lipstick had worn away and her lips were no longer stained with color. Plain and unpainted, they looked even lovelier to him than before. She shook hands with Blake. "So, how is Jesse?"

Blake rubbed a thumb and forefinger over his scruffy stubble. It was clear he'd been at work for hours. "Well, he's still with us. He made it through the night. The last procedure seemed to stop the rest of the internal bleeding."

Thomas let out a sigh of relief.

"I get the sense that you led with the good news," Darcy said shrewdly.

Blake gave her a tired smile. "You'd be right. I'm afraid not all of my news is good."

"So what is the bad news?" she asked.

"Jesse has slipped into a coma."

Chapter Four

A coma? Thomas was thankful Jesse had lived. But for Darcy's sake, and for the sake of Jesse's continued safety, he sure wished he could ask his old neighbor a few questions. From the look of disappointment on Darcy's face, Thomas guessed she was thinking the same thing. How were they going to get to the bottom of this without Jesse's help?

"A coma?" Darcy repeated. "How long will that last?"

"I can't say," Blake answered. "But this can happen when recovering from such trauma to the brain. In many cases, the patient is able to eventually make a full recovery."

"So he *will* wake up?"

"I can't make any promises, but we certainly hope so. There's a very good chance, and many of his indicators look positive. Still, he won't be out of the woods completely even after waking up. There was a lot of hemorrhaging and we won't be able to gauge the full extent of the damage until we can communicate with him." Blake looked at Thomas.

"So…what? What does that mean?" Darcy dropped her arms by her sides, demanding the rest of the news.

"There is always some potential for brain damage. He may end up losing some or all of his cognitive and motor skills, and it's very possible his memory will be affected."

"So he won't remember who he is? He won't remember me? Or Thomas?"

"Every case is different," Blake said, trying to console her. But Thomas knew what Blake was really saying was that he had no idea what was going to happen to Jesse. And Thomas could see Darcy's tiny light of hope extinguishing. He couldn't imagine how she felt, reconnecting with her father after all of these years only to run the risk of losing him again so soon.

"Doctors have to tell you all of the possibilities," Thomas said, trying to sound casual. "It doesn't mean that's what will happen. God will decide what will happen to Jesse."

"So you've said." Darcy's expression soured. "But isn't there anything you can do medically to help him heal faster or better? To wake him from the coma?"

"Unfortunately no," Blake said. "His body is already doing what it needs. It's trying to heal, to live. He's breathing on his own. We just have to wait now."

"So he stays here? In this hospital? Can I move him to a hospital in the city? Closer to me?"

"Moving him right now…" Blake shook his head. "Well, that could set on a temporary decline in body function and when he's already functioning at the lowest level, that would be taking a very unnecessary risk. We should avoid anything that would stress or strain his system more."

"Can I see him?"

"Of course you can," he said. "Anytime you like."

Darcy nodded. "How about now?"

"He's in the ICU," Blake said. "Room 11."

"Thank you, Doctor." She started toward the door, but turned back to them. "Thomas, may I join you and your friends at Jesse's later today? I'd like to help clean up."

"You would be most welcome," Thomas answered with a nod.

Blake and Thomas watched her move away toward the elevators.

"Why don't you go home and get some rest?" Blake put a hand on Thomas's shoulder.

"I was going to say the same to you." Thomas tried to muster a smile but the heaviness on his heart wouldn't allow it. "You are working yourself too hard, Blake, but thank you. Thank you for fighting so hard for my friend. I know you are doing all you can to help Jesse."

"He's a tough old bird," Blake said. "But he was beaten up like I've rarely seen. And I've seen more than a fair share of beatings working in the ER."

Thomas shut his eyes as he thought of the state they had found the old man in. The pain he must have been in. At least now Jesse could not feel the pain. He could be thankful to God for that.

"It's good you found him when you did," Blake continued. "Without blood and other fluids, I don't think he would have lasted much longer..."

"Then he must live," said Thomas. "And I pray that he does. Even apart from his value to the community and to me, it would be so sad for his daughter to lose him now, when she only just found him again."

Blake's eyes looked intrigued under the shadow of exhaustion. "What do you think of Miss Simmons?"

Darcy Simmons? Heat rose to Thomas's cheeks as he remembered the feel of her soft hand and the way her long brown waves framed her sweet face. "I—I think she is scared and confused. And…I think she is in a lot of danger."

Darcy stayed with Jesse for most of the morning. He looked so small and weak and old, lying there lifeless in the hospital bed, with tubes running in and out of him. The nurses said he was blessed to be alive. But he hardly looked it.

She wished he would wake up. She had so many questions. She no longer believed anything her grandparents had told her as a child about her parents. Was her mother really killed in a car crash? Why had Jesse started a life with the Amish? It was clear from all the photos of the past that Jesse had not been born Amish. Why hadn't he stayed in the non-Amish world and raised her? Or at least taken her with him?

There had to be reasons for his choices. There had to be something that caused him to choose this path—a path that had not included her in his life. She tried not to let her questions and confusion cause anger toward her grandparents. But it was hard not to feel betrayed by them and all the lies. She'd probably be upset with Jesse, too, except that he looked so helpless lying there all but lifeless in the hospital bed.

Please wake up, Jesse. Please tell me what happened. Tell me who did this to you and what they want.

Darcy hated to leave Jesse but she was determined to get to the cottage and help clean up. Maybe, just maybe, there would be something there that would tell her more about her father—or at least give her a clue as to who was after him. And now her.

Darcy called a close friend and colleague who was kind enough to use a spare key to her town house and deliver a change of clothes and her makeup bag to the hospital. After breakfast, Darcy felt revived with a clean suit, fresh makeup and some food in her belly. She headed out to Willow Trace, driving through the beautiful back roads of Lancaster County. Her friend had asked her lots of questions when dropping off the clothes, which Darcy had answered merely by saying that a close family member was in a coma and she'd be away from work until further notice. Hopefully, that wouldn't be long. Funny, though, she thought as she passed an Amish man driving a horse-drawn buggy that was moving at a snail's pace compared to her, how time seemed to move slower here. Even with all that had happened in the past twenty-four hours.

When Darcy drove up in front of the cottage, there were already several Amish buggies parked in front. And there was Thomas. He was seated on the front porch, head down, a large book in his hand.

"Good morning," she said.

He looked up at her. "Good day, Miss Simmons. You look all cleaned up and fancy."

Heat rose to Darcy's cheeks. She looked down at her designer suit. "I guess it's a little dressy for cleaning."

"We are just finishing up," Thomas said. "It is time for lunch."

"Oh. I'm so sorry. I should have come earlier." Darcy was truly disappointed. She had really wanted to help. She had wanted to be a part of this. She had wanted to

see Jesse's home and feel closer to him and his friends.
The wave of emotions made Darcy shift her weight over
her heels. Life had taught her that depending on anyone
made her vulnerable to getting hurt. She couldn't allow
herself to get attached to Thomas or the others in this
community just because they were being kind. Maybe
she should have just stayed at the hospital.

Thomas stood, folding the book closed. A Bible,
from the looks of it, which he tucked under his elbow.
"Come. There are people who would like to meet you."

She followed him into the small living space, which
was all tidied up. There were two women inside, along
with Elijah, Thomas's friend whom she had met at the
hospital, and one other elderly man. All of them were
Amish.

The two women were dressed similarly in homespun
dresses, dark aprons and thin white caps set over their
hair, which was parted straight down the middle, then
tucked up and hidden away in a tight nest on the back
of the neck. Darcy felt awkward in her stylish pantsuit
and heels. But the ladies didn't seem to pay her or her
clothes any mind. They were all smiles, happily humming as they finished their work.

"Miss Simmons, how is Jesse?" Elijah asked as he
approached her. "Any change?"

"No," Darcy said, shaking her head. "Though that's
not necessarily a sign of trouble. Dr. Jamison said he
didn't expect there would be any change today. And he
is stable. So that is good."

"We will hold a prayer gathering for him," the older
of the women said as she turned to her. She was completely gray headed but had the same warm golden-
brown eyes as Thomas. "I am Nana Ruth, Thomas's

grandmother. You must be Miss Darcy. I think it is *wunderlich* that Jesse has a daughter. I just—"

"Nana…" Thomas glared at the old woman.

"*Ach*, Thomas." Nana held her nose up defiantly to her grandson, who towered over her by more than a foot.

"It's nice to meet you, Mrs. Nolt." Darcy offered her hand to Thomas's grandmother.

"Just call me Nana. Everyone does. And this is Hannah, Elijah's wife."

"Nice to meet you," Darcy said to the other woman, who was close to herself in age. Elijah's wife had flawless skin, shimmering green eyes and a look of genuine sympathy in her expression.

"They were teenage sweethearts," Nana explained. "Reunited by—"

"Nana," Thomas interrupted again, this time whispering something to her in their Germanic language.

Again the old woman dismissed Thomas's unsolicited guidance with a wave of her hand. "I was just going to invite her to the prayer gathering."

A change in subject was definitely in order. "Wow. This place looks great," Darcy interjected. She didn't want to be rude to the woman who had worked so hard to clean Jesse's home and who had been so kind to her already, but Darcy did not want to go to a prayer gathering. She didn't even know how to pray or if she even could. Faith had never been a part of her life. In any case, even if changing the subject had been her goal, the compliment was sincere. The transformation of the cottage was stunning. The home had been completely cleaned and organized. "It's so warm and homey."

"Just like the man who lives here." Nana glared back at her grandson. Darcy had to hold back the urge to laugh at the comical exchange between Thomas and his grandmother.

Darcy looked to the older man who sat nearby. He'd seemed uninterested in the conversation, but now rose and moved toward her.

"This is Bishop Miller. He's one of the Elders, or leaders, of our Ordnung," Nana explained. "He's also Elijah's father."

Darcy nodded at the man who was slow to make eye contact with his piercing blue eyes. There were no smiles from this person. No handshake. Yet he did not seem harsh, simply solemn. He looked like a man who carried a lot of weight on his shoulders. He stopped just a few feet from her and stood silent.

"It's very nice of you all to do this for Jesse," she said. "So very kind. I'm sorry I wasn't here to help."

"You had a long night. You must be exhausted," said Nana.

"Which is why we'd like for you to join us at lunch at Nolt cottage," said Hannah.

They didn't wait for her answer, but swept through the front door as quick as a second. Only Thomas and the bishop stayed. Thomas still held the Bible in his hands. She wondered if he took it everywhere with him. And why did its presence in his hands make her so uncomfortable? She'd seen plenty of Bibles in her life.

"Bishop Miller would like to speak with you, if that's okay," Thomas said.

Darcy nodded to him as a wave of dread washed over her.

"Then just follow the bishop to our place," Thomas said. "It's not far. About a mile or so."

She nodded again and tried to swallow down the dry lump that had formed in her throat.

The bishop remained behind as Thomas exited. It was obvious he had something to tell her. Had something changed in Jesse's condition since she left the hospital? She knew it was unlikely—the hospital had her contact information—but she was too worried to be rational. Her pulse spiked as she feared the worst of news.

"You know something about Jesse?" Darcy asked, trying to be brave.

"About his past, yes," the old man said. "Just a little. But I will share what I have been told as my son thinks it is important for you and the police to know."

"The police?" Darcy could feel her heart pounding against her ribs. So this past might have something to do with Jesse's beating and her phone call? Did he also know why Jesse had abandoned her? Did she even want to know?

Bishop Miller cleared his throat. "When Jesse came here he was a broken man. A man running from many things. He was very scared. But he was also searching— for God and for the forgiveness that can only come from the Lord. And he opened his heart and found peace."

"Until yesterday?" Darcy asked.

He nodded.

"What was he running from? From the people who beat him? From the law? From…me?"

Darcy tried to swallow again, but her tongue felt glued to the roof of her mouth.

"He was not running from you, child, but from himself. He made many mistakes, Miss Simmons. Although it is not for me to judge." The bishop remained solemn but his tone was kind. "And please know that Jesse has had to pay dearly for his past decisions through great loss and sacrifice."

"What sacrifice? Looks to me like he came here and lived a pretty great life…"

"His sacrifice was you. And your mother."

"My mother? What do you know about my mother?" Darcy fell back into one of the upholstered chairs. None of this made her feel any better. Only more confused and sick inside.

Bishop Miller locked his sea-blue eyes on hers. "From what I was told, it all began when your father helped put a man in prison many years ago—a very bad man. Now that man has been released."

The phone call. The voice. The man who was coming after her. The man who'd already viciously beaten Jesse. Darcy's head was spinning. It felt as if all the blood had drained from her body. She tried to breathe and calm herself down, but it was like some invisible force had gripped her chest. "What did this man do? What has this got to do with my mother?"

"This man… He killed your mother."

Chapter Five

"Why, Darcy, you've hardly touched your lunch," said Nana Ruth as she cleared away the plates.

"I had a late breakfast," she explained. Thomas watched Darcy stand and begin to help Nana and Hannah clean away the dishes. He knew the real reason she hadn't touched her lunch. On the way from the cottage, when Darcy had stayed behind to talk to the bishop, Elijah had shared with Thomas what the Elders knew about Jesse Troyer's past.

Thomas supposed he shouldn't feel so mixed up about what he had learned. After the beating and the phone call to Darcy, he should have expected that Jesse had some dubious connections. Still, it created a cloud of mistrust to discover that Jesse had kept secrets for all these years. For Darcy those mixed emotions must have felt even heavier.

He glanced through the kitchen window. In his office in the stables, where he managed his business of raising and training horses, he'd stowed away Jesse's Bible, which he'd taken from the cottage. He was going to take it to the hospital the next time he went to visit

Jesse so he could read to him. But now, he felt compelled to share it with Darcy. She should be the one to take it to the hospital and share God's word with her father. Maybe it would give her some peace in all of this confusion. By the look on her face, she could certainly use some.

"Your home is lovely." Darcy brought him a cup of coffee that Nana had poured out.

"Danki." Thomas felt a brief grin slide over his lips. He took the coffee from her hands, thinking how this woman was not quite what he had thought when he first saw her on Jesse's front porch. Fancy and sharp-witted, yes. But there was something softer there, too, although Thomas guessed it wasn't a side of her that she was comfortable revealing to many people, especially to a stranger like him.

"Well, if you like the old house, Miss Simmons, please allow me to show you the even older stables." He glanced over to Elijah. "Eli and I were just heading there to look at the filly."

Eli raised an eyebrow at the unexpected invitation, but followed Darcy and Thomas out of the white clap-board home toward the great red stable.

"So your grandmother lives on one side of the house and you on the other?" Darcy asked.

"When the house was more crowded, we definitely needed the space," Thomas said, thinking back to a time not so long ago when his brother's child and wife had lived there under his roof, dependent on his protection—protection he'd failed to give. "Now it's just the two of us. Frankly, I don't know how Nana keeps up the place all by herself."

"That's why Nana is always on the lookout for a new granddaughter-in-law." Eli slapped him on the back.

Thomas clenched his teeth. He knew his friend meant no harm, but somehow the comment rubbed him wrong. To redirect the conversation, he started to explain to Darcy that Hannah—Elijah's wife—used to live with him, along with her stepdaughter, Jessica, when Hannah was widowed by his older brother, who'd died in a buggy accident. And so it was really Eli's fault that Nana had lost her helper, when he'd come back to town to investigate the case of Jessica's murder and married Hannah. But the memory was so bittersweet. As happy as he was that his friend and his sister-in-law had found love together, the losses of his niece and brother weren't happy topics. After all, the whole point of taking Darcy to the stable was to lift her spirits, not add to the weight of what she already carried.

Thomas led Darcy and Eli through the aisles. "These are the Morgan breeding mares. On the other side are the draft mares. I have two stallions, which are housed in a separate stable on the far side of the property. And this—this is Gilda. She was just born two weeks ago."

Darcy looked over the stall door, down at the little bay filly, who tried to put her nose over the door to greet them.

"Oh, my, she's so sweet." Darcy smiled. And Thomas thought he saw at least a little of the weight from her shoulders lift. "Can I pet her?"

"Ja. Ja," he said. "She's very friendly. And already used to people. She's going to make a great driver."

He and Eli watched Darcy pet the playful filly, who snorted and nipped at Darcy's hand. "I've never really been around animals much. My grandparents wouldn't let me have a pet."

"It's sort of a mandatory experience around here." Eli laughed.

Darcy's smile slipped a little.

"I have something for you," Thomas said. "It's in the office."

"For me?" Darcy looked stunned as she followed him into his small office.

He lifted the Bible from his desk and placed it into her hands. "This is Jesse's. I found it on the table when we first started cleaning. I was going to take it to the hospital and read it to Jesse. But then I thought that he would want you to do that."

"Oh." Darcy looked frozen for a moment, then she finally extended her hands to take the great book. "I'm afraid, like the animals, I don't know much about the Bible, either."

She held it delicately in her hands, as if it was made of glass. Thomas felt a lump form in his throat. Had he gone too far? He had only meant to make things better.

"What would I read to him?" she asked.

"Just trust your heart." Thomas smiled.

She nodded. "Jesse did share some verses with me in a letter. I guess I could look those up."

Eli reached for the Bible. "Really, you can't go wrong with any part of it. For example, sometimes I'll just flip it open…"

As Elijah turned the pages, a note fluttered out from the book and fell to the floor.

Thomas reached for it and unfolded the small letter, his eyes glancing quickly over the message. Then his heart sank to stomach. He looked up at Darcy. "We need to call the chief."

* * *

Darcy pulled at the ends of her hair. How much more could she take? She wasn't sure. The note had been addressed to her to give to Jesse. It had been meant to terrorize them both. The man who had left it wanted her to know that he was coming for what Jesse had stolen. And if they wanted to live, they wouldn't get in his way. It had been signed W.W. She agreed with Thomas that they needed to call McClendon. She needed to tell the chief what Bishop Miller had told her about Jesse's past, too. Hopefully once he had all the information, the police chief would be able to piece together what was going on and stop this W.W. from hurting anyone else.

Darcy hurried from the stable to her car, where she'd left her phone in her bag. Her hands were shaking. Another threat and in a Bible of all places and... Where was her phone?

She searched her clutch bag, which was sitting in the passenger seat. The phone wasn't there. She looked under the seats. It wasn't there, either. She knew it wasn't in the Nolts' home. She hadn't taken her purse or the phone inside.

Darcy's mind flashed back to her enlightening conversation with the bishop. She remembered how the shock of his words had caused her to fall back. She had dropped her bag into the chair. Her phone must have fallen out then. It was probably right in the seat where he'd delivered the news that her mother had been murdered and the killer was now out of prison and on her trail. Now, thanks to the note in the Bible, she had yet another reminder of just how close that killer was.

She looked around, reminded of the isolation of

the Amish farm. The cottage was only a mile away. It wouldn't take long to go back and get it.

She hopped into the driver's seat, her mind still spinning with all new information. Her grandparents had always blamed her father for her mother's death—for the car crash that Darcy had always believed killed both of her parents. They had lied about her father dying. But were they telling the truth when they said it was her father's fault? Had they known their daughter was murdered? And that her father had helped send the killer to prison? *Murder... Killer...* The words made her cringe. What else had everyone lied about? Had she ever known the truth about anything? Darcy felt like she didn't even know who or what she was anymore.

Darcy passed through the woods separating Jesse's land from Thomas's. The cottage looked desolate as it came into view. Jesse's horse wasn't even in the field. Probably taken to a neighbor's while Jesse was in the hospital. The thought of others pitching in to help in different ways touched Darcy. Jesse's friends and neighbors were so loyal and devoted. Darcy wasn't even sure who her neighbors were. And she was certain that if she'd been the one in the hospital, there would not have been a constant flow of visitors like there had been for Jesse.

She pulled up in front of the cottage, leaving her car running. Grabbing her phone wouldn't take a second. She jiggled the door open and headed over to the chair where she'd been sitting. The phone was nestled between the arm and the seat cushion. That was a relief.

She tucked the phone into her jacket pocket. But as she began to turn, the front door suddenly slammed behind her.

Darcy jumped at the sudden sound, but tried to calm her nerves as she reasoned that it was simply a drafty house and that a change in pressure had caused the door to shut.

But a change in pressure where? And why? She turned toward the kitchen. Was there a back door that had opened? She spun back around. Everything looked in place. She was worried over nothing. She just needed to get back to Thomas's. The sooner the better.

As she stepped toward the front door, something fell in the kitchen. The clank of a tin pot hitting the hardwood floor reverberated through the house.

Her heart froze. Darcy couldn't breathe. Someone else was in the house. She took a step back. She looked left. She looked right. She saw nothing.

She hurried back toward the open door, but a figure appeared in her periphery.

She was not alone.

Chapter Six

Inside the barn, Thomas was pacing, trying to make sense of why he'd heard Darcy's car drive away. He hadn't joined her when she left the barn because he'd thought she was just stepping out to grab her phone—she hadn't said anything about departing yet. Darcy didn't need to be going anywhere alone. "I thought she meant her phone was in the house."

"Me, too," Elijah agreed. "Do you have your business phone?"

"Of course. It is still in the buggy we took this morning to Jesse's. I'll go get it."

Thomas jogged out to his buggy, which was parked on the other side of the stable. He would have offered his phone earlier but Darcy had been so keen to get her own. If he'd known she was going to drive off...

His little flip phone was tucked away inside the console of the buggy. It still had some power. He brought it back to Elijah. "I don't know her number."

"Call McClendon," Elijah said.

It took a few minutes but Thomas finally got the chief on the phone.

"Miss Simmons left here alone," Thomas said after explaining the rest of what they'd learned and the contents of the note they'd found.

"I'll call her," the chief said. "And I'll have my assistant forward you her number, as well. We can try to locate her by using her phone, too, if it's on and powered up."

Thomas disconnected.

"Maybe she's on her way back to the hospital to see Jesse?" Elijah suggested.

Thomas shook his head. "Why would she leave without saying anything?"

Thomas stared at his phone screen waiting for Darcy's number to come through. When it did, he dialed the number immediately. *What was that woman thinking, driving off without saying a word?*

Darcy's line rang and rang but she didn't answer. Thomas left a message asking her to return the call.

"Maybe she needed a minute and went for a quick drive?" Elijah offered.

"I know there could be a million legitimate reasons for her to drive off," Thomas admitted. "Maybe she saw the phone and realized she needed to call someone and drove away for some privacy."

He didn't believe a word of it. No matter what her reasoning, he couldn't imagine why she hadn't come back by now or said something to them first.

Thomas felt his heart jump when his phone rang in his fingers. "Darcy?" He lifted the phone.

"No. It's the chief. We can't get her to answer," McClendon explained. "But we were able to track the phone."

"Where is it?"

"Fourteen-oh-one Waking Lane."

"That's Jesse's cottage. I'm going to go take a look."

"She may not even be there," Elijah said to him. "Just because the phone is there doesn't mean the person is."

"Well, it's worth taking a look." Thomas shoved the phone into Elijah's hands. "You keep calling."

"Right," his friend said. "Take my buggy. Perry is still hitched up."

Thomas untied Elijah's horse from the hitching post and climbed inside the buggy. The trip through the woods seemed interminably long.

A large man grabbed Darcy's arm from behind. With tremendous strength, he pulled her back into the center of the cottage.

Darcy's blood raced through her veins. She screamed as she tripped backward. She braced herself and tried to whip her arm free, but his grip was too tight. Then a second man closed in on her from the other side. What could she do? They had her surrounded.

"What do you want?" The strength of her voice surprised her. She felt anything but strong at the moment. "This isn't your home. You're trespassing."

"Where is it? Where did he leave it? With you, no doubt." The voice was low and angry but with a distinct accent that she couldn't quite place. Was this the man from the phone call? Were these men responsible for the note they'd found in Jesse's Bible?

"I don't know what you're talking about, I assure you. Jesse didn't give me anything." Darcy thought of the phone inside her jacket. If she could just get the call to 911…but she'd have to do it carefully to keep her attackers from noticing. She reached her free hand slowly into her jacket pocket as her eyes darted back and forth between the two men—she needed to find a way to escape them.

"She's got a gun!" one of them yelled.

Darcy felt it before she knew what had happened. A sharp searing pain ran from the top of her head down the length of her body. She buckled to the floor. Warm blood trickled over her forehead. She fought to keep her eyes open but it was no use. Her vision blurred. Words swirled in the air above her and then the world turned black.

The cottage looked dark as it came into view, but Thomas breathed a sigh of relief when he saw Darcy's small red automobile parked in front. Thomas slowed Perry to a trot.

But the closer he got to the cottage the more Perry pranced and pulled. He sidestepped. He flung his weight around. He shook his thick, black mane and began to exhale with sharp, strong breaths.

"Easy, boy. Easy." He tried to reassure the frightened animal, but a spooked horse was hard to settle. Especially when Thomas felt a little out of sorts himself. He knew what was bothering him—he was worried about Darcy. But what had the horse so unsettled? Thomas halted the buggy and tied Perry to a hitching post in the back. He moved silently across the back lawn, nearing Jesse's cottage, then froze when a woman's loud scream echoed out of the house and across the field.

Thomas ran along the side of the house toward the front porch. Low, deep, masculine voices sounded in the cold air. Though he couldn't make out everything they said, they didn't sound familiar. And from the stray curse word he caught here and there, they certainly didn't sound Amish.

Thomas turned the corner of the front porch, just in time to see two men rush out the front door. They hopped into Darcy's running car and drove off in a red blur.

Thomas flew through the open front door and scanned the cottage. "Darcy?"

Then he spotted her lifeless body sprawled over the floor near the kitchen. Her thick dark hair was splayed around her face with bits of blood splattered around her in almost every direction.

Oh, please, Lord, no! Don't let her be dead...

For a millisecond, Thomas staggered, unable to breathe as if he himself had been struck over the head. But just as quickly he shook off the horrible surprise and made his way to her in two broad steps. Kneeling beside her, he steadied himself to check her pulse. The gruesome gash on the front of her head looked deadly and she wasn't moving.

He glanced down at the creamy skin of her delicate hands. Her painted nails glinted in the afternoon light.

He swallowed hard and pressed his fingers against her skin. *Please, please be alive. I could never forgive myself if...*

He felt her heart's rhythm stroke his fingertips. Danki, *Lord*. Danki!

He touched her cheek with the back of his hand. She didn't react. She was out cold. It was like finding Jesse all over again.

A soft buzzing sounded from the floor beside him. Her phone. He pulled it from her jacket pocket and recognized his own business number displayed on the screen. Elijah—continuing to call, as he'd promised.

"Elijah, it's Thomas. I found her," Thomas said when he answered the phone. "We need to call 911."

Darcy heard words floating over her but she couldn't concentrate on them enough to understand. A gentle hand on her forehead pressed a damp cloth against her hot skin. Her eyes fluttered. Light struck her like a club against her skull. Pain radiated from her head all the way down to her fingers.

"Hey, she's coming to," a voice said above her. A voice she didn't recognize.

Slowly, Darcy squinted and gazed up. A slender, blonde woman stood, looking down with concern. The woman wore nursing scrubs and her hair was neatly braided into one long strand, flipped over her shoulder. She was pretty and natural. Her deep blue eyes looked sharp and intelligent.

Darcy glanced over the room, recognizing Jesse's home. She was on the couch. And there were two Amish men standing by the woodstove. She knew them— Thomas and his friend. They had had lunch together. They had been at the stable. Thomas had shown her that adorable baby horse. Then what? Everything after that was a foggy—and painful—blur.

The throbbing in her head intensified with the light and movement and sound of voices. She closed her eyes and willed the horrible ache to go away. It hurt to think.

"Hi, Darcy. I'm Abigail. Abigail Jamison. I'm a nurse and I'm taking care of this head wound of yours until EMS gets here. Then we will get you to the hospital."

Hospital. Jesse. Beating. Bible. Message. Phone. The

progression of thoughts strung together one by one until she remembered what had happened. Images of two huge men flashed through her pain-filled mind.

"You have a serious head injury," the nurse continued. "And probably a concussion. Is there someone we can call for you?"

Darcy felt sick from the horrible pounding in her head. She wanted to vomit, but she didn't think she could bear the pain of moving her head in order to relieve the nausea. It hurt even to think. "No. Please, don't call anyone. I'm fine. I just need to…" *Go home and forget this place. Forget Jesse. Forget this nonstop nightmare I can't wake up from.*

"It's okay. Just try to be still. I hear sirens. The emergency crew must be close. You're going to need a doctor to stop that bleeding. It's under control now, but as soon as you move it will start back up again. I know it hurts."

Darcy closed her eyes again. She felt exhausted, but too adrenaline charged to relax. She could hear Thomas and Elijah speaking to each other, whispering in a language she did not understand. Pennsylvania Dutch, most likely. The soft sounds soothed the edges of the sharp pain. "Thomas…" she said, trying to sit up, wanting to ask if he'd seen those men. But moving made her head spin. She dropped back against the pillow, and Thomas stepped up to her side.

A gentle smile cracked over his dark face. "Glad to see you awake and talking. You've had us worried ever since you went out to get your phone and did not come back."

Someone had attacked her. Fear seized Darcy's whole being. "Yes, I did. I remember. When I went to the car,

I realized my phone had fallen out and I came here to find it. But…"

She closed her eyes and turned her head away from him. The nausea was overwhelming. The ability to keep her stomach from rebelling grew weaker and weaker.

"Just let her rest." The nurse shooed away the two men.

"There—there were men in Jesse's house. They attacked me," Darcy told the blonde. "Did Thomas see them?"

"He did. He's called the police. Now, you just rest," Abigail said.

"You talk like they do," Darcy said, her mind swirling in and out of the moment, not sure how to describe the accent the woman shared with the two Amish men.

"I'm Elijah's sister. And I'm Jesse's friend, which means I'm your friend." She turned the wet cloth on Darcy's head. "I also happen to be a nurse. I have a clinic nearby. So Thomas called me to come and help make you comfortable while we wait for the EMS."

Darcy tried to speak but couldn't. Tears slid from the corners of her eyes. She gasped for air before the words finally emerged. "I don't know what they want from me. I don't know how to make this stop."

Thomas was back at the hospital. He'd come with Abigail. While doctors patched up Darcy, he decided to visit Jesse. The old man lay in front of him, lifeless. His status had not changed, for better or for worse. Thomas touched his friend's cold hand. A tear trickled down his cheek. He could not help but think about what life might be like without Jesse. He was much more than a friend. More than a neighbor. In many ways, Jesse had been like a second father to him after his own had passed away. He didn't want to lose Jesse. He'd already lost too much.

"I heard you were here," Dr. Blake Jamison said as he stepped into Jesse's room. "No change, but Jesse's holding on. He's strong. We just have to keep waiting."

Thomas hadn't heard his friend enter. Quickly, he dropped his head and wiped the tears away.

"Darcy is ready to go home," Blake continued. "But McClendon is here and wants to talk to her. And to you. They're waiting for you downstairs in a conference room. I'll show you."

Thomas nodded and followed Blake to a second-floor conference room. He knew that he and Darcy needed to talk to the police, but after being with Jesse he found it hard to transition his thoughts back to the attack on Darcy as he entered the room. What if Jesse was lost to him forever?

Thomas shook away the dreaded thought. McClendon, Darcy and another woman were seated at the conference table. He paused in the doorway as there seemed to be some dispute between McClendon and the woman as to whether or not he should be allowed in the meeting. Before he could say anything, Darcy interrupted them.

"I want him here," she said firmly. "He can answer questions about Jesse that I can't."

McClendon and the woman accepted Darcy's decision.

Thomas walked farther into the room, focusing his attention on Darcy. "How's the head?"

"It hurts," she answered with a half smile.

Thomas could tell by her speech, her clear eyes and

her attitude that she was feeling much better. He was glad. And glad he'd arrived at Jesse's when he had or she might have been hurt even worse.

"But I'll be fine. Just a mild concussion and a couple of stitches. I'm not supposed to drive for twenty-four hours, which is fine since I heard the two men made off with my car."

"Your car has been found," McClendon said. "Abandoned only a mile from Jesse's cottage. The perpetrators most likely used it to get back to their own vehicle as fast as possible. It's at the station now under examination of my forensics team. Maybe they left prints. At any rate, our guys will check it over to make sure the car hasn't been tampered with in any way before returning it to you."

Darcy smiled. "Thank you. I guess that's at least one thing less to worry about. But why would they have left their own car so far away?"

McClendon shrugged. "So that you couldn't hear them approach? Or, since Mr. Troyer is Amish, they might worry that a vehicle out front would be cause for concern."

"Hi, I'm Agent Susan Danvers with the US Marshals office." The other woman in the room stood and offered a hand to Thomas. It was clear that she did not like being left out of the conversation. "We were just discussing you, Mr. Nolt."

Thomas could also tell she disapproved of his presence. "Yes, I heard the last bit. But I'm Jesse's neighbor and closest friend. I would like to be here. Thank you."

The woman was in her midforties. She was tall and dressed all in black with a tight-fitting jacket that read United States Marshal on the left side. Her short blond hair had been purposely spiked out in every direction. He would like to believe that she was truly only interested in helping, but he noticed that she seemed overly official and self-important.

"US Marshals? Doesn't your agency transport criminals?"

"Among other things," Danvers snapped. In front of her was a large, open leather case. Its contents had been spread across the table. In her hand was an identification card, which she flashed at Thomas.

As they shook hands, Thomas caught a sense it wasn't just *his* presence that was upsetting her.

Thomas took a seat across from Darcy. Agent Danvers and McClendon began to speak at the same time. When he didn't immediately gesture for her to go first, Danvers looked over at McClendon with great annoyance.

"Excuse me, Chief." Agent Danvers's tone was snippy and arrogant. "Let me tell you what I know and then I have to be off. I have other cases to handle that aren't twenty years old."

McClendon inclined his head.

"Before Jesse joined the Amish church, he was in possession of some very valuable material."

"I thought he helped to put a murderer away?" Darcy asked.

"He did." The woman looked slightly surprised that this information was already known, but she recovered quickly and smiled at Darcy. Her expression was tight. "He was a key witness in the William Wissenberg murder trial."

"So Wissenberg is the man who killed my mother?" Darcy said.

Danvers's smile dissolved into a frown. "Your mother died during the trial in a car crash. Your father claimed that the crash was orchestrated to scare him out of testifying. Of course, the authorities were unable to find any proof of that, but your father's fear for you endangered his willingness to testify, so you, your grandparents and your father were entered into the witness relocation program."

"But why were we separated?"

"I think that was a stipulation your grandparents made," Danvers replied. "Something about them blaming him for your mother's car crash. I don't know the details. This all occurred before I came to work for the department…" She paused and pressed her lips together. "Miss Simmons, did Jesse Troyer pass along anything to you before…?"

"Before he was beaten into a coma?" Darcy looked at Danvers. She seemed to struggle with her emotions as she crossed her arms over her chest. One hand raised to the locket hanging around her neck. She rubbed the charm between her finger and thumb. "We exchanged some pictures and letters. He bought me a coffee and—"

A buzzing sound filled the small room.

"Oh, that's me," Danvers said, checking the phone hitched to her waistband. "I'll need to take this. Excuse me for just one second."

She answered the phone and left the room. Thomas felt like the front of opposition had departed with her.

"Wi-ssen-beeerg." McClendon wasted not a second before typing the name into his small tablet. "I guess that's who the W.W. on the note could be. Says here that he was released one week ago after serving a twenty-year sentence for the murder of a private security guard.

If Jesse helped put him in jail, maybe this is all an act of revenge?"

"Except revenge would only motivate one person, and there were two men who attacked me." Darcy looked over at the screen on the tablet. "And they were both way too young to be that guy."

Thomas nodded. He agreed with Darcy. The two men he'd seen leaving Jesse's house were much younger than the man who'd been released from prison.

"Perhaps, they were hired muscle," added McClendon.

Agent Danvers burst back into the room and began gathering her things. "Well, it turns out, I'm going to have to go, so let me get to the point, Miss Simmons. Your location has been compromised. So, I'm here to ask if you'd like to be relocated to ensure your safety."

"What about Jesse?" Darcy asked. "What about my grandparents?"

"We don't believe your grandparents were ever in any danger. They were only relocated because they took over custody of you," she said. "And Mr. Troyer? Well, we will see if he wakes up.

"You don't have to decide right now." Danvers snatched the large leather case into her left hand and handed a small business card to Darcy with the right. "Here's my card. Let's meet again soon." With a glare at McClendon, she added, "In private."

Darcy looked even paler than when Thomas had found her on the floor at Jesse's.

Danvers was halfway out the door, then she paused and looked back. "Call me, Miss Simmons. I can get you to safety and you can leave this all behind."

Chapter Seven

Darcy dropped her head into her hands as she desperately fought the onslaught of tears building. Her head spun and it wasn't just from the injury. She had been in the witness relocation program her whole life? Then who was she, really? Or who had she been? What were her parents' real names? Where had they lived? The questions devoured her. She wanted to curl into a ball and will all of these horrifying truths away. Truth was supposed to mean freedom. But these truths felt more like they were destroying everything she believed about herself and her past.

Thomas and McClendon fidgeted in their seats. They probably didn't know what to say after the whirlwind visit from Agent Danvers.

How strange her life had become. She couldn't even imagine what Thomas must be thinking or feeling about Jesse. And her. "Well, that was enlightening," she said.

"Actually, it answers a few questions that I had," Thomas said, his voice heavily coated with emotion.

Darcy suspected that Jesse must be much more than just a neighbor to Thomas. The thought made her a little jealous. She'd barely had a chance to form any kind of relationship with the man through their brief meetings—and now she might never have the chance.

"You weren't abandoned by your father," he continued.

"Nope. Stolen away by the grandparents, it would seem."

"I wonder how Jesse found you?" McClendon asked.

"And how this Wissenberg found Jesse?" added Thomas. "Do you really think this is about revenge?"

McClendon nodded. "Partially, but there must be more than that at stake here. Wissenberg is clearly after more than simply hurting Jesse. He seems to be after whatever it is that Danvers claims Jesse had."

"*Stole* was the word used in the letter." Darcy didn't care that her tone sounded severe and unforgiving.

"Danvers asked you about receiving gifts from Jesse," McClendon continued. "And she mentioned believing that Jesse has something of great value."

"Well, he didn't give me anything like that," she said.

"As far as I know, he doesn't possess anything like that—not anymore. Jesse lives very plain. He may not have been born Amish but he lives the life to the letter," Thomas said.

"But by finding you," McClendon said to Darcy, "he has inadvertently put you in harm's way. If you don't know what these people are after then maybe you should consider what Ms. Danvers said about going someplace else where you can be safe."

Darcy didn't want to start her life all over again. Did she? What about Jesse? What about her grandparents? They may have lied to her, but they did love her in their own stiff way. She was certain of that. And she loved them.

How had all this happened? If only Jesse could wake up and tell her what they wanted, then she and her father could relocate together and live the life that was taken from them...

Thomas excused himself from the room while Mc-Clendon continued to question Darcy and warn her about her own safety. Thomas must have sensed how tired she was because he came back with a nurse. He was rescuing her again. And she was very grateful.

"You need rest." Abigail, the pretty nurse from the cottage, entered the conference room with a smile. "You're welcome to come stay as our guest tonight at the clinic. We have plenty of room."

A safe place to stay. Darcy hadn't even thought about that. Her attackers had known her phone number—she doubted it would be that difficult for them to find her address. Still, she didn't know Abigail at all. On the other hand, she couldn't drive and asking a friend to come pick her up would mean explanations that she didn't feel like giving.

"Are you sure? There could be trouble," Darcy said. She didn't want to bring her problems, her dangers, to someone else. But what else could she do?

"I'm positive. Thomas, Chief McClendon, you are welcome to join us for dinner," Abigail offered.

"Not me. Thank you. I've got piles of work," Mc-Clendon said. "But I will send a squad car by the clinic every hour through the night. No more uninvited guests for you, Miss Simmons. I'll be in touch."

"Thank you," Darcy said. McClendon nodded and left. Thomas accepted the dinner invite but said he had a few things to do first and would meet them at the clinic later.

Darcy wanted to walk out to Abigail's car, but the nurse insisted she stay in a wheelchair.

"Hospital policy," Abigail said as they exited.

"This is awfully kind of you," Darcy told her a little later as they drove along the single-lane country road.

"Well, Jesse is like one of the Nolts. And the Nolts and the Millers are like—well, our families have been friends for ages. So that kind of makes you like family."

Darcy felt a lump the size of Kansas form in her throat. She wasn't used to all of this sentimental talk. "You and Thomas seem close."

"Ach. Ja," she said, throwing a hand in the air. "Growing up, it was hard to get away from him and my big brother. They were such a pair. Always into trouble."

Darcy tried to imagine Thomas not behaving. But it was hard to imagine him as a mischief-making boy. He was all strong, serious man. "Really?"

"Really. And Thomas instigated most of it. Nearly gave his Nana a stroke a few times."

Darcy's mind wandered quickly back to the meeting with Danvers and McClendon. "I suppose Thomas shared with you what Agent Danvers came to the hospital for. Is that why you offered for me to stay over?"

"Well, Thomas did tell me, but I would have offered anyway. You don't have a car. And even if you did, I wouldn't let you drive it. Not with a head injury like that."

"I could have called a cab," Darcy said.

"And gone where? Home alone? Thomas wouldn't have let that happen."

Thomas would not have *let* it happen? What business

of it was his? Mixed feelings settled over her. On the one hand, Abigail was right. She shouldn't go home alone. Not even after that first phone call had come through, but especially not after what Agent Danvers had told her. On the other hand... "Thomas shouldn't feel responsible for me. He doesn't even know me."

"Knowing you has nothing to do with it. You're Jesse's daughter and Jesse can't look after you so Thomas feels that it's his duty. Thomas and Jesse are pretty tight. Both being widowers and all."

Thomas was a widower? That meant Thomas had been married and in love. Darcy swallowed away the strange taste in her mouth and forced a laugh. "I don't think in my adult life I've ever been called someone's duty."

Abigail laughed, too, though hers sounded more sincere.

"So, one of the other nurses told me about you and Dr. Jamison. And then I remembered reading in the *New Yorker* about your husband's search for his biological parents," Darcy said. "I never thought I'd meet someone featured in such a prominent magazine."

"Blake hates all of that nonsense. Thankfully, it's all died down since we got married."

Darcy decided that she liked Abigail. She was intelligent and married to a very wealthy man and yet she was so down-to-earth. "I like how everyone is so uncomplicated here. I don't meet many people like that. Not in my business. In fashion everyone is complicated— or pretends to be."

Abigail nodded, but Darcy got a sense she might not agree with her statement. They rode on a few minutes in silence.

"Do you have a computer I could use?" Darcy asked.

Abigail nodded. "I do. But you shouldn't be looking at a computer screen with a head injury. Your work will have to wait."

"It's not for work," Darcy said. "I want to know more about who Jesse used to be. If he testified in a trial that put someone in prison for twenty years, there has to be something about that on the internet, right? We know who he put in jail, so maybe Jesse's former name is out there to find, as well. Or even better, we could find out what these men who beat Jesse up are after."

"In that case, you tell me what to look up and I'll work the computer for you."

"Deal."

Thomas had gotten a ride home from the hospital by calling a local business that provided a sort of taxi service to the Amish. He was anxious to get home and take care of his horses. As soon as he returned, he pulled some from the fields. A few he turned out with heavy blankets. Others he led to their stalls. Then he provided fresh hay, clean stalls, water and feed for his herd. Most days, he had a teenage boy come and work for him. But today he was solo, just him and the horses. Thomas liked the time it gave him to think. To pray. And to be patient as he waited for an indication of God's will.

He was thankful he wasn't a person like Agent Danvers—attached to a cell phone, constantly talking, constantly moving on to the next thing without having taken care of the one before. But it wasn't just that endless busyness that set Thomas's teeth on edge when he thought of the government worker. Sure, she could have been a little more sympathetic when asking

Darcy to consider upending her whole life. But there was something else about her that had rubbed Thomas the wrong way. Something about the way she asked Darcy if Jesse had given her anything. What was that all about? What business was it of hers what Jesse had given his own daughter?

Then again, what did Thomas know about such matters? Nothing. His life was faith, family and his four-legged friends. Not beatings, intrigue or danger.

Thomas locked up the feed room then checked on Nana, telling her that he would be eating with Blake, Abigail and Darcy. The sun had already set and Thomas decided to park the buggy for the evening. Sadie had already trotted all over Willow Trace and he had put her away for the night. Instead, he called the same car service that he had used earlier. As he was getting into the back of the driver's car, Nana came running out of the house. One would have thought the place was on fire. But she was only there to hand him some fresh baked bread to take over for the dinner. She didn't believe in going to someone else's table empty-handed.

On his way to the clinic, he passed the Miller farm, which bordered his land on the opposite side from Jesse's. He asked the driver to pull off and drive up the lane. He found Elijah out chopping wood. Elijah smiled when he saw Thomas emerge from the back of the small commuter car. Thomas quickly updated his friend on what had transpired in the conference room of the hospital.

"I can't get over Jesse being in witness protection." Elijah slammed down his ax and split another log in half.

"Well, that's what I wanted to ask you," Thomas said.

"Why would Jesse go into hiding after he testified and the guy was convicted? And how would anyone have found him once he did? How did he find Darcy if they separated when they got new identities?"

Elijah stopped and leaned on his ax. "I think it makes sense after what my father told us. That Jesse blames himself for his wife's death. Whether that car accident was before or right after he testified, it doesn't really matter. If someone is powerful enough, they can have people found and killed whether they are behind bars or not."

"Hence why Darcy and her grandparents also got new identities," Thomas said. "So this Wissenberg person must be pretty powerful. Or at least he used to be."

Eli nodded.

"But how would this guy find Jesse after all these years?" Thomas said. "And how did Jesse find Darcy?"

"I don't know, but his timing sure was bad, getting in touch with her right before Wissenberg was released."

"He must not have realized it was happening. No way Jesse waited all this time before contacting his daughter just to put her in danger," Thomas said.

"The US Marshal didn't tell you anything more?" Elijah asked.

Thomas shook his head. "She did not say much. She offered Darcy a new identity. Then she left in a big hurry. I got the feeling McClendon had more questions for her. Darcy, too. But the agent wasn't going to answer them. She said she couldn't talk in front of me. Maybe I should have left the meeting."

"I'm glad you didn't." Elijah rubbed the tip of his beard. "I still have friends in the FBI. Especially one—a guy by the name of Frank Ross. You've met him. He may be able to help us fill in some of these blanks."

"I don't know…" Thomas hesitated. It was not the way of the Amish to meddle in police or government affairs. Shouldn't it be left up to God? "What if we find out things about Jesse that he doesn't want us to know?"

"I think it's far too late for discretion," Elijah pointed out. "The information we don't know is putting Jesse and Darcy in danger. We can't protect them without learning more of what's going on. Anyway, it's Jesse. And Jesse's daughter. He would want us to help, even if it meant revealing things about his past."

"She's staying with your sister tonight," Thomas said. "I'm headed there for dinner. McClendon is sending a car by every hour, in case there's trouble."

"Even more reason to get some information for ourselves. I'll call Agent Ross," Elijah said. "You go to dinner. Call me if you need me."

"I always do." Thomas smiled and returned to the back of his driver's car.

Dinner was pan-seared chicken with potatoes and fresh vegetables, served with homemade iced tea and chocolate pie for dessert. Darcy surprised herself at the quantity of food she was able to consume after having spent most of the day nauseous.

Her nerves had calmed some, but the US Marshal's unveiling of her secret life weighed on her mind like a pile of anvils. As did the agent's offer for Darcy to be relocated again.

Should she really start a new life? Never talk to Jesse again? Never talk to her grandparents or coworkers again? It seemed such a terrible price to pay, but would it be worth it if it meant she'd be safe? She was glad she had more time to think about it. With her head pounding and her mind reeling from the attack, she was in no shape to make a decision that would change her whole life.

Conversation over dinner had been light. Lots of stories about Jesse. While she couldn't repress lingering jealousy that these people had known her father so much better than she had herself, she was still grateful for insights into the kind of man he was. Abigail and Blake were the perfect host and hostess. Their home was well decorated and had every modern convenience— a great contrast to Jesse's cottage, and even Thomas's larger but still simple home.

"I can't believe how kind you are to have me over like this," Darcy said. "And it's so great that you're Jesse's doctor."

"Happy to do it," Blake said.

"But I wasn't thinking when I agreed to stay here," Darcy continued. "You guys are newlyweds. I'm totally imposing on you. Not to mention the chance that I could be attacked again, putting you at risk. I should get a room at that B and B I saw on the way in yesterday. It looked charming."

"It is," said Blake. "I lived there when I was working as a visiting doctor at the hospital. But we don't mind you staying here at all."

"In fact, we insist you do," Abigail added.

She had to credit their enthusiasm to their loyalty to Jesse and Thomas. They were doing this to please them.

"So, how did that meeting go with McClendon today?" Blake asked. "Any leads on who beat up Jesse and tried to do the same thing to you?"

Darcy was surprised when it was Thomas who let out a low grunt of disapproval. "That was not what the meeting was about."

Blake's eyebrows shot up. "Really?"

"Oh, my, Abigail, you haven't even told him what he's gotten himself into inviting me over," said Darcy.

"He already knew about the attack," Abigail said. "It's not going to make any difference to us that you and Jesse were part of WITSEC."

"What? Wow! That's not something you hear too often," said Blake. "Witness relocation… I would have never thought of that. Do you know why you all had to relocate?"

Darcy shrugged. "Not completely. I only know the basics. I was hoping to use your computer and do a little research?"

"Sure." Abigail stood from the table and began gathering dishes to take to the sink. Blake followed her lead. "It's in the clinic area. Help yourself but make sure that Thomas reads the screen for you."

Blake grabbed his young bride and pulled her close, giving her a kiss. "Nurses are the worst, right? They don't let anyone do anything."

"What's that supposed to mean?" Abigail pushed him away playfully, and whipped him with the drying towel.

"The computer is through there," Thomas told her, lifting his arm to direct her.

There was plenty of information to be found online about Wissenberg. Years before, he had been the director of the Gregorian Museum of Fine Art. Then he was arrested and convicted of murder, international smuggling and fraud. One article stated that it was believed that he had illegally sold over one hundred million dollars worth of museum-quality art.

The Gregorian? That was one of the most prestigious museums in the United States, located right in the heart of the nation's capital.

The more Darcy found out about this mess, the less she really understood. How had her father gotten mixed up in this?

Thomas read the article aloud.

"'Smugglers at the Gregorian—William Wissenberg, former director of the Gregorian Museum of Fine Art, has been convicted of murder, international smuggling and fraud. He was condemned to a life sentence and a fifty-million-dollar fine for having "displaced" hundreds of important works of art over the past ten years. Sources say that his operation was so well constructed that if it had not been for the testimony of a former Gregorian employee, who was also the lead member of the Wissenberg smuggling ring, that Wissenberg would never have faced charges. Instead, he was convicted of killing security guard Kevin Loewer, age sixty-five.'"

Thomas glanced over the rest of the old article. "Director of the Gregorian? That's something. Elijah said that Wissenberg must have been important… So, you think that it's Jesse who is mentioned at the end of the article? The former employee? The reporter never reveals his name."

Darcy let out a low exhale. "Yes. I guess he must have worked at the Gregorian, too."

Thomas tried searching Gregorian employees during that time frame matching the ten years in question, but in all of the news coverage they could find, everything seemed to be about Wissenberg.

"Thinking I was born with a different name than Darcy Simmons is pretty strange."

"A name is just a name," Thomas said. "It does not change who you are. I only knew your father as Jesse Troyer, but I can see in him the man who used to work for a grand museum. He is definitely a very educated man. I'm not surprised he did something scholarly. He is always reading. Taught me a lot. He could approach things from a different perspective that challenged me to think about why I believe what I do. And he always knows how to explain things in relationship to his faith."

Darcy felt a pang of mixed emotions, which quickly turned over to anger. "But what you just read about the employee who testified—if that's Jesse who gave the evidence against Wissenberg, then that means he was also a large part of a smuggling operation. That doesn't bother you? I know he's in a coma, and I shouldn't feel angry at someone in a coma but…"

Thomas dropped his hands from the keyboard. "I don't know who Jesse was before he was Jesse. But the man I know is a good man, Darcy. I thought of him as a second father after my own passed away. And I can't stand the thought of losing him. It does not matter what he was, or what he did. Our God forgives. And so must we."

"I'm sorry," Darcy said. "About your father." *About my outburst. That I'm scared out of my mind. That I don't even know who I am.*

Thomas looked over at her and smiled. "*Ach*, that was a long, long time ago. But my *datt* and yours, they were good friends, too."

Jesse was still a thief and his association with criminals got her mother killed. She couldn't forgive that so easily. Darcy shook her head slightly, tears rolling down her face. "I was really looking forward to getting to know him. But now to find out that he was a thief? That he conspired with a murderer? No wonder my grandparents hated him. He ruined our family by being a part of some crime ring. How can you forgive someone for that?"

Thomas touched her wrist with his big calloused hand. Warmth shot through her skin and she stared down at her small hand under his. For a moment, she didn't feel the pain in her head.

"Do you think that maybe that's unfair?" he asked gently. "You told me yourself that Jesse never got a chance to explain himself to you. Wait until you hear his side of the story before you condemn him."

"How do you only see the good in everything?" She thought about turning her hand and lacing her fingers with his. Instead, she pulled her hand away and shook off the crazy idea. What was she thinking? She felt close to him—but it was only because of the circumstances. Once this situation was over and she was no longer in danger, there would be no reason for her path to cross the Amish farmer's again.

Thomas left shortly after, with Blake giving him a ride home. Darcy took a quick bath and settled into her luxurious guest room. But sleep eluded her. She couldn't relax. Not with all that had happened. Not knowing what she now knew. How was she ever going to accept it all?

She continued to struggle with the idea the next morning, sitting in the passenger seat of Abigail's car.

"I feel silly being babysat," Darcy said to Abigail as they pulled up in front of Nolt cottage.

"Nonsense," Abigail said. "Someone needs to keep an eye on you to make sure you don't experience side effects from your injury, and Nana Ruth absolutely loves to have company. Let her fuss all over you today. You need to rest up if you expect to get back in the swing of things. And your car should be ready by the time my shift is over."

"Are you sure? I do have a friend or two in the city. I can call one to come pick me up, and I'm sure they'd be willing to keep me company for a few hours." Darcy felt ashamed to keep depending on the kindness of Jesse's community. "I really think I've outworn my welcome."

"Don't you want to check on Jesse later?"

"Well, yes, but—"

"Then why call in someone from the city when we are all here to help you?" Abigail said—the woman knew her reasoning was sound.

"I really can't thank you enough," Darcy said. "Your kindness. Everyone's kindness here. I don't think I've ever needed it more."

But what price would they pay for that kindness? Would they get hurt simply because they were helping her? How could she live with herself if that occurred?

Chapter Eight

Thomas didn't have to like or dislike what he and Darcy had uncovered on the internet the night before, because he didn't dare let himself believe it. Not yet. Jesse had been his good friend—to think him anything but a good and honorable man hurt something deep inside Thomas.

More than ever he wished Jesse would wake up. Tell them the truth. Set this all straight. But he knew God would take care of things in His time, not Thomas's.

Darcy had spent the day at his home, working inside with his grandmother. He had stayed away, mostly getting his own work done. But he knew that it was about time for Abigail to come and pick her up. Where would she go? Would she stay another night at Abigail's? Had she heard anything from Chief McClendon? Had she decided to accept the US Marshal's offer to relocate her?

Thomas was anxious to hear something from Elijah and his friend at the FBI. But as Elijah always told him, calling in these types of favors took time and it hadn't even been twenty-four hours. He was glad he had work to keep him busy.

Thomas grabbed a tiny halter and took a filly out of the large pen away from her mother. She didn't like that too much but the youngling would have to learn.

He led her down the aisle, slowly but firmly, as he whispered sweet words to her. Calming words.

"You'd make a good father." Darcy's voice sounded from the front doors of the stable. "But isn't she a bit young to take from her mother?"

"No, this is good for her. She has to learn to trust humans." Thomas turned and smiled. He was glad she'd come to the stable. In fact, he had hoped that she would. With his closeness to her over the past couple of days, he had begun to grow attached to her in some capacity. It was silly. A fleeting emotion, probably born out of his loyalty to Jesse. Nothing to linger his thoughts over. He smiled at her. "What have you and Nana been up to?"

"Sewing," she answered.

"You can sew?" He had not expected that. Even though she had said she worked in fashion, he had pictured her in an office, in meetings, surrounded by models and designers, not behind a sewing machine.

"Yes, how do you think one designs clothing if one can't sew?" Her gray eyes looked up at him.

She had a playful smirk on her face. He had to stop himself from staring at her, focusing his attention on the filly.

"So do you do this every day with her? Get her used to people?"

"Not every day," he said. "Not yet."

Darcy walked up beside him and reached her hand out to the baby's muzzle. The filly sniffed around her fingers then nipped at them. Darcy squealed and let out a little laugh. "She's going to bite me."

"Maybe." He laughed back. "But I don't think so. I think she likes you."

Their eyes locked for a moment. "Come. It's time to return her to her mother."

"Thomas, can I ask you something?"

"Sure. I've certainly asked you enough questions." He walked the filly to the enclosed pen with her mother.

Darcy was silent. He looked back at her to find a grim look on her face.

"Well, it's none of my business really..." She hesitated. "But I was just wondering, because Abigail told me that you..."

"She told you that I what?"

"That you were married once." She looked down and away.

"Is it so hard to believe—that someone would marry me?" He couldn't stop the wide smile that spread over his face and he laughed.

She looked up with wide eyes, her lips quickly spreading into grin that was laced with relief. "No. Not at all. I'm sorry. That's not what I meant."

"I know." He looked down at her and stepped close.

"Like I said, it's really none of my business. I didn't mean to be disrespectful but... I was curious."

"It's okay. It is a good question." He got control of his laughter and suddenly became serious again. "I was married. But it was a long time ago."

"What happened?"

"Cancer."

Darcy closed her eyes. "Oh—oh, I'm so sorry. I shouldn't have asked."

She started to turn away, but Thomas didn't want her to leave. He reached out and grabbed her gently by the wrist. "Don't be sorry. As I said, it was a long time ago. All is as God planned."

"You really believe that?"

"I do. Do you doubt it?"

"I don't know. I guess I never really thought about it. About God." She pulled back from him. "So what's up with the beard? I thought a beard meant that you are married?"

She had changed the subject away from the topic of faith. Thomas didn't press her. God would open her eyes in His time. If she wanted to talk, God would provide the moments. He didn't have to force them.

"*Ach.* So you do not like my Amish beard?" He laughed out loud again. "It is different, no? Without the mustache?"

"Yes, it's very different."

"Once married it is custom to keep the beard. And frankly it's easier than shaving all of it every day."

"Doesn't look like you have all that much to shave," she teased.

"That is true. Just like my *datt*."

"You must miss him."

He missed them all—all those that he'd lost. It was something he and Jesse had always had in common— loss. "Like Jesse missed your mother—and, I guess, you, too. He didn't tell me about you but as I said before, he used to talk about your mother.

"Her name was Margaret, right? He really loved her. A lot of Amish ladies have tried to catch his eye over the years, but Jesse was true to his one love. And to you."

"What do you mean?" Darcy felt like no one was true to her and especially not Jesse.

Thomas shrugged. "Just that he gave you up to keep

you safe. Giving up a child—that's a sacrifice no parent wants to make. I think that may have been part of the reason he never tried to make a new family for himself."

"I'm not sure how I feel about it all. He wanted to protect me...but he left me. I should be so angry. But, mostly, I'm just confused. Why did he do those things? Why *would* he do those things?"

"I don't know." Thomas could almost see the battle within her. The struggle to love a man who should have protected her, raised her, loved her, but who made decisions that prevented him from being in her life at all.

"And how did they find us?"

"I don't know that, either. But I suppose secrets are only as secret as the people who keep them."

"Who do you mean... Do you mean Jesse?" Darcy tilted her head.

"No. I mean the government. WITSEC should be safe. But I guess there can be corrupt people anywhere."

She took a minute to process that. Then she said, "Thomas, what am I going to do?"

Thomas paused, pressing his lips together. He wanted answers, too. He couldn't stand seeing the pain and fear in her. He wished Elijah would call with news. "Trust in God."

"Easy for you to say. You don't have people trying to..." She touched her hands to her head. "My head is starting to hurt. I think I need to sit down for a while."

"I'll walk you back to the house."

Darcy closed her eyes. She needed rest. And though she had enjoyed her time with the spirited Amish woman, spending the day with Nana Ruth hadn't provided her with much downtime. Only those few minutes in the stable with Thomas had made her forget about the problems in her life. But even that had ended when Thomas began speaking of her mother. It seemed he'd heard more about her than she had. Her grandparents had rarely spoken about their daughter, saying they found the memories too painful.

It was late afternoon now—almost time to go. But go where? Where could she go that would be safe? She felt safe at Thomas's home, but she couldn't stay there.

She could feel him so close to her as they walked back across the yard and to his house.

"Darcy…" He stopped her with a hand to her shoulder.

She turned and slowly looked up. She was so tired and he was so…so handsome. And kind. And strong. It was his strength that was most appealing.

"What is it?"

"Well, I do not know why, but I cannot stop thinking about that Agent Danvers from the US Marshals."

"Me, either. She was sort of unforgettable." The reminder of her looming decision hovered in the air.

"No. It was something she said. Something she asked you that I keep thinking about."

"About my relocation? About your neighbor being a big phony?"

"No, Darcy." There was disappointment in his eyes.

She dropped her head. She shouldn't have said that about Jesse—not to Thomas, who cared for the man so deeply.

"It was her question about what Jesse gave you."

"Yeah, well, he didn't give me anything of value. I looked at the locket. It's silver plated. It's not valuable to anyone except me."

"But what if what Jesse gave you wasn't actual valuables, but information?"

"Information? But he didn't tell me anything, either. Not even that we were in witness protection. He said very little about the past. We just talked about our lives now…and mostly we talked about me."

"But he sent you letters?"

"Yes, but there wasn't anything special in them."

"Do you still have them?"

"Yes, they're at home. But I'm telling you, there's nothing special about—" Darcy stopped as she heard the faint pulsing of her phone on vibrate.

She pulled the phone out of her jacket with trembling fingers. "I don't want to answer it."

"But you should. We need to know what the caller wants if we're going to keep you safe. Remember the police are tracing your calls."

"You answer it then." She held the phone out to him. Thomas pressed the screen to answer the call.

"Hello."

The line went dead.

Chapter Nine

"You think it was the same person that called before?"
Darcy asked later that evening, as she drank a cup of
tea with Thomas and Nana while waiting for Abigail.
Nana had brewed it to help calm her nerves, but so far
the tea had done little to help her mind settle.

Thomas shrugged. "I don't know but whoever it was
didn't want to talk to me."

Maybe, Darcy thought, unsure whether or not she
should be grateful that the call had ended before it had
really begun. On the one hand, they needed all the information they could get. But on the other hand, she
couldn't take hearing that horrible distorted voice again.

"I'm sure Abigail will be along any minute now,"
said Thomas. "Where are you planning to stay tonight?"

"You can stay in *Dawdi* house with me," offered
Nana.

Darcy's eyes shot over to Thomas. By the way he
was looking at his grandmother, she guessed he wasn't
too keen on that idea. Neither was she.

"I need a change of clothes, so I thought first I'd drive

home," she said, hoping that would be good enough for Nana. But it wasn't.

"Well, you can't do that all by yourself," Nana said. "If these men know who you are, they might know where you live. Thomas, you'll have to go with her. And then if you're not going to stay with us or with Abigail, then you'll just have to spend the night with the Millers."

"Or at the B and B," Thomas offered. "And I'd be mighty obliged if after we gather your things at your home, you would drive me to the hospital. I would like to visit with Uncle Jesse for a bit."

While Darcy turned the idea over in her mind, Thomas stood and walked to the back door. "Here's Abigail now," he said, "and another car following her."

Darcy turned and glanced out the window behind her. "That's my car. I thought she was going to take me to it, not bring it to me?"

A few seconds later, Blake and Abigail walked through the back door.

"I hope you don't mind," Abigail explained. "The car was ready early so Blake and I went on a lunch date to pick it up, went back to the hospital and finished our shifts, then thought we might as well just bring it straight to you."

"Thank you," Darcy said, taking the key from Abigail.

"We also wanted to offer for you to spend the night again."

"Oh, thank you. You're so kind, but I need to get some of my belongings from home. We were just talking about the B and B. I'll probably stay there."

Abigail and Blake stayed and chatted for a few minutes. Darcy thought they paid particular attention to her, probably trying to get a feel for whether or not she could drive. She must have passed the test, because they took their leave and said they hoped to see her soon at the hospital when she comes to visit Jesse. Darcy liked that it didn't seem like a goodbye. Even though she knew that once she called Agent Danvers back, it very well could be.

Thomas turned to her as soon as the couple had left. "If you're ready, I'm ready."

Darcy nodded. "Then let's get going."

Thomas followed her out to the car.

"Would you like to drive?" she offered.

"I can't."

"Sure you can. You'll like it," she said. "It's a zippy little thing."

"No. Really, I can't. I don't have a license."

"Oh." Darcy climbed into the driver's seat. He scooted in beside her on the passenger side. He was so big he filled in the whole space. He carried Jesse's Bible.

"I thought we'd finally take it to the hospital to read to Jesse."

"Good idea." She took it from his hands and placed it behind the seat with her other things. "I've been thinking about what you said."

He lifted his shoulders. "About what?"

"About Jesse giving me information," she explained. "I was thinking when I get home I'll grab the letters Jesse wrote to me. I figure it can't hurt to look at them again. Right?"

"*Ja.* You should. But, Darcy, you don't plan to stay there, do you?"

"At my town house? No. Not after being attacked.

Your grandmother is right that it would be easy for them to figure out where I live. I like the idea of the bed-and-breakfast. You think they'll have a room available?"

"One way to find out."

Darcy called as they drove out toward the highway and made a reservation.

After that, the drive seemed to go by in a blur. Darcy was tired and her head ached. It was a relief to arrive at their destination. She parked right in front of the town house. It seemed unusually dark. She exhaled slowly. *Home. Finally.*

She collected her purse and started to climb out of the car. "You coming?" she asked Thomas.

Thomas lifted his flip phone from his pocket, which had just started ringing. "I'll be right there."

She gathered up her things from the backseat and made her way up the narrow walk. She clutched at her unzipped coat as the wind whipped through the town house complex. Stepping onto her stoop, she held out her keys to unlock the front door. It was so dark, she could barely see to insert the key into the lock. Squinting at the doorknob, she stumbled forward. Her shoulder brushed against the door and it swung wide open.

Darcy gasped. She straightened herself and grabbed onto the door frame for balance, but she slipped. Her head pounded, as did her pulse. Never in a million years would she have left her town house unlocked. Someone had been inside her home.

"Hi. I was hoping to hear from you," Thomas said into his old flip phone as Darcy walked up to the front of her town house.

"I just heard from my friend at the Bureau, Agent Ross," Elijah said.

"Anything helpful?"

"I think so… Agent Ross was able to get access to sealed courtroom records. He found out that the man who testified against Wissenberg was named Michael Finlay. And he was a curator at the Gregorian Museum in Washington."

"Now that we know Jesse's real name," Thomas said, "does that help us know what these people are after?"

"To a certain extent. Wissenberg had a huge operation going. He stole art from private collectors around the world. Being the director of such a prestigious museum, he would easily get invitations into people's homes. His team would study and copy the works. In many cases, they bribed the owners' own cleaning staff or housekeepers to replace the original for the copies. It was sometimes months before an owner would realize he'd been robbed. Plus, Wissenberg took his time. He'd sometimes wait a year before executing a theft. It took a private art-insurance company doing years of legwork to even have a clue about what was happening, or how it was all connected. Wissenberg was so well-known and his work at the museum was so well respected that no one could believe it at first."

"Do you know how Jesse played into it?"

"Yes, in addition to working as curator, he was a talented artist himself—and he knew plenty of other painters willing to create forgeries for the right price. He recruited the team of artists who often made the reproductions. Very good reproductions," Elijah explained.

"Do you think Jesse knew what his artists were doing?" Thomas dropped his head into his hands.

"He knew about the forgeries, but I don't believe he was willing to be complicit in anything more physically harmful. After Wissenberg shot that night guard right in front of him, Jesse went to the authorities and agreed to testify against him. Jesse admitted to his own role in the fraud and thefts, but charges were dropped in exchange for his testimony. Reports indicate that Wissenberg possibly threatened him. The day before the trial, he and his wife were in a suspicious car accident. Margaret Finlay was killed instantly, although it's more likely that Michael—Jesse—was the real target."

"To keep him from testifying," Thomas said.

"Yes."

"But he testified anyway. And now Wissenberg is after him for revenge," Thomas said, still trying to make sense of it all. "But how does that explain the threats?"

"That's where it gets more complicated," Elijah admitted. "Apparently the system was that Wissenberg would pick the targets, commission the forgeries and then resell the originals, but the actual theft was handled by Jesse, working with whomever they had bribed inside the house. He'd take the frame off the original painting and replace it on the fake, then rehang it—he was the one with the experience and training to make the swap virtually undetectable. And then later, he'd turn the original paintings over to Wissenberg to resell. Wissenberg was the type to want to keep his hands clean—he was never actually there for the theft itself… except for one time."

"The night he shot the security guard," Thomas said, realizing what had happened.

"That's right. Apparently, it was a special commission— he had a buyer lined up who didn't want to wait. So

Wissenberg went along so that he could deliver the painting directly to his buyer afterward. He wasn't as used to slipping in unnoticed as Jesse, though, and the security guard caught them. You know what happened from there."

"But what does that have to do with the threats?" Thomas asked again.

"The authorities were able to track most of the trafficked paintings, but Ross also found out that quite a few of the stolen originals were never recovered. There was some suspicion that Jesse had them, and never gave them to Wissenberg or the authorities."

"So Wissenberg thinks Jesse still has them." Thomas closed his eyes. "How much artwork are we talking about?"

"Ten million dollars' worth."

Thomas shook his head. He was about to reply when he heard a scream come from the still-dark town house.

Darcy!

Chapter Ten

"Elijah, I'll call you back."

Thomas folded himself out of the small car and tossed his phone onto the seat as he raced to the town house's entrance. "Darcy? Are you okay?"

The front door was wide open and inside was nothing but darkness. Thomas stumbled over the threshold. "Darcy?"

A scuffling of feet sounded from the back of the home and then there was silence. Thomas lunged forward, tripping over a mass in the middle of the floor. When he heard the whimpering noise below him, he realized it was Darcy. He spread his arms out over her to keep from landing on top of her.

"Someone's here," she whispered.

"I think they just left. Are you okay?"

"Yes, I was just knocked down." Her voice sounded weak.

"Where's the light switch?"

"It wasn't working when I came in. They might have flipped the breakers, which are in the kitchen. All the way to the back," she said. "Take my phone. It has a flashlight."

Thomas groped around for her bag. "This is your bag, but it's empty."

"I guess whoever was here dumped it all out. Took something and ran."

Thomas felt around the floor and finally wrapped his hands around her fancy smartphone. "How do I—"

"Swipe up," she told him.

The bright flashlight illuminated the small entryway. Using its light, Thomas first checked Darcy. He slid his free arm under her shoulder and lifted her from the floor. She clung to him. He wanted to pull her tighter and take away all her pain and fear. He was starting now to understand her anger. She hadn't asked for any of this. She hadn't done anything to bring this threat to her doorstep. And yet, here was this horrible danger. And it was sounding more and more like Jesse was to blame for it.

"Here. Let's get you to a more comfortable place," he said.

"There's a couch. This way," she said, directing him.

He placed her down gently. "Whoever was here is gone now. But I'm sorry I didn't walk in with you—"

"Don't be," she interrupted. "You were here when I needed you. That's what matters."

When she looked up at him with eyes of thankfulness, his heart melted. She was so beautiful. So strong and yet so vulnerable. He tore his eyes away. "I'll go get that breaker."

He followed her directions to the kitchen, making his way around strangely placed items and furniture. He flipped the switch and the home lit up with soft lighting throughout, revealing a scene of absolute devastation. Ransacked. He made his way back to Darcy, who was already tearing up. "I'm calling the police now."

Darcy pulled herself up to a sitting position and swung her legs back around to the floor. Her home looked like a wreckage site. Chairs had been toppled over, drawers opened and emptied on the floor, the contents of closets strewn about. She could barely process it all. Thankfully, Thomas had known what to do. He had called the police and was talking to them now. He'd also called Elijah, who was on his way.

"Did you see who did this?" one of the officers asked Thomas.

"No. I could hear the intruder leaving by the time I came in."

"And you, Miss Simmons? Can you describe the intruder?"

Darcy shook her head. "No. He was behind me and it was very dark. But it didn't seem like he was alone. I think one of them had a gun to my neck."

"And they left through the back door?"

"Yes."

Darcy was growing tired. It was exhausting to have to answer questions about everything all over again. Thomas tried to intercept as many of the questions as he could. She was thankful for that.

"Miss Simmons, we are almost finished here, but since you've been part of the witness relocation program, you'll have to wait for an agent from the US Marshals to arrive. They'll take care of you."

Darcy swallowed hard. She didn't want to be taken care of. It seemed like the words were hardly out of the officer's mouth before Agent Danvers was standing at her door.

Just like at the hospital, she came blustering in, taking over the questioning and ordering the local authorities around. Darcy almost felt sorry for them except that at least the agent's attention was focused on them and what they were doing in her home, instead of on badgering or pressuring her.

"Elijah should be here soon. Blake is bringing him," Thomas whispered to her. "They will take us back to Willow Trace."

"You think their offer to stay at the clinic still stands?" She looked over at him. What would she have done through all of this without him?

"For sure." Nodding, he smiled and the warmth in his expression spread all the way to her own lips, which she felt curl up into a grin.

She reached over and touched her hand to his. "Thank you. Thank you for all you've done. You and all of your friends."

"The police are wondering what has been taken from your house. They want you to look around but I told them you couldn't."

"Darcy," Agent Danvers said as she came up behind them. "Did your father give you anything? Did he tell you about your past or about his past? Did he ask you to do anything for him?"

"You've already asked her that." Thomas stood and turned to face her.

Danvers took a step back. Darcy didn't blame her. Thomas was physically intimidating, even to someone as tall and fit as she was.

"Mr. Nolt, I appreciate your…help. But I am going to need to get Miss Simmons to a secure facility."

A secure facility? Darcy had been scared before, but it was nothing compared to the panic that rushed through her now. *What is this lady saying? A new identity?* Not yet. She wasn't ready for that. Darcy dropped her head between her hands. The pain seemed to triple. "Right now? I thought I had more time."

"Miss Simmons, surely this proves that you're not safe. You need to leave with me. The sooner the better. I was trying to give you more time, but…well, it's clearly too dangerous."

"You don't have to go with her," Thomas whispered to Darcy.

Darcy shut her eyes tight. If she could have, she would have willed herself to disappear off the sofa and escape all of this. But wasn't that what Agent Danvers was offering? So why not just go with her?

Thomas was glad to see Elijah and Blake pulling up behind the police cars in the complex's parking lot. He hoped they could help convince Darcy not to go with Agent Danvers. Not now that they knew what Wissenberg was after. There was hope that they could get this figured out and everyone would be safe. Both Jesse and Darcy. Without anyone needing to start his or her life over. At least, it was worth a try. Maybe they needed to search Jesse's cottage again. Maybe they needed to look at the letters Jesse had sent Darcy. But there were clues to follow—things they could do. He didn't want her to go. What would he tell Jesse when he woke up if he had let his friend's daughter walk away forever?

Thomas hated seeing Darcy struggle so with the decision. He supposed Danvers was doing her job, but she was such a bully. And he was certain that Blake and Abigail could keep Darcy safe for at least one more night. Thomas filled in his friends on what had happened and why Danvers was there.

"Well, I know how to put a stop to that," said Blake. He stepped away and headed straight to the US Marshal.

"She's in shock," Blake declared. "You can't expect her to make a life-altering decision like this in her condition."

"This is exactly how these decisions are made," the agent insisted. "If everything was all hunky-dory they wouldn't need to be in the program."

"She has a head injury and is under my care," said Blake. "I will not release her over to any agency until she's had further treatment and an exam."

If Blake was bluffing, Thomas thought, he was doing a pretty good job of it. Thomas hoped it would work. He at least wanted to have the chance to tell her what Elijah had learned. She would want to know.

"And you are?" Agent Danvers lifted an eyebrow.

"Dr. Jamison, head of ER at Lancaster General," Blake said.

"I thought Miss Simmons was released yesterday after I met with her," she said.

"That is correct. However, we are waiting for some of the swelling to go down before doing a second exam," Blake said.

"So you're taking her back to Lancaster?"

"Yes," said Blake.

Danvers sighed and dropped her arms to her sides. She turned to Darcy. "Then I'll expect a call from you as soon as this exam is over. I'll pick you up at the hospital."

Darcy did not respond. She actually did look like she was in shock. Perhaps Blake's words had been the truth.

Danvers took her leave in a mad rush. Her frustration seemed to be oozing from her hard glare at Thomas and his friends as she walked out. Thomas was not sorry she was leaving alone. Darcy didn't belong with her. That he was sure of.

"I'm glad you got here when you did," Darcy said. "Maybe I should go with her, but—"

"No. You shouldn't. Not today, at least," Elijah said.

"You have a better idea?" she asked, lifting a hand to her head.

Thomas smiled. His friend Elijah always had a better idea.

"Okay. Okay," Blake said. "Clearly there are things we all need to discuss. But first let's get Darcy some fluids. And by the looks of it, some pain meds."

The medication Blake administered started to take the edge off her pain. Darcy was able to stand and gather a few personal belongings. She was so thankful she had stayed behind. Saved once again by her three musketeers of Willow Trace. They had even straightened up her town house a little. And she'd learned what Wissenberg was after and why. She even knew Jesse's former name now. Finlay. Michael Finlay. And her mother had been Margaret Finlay. That would have been her last name, too. Not Simmons. She wondered what her own first name had been.

"Do you think anything is missing?" Thomas queried as he walked into her room. "I know you've been asked that a million times tonight, but Elijah says it's really important and I figured maybe now you've had a chance to look around."

"It's a mess, but I don't really notice that anything is gone. Certainly not any of the things a thief would usually target, like my computer or TV." Darcy blinked and concentrated on his question. "But you're asking about the things that Jesse gave me?"

He shrugged. "You were going to look for the letters."

"Right." She reached around her neck. The locket was still there. "The letters would be in the front hall. I kept them in a basket."

He followed her to the foyer. The basket had been toppled. Some of its contents were on the floor. But no letters. Darcy crouched and looked around.

"Allow me." Thomas swept the floor with his big arms. He pulled up a few bills, some junk mail and a magazine. But none of Jesse's letters.

She opened the drawer to the console table. Empty.

"They're gone. All of the letters Jesse wrote to me are gone."

Chapter Eleven

Darcy slept all the way back to Lancaster County. Thomas was glad for that. After what she'd been through, she deserved the chance to rest a bit, surrounded by people who made her feel safe. He only hoped they wouldn't let her down.

Elijah was on and off the phone, talking to McClendon and to his agent friend at the FBI. The more Thomas overheard the conversations, the more he worried.

Elijah had suggested that Darcy leave both her phone and her car behind. There could be a tracking device on the car, to say nothing of the ways to trace an unencrypted phone. Darcy had readily agreed. Thomas had her cancel her reservation at the Willow Trace Bed-and-Breakfast. For this night, she would sleep again at the clinic. Blake truly did want to reexamine her head injury in the morning. It was a needed precaution after she'd fallen again. But after that, what would or should they do?

"Where are we?" she said, half waking up.

"Almost to the clinic," Thomas said.

Abigail came out to Blake's truck and helped to escort Darcy back to the guest room.

"She's changing," Abigail said, returning to the kitchen, where Thomas, Elijah and Blake sat discussing the evening.

"I'm glad she's safe," Thomas said.

"She wanted to know if she could visit Jesse tomorrow. I didn't know what to tell her," Abigail said.

"I don't know if she should go anywhere," Elijah said. "At least, not as Darcy Simmons."

"You think she should go with Agent Danvers, take on a new identity somewhere else?" Thomas felt his blood pressure rise. How could Elijah suggest such a thing?

"No. I don't," Elijah said.

That was a relief, Thomas thought. "So your solution is just to keep her inside until all of this is over?"

"No, I don't even know if that would be enough," Elijah admitted. "If Wissenberg was able to find Jesse and Darcy once, what's to stop him from finding her again? Staying home wasn't enough to protect Jesse."

"So, you have a better idea?" Abigail lifted her eyebrows at her brother.

Elijah grinned. "Of course I do. But I don't know if Darcy will agree to it."

"You want me to do what?" Darcy could feel her eyes practically popping out of their sockets. It seemed Elijah had come up with an interesting idea to keep her safe while she had been changing her clothes. He was now sharing the plan with all of them as they sat around Abigail's kitchen table. Darcy, stunned, had had to ask him to repeat it again.

"It's called hiding in plain sight," Elijah explained. "It's just for a few days."

"No. I can't do that," Darcy shook her head. She could not—would not—do what they were asking. "I've already depended on you way more than is fair to you. It's not your job to keep protecting me."

"Well, we kind of think it is," Thomas said. "It is for Jesse. You're his daughter after all."

"I don't know." Darcy tried to come up with a good alternative plan. But what could she do? Call Danvers? Stay with a friend in town and put them in danger? Stay in a hotel? Run away?

She didn't like any of those options, either.

"Do you really think it will hide me? These people know what I look like," she said. "They got a pretty good look at me at Jesse's yesterday."

"Yes, but in your *Englisch* clothes. In those you're pretty easy to identify. If you dress Amish, you will blend in with us. From a distance or in a crowd of other Amish, you'll be pretty tough to spot. They won't be looking for you in a frock. And like I said, it's just for a few days."

"What's going to change in a few days?"

"Hopefully Jesse will wake up," said Thomas. "And while we are waiting, we are going to comb through Jesse's cottage and find any and every clue we can. There could be something in his cottage from his past. Something besides pictures."

Darcy didn't like the idea of dressing Amish and staying with Elijah and Hannah, putting them in danger. In fact, she hated the idea. But she did not have a better one, and she could see the logic in the decision. Elijah was a former policeman, able to take care of himself and trained in providing protection. Hannah was aware of the danger and had agreed to this. Hiding with the Amish would let her stay close to Jesse and help search for answers while keeping her hidden.

"Okay, then," Darcy said. "I hope you're good at makeovers."

"I can't do this." Darcy leaned into Abigail's mirror. "Look at me. I look ridiculous. I *feel* ridiculous."

After a morning shower, Abigail had helped Darcy get into her Amish costume—blouse, frock and *kapp*. Her bandage was gone and with her hair parted straight down the middle, the stitches were barely visible.

Abigail smiled at her. "Actually, you make me a little homesick. I mean I didn't really leave home, but when I made the choice not to be baptized, I left that lifestyle behind. But before that, I'd dressed like that my whole life. You look like home to me. I think you look beautiful."

Darcy looked to Abigail with an apologetic frown. "I'm sorry. I didn't mean to—"

"No, no, no." Abigail walked over to her and tied her *kapp* in a loose bow, leaving the straps to hang to her chest.

She looked again at herself in the mirror. They were right. She would be hard to recognize. She wasn't even sure she recognized herself. "It feels like a costume."

"I understand. It's not what you're used to. But trust me, you look just fine. And this will keep you safe until my brother and Thomas work this all out."

"You sound pretty confident in their abilities." Darcy wanted to believe her, but she had little hope.

"You really think they can solve a mystery that has endured over two decades?"

"Anyone can if they look in the right places. There are always signs around us that lead to the truth."

"I hope you're right," Darcy said. "Okay, tell me what to do. What do I say when people talk to me?"

"Just be yourself. Remember, we are not people who ask a lot of questions."

"Right."

"And be useful, wherever you can," Abigail advised.

"But I can't cook. I know nothing about horses and farms. And I really know nothing about God."

Darcy knew she had just a few minutes before it was time to go to the Millers'.

Why was she so nervous? Everyone was there to help her through this. Still, she could feel her heart pounding and her palms sweating.

What if her presence brought harm to these good people? What if Jesse didn't wake up? What if she never discovered the truth and she would have to leave and start her life anew?

"God loves you, as He loves all of us. And when we do His will, we know Him. This will be a good time for you, Darcy. I am sure of it. We should go now."

Darcy closed her eyes. How was she going to get through this?

Abigail put her arm around Darcy's shoulder and began to lead her toward the front of the clinic. It was time to go.

"Don't worry. All will be well, Darcy."

At the designated time, Thomas drove his horse and buggy over to the clinic to pick up the Millers' new houseguest. Thomas had offered to pick her up since it seemed everyone else was busy. Elijah had business with his father. The women were all excited to show off their great cooking to Darcy. Nana had even gotten up early and headed to the market with the bishop's wife in order to get extra provisions for the evening meal. Thomas was glad that he and Nana had been invited to dinner, too. He wanted to keep an eye on Darcy as much as possible. He was very glad she'd decided to accept Elijah's plan and he was happy to drive her to the Millers'.

Thomas pulled Sadie up in front of the clinic and hitched her to the post. He paced across the front porch, sweating slightly despite the cold winter air. The morning sun peeked occasionally through a fluffy band of clouds headed north and east. The year's first snowfall would be upon them soon.

When Abigail appeared at the front door, Thomas wiped his palms against the front of his trousers. Darcy was standing behind her wearing one of Abigail's old dresses.

"I know," Darcy said. "I look so—so…"

"Plain." Thomas was careful not to stare but it was hard. It was strange to see her in plain clothing. He could only imagine how strange it must have felt to her.

"She worked on it all morning," Abigail said. "My clothes were way too big for her. She's pretty handy with a needle and thread."

"So I've already heard," Thomas said, daring to look up again at Darcy. She wore a dark gray frock that accented the color of her big eyes. Over the dress was a neatly pressed black apron. On her feet she wore a pair of old leather lace-up boots.

She laughed and pointed to her head. "I don't think I've parted my hair down the middle since I was in the first grade."

She hardly looked like a first grader, Thomas thought. "It suits you. Not a trace of *Englisch* about you now."

Darcy looked desperately to Abigail. "What? What does that mean?"

"*Englisch* are what the Amish call everyone who's not Amish." Abigail showed Thomas to Darcy's bag before giving Darcy a reassuring hug. "Just relax and enjoy your time with the Millers."

Darcy flushed. The creaminess of her complexion highlighted her dark eyes and high cheekbones more than any store-bought makeup could have. He swallowed hard and looked away, while Darcy thanked Abigail for her help.

"Remember, Thomas, she still needs to take it easy," Abigail said, then looked to Darcy. "If you get the least bit dizzy, stop what you're doing and give me a call."

Darcy nodded.

Abigail gave her one more reassuring glance then waved goodbye from the front porch.

"Well, then," he said. "I suppose we should get going. Hannah is anxious to see you."

She followed him out to the vehicle. He gave her a hand into the front seat. "My first time in a horse-drawn buggy."

"It's a little chilly today," he noted as he untied Sadie and climbed into the driver's seat. "You're gonna want this blanket." He reached into the back and handed her the thick wool coverlet that he kept there for the cold days.

He gave Sadie a tap with the reins and the mare took off onto the highway. Darcy was quiet at first, fidgeting with her hands. Then she tucked the blanket around herself tighter.

"You weren't kidding," she said as she shivered. "It's cold."

Thomas passed the reins to her. "Here. Take them."

"What? I don't—"

"One second. Just hold them."

Reluctantly, she took the long leather straps into her hands.

Thomas waited another second, then he took off his coat and placed it around Darcy's shoulders.

He wasn't sure, but he thought he saw a few tears in her eyes.

"Thank you. Thank you for everything you're doing for me."

Thomas took the reins back into his left hand. Then he took his right arm and placed it around Darcy's torso. He pulled her next to him on the bench.

"This way I can stay warm, too," he said, but that wasn't the only reason he wanted her close.

Darcy was the one to protect, but Thomas knew if he wasn't careful with his heart, he was going to be in more danger than Darcy. Just a different sort of danger.

Chapter Twelve

It was a whole other perspective of the Amish country-
side, seeing it from inside Thomas's buggy. The *clippity-
clop* of the horse's beat. The cold air. The smell of the
outdoors, fresh and wild and clean. And Thomas, so close
beside her. Darcy watched him tap the reins on the back
of his horse. "What's he like?"

"Who? Jesse?" Thomas asked.

"Yes, I mean more like what does he do? What did
he do for a living?" she said.

"Well, when he first came here, he secured a job at
Millers' Furniture immediately."

"As in Elijah Miller?"

"His father, the bishop, owns an Amish furniture-
making business."

"What did Jesse do there?"

"He made and designed furniture."

Darcy swallowed hard. Her father was so interesting
and it was fascinating to discover that she shared some
of his interests. She loved art and design. *He* loved art
and design. Maybe it was a silly thing to cling to. But
she'd lived her whole life knowing nothing, so now

every little thing she heard, she couldn't help but try to relate to herself in some way.

"Yes. He was really good at it. He made all of the furniture in his cottage," Thomas said.

"It's beautiful. He must have done well."

"He did but he quit and went to work for my father after a while," Thomas said.

"Why?"

"He got a little too creative. He varied too much from the traditional Amish style. Too much detail. Too fancy. So Bishop Miller couldn't sell what he made in his store. Jesse considered selling through other vendors, but being a part of the community was more important to him than his gifts and skill with wood. So he apprenticed as a farrier with my father and he became one of the best in the county."

"My dad worked with horses?"

"Yes, still does. He stays busy, too. All the Amish buggy horses have shoes."

"It's a shame about the letters," she said.

"Well, at least you still have your locket."

"Yes, Abigail said it would be okay to wear it as long as I keep it under the dress."

He nodded. "You know… Jesse's going to wake up."

"How do you know?" He seemed so sure.

"I don't. I just hope and I pray."

"And God answers your prayers?"

"Always. It's not always the answer I was hoping for. Sometimes it's even better." Thomas cleared his throat. "Do you think there was anything in the letters that could be useful? Can you remember?"

"I don't think so." Darcy thought hard, trying to remember the contents. "But I was so overwhelmed by the whole idea of having a father who was alive that I might have missed something."

Thomas took off his hat and ran his hand through his dark curls. "I have a hard time believing that Jesse would have done anything purposely to put you in harm's way. Most likely, he had no idea that Wissenberg was going to get out of prison so soon."

"Do you think it's possible that Jesse really has millions of dollars' worth of stolen artwork hidden away somewhere?"

"I don't want to believe it," Thomas said. "But all these attacks would seem to prove that Wissenberg is convinced."

Darcy hated that. She hated thinking that her dad was a selfish crook, hiding away art instead of returning it to the rightful owners.

"Do you think it's worth going back over to the cottage to see if anything is there that the police didn't find?"

"I don't know. Maybe." Thomas looked up. "That's the Miller house up ahead."

A gray farmhouse came into view. Unlike Thomas's home, the stable was a long distance from the house and much smaller. Hannah met her at the door holding a six- to nine-month-old baby boy in her arms.

"Where was this fellow the other day?" Darcy asked.

"With my mother-in-law," Hannah said. "Please come in and let me show you to your room. I've been instructed that you need a lot of rest."

Darcy nodded. She had to admit she was tired. She said goodbye to Thomas and followed Hannah through the house. It was an old place, with low ceilings and tiny rooms. "This house must have been built before the Civil War."

"Before the Revolutionary War." Hannah laughed. "It's been in the Miller family for a long time."

"It's charming," Darcy said. And it was, in its own way. The Miller family had done well to preserve the old wood and trim. And it was surprisingly warm.

"You'll be in here." Hannah showed her a small bedroom that had little more in it than a single bed, a wooden table with a lantern and a chair. "Please rest up and I'll call you for lunch."

Darcy went inside. Hannah closed the door behind her. As grateful as she was for a safe place to stay, a big part of her wanted to put her own clothes back on and reclaim her life. But that wasn't an option just now, so she gave in to her other temptation. She lay down and slept.

Thomas hoped Darcy would get some rest. He knew Hannah would take good care of her, as would Elijah and the bishop. So why did he not like leaving? He would be back for dinner, he reminded himself.

As Sadie trotted thought the forest, Thomas couldn't help but think about the drive over to the Millers'. In fact, he thought over everything that had transpired recently. To think that it was just several days ago when he was riding to Jesse's to take a look at his well. It seemed like decades had passed.

Jesse's well. Come to think of it, he never had taken a look at it. He would have to do that before Jesse came back home from the hospital. Just thinking of Jesse filled Thomas with a powerful urge to see his friend. Thomas had chores to do but nothing that couldn't wait.

Instead of driving Sadie back home, he went to the hospital and sat with Jesse. He'd been there for a few minutes when the quiet was interrupted by a voice from the doorway.

"So where is she?"

Thomas turned around to find Agent Danvers. She was wearing the same dark US Marshals coat and sporting the same spiky hairdo. "Where is who? Miss Simmons?"

"Yes, Miss Simmons." The agent crossed her arms over her chest and widened her stance. "Who else?"

"Why would you think I might know where Miss Simmons is?" He turned his back to her and looked down at Jesse, lying there helpless in the hospital bed.

"The two of you have seemed inseparable," Danvers snarled.

"She's not with me now," Thomas answered.

"I know you know where she is," Danvers accused as she stepped into the room.

Thomas struggled to control his temper. He really didn't like this woman. "I do know where she is. And I know that she is safe. That's all you need to know, as well."

Thomas stood. He turned around and headed out of the small room, forcing the agent to move backward.

"I'll just follow you," she said, as he walked past.

"It's a free country," Thomas replied over his shoulder as he walked on.

"You can't keep her safe, farmer boy," she yelled after him.

Turn the other cheek. Turn the other cheek, Thomas repeated in his mind. Danvers's behavior had crossed the line. But he walked on in silence. In a way, he hoped she did follow him. He was headed straight to Jesse's cottage and if she trailed him there, he would call Chief McClendon and whoever else he needed to put an end to her bullying.

Still, as he left the hospital, her words rang over and over through his head. Mostly because he feared that she was right.

He couldn't keep her safe. He was just a farmer.

Thomas drove his buggy down the highway, more determined than ever to help Darcy and Jesse. He reached for his phone.

"How is she?" he asked Elijah.

"She's been sleeping all day," his friend said. "Hannah's been checking on her regularly. She took her some stew for lunch. She's fine."

"I saw Danvers at the hospital. She threatened to follow me. She wants Darcy."

Elijah was silent for a moment. "Where are you now?"

"I'm heading home, but I'm going to stop by Uncle Jesse's first. It looks like snow and I just want to at least turn off his water so that he doesn't come home to a burst pipe."

"I'll meet you there. You shouldn't go there alone."

"I'll be fine. You stay with Darcy. I'll see you at dinner."

Thomas felt exposed as he pulled up to Jesse's cottage. But he reminded himself that Darcy was safely tucked away at the Millers' and that he was just there to turn off the water and take a peek at the well.

He parked his buggy at the house. As the wind whipped across the open hills, Thomas pulled his coat collar up around his neck. It was definitely going to freeze tonight. He walked around to the back of the building, removed the side panel, which led to under the house, reached in and turned off the main.

Sadie whinnied and snorted at the front of the house. Was someone there? Thomas's thoughts flashed back to the past few days. Maybe Elijah was right. He shouldn't have come there alone.

No. Thomas shook away his fear. *If the Lord is for us then who can be against us? Romans 8:31*

Thomas scanned the fields. He saw nothing but he distinctly felt as if someone was nearby. Someone was watching him. Had Agent Danvers really followed him? Or was he just being paranoid?

He headed to the well. He slid off the lid and looked down inside. Everything seemed to be in order. Thomas was ready to slide the lid back over when his eyes spotted a little box attached to the inside wall.

What was that?

Thomas reached inside and unhitched the box. He tried to open it but the little box was locked. Thomas took it back to the buggy and headed home. Whatever was in the little chest was sealed up tight. Maybe he could open it later with tools.

Was this what Jesse had called him over for? Did Jesse know it was there? Did it have anything to do with Wissenberg and the missing art?

Thomas didn't know, but as the buggy entered the woods, he was sure that someone was watching him.

Chapter Thirteen

"Darcy?"

There was knocking. Someone was at the door. But Darcy could barely focus. Her head was clouded with sleep.

"Darcy? Time for supper. Everyone is here."

What? Supper?

The voice had an accent that was both strange and familiar. Where was she? Darcy blinked her eyes open. She was enveloped in darkness. What time was is? She sat up. This was not her bed.

"Darcy? Are you awake?"

It was Hannah. She was at the Millers' home. In the middle of Amish country. Dressed like she was Amish. She put a hand to her head. Her hair was still pulled tight at the base of her neck.

"Yes, I'm awake. Barely." She swung her feet around to the floor.

"Let me come in and light the lantern for you," Hannah offered.

The auburn-haired Amish woman floated across the

old wooden floor and grabbed something off the table. Soon the tiny room filled with a soft yellow glow.

"To the left is the bathroom," she said. "If you'd like to wash up before dinner."

She turned back to the door but paused before leaving. "Darcy? Are you okay?"

Was she okay?

"I'm fine. I'm just a little disoriented," Darcy said. "You know how it is after a deep sleep."

Hannah nodded. "Thomas is here. He has something for you."

Darcy rubbed her eyes, still foggy from sleep. Thomas. She'd dreamed of him—of his brown eyes and his wide smile. She'd dreamed of his soft, deep voice and the weight of his arm around her shoulder. *He had something for her?*

Darcy shook her head. She was awake now and remembering everything that had happened over the past few days. She hoped whatever Thomas had was what they needed to end all of this, so that she could go home. She needed to get out of here. Back to her life. Back into her clothes. And away from Thomas and his big brown eyes. Thomas could never be interested in someone *Englisch*. And she shouldn't be interested in someone Amish. She didn't even know how to pray. How could she fall for a person whose whole life revolved around faith? How could that ever work?

It couldn't.

"It was in Jesse's well." Thomas handed the small wooden box to Darcy. He had stayed behind with her in the Millers' kitchen so that he could give it to her without so many others around. He had no idea what was inside. Maybe nothing of importance. But the more he had thought about it, the more Thomas had decided that it might not have been a coincidence that Jesse had asked him to come over "to look at the well" at the same time as he'd been expecting Darcy.

Then again, he was probably just overthinking it all in the hope that he would find answers.

"It's a nice box." She took it from his hands. "You found it inside Jesse's well?"

"*Ja.* I just went by there to turn off the water so the pipes don't freeze tonight and I remembered that the day I met you, he had asked me to come look at the well. So I thought I might as well have a look at it. And I found this."

"It looks handmade." She turned the box over in her hands, touching the complicated pattern of inlays.

"I'm sure Jesse made it."

"It's beautiful, but why did you bring it to me?"

Why had he brought it to her? Thomas felt heat rise to his cheeks. "I started to open it at home with tools, but I knew that might ruin it. And I wanted you to see it before that, since we had been talking about his craftsmanship."

But that wasn't the only reason why he'd waited. It had also been an excuse to spend a moment with Darcy. An excuse to speak with her again. "Plus, it just seemed wrong to open it up without you."

"Speaking of opening it," she said. "How are we going to do that? It's locked up. Looks like it needs a key."

Thomas took the box back from her, his hand lingering maybe a moment too long as his fingers grazed over hers in the exchange.

"See these inlays?"

She nodded.

"These are the reason that Jesse's furniture could not be sold as Amish."

Thomas turned the box over in his hands, touching each one of the inlays. "Once Jesse told me that fancy things were just a way for the *Englisch* to hide the real truth in their life."

He used his fingernail to pry at each of the inlays. One of the pieces popped out with ease.

Darcy picked up the block of polished wood and turned it over. Inside was a tiny key.

"You do the honors, please," Thomas said.

"Okay." She smiled and placed the key delicately into the box lock. It opened on the first try. Slowly, Darcy lifted the lid.

"It's pictures. Old Polaroids."

Thomas put the box down on the table and held the lid back. Darcy reached in and pulled out the stack of photos.

"Oh, my," she said, turning through them one after the other. "They're pictures of paintings. Really nice paintings."

"There's something written on the back of each photo, too."

She flipped the pictures over one at a time. "Phelps. Thurston. Davies. Beauchamps. Geigenhaus…"

"Could those be the names of the artists?" Thomas mused.

"I don't know." She shook her head back and forth, her eyes wide with excitement. "But are you thinking what I'm thinking?"

Thomas nodded. "That this could be the missing art everyone is hoping to find…or at least pictures of it."

"Exactly!" Darcy stared up at him. "I don't know whether to be happy or sad at finding this."

Thomas wanted to hug her and comfort her through the disappointment she was feeling in finding yet another clue that shed more suspicion over Jesse. He felt it, too. "I think we can be thankful for more information. In any case, we don't know what these mean. Not yet anyway."

She nodded. "I guess we should call the police. Again."

After dinner, Chief McClendon and another man named Agent Frank Ross of the FBI sat with Thomas, Elijah and Darcy at the Millers' kitchen table. The FBI agent was a small man in his late forties, dressed informally in jeans, a T-shirt and a big blue jacket that said FBI in huge yellow letters. He looked at each of the pictures quickly then scanned them into a tiny handheld scanner, which was hooked up to his laptop.

After each photo he was able to quickly identify the painting. "This is *Sunny Day* by the artist Florence Ko. Stolen from Mrs. Deveraux of McClain, Virginia, twenty-five years ago. Never recovered."

"*Deveraux* is the name written on the back of the photo," Darcy said.

Elijah stood from the table and began to pace. "There are fifteen photos. Fifteen stolen paintings. None of them were ever recovered. Jesse clearly had them in his possession at one point, and kept a record of them all. But why?"

Thomas fidgeted with the empty box that had contained the photos. He hated how guilty all this made Jesse seem. Why had he had these paintings? Why had he kept pictures of them? And why had he asked him to come and look at the well? Jesse would have known that Thomas would have spotted the box. Jesse must have wanted him to find it or to retrieve it for him. But why?

The FBI agent pushed his equipment aside and cleared his throat. "The good news is that the statute of limitations would be in effect for all of this stolen property. So Jesse cannot be tried for possession of these, if indeed he does have the actual works. But honestly, there is no evidence of that here. It seems likely that he took these pictures a long time ago, and that the artwork was in his possession when he did so, but we can't know that for sure. It doesn't mean he has the paintings now. These photos don't prove anything except that Jesse knew whom the artwork was stolen from."

"And why would a thief care about that?" McClendon asked, his voice dripping with sarcasm.

Jesse was far more than just a thief, Thomas thought to himself. Thomas refused to believe that until the day that Jesse told him otherwise. Maybe he was blinded by his love for the old man. But better that than thinking so single-mindedly.

"He wanted to remember who the works belonged to," Thomas said. "You're right. I wouldn't think your everyday thief would care about knowing that. In fact, he'd probably want to forget whom he stole from. But Jesse wanted to remember, because…"

"Because he wanted to return them?" Darcy suggested hopefully.

Thomas looked across the table at her and smiled. She didn't want to think badly of her father, either.

"That's really irrelevant," Elijah said. "What we need to know is where Jesse put the actual paintings. Did he pass them on to another party? Maybe he sold them?"

"First thing tomorrow, I'm sending a small investigative team to Jesse's cottage," said Agent Ross.

"We've already had a team there," said McClendon.

"Yes, but they were investigating a break-in and a beating," said Elijah. "Agent Ross is right. We have a lot more information now. A new search will be much more focused."

"Could Elijah and I be there?" asked Thomas.

"Me, too?" said Darcy.

"Is that a good idea?" Thomas said. "I mean, is that safe?"

Agent Ross collected his things from the table. "I can't think of a safer place for her to be than surrounded by a crew of FBI agents. Right?"

Right. But why did Thomas still feel like it was a bad idea? He kept his mouth closed. Darcy looked happier than she had all evening.

"Okay, see you bright and early tomorrow." Agent Ross took his leave.

McClendon followed.

Thomas called Nana and they, too, headed out into the night to make their way home.

Again, he felt as if someone was watching him.

You can't keep her safe, farmer boy.

Chapter Fourteen

The new search at Jesse's had turned up nothing. And to make matters worse, Blake had called with the news that Jesse's stats had taken a slight turn for the worse.

The Elders would soon have to decide how long they would keep Jesse on life support.

"What will happen to all of this beautiful furniture if Jesse…" Darcy looked around at the cottage and all the pieces inside it that her father had made.

Thomas swallowed hard. "If Jesse passes? Normally it would all be auctioned or go to families in need, but I suppose now it could all go to you. You'd have to speak with the Elders about that. They make those sorts of decisions. But, Darcy, Jesse may pull through yet. Have a little faith."

Elijah came into the room. "The FBI team is heading out. And I have to go, as well. My father called and he needs help with a delivery. Thomas, is Nana still hosting that barn singing tonight?"

"*Ja*. As far as I know," Thomas answered.

"Barn singing?" Darcy asked. "What's that?"

"It's a social meeting for the young folk," Thomas

said to Darcy then turned to Elijah. "You're coming, aren't you?"

"Of course, I think my dad still has the buggy with all the benches so we will be there early. Though that's a lot of buggy riding for Miss Simmons—riding all the way home with me now and then heading back this way later."

"Darcy can come spend the afternoon with us," Thomas offered. "Stay for the singing and ride home with you and Hannah? If that's okay with her?"

"Sure," she said.

Darcy was actually relieved. She liked the Millers and was more than grateful for their hospitality, but she felt like an imposition. She should probably feel that way about going to the Nolts' home, but with Thomas and Nana, it just didn't seem as awkward.

"Okay, then. We will see you later. I'm sorry this didn't pan out today, Darcy. But we just have to keep thinking." Elijah turned and was gone.

The house cleared out quickly, leaving Darcy and Thomas alone to close up.

"We should get going," Thomas said. "Nana is going to love having you over today. And there will be a lot to do to get ready for the singing."

"And what about you?" she asked. "I hope you don't mind my being there. Elijah didn't really leave you much of a choice."

Thomas grinned slightly, but he wouldn't look up to meet her eye. "You will always be welcome in my home, Darcy."

"Thank you but I don't think I'll be much help to either you or Nana. I don't sing."

Thomas burst out laughing. Darcy felt heat rise to her cheeks.

"We won't be singing," he said. "Only the youth. It's really more of a social thing. But there is lots of food to prepare. And a little extra work to do in the stable."

"Sounds like I can pitch in. And it is the least I can do after all the help you and your friends have given me," she said.

"You know I'm really sorry we didn't find anything else here today," he said. "I just thought that if Jesse left those photographs behind then he probably left something else."

"You're right. We just have to stay focused." Darcy looked around the cottage at all of Jesse's belongings. Thomas had been right about the furniture designs not quite being suitable for the Amish. They were in the same style as the ones in his home and in the Millers' home, but the extra flourishes meant they did not exactly fit. All of the pieces had inlays like the box Thomas had found in the well. An idea occurred to her.

"Thomas, does the FBI know that Jesse used to make furniture?"

"I don't know," Thomas said. "I think I mentioned that he'd made that box I found the photos in. Why do you ask?"

"It's nothing really," Darcy said, but the idea she had kept coming back to her. "I guess I was wondering about the possibility that Jesse may have built something special into one of these pieces of furniture that he made."

"What do you mean? Like a hiding place? A secret compartment?"

"Yes, exactly. I did that once for a friend of mine who

was getting married." Darcy smiled as she remembered the beautiful dress she had sewn for her friend. "She wanted a hidden pocket in her dress so that she could put her 'something blue' in it. It was this huge sapphire that had belonged in her family for years and she didn't want to worry about losing it on her big day. Anyway, I loved the idea. It was easy to do. In fact, after that dress, I ended up selling the idea to a large bridal dress manufacturer. Now those 'something blue' pockets are sewn in a whole line of dresses."

"Sounds impressive," Thomas said.

"Thanks. But actually, my point is that maybe Jesse hid something in his furniture. Like the secret key in the inlay last night. Maybe there's another one in here?"

Thomas was nodding. "Won't hurt to look."

Both of them started running their hands over each piece of finely made wooden furniture, tugging at every joint and pressing on every fancy detail. They worked their way through all the downstairs furniture and found nothing.

"Might as well try the loft, too," Darcy said.

Thomas followed her up the narrow wooden steps. "You take the left. I'll take the right."

Darcy started with a small chair and a nightstand. Thomas went to what was probably the largest and most ornate piece in the whole house. But instead of running his hands over it, he took off his hat and turned it in his hands.

"It's this. It's the highboy," he said. "Come look."

"How do you know?" Darcy walked toward him. "You haven't even touched it."

"I should have thought of it before," he said. "Someone wanted to buy it from Miller's shop. It was a long time ago."

"Buy what? This highboy?"

"Yes, but Jesse wouldn't sell it. Bishop Miller was pretty put out with him. He said he shouldn't be building pieces at the shop that weren't actually for sale. I don't think they talked to each other for a week after that." He grinned at the memory.

Darcy ran her hands over the piece. She pried at the inlays but there weren't that many. This piece was hand carved and had amazing detail on the legs and feet. "Nothing's moving."

"Here, take a look at this." He leaned over and pointed. At the bottom of the highboy was a long piece of intricate trim, on either side of it a small drawer. "Why put a panel here instead of another drawer?"

"You think there's something behind the panel?"

Thomas shrugged. "I think it's worth checking."

He loped back down the stairs.

"Where are you going?"

"Jesse kept his carpentry tools down here. I don't want to just rip the panel off," he called from the stairs.

Thomas soon returned with a small wooden chisel and a soft cloth in his hands. He went back to the highboy. She moved out of his way and watched as he covered the tip of the tool with the cheesecloth so as not to damage the beautiful piece of furniture before prying open the panel. It took some maneuvering, but slowly, steadily, he worked the thick, decorative plank loose.

"Oh, my, Thomas, look. You were right. There's a secret shelf." Darcy felt her heart pumping hard.

Thomas reached in slowly then stopped, hand in midair. "Did you hear something?"

"No. I don't think so." Darcy shook her head. All she could hear was her pulse throbbing through her veins, strong with excitement.

"Well, then, what are you waiting for?" He smiled at Darcy.

"Of course." She nodded and moved in front of him. Her hand trembled as she reached forward into the dark, narrow space. Her fingers fell over a familiar object. "Feels like a book."

It was indeed a book. Her eyes swept over the cover, her heart practically skipping a beat as she read it.

Thomas raised an eyebrow at the item she'd pulled out. "It's a Bible. Why would he hide that? It's just like the one he had downstairs. The one I gave you to take to the hospital."

"No. This one looks less worn. Maybe like it's never been used."

Thomas lifted the book from her hands and shook it from the binding to see if anything had been tucked inside. A key and an envelope slipped out from between the pages and fell to the floor. Darcy swooped down and scooped them up. She turned the items over in her hands. Neither was marked and the envelope was sealed.

"Wait," Thomas whispered, putting a hand to her shoulder. "This time, I'm sure I heard something. Stay here."

Darcy nodded and watched as Thomas glided across the loft then slinked down the stairs.

Thomas came to a sudden halt at the bottom of the stairs. Someone was there. A man. Tall and slender. He was dressed all in black, including a stocking cap over his head, which prevented Thomas from being able to see his face.

"You're trespassing," Thomas said, stepping closer. The man was big. But Thomas was bigger. Much bigger. Of course, Thomas knew that the intruder could have a weapon, but there really wasn't much of a choice. He had to stand his ground and try to make this man leave. Then he had to get Darcy out of there. And call the police.

Without saying a word, the man pulled a gun from his jacket. Thomas could hear the hammer click to a ready position. He was going to fire.

Thomas stopped in his tracks, then dove over the sofa and hid behind it. The shot fired out. But it missed him.

Thomas scrambled to his hands and knees and peeked out from behind the furniture. The masked man aimed the gun at him again. Thomas shoved his hands up under the frame of the couch, grabbing on to the back of it with a hand at either end. It was even lighter than he'd thought. With a grunt he lifted the upholstered love seat and sent it sailing through the air toward the intruder.

The man lurched backward, trying to escape the giant projectile. The gun fired again.

This time Thomas felt something stinging through his flesh. He'd been hit on the top of his right leg. It wasn't going to kill him, but it stung fiercely. He howled and watched as the love seat crashed into the intruder, throwing the man off balance. The masked man stumbled backward and crashed into the wood-burning stove, knocking it over.

In an instant, the logs and embers that had been lit that morning to warm the team while they searched spread through the living space. The dry materials of Jesse's cottage caught fire almost instantaneously.

The intruder fled through the front door. Thomas hurried up the stairs. He had to get Darcy out of there. And fast. That old wood inside was going to burn like the sun.

Darcy had always heard that dry wood would practically combust given the proper conditions. It must have been true because that was exactly what seemed to be happening to Jesse's home. The cottage had suddenly become an incinerator.

"We've got to get out of here. Come on!" Thomas grabbed hold of her arm with such strength that she dropped the key and envelope.

Smoke already swirled through the loft. The flames would soon follow. Keeping his grip on her arm, Thomas pulled her to the edge of the stairs.

But then he stopped. The bottom of the steps was already knee-high in flames. There was no way out.

Darcy stared into the flames. Thomas hobbled around her. Why was he moving so stiffly? Then she saw his leg. A hole in his trousers. Fresh blood.

"Thomas, you've been shot!" Panic filled her words. This was all her fault. They should have left the cottage when everyone else had. Now how were they going to get out of there?

"I'm fine," he insisted. "Let's focus on getting out of here for now."

Get out? How could they? The only way left was out the window. "Please tell me Jesse has a ladder under the bed," she said.

Thomas hobbled away from the stairs toward the one

and only window in the loft, pulling her along with him. "No. But I know how we can improvise one."

They reached the small window. Thomas yanked the curtains away from the wall and handed them to her. "Tie those together. End to end. Make the knots strong."

Darcy dropped to her knees and set to the task at hand. The smoke was growing thick. Thomas limped away again toward the bed. He grabbed the sheets and bedding and tossed them to her. He caught her looking at the window. "Don't open it yet. As soon as you do, flames will get sucked up here with us."

Thomas came back to her side and worked the other pieces of the cloth, tying ends together as quickly as he could.

Darcy coughed and tried to cover her mouth and nose with her starched apron.

Thomas tested each of the knots. He tightened a few of them and when he seemed satisfied he wrapped one end of the makeshift rope around the bottom leg of the highboy, then pinned a good portion of the material under the leg of the massive piece of furniture.

"It might not hold me all the way down, but it will definitely slow the fall and that's all I need."

He opened the window. Fresh oxygen was sucked into the house with amazing force. Darcy braced herself against the wall. More smoke rolled through the bedroom, following its new escape route to the outside. Underneath, the heat felt as if it would liquefy the cottage altogether.

Thomas threw the tied pieces out the window. They reached a little more than halfway down the side of the house. Not quite a real ladder, but better than nothing.

"Okay. So you go first," he said.

Darcy froze. "I—I—can't."

"It's fine. Just wrap the material around you and lower yourself down."

Darcy could feel her head shaking. She couldn't jump out of a second-story window. Not even with a blazing fire at her back. "Wait. Jesse's Bible."

She bent over and scooped their findings into her hands and clung to them.

He positioned Darcy at the side of the window. "Okay. Sit down and swing your legs over the ledge."

She sat and slung one leg over the window ledge and then the other. Thomas took the bedding and swirled it once around her left leg. He took the Bible, key and letter and tossed them outside. Then in one quick motion, Thomas grabbed her off the ledge of the window and started to lower her.

Darcy closed her eyes. Her heart was pounding. The quilt around her leg tightened slightly as he lowered her.

"Grip the quilts and slide," he coached her.

Darcy held her breath. She opened her eyes and looked up. Smoke was swirling around Thomas's head. She had to forget her fears and move quickly so he would have time to escape, too.

The makeshift rope held. She slid down it until she was only ten feet from the ground and then she let go and dropped the rest of the way to the ground.

Wasting no time, she turned around and called to him, "Okay, now, your turn."

Darcy was safe. Thomas let out a sigh. Part of him wished he'd just carried her down with him. She didn't weigh that much and then he'd be down there, too, instead of in this inferno with a bleeding leg and a head full of smoke.

The old cottage was burning at an incredible rate. He doubted they would be able to save any of it. Flames ravaged the dry wood like a hungry wolf.

He had to get out of there now, but getting his body through that tiny window was going to be much more of a challenge than it was for Darcy.

Thomas wrapped the quilt around his good leg. He checked the knot around the high boy. Then he put a hand on either side of the window frame and pushed himself through, feet first. His weight tested the make-shift rope. Thomas slid fast. Too fast. The quilt was slipping from inside. His fingers were losing their grip on the outside.

The thick material ripped through his hands then ended. His shoulder and hip slammed into the side of the house. He bounced out and away from the cottage. The ground was rising up to meet him. He tucked into a ball and tried to break his fall with a roll.

"Thomas? Are you okay?"

He felt his lungs fill with air again. He felt the feeling come back to his body. Pain. His leg was screaming with it. But he was alive, and so was she.

He opened his eyes to find Darcy perched over him on her hands and knees. She was staring right into his face. "I'm going to be fine," he said. "How about you?"

"You saved me. Again." She grabbed his hand and tried to help pull him up.

Thomas lifted his torso off the ground and sat up beside her. They both looked down at his leg.

"It's going to be fine," he told her. "Can you go get

my phone? It's in the buggy. We need to call the fire department."

"Of course," she said. But she didn't move away at first. Instead, she put her hands on his cheeks and leaned close to him. He could feel her soft breath on his face.

Thomas could see and feel the emotion in her huge eyes as they searched his. Without thinking, he cupped her cheek in his big hand and leaned his head into her, touching their foreheads together.

"Thomas," she whispered, like a warning. She dropped her gaze away and started to pull back.

His heart pounded. He tightened his hand on her and he pulled her to his lips. They were soft and warm and for an instant he forgot about his leg and the fire.

And then she was gone, running around to the front of the house, no doubt to get his phone from the buggy and call 911.

Chapter Fifteen

The fire department came quickly and doused the rampant flames, but not before the front porch fell in. Tomorrow they could comb through the ashes and see if anything was salvageable, but from the looks of it that was doubtful.

Thomas's leg has been treated. He moved easily now, but Darcy imagined there must still have been some pain.

She, too, had been to the EMS vehicle. Fortunately, the stitches in her forehead had stayed intact and she'd gained nothing worse than a few bruises. She sat now on the front bench of his buggy, where Thomas had wrapped her in heavy blankets. But she couldn't stop shivering. Mostly from the cold, she told herself. And perhaps a little from residual fear. But she also knew it was from Thomas, from his gentle touch. From his kiss. She could feel it still as he breathed against her. He'd tasted sweet, like apples. His beard had brushed against her chin. He had kissed her. And she didn't know what to make of it. If anything…

She watched Thomas while he talked to the firefighters, the police and the EMS team. He moved with self-assurance, seemingly unruffled by the chaos that surrounded them. A man of great strength, both physical and emotional. A man she hardly knew really, but who'd agreed to help her through this nightmare with no hope of getting anything in return but this headache of problems and a bullet through his leg. And he had kissed her.

A kiss she really needed to forget about. Thomas couldn't possibly be interested in her romantically. No way. He was so…Amish. And she was not. The kiss was just one of those things that happen in an intense moment. That was all. Nothing more.

What she really wanted to concentrate on was the Bible, envelope and key they had found in Jesse's highboy. She was too anxious to open the envelope to wait for Thomas to be able to join her. He probably wouldn't care.

Darcy picked it up. She slipped a finger through a gap between the flap and the top edge and ripped it across the top with her finger. There was a single sheet of paper inside. She opened it to find a typed letter with an old photo tucked inside. Another Polaroid—the exact picture Jesse had shared with her weeks ago. Her as a small child, with both of her parents. But this was clearly the original as opposed to the copy, on regular printer paper, that Jesse had provided. The photo had yellowed and faded with age. But there she was being held between the mother and father that she never knew. Darcy turned her attention to the letter and read.

It is not destroyed, but hidden where only the righteous and pure of heart may find it. These places hold the answers and the beauty and the destruction of the responsible.

After those cryptic words, there were two quotes that didn't make any sense to her.

Darcy shook her head as she read the letter through a second time, her heart sinking into her gut. Then she folded the paper back around the photograph and slipped them back into the envelope.

"How are you holding up?" Thomas appeared at the side of the buggy.

Darcy nearly jumped from her skin. She had not seen him walk over. "I'm fine."

"We can go home now." He climbed into the buggy beside her and pulled up the brake. His leg brushed against hers and the contact sent a shiver up her spine. She scooted over an inch to make more room for him.

With a couple of clicking sounds and a light tap of the long leather reins, his horse set off in a fast high-stepping trot.

"How's the leg?" she asked.

"It's nothing. I've had worse from falling off a horse." The warm sound of his voice resonated deep inside her.

"When we get home, Nana can you fix a hot bath. She also makes the best apple pie in the world."

"A bath sounds nice. But what would I change into?"

"Abigail may have something else for you to wear. And you can borrow something from Nana in the meantime. It might not fit but you can't stay in that."

Darcy pulled the blankets tighter around her torso and forced a smile. "It's funny how after being trapped in a fire, I now can't seem to get warm."

Thomas didn't respond. Immediately, Darcy wished

she had worded that differently. He'd shared his coat with her the day before. He didn't have a coat on now, of course. It had burned in the fire as had her wool wrap. So it sounded like she'd meant for him to put his arms around her again. Ugh. Why did a kiss make things so awkward?

Darcy cleared her throat. Time to move on to another topic. "It's a real shame about the cottage. Did Jesse have insurance?"

"The Amish don't—"

"Have insurance… Of course you don't." Darcy pressed her lips together. "Then how does Jesse get medical care?"

"The community has funds put away for such things. To cover unexpected costs such as Jesse's hospital bills, or for when a house burns down or gets damaged in a storm."

"That's amazing. You really take care of each other."

"Isn't that what we should do? Help those that we love?"

"Well, yes, it's what people *should* do. But trust me, I don't think too many people actually do it." Then again, what did she know? She hadn't exactly grown up in a normal loving home. In any case, she didn't want to talk about it. "I opened the envelope."

"I thought you might."

Darcy shrugged. "I didn't understand any of it. It was very cryptic. Some quotes. A weird message at the top. And a picture inside. It was the original of the same picture he gave me a copy of when we first met—him and me with my mother when I was little."

"Where was that picture taken?"

"I don't know exactly," she said.

"Maybe it's important."

Darcy frowned. "Thomas, I know you're trying to help me and I appreciate it more than you know. More than I'm showing you, but… I should just go. We should just call Agent Danvers—"

"Agent Danvers? Don't you mean Agent Ross?"

"Come on, Thomas," she said. "You were nearly killed today. I'm just putting all of you at risk by staying here. I can't keep doing that."

"I don't think that man today was hunting you," Thomas said. "He was looking around the house. And he definitely didn't mean to set it on fire. That just happened in the scuffle—"

"In the scuffle of him shooting at you."

"Well, now that the house is practically destroyed, I don't think they will be back again. They don't know where you are. And they wouldn't even recognize you if they did."

"Do you think Jesse had some of the art stashed away there, in the cabin?"

"If he did, then it's gone now or at least damaged." Thomas shook his head. "But no. I don't think there was any artwork there. The FBI team would have found it. Plus, if Jesse did keep all that artwork, I don't think he would have kept it nearby."

"Kind of like how he had the photos in a box all the way out at the well?" she asked.

"Yes, but the pictures aren't worth anything. Paintings worth millions of dollars? Well, you would think he would have put those somewhere really secure."

"Like a vault."

"Right," he agreed. "Anyway, don't call Agent Danvers. At least not today."

"Okay, I'll see what McClendon and Agent Ross have to say. I just don't want to put anyone in danger. I mean, look at you." She glanced down to his wounded leg. "Does it hurt?"

"This isn't your fault, Darcy," he said. "None of this is. Just remember that."

His voice was full of emotion, but for what she wasn't sure. For her? For Jesse? For the destruction of the cottage? For the discovery that someone he loved was a thief?

He was right. Nothing about this situation was her fault. But that wasn't the only thing she was thinking about. She was thinking about Thomas. Was she starting to have feelings for him? Her heart was pounding. Darcy had to remind herself to breathe.

"Would you let me have a look at it? The letter, that is."

"Of course you can. You're the one who found it. And you're right. We should show it to Agent Ross."

"Good. I'm glad you agree because I already called him and told him about it."

For someone who'd been attacked and nearly burned to death, Darcy was amazingly resilient. He liked that about her. Actually, Thomas liked a lot of things about Darcy Simmons. He liked her small frame and her huge round eyes, especially now that he could see them in all their natural beauty, uncluttered by dark makeup. He liked her quick mind and her outspoken opinions.

What he didn't like was that she didn't like to talk about God. He didn't like that she didn't understand that some people were willing to help one another without expecting anything in return. He didn't like that she was going to leave. Which brought him to the real doozy that he didn't like—that he'd kissed her. Of course, that was his fault, not hers.

A rush of emotions flooded through him at the thought—emotions he would repress and ignore, as they had no possible hope of further development.

Anyway, the kiss had been just an expression of thankfulness that God had saved them from the fire. That He'd delivered them once again from a dangerous intruder. Right. Thomas swallowed hard. Although holding her close might have filled him with a feeling that was not exactly thankfulness. Not that Thomas wasn't thankful, of course—he was. But he knew what had really happened. He had gotten caught up in the moment. That's what had happened. And what a moment it was…

"You must be exhausted," he said, forcing his thoughts in a different direction.

"I would imagine no more than you are," she said. "Thomas, what if the letter and the pictures and the key all lead to nothing? What if Jesse never wakes up? What will we do?"

A sadness swept over Thomas at her words. He wanted to reach over and draw her close. But he couldn't. He wouldn't go there again. Anyway, thankfully they were home. Nana was standing on the front porch looking at them like they were a pair of teenagers that had stayed out too late.

"I have been waiting and waiting. I heard all those sirens," she began. "And I saw smoke. What were you all doing over there? I thought it was going to be just a small investigation. You know Jesse wouldn't like all these people rummaging through his belongings…"

There was a distinct pause as they got close enough for Nana to see the condition they were in and then Nana started again. "Oh, my! What has happened to the two of you? You're covered in soot and it smells like—"

"The cottage caught fire," Thomas announced.

"With the two of you in it, from the looks of it."

"Wait until you see his leg," Darcy said as she climbed out of the buggy.

"Thanks for that." Thomas eyed her as she jumped down. There was a twinkle of mischief in her stormy gray eyes. *Ja*, he liked that about her, too.

Chapter Sixteen

When Darcy walked into the kitchen she looked clean and refreshed, except for her slightly soiled frock. Thomas, on the other hand, had not moved far from the stool, where he had his leg propped up. He still smelled of smoke and sweat.

"Elijah and Agent Ross are on their way. I think they have more news," Thomas said. "Nana left out some coffee and sandwiches. I guess Nana's clothes don't fit you?"

Darcy pressed her lips together and shook her head. "Is she not joining us?"

"No, she thought she'd be in the way. Do you mind serving?"

Darcy poured both tea and coffee and filled a plate with the turkey sandwiches that Nana had made. Thomas liked watching her work. Plus, the smell of food was reminding him of how hungry he was.

Darcy was just putting things on the table when Agent Ross entered along with Elijah and Bishop Miller.

"Bishop Miller?" Darcy tried to hide the surprise

in her voice, but Thomas could still hear it. "I—I don't think I have enough sandwiches."

"Not to worry, Miss Simmons." The bishop's voice was calm and kind. "Elijah and I were able to reschedule our deliveries. How's the leg?"

"Kind of sore," Thomas admitted reluctantly. He hated being physically weakened. *You can't protect her, farmer boy.* Agent Danvers's words could not be truer. Thomas clenched his teeth. He should not be so proud of his strength. "Please sit down, everyone. And forgive me for not getting up."

"We understand you found something in Jesse's house," said Agent Ross. "But before we take a look at it, Bishop Miller wanted to tell you something."

"Jesse…" Bishop Miller paused. "Jesse told me a little more than what I shared with you the other day."

Thomas and Darcy both exchanged a glance then looked back to the bishop.

"Darcy, your father loved you. Leaving you with your mother's parents ripped him apart. But your grandparents wanted custody and he thought with what he'd done that he would never be able to win a custody battle in court. Plus, it was a question of safety. And I can assure you, he felt guilty about your mother's death. But he prayed for you every day. No earthly father could have loved you more. And he always knew where you were. One of the agreements he made with your grandparents was that he was allowed to know your identity and whereabouts as long as he promised not to contact you until after your twenty-fifth birthday."

Darcy looked ready to burst into tears. But she had to have been relieved to hear more about her past.

"I turned twenty-five two months ago," she said.

The bishop smiled. "I know. Jesse came to me and asked me what he should do. He wanted to contact you but he was afraid. Not of any of the danger that's been happening—I believe he never would have considered contacting you if he'd thought it would place you in danger. He was afraid you wouldn't love him. That you wouldn't forgive him."

The bishop paused for a moment, giving Darcy a chance to regain her composure, which she looked quite close to losing.

"Anyway," the bishop continued, "he decided it would be better to have tried and failed than not to have tried at all. And that's all. I heard that he had taken a turn for the worse and I just wanted to tell you how much you mean to him in case he doesn't get the chance to do it himself."

No one spoke for another minute, as Agent Ross set up his computer on the kitchen table.

"Should we take a look at what you found?" Agent Ross said.

"Wait a minute," Thomas said. "Of course we will look at the letter and key but I just got to thinking… Well, even if these new clues lead us to the paintings, then what? Darcy and Jesse are still in danger. What can we do about Wissenberg? What about the people that helped him find Jesse?"

"You're right. That just as important, which is why I've been on Wissenberg's whereabouts 24/7. But he is gone."

"How can he be gone? Wouldn't he still be on parole?" Elijah asked.

"Yes, but that doesn't always keep people who are well connected from disappearing."

"So how do you figure out who is doing his dirty work for him?" Darcy asked. "Like who told Wissenberg where Jesse was in the first place?"

"Right, well, we've worked on that, too, but like I told Elijah, it's touchy when an FBI investigation involves another government agency. Everyone is sort of territorial. What I have been able to get is a record of all of Wissenberg's visitors and phone calls while he was in prison."

Thomas nodded to show he was following. "Anyone of interest on that list?"

"My biggest hope is the three visits from someone who didn't sign in properly. My team is looking through footage of the prison video surveillance tapes. We hope to match a face up to a name and go from there. We also have leads on Wissenberg's two sons. They left the country after their father's trial. That makes it harder to find them. But there is a money trail. I think we may be able to get that nailed down soon. And there's also an unregistered phone number that he called almost every week. There is no locator on the phone, which means the calls are being filtered through some sort of computer program designed to keep people like us from locating phones."

"But it's not impossible to track down the phones," Elijah said.

"No. Not impossible," Ross acknowledged.

It was all so complicated, Thomas thought. But he was thankful for Elijah's friend. It sounded as though he was doing everything he could.

"What about other angles? Like other people who were involved in the smuggling? Or other people who worked at the Gregorian?" Thomas suggested.

"Exactly," Elijah said. "I thought of that yesterday morning and called Frank. That's why I told you we have news."

Agent Ross nodded. "We are tracking down a woman named Lenore Moon. She worked for Jesse and for Wissenberg and was part of the art-theft ring. She went to jail for fraud but only for six months. We think she's changed her name and her look. We are trying to get a location on her. There were rumors of a romantic interest between her and Wissenberg. It's likely that she knew about the paintings that Jesse held back and could be in on this."

"Why would she wait until now to look for Jesse if she knew he had the paintings all this time?" Darcy asked.

"Probably because she couldn't locate Jesse without Wissenberg's help. Or needed him to provide muscle, which he wouldn't do until he knew he would get his cut. Or she had nothing to do with it. It's just a lead. That's what all of these are…just leads."

"The coffee is getting cold," Darcy said, needing a break from the conversation.

She had been listening and asking questions, but her heart was so full of emotion that it was all she could do to keep from crying. Part of her wanted to run out of the room and escape all she was feeling. The other part of her wanted to run to the hospital and tell Jesse that she forgave him. No part of her could bear to look at Thomas. She knew if she did she would lose what little bit of control she had left. And though they had been nothing but kind to her, she did not want to cry in front of these men.

Darcy left the table to pour the tea and coffee. She returned and placed the sandwiches on the table and passed out some plates and napkins. She felt a little bit more in control when she sat back down again.

"Let us pray," the bishop said. "Our Heavenly Father, hear our thanks. Hear our praise. Know we are Your people. Give us ears to hear Your will and guide us along the path of the righteous that we may be found acceptable in Your sight."

Darcy whispered the words of Bishop Miller as he said them. She said amen as she thought about the bishop's words. *Was she one of God's people? How could that be? Was this feeling inside her what it meant to be called to God?*

"Thomas, where are the things we wanted to show them?" Darcy did not look his way as she stood again and began to clear the empty plates.

"On the counter by the back door."

Darcy went to get the items and spread them out across the table.

Elijah picked up the key and turned it in his hands. "Looks like a bank key. Or a mailbox key. And the letter?"

"It's just a cryptic line about something hidden and then a couple of random Bible verses," Darcy said. She read the first one aloud.

"'Next they made the courtyard. The south side was a hundred cubits long and had curtains of finely twisted linen.' There's no reference."

"That's from Exodus," Bishop Miller told her. "It's from the building of the tabernacle under the direction of Moses. Everything was very exact. Every inch of the instructions. Fascinating."

"What's the other verse?"

"It's just as fascinating," said Thomas. "Read it."

Darcy cleared her throat. "'He gave two carts and four oxen to the Gershonites, as their work required.'"

"And that would be from Numbers," the bishop said. "Still about Moses. But I believe this is dealing with offerings."

Agent Ross was typing into his computer. "I got the references," he said. "Exodus chapter thirty-eight, verse nine and Numbers chapter seven, verse seven. I'll have my team look into code possibilities."

He read the rest of the letter. "Most likely the top part is a message and the bottom tells us how to decode it."

"Well, if everything you need for the message is in the letter," Darcy said, "why also leave the Bible?"

"Right," Elijah said. "He wrote the verses out and specifically left off the references."

"And the key? How do we figure out where that fits in?" Thomas struggled to get up off the stool. Darcy flinched watching him move so stiffly. "I don't know about any code or secret writing. In fact, that all sounds a little too fancy for Uncle Jesse. What if it just is what it is?"

"Which would be?" asked Agent Ross.

"A bunch of numbers and instructions. Directions. An address."

"Telling us where to go to use this key," Darcy said. *And to how to end this nightmare.*

Chapter Seventeen

"We will look at every possibility," said Agent Ross, packing up his notes and computer. "The FBI has the best cryptographers in the world."

Darcy appreciated Agent Ross's help, but she knew the FBI's top cryptographers would not be focusing all of their attention on a twenty-year-old art smuggling case. She was surprised he'd been able to help as much as he had. Surely he had other cases requiring his attention, and yet he had come up with several leads for them, and had come willingly to help whenever Elijah called. She just hoped one of the leads would pan out soon. Soon enough that she would not have to go into WITSEC. She couldn't even bear the thought of it. If only she could just go home. But after the break-in, home didn't feel particularly safe anymore. In fact, the only place she'd been in the past few days where she'd felt truly safe had been Thomas's arms.

Thomas walked the guests to the door. Darcy hung back in the kitchen. She was glad not to have to leave with Elijah and go back to the Millers' just yet.

But poor Thomas. She knew he was in pain. She also

knew he had a lot of work to do—his regular chores on top of the preparations for the singing—and it would be extremely painful, with no one to help him other than his eightysomething-year-old grandmother.

"*Ach!* That was a long meeting and I need to be in my kitchen. So much to do for the singing tonight." Nana Ruth came busting into the kitchen. "And you, my dear, will need another change of clothes. You can't wear that old smoky thing tonight. I'll have Thomas phone Abigail. Hopefully she has another dress still hanging around."

Darcy looked down at herself. She had washed the grime from her hands and face before the meeting, but Nana was right. She smelled like smoke and fear, and her dress was streaked with dirt. And since Nana was about as wide as she was tall, sharing with her hadn't worked out. Darcy made a mental note to be careful from now on of how much Amish food she stuffed away while she stayed there. Hopefully, it wouldn't be for much longer.

"So, what can I do to help?" she asked.

"You can get out there to that stable and help my grandson." The old woman turned to her, her little spectacles sliding down her nose. She put her hands on her hips. "Don't wait for him to ask you for help. He never will. But he needs it."

"Of course," Darcy said. She hurried out of the kitchen and across the courtyard. The temperature had dropped dramatically. And somehow the inside of the barn seemed almost colder than the outside. She walked up and down the aisles. It was a large stable. She found Thomas hobbling forward with a wheelbarrow. "Tell me what I can do to help?"

"What? You? Come to help me with the horses?"

"Yes. Me. Why not? I'm already dirty."

He smiled. "Okay then, come on. I'll show you how to muck out a stall."

"I don't think there's too much to it," she said, grabbing the wheelbarrow away from him.

"Hey, I was using that to help me walk," he teased.

"You shouldn't be walking at all," she countered. But she couldn't stop him from following her from one stall to the next. She mucked. He filled the water buckets and placed blankets on some of the horses.

"What did you think about the meeting?" she asked him.

Thomas twisted his face in thought. "Lots of angles. Complicated. But I know Agent Ross is doing what he can. And the fire department and police will be back out at the cottage tomorrow. You never know, they may uncover something about that intruder that gives us another clue."

"I don't know. Whoever it is has been pretty careful so far. No prints at my house or Jesse's previously… though he might have been distracted enough today to drop something without meaning to. I can't believe you threw a sofa at him." She tried to picture the couch flying through the air.

"Well, it seemed only fair. He had a gun and I didn't." Thomas laughed and leaned against the wall. "I think I must have had a lot of adrenaline going. Anyway, it was a small sofa."

"Do you think we will ever figure out what that letter means?"

"If God wills it." He looked her dead in the eye. "Then yes, I think we will figure it out."

God... Is that who had led them to the message and the box with the pictures? Well, she hoped if He was there and listening that He would bring an end to this sooner than later.

Thomas watched Darcy dodge hungry horse heads over the stall doors. Getting around the stable with a shot-up leg was slow going and it hurt. He probably should have gone to the doctor, but there was no way he would leave Darcy and Nana alone at the house, unprotected. And now it was good to move around. He was certain Abigail would take a look at it when she arrived with another dress for Darcy to wear.

"This is the feed room. It stays closed up or critters will wander in. Now, we have several types of grains—some for horses in work, some for horses in foal and some for..." He looked back at her. "Well, you get the idea. So first we fill the buckets and then you distribute."

"Sounds easy enough."

Thomas handed the grain-filled buckets to Darcy and she put them in the wheelbarrow and rolled it down the first aisle. "We'll start here."

He handed a bucket to Darcy and opened the first stall for her to enter. She held the bucket loosely, between her thumb and forefinger. Thomas repressed his desire to smile.

"Watch out, now. This is Princess. She doesn't have very good manners."

Princess turned around and whacked the bottom of the bucket with her head. Darcy squealed. The bucket of grain went flying through the air and Darcy landed right on her backside.

Thomas pressed his lips together to muffle his laughter. "You knew she was going to do that, didn't you?"

"I was trying to tell you she has terrible manners. She was very poorly named," he said. "I'm sorry about that. But perhaps you'd do better to keep your eye on the horse and not on the ground."

"Point taken. But they didn't do that when we were mucking."

"You didn't have food in your hands then."

Darcy stood up and brushed her skirts off. Princess nibbled up the spilled grain around her feet. "She's beautiful, isn't she?"

"My most valuable mare," he said. "Would you like to ride her?"

"Me? Ride?"

"Yes, you. Ride." He crossed his arms over his chest. "One of my favorite things to do is ride bareback in the snow."

"Snow? What snow?"

"Oh, it's going to snow for sure."

"So you're a weatherman and a horse whisperer," she teased.

"I'm just a simple God-fearing man, Miss Simmons." He smiled and handed her another bucket. "Next up, Storm."

"Storm? If she lives up to her name, then maybe you should feed her."

They made their way through the barn. Thomas loved the flow of their rhythm. They didn't speak much, but still anticipated the movements of one another. It was like their hundredth time feeding the horses together, not their first. He couldn't help but think about the kiss, too. That had been foolhardy of him. Still, regret was not what he felt over it. It was more a feeling of grief that it could never happen again.

"I come bearing gifts." Elijah's voice sounded through the stable, loud and, to Thomas, a bit unwelcome as he knew his time alone with Darcy was now at an end.

"Back here," Darcy shouted.

Elijah came jogging around the corner. "A dress for you," he said to Darcy. "And pair of crutches for you," he said to Thomas.

"Any word on Jesse?" she asked.

"Abigail says he's steady," Elijah answered. "She will be here later to see this patient. As for you—" he turned to Darcy "—Nana said she will draw you a bath, but only if you hurry because then she needs you to help carry the food out to the barn."

"Thank you." Darcy hurried away.

Thomas should have thanked her but the words somehow stuck in his throat. He watched the back of Darcy floating away from him until she turned and disappeared around the corner of the stall. He didn't like watching her leave.

Remembering Elijah standing there, Thomas shook away his thoughts. He put a crutch under each arm and took all the weight off his bad leg. "Hey, these are great."

Elijah nodded readily.

Thomas swung his way to the stable office and lit a lantern. Elijah followed. "Let's go grab those benches."

This time, Thomas followed Eli out to the large trailer that housed all the church benches and tables. Every other week they traveled to a different home for

Sunday church. And occasionally they were used for weddings and funerals and other events like the singing.

Tiny flakes of snow floated through the air.

"I knew it was going to start soon," Thomas said. "How much are we getting?"

"Maybe a foot." Elijah got into the trailer and slid out the benches.

Thomas put down his crutches and helped to set the benches on the ground. "You'll have to get one of the boys to help you carry them inside."

"No problem. I'm sure some kids will start showing up here in no time."

"I'm glad for the singing. It's good to get our minds off Jesse and these break-ins."

"And the fire," Elijah mumbled. After unloading the trailer, he hopped down. "Do you think Darcy can keep her cover with a whole barn full of Amish?"

Thomas nodded, trying to keep his facial expression neutral. "*Ja*. She's pretty, uh…pretty good, *ja*?"

Elijah slapped his friend on the back. "I saw the way you looked at her."

"The way I looked at her?" Thomas tried to play dumb. "You mean a worried look."

"I wouldn't call what I saw a look of worry," Eli teased.

"What would you call it then?" Thomas sighed and picked his crutches back up.

"I'd call it a look of admiration. Affection. Thomas, I'd call it chemistry." Elijah smiled, but his eyes were focused, making it clear that Thomas should listen closely.

"Chemistry?" Thomas repeated casually. "Elijah,

I think you've been smelling too much shellac at the furniture store."

Eli's smile went flat. He was not joking and he wanted Thomas to know it. "I suppose I'd only call it chemistry, if I didn't know better. But I do. The Thomas I know is much too smart to fall for an *Englischer*, even if she is all dressed up in a nice plain frock."

If his friend could see through him, who else could? He would have to be more guarded. More careful with his eyes and his attentions.

Thomas met Elijah's eye. "Advice taken."

"Now, go get cleaned up before that *Englischer* uses up all the hot water."

A little while later, Thomas tried rinsing the smoke and an entire day's worth of grime off his aching muscles. It wasn't easy to keep the bullet wound dry.

Darcy had helped him today, but he'd have to get his cousin's son to come lend a hand in the stables for the next few weeks until he healed. After washing up, he dressed in a clean white shirt and his best pair of trousers. He ran his fingers through his dark curls and then down his beard. Darcy was right. It had never grown in too well. It was strange that she had asked him about it. When his marriage had not worked out, he had wanted to shave it off, but his father had said that was not the way.

Thomas had never kissed a woman since Mary. Not until today. He supposed over the past ten years he had never met one he wanted to kiss. And now that he had, she was an *Englischer*. Elijah was right to remind him. There was no future with Darcy. Thomas knew that and he needed to act accordingly.

* * *

Darcy couldn't remember when a hot bath had felt so good. She only wished she could have lingered in it a little longer. It had been fun working the stable with Thomas. But she could tell she was going to be sore tomorrow from all that shoveling. And sore from falling out of a two-story window.

After toweling off, she dressed in another of Abigail's frocks. She combed out her hair, parted it and pulled it back. She fit the white prayer *kapp* on her crown, surprised at how quickly she'd grown accustomed to dressing herself in these clothes. It wasn't easy. There were no buttons. No zippers.

Next, Darcy lifted the lovely silver locket and turned it over. There was a small inscription on the back:

Forever yours, October 4

She wondered what the date could be. Their wedding? The day they met? Ten…four. The number date made Darcy think about all the numbers in the verses that Jesse had written in the note she'd found. She wanted to get her hands on that Bible. She disagreed with Agent Ross about the letter being a code in and of itself. She was certain that the letter and the Bible had to work together. She just needed some time to look through the Bible. Find the verses. Study the pages. Maybe, just maybe, something would pop out at her.

Darcy fastened the locket around her neck and slid it under the collar of the dress, then hurried down to help Nana Ruth with the evening's festivities.

Chapter Eighteen

It was after six o'clock when the kids had started to show up in groups and pairs. Darcy and the Miller family had placed tables and benches and plates and mugs and napkins out. Nana had made obscene amounts of food. The whole time, Darcy had wrung her hands and worried.

It was one thing to disguise herself as Amish when she was with people who knew she wasn't like the Millers and Abigail. It was another to keep up the act in front of a whole community of Amish folk. There were over thirty Amish teenagers plus friends and family gathered in Thomas's indoor paddock for what everyone called the "singing."

The boys were lined up on one side of the table and the girls on the other. The girls outnumbered the boys almost two to one. But no one seemed discouraged. Most of the adolescents had arrived in small open carriages and carts. Others had walked through the snow. With no musical instruments for accompaniment, the adolescents began to sing songs of praise and worship, sometimes in harmony, sometimes in unison. Sometimes in English, sometimes in Pennsylvania Dutch. Their glorious voices lifted to the roof and beyond. Darcy couldn't remember when she'd heard anything so wonderful in her entire life. All her worry and fears melted away with their voices.

"Gelobt Sei Gott im hochsten Throne... Hallelujah, hallelujah, hallelujah...

"Praise God on the highest Throne... Hallelujah, hallelujah, hallelujah."

"We haven't had a singing here for a while," Thomas told her as he sat down beside her.

"It's wonderful," Darcy said. "At first, I couldn't believe these kids came here through the snow to sing worship songs. But now that I see how much fun they're having…"

"I'm glad you're enjoying it. You know, there are usually at least ten more kids attending. So I do think the snow may have stopped a few from coming. But at least our place is more centrally located than the home of the family who was originally going to hold the singing tonight. Nana got wind a few weeks ago of someone wanting to relocate, so here we are."

"And it's the finest barn in Lancaster County," said a tall boy who had just entered. He shook hands with Thomas. A frail dark-headed girl stood shyly behind him. "Thanks for having it here. You saved my parents." He looked to Darcy and tipped his hat.

"I'll take that." Darcy reached for the fresh bread in his arms.

"Thank you, ma'am," the boy said with great enthusiasm. "I'm Amos Beiler. And this is my girl, Lucy King."

"Nice to meet you," Darcy said.

"Now, go join the fun," Thomas urged them. As they

walked away, he leaned over to Darcy and whispered, "They will get married come next November."

"They're engaged?"

"No. They won't announce it formally until the end of the summer. But they've been steady for years."

"For years? They look so young."

"Lots of couples marry at eighteen or nineteen. It's not so young when you're already working and making a living."

"So I guess I'm pretty much an old maid according to your standards?" she asked.

"The oldest," he teased.

Darcy gave him a sideways glance and punched him in the arm.

"But don't worry. None of the boys will ask you to go for a buggy ride after the singing. They all think you're with me," he said. His gaze was on her, obviously waiting for a reaction. She'd give him one. But it wouldn't be the silly girlish blush that he might be expecting. Yes, he had kissed her. Yes, she was attracted to him. But she and Thomas were like milk and soda—not ever meant to be together.

"Well, maybe you should set them straight." She stood with Amos's bread in her hands and a flat expression on her face. "I'll go put this on the table with the others." She scurried away from him to the food table.

Thomas used his crutches and swung over beside her, closer than he needed to. His scent wafted over her, a mixture of manly musk and homemade soap. Whether he was the soda or the milk, there was no denying his appeal. His fingers brushed her upper arms, sending a chill through her entire body and something else. Something she hadn't felt in a very long time—in fact, maybe it was something she'd never felt.

"Meet me outside," he whispered through the thin layer of her prayer *kapp*. "I want to share something with you."

Her heart beat wildly. What could it be? He must have had news about the intruders or about Jesse. Whatever it was it sounded good. Darcy put the bread on the dessert table with the other treats. She and Nana had made several gallons of hot chocolate for the kids, too. Nana stood guard by the table, refilling mugs and loading plates with cakes and cookies.

Darcy grabbed a wool wrap that Abigail had brought over for her and threw it around her shoulders. As she walked through the aisles of the stable, she wondered if Thomas had heard from Agent Ross. Maybe he had figured out the verses in the letter. She passed through the front door and out into the courtyard.

Thomas stood a few feet outside next to one rather large gray horse. The horse was bridled but wore no saddle. His light-colored coat shimmered like stars in the night. Thomas looked as handsome as a movie star. He wore a smile that was brighter than the blanket of snow covering the ground.

"I thought I'd better get you out here in the snow before you decided to go on a buggy ride with one of those fine fellows at the singing. How about a ride?"

"Me?" Darcy shook her head slightly. What was happening? "I—I was expecting information about the case, not… But what about your leg?" She looked down at the ground. Her heart was racing. Her hands trembled.

"No information. Sorry. Just me and a horse. But I'm not going to ride. Just you."

"Just me? Oh, I don't think so. I don't ride," she informed him. "No way."

"Well, not really all by yourself. I will lead him. You just get to sit and look pretty."

"Thomas, I don't know... Shouldn't we stay and oversee the singing? You are the host."

"*Ach,* no." He waved his hand through the air. "Nana's inside. Anyway, we are riding patrol."

"Patrol?"

"*Ja.*" His voice was mocking, so she knew his words weren't the least bit serious. "Sometimes the couples want some alone time. They wander off into the woods for a kiss or two."

"Sounds like you know from experience."

"Maybe." He winked, smiled again and waved her to him.

"What if I fall?"

"Are you going to fall?"

"No."

"*Gut.* And just in case, I brought you a helmet." He placed the rider's helmet on her head and fastened it around her chin.

"Well, there's one more problem." She put her hands on her hips. "I'm wearing a dress, in case you hadn't noticed."

"You think Amish girls don't ride horses?" He paused for a moment. "Well, they don't too often actually. But it's not unheard of."

"Okay, fine. I give in."

"Here, let me give you a leg up."

The next thing she knew Thomas had slung her over

the back of the horse. She balanced herself and took hold of the reins. Thomas put another halter over the horse's head and connected a lead rope to it.

"How do you feel?"

"A very long way from the ground." She glanced over her horse's shoulder toward the snow-covered ground.

Thomas grinned. "He's a gentle giant of a plow horse. I'd put my own baby on him."

Darcy hadn't ridden horses since she'd been to summer camp as a girl and she'd never ridden bareback. Nor in the snow under the stars. She had forgotten how much she'd loved it.

"You have ridden a horse before." Thomas couldn't take his eyes off Darcy as she sat astride the big gray. She was tense and clung onto the horse's reins but she kept her head up and her legs still. He only wished he could have ridden, too.

She laughed. "I haven't been on a horse since I was thirteen at summer camp. My grandparents sent me every summer. It didn't take me long to realize that they were just getting rid of me for the summer."

"That must have been hard. Not knowing your parents. Having grandparents that weren't close."

"Oh, don't feel sorry for me. My grandparents spoiled me. Anything I wanted, I got."

Except love, he thought.

"I'm glad you brought me out here."

"Me, too." Thomas stopped and stared up at her. He was falling for Darcy Simmons, harder and deeper each moment. Did she feel at all like he did?

Not that it mattered. She would go home soon and he had to remind himself of that. This wasn't her life.

He wasn't going be anything to Darcy. And she wasn't going to be anything to him. Anyway, who would be stupid enough to fall in love with someone who was destined to leave him? He'd already done that once. He certainly wasn't going to do it again.

Darcy looked back down at him. "You okay? Your leg must be killing you. We've walked a long way and you're only using one crutch."

"No. I'm good. Abigail took a look at my leg and said the EMS guy did a really good job cleaning it up. It really was just a graze."

"You don't feel pain, do you?"

"Oh, I do." He saw a movement in the distance. He turned his head to follow it.

"Are you sure you're okay?" she asked again.

"Yes, I just thought I saw something in the woods." He shook his head. "It was probably just a deer."

And yet, Thomas was pretty sure what he'd seen was on two legs. It might be nothing. Or it might be someone dangerous, come to harm Darcy again.

He turned the horse around and led them back toward the barn as fast as his leg would allow. The stable glowed like a beacon as a light snow fell. The singing was a faint hum in the distance, floating over the snow-covered fields. It was a terrible thought to consider that danger might still be lurking at their doorstep. And why *his* doorstep? He searched the woods again. All seemed still. He was just tired and imagining things. After all, who would risk coming around with all these people here?

Darcy didn't seem to be listening. She was staring up at the night sky. Her face glowed in the soft moonlight as a few lucky snowflakes kissed her soft skin.

"Did you ride a lot with her—your wife?"

His wife, Mary? Mary was the furthest thing from his mind. "What made you think of that?"

She shrugged. "I don't know… It's just sort of romantic, I guess. You know, the barn singing. The ride in the snow."

"No. Mary didn't ride." His jaw tightened. "She didn't really like much about life in the country."

She looked down at him and smiled apologetically. "I shouldn't have asked. But…" She hesitated, and he figured she was torn between good manners and curiosity. Finally curiosity won. "It's just that you seem so content. Aren't you sad? Aren't you angry that you lost your wife? Aren't you lonely?" The words came out in a rush, and as soon as they were out, she looked uncertain. He figured she was worried she'd said too much, and he hastened to reassure her.

"I don't mind talking about Mary. I am very sad that she died so young from cancer. But the saddest part is that she spent so much of her life unhappy. Not because of me, but because she didn't want this life. Her family pressured her to take vows and marry. She wanted to leave here. And eventually, she did. Not long after we married. You see, she got sick after she left me—not long after she finally had the life she wanted."

"Wow." Her eyes were wide. "How you can be so okay with that? Didn't that hurt? I don't know anyone who could talk so calmly about someone who treated you like she did. How could she have done that to you?"

"It's called forgiveness," he said. "It's a way to show love. Sometimes when you love something, you have to let it go. It's the only way to have peace in this life, Darcy. Love and forgiveness."

She pressed her lips together and nodded. "I've never met anyone like you. Like all of you—your friends and family. You're all so…accepting. So comfortable with who you are."

"How about you?" he asked. "Any lost loves? Someone special in your life now?"

"Ha. No. Never. I go on a lot of first dates."

"So, you're content being single, it seems. I'm not so unique after all."

"No. I'm not. I'm not content. Or at least I haven't been." She looked off into the distance.

Thomas stopped walking. He turned around and looked up at her. Tears filled her eyes. A few had spilled over her lids and down her cheeks. It pained him to see her hurting. He wished he had not asked her.

"I am so sorry. I did not mean to upset you," he said.

"No, it's just that when Bishop Miller told me about my father, that he asked for my forgiveness. It dawned on me how different my life would have been if I had had my father in my life. If I had lived here with him instead of my grandparents. I had…"

"Had love?" Had *Gott*, he thought, but did not add. God was working in Darcy just fine without his interference. Maybe there was no future for him with Darcy. But there was one for her with God and for that he was so glad she had come here.

She nodded and turned to him, her face streaming with tears. "Can you imagine? What if he had brought me here with him like he'd wanted to? Then I'd have been…"

"You'd have been loved," he said. *And Amish*, he thought to himself, *and not off-limits to me*. "But you are loved, Darcy. You have friends. You have an important job."

"I have a good life. But Thomas, I've never been happy." She pointed to her heart. "And I never really knew it until I came here, because I didn't know there was more. Seeing life through the eyes of you and your people, it makes my world seem so small and unimportant and empty." She chuckled at herself. "I sound crazy, don't I?"

Thomas reached up his arm and closed his fingers over her hands that clutched the reins. "Crazy? No. You do not sound crazy at all. You sound like you have found *Gott*. And in *Gott* you are finding peace."

She laughed again and wiped away the tears. "Maybe you're right…"

He let go of her hand but he didn't want to. "Accept what you have found, Darcy. Never let it go. It won't matter where you are or who you're with."

They rested in silence for a moment. Darcy wiped her eyes and looked away, then she stiffened, causing even the docile plow horse to stir.

"What is it?" he asked.

"You were right, Thomas." Her voice was as cold as the air around them. "Someone *is* in the woods."

Chapter Nineteen

❦

Darcy sat rigid on the back of the giant draft horse. Her tension no longer had anything to do with riding bareback or finding God. She had seen someone in the woods.

"It could be some of the kids from the singing," Thomas suggested. But she could tell by his stern expression and the way he'd quickened his step that he knew it was an intruder. *The intruder.*

But how? She understood an intruder at Jesse's, or at her town house, but here? At Thomas's? Why would they come here?

"Oh, no," she cried. "Thomas, where did you put the Bible and the other things we found at Jesse's?"

"Agent Ross took them," he said. "Why?"

"Because why else would someone be here?"

The intruder at Jesse's cottage had fled the house and the flames, but he might not have completely fled the scene.

"What if the man who shot at you stayed near the house during the fire and watched us leave? What if he saw us throw those things out of the window to save them? What if he knows we have that key? And what if he already knows what to do with that key?"

"Slow down, Darcy."

"No. Thomas, the person I see is running. And he most definitely does not look Amish. Do you see him?"

Thomas followed her gaze. She could see his expression of concern amplify as his eyes found the dark figure.

"*Ja.* I see him. Here, Darcy." He lifted up an arm. "Slide down. I'm going to go see who it is."

"After he shot at you?" Darcy slid off the big horse. "You can hardly walk. Plus, what if he has a gun again?"

Thomas wasn't even listening. She might as well have been talking to the horse. She knew Thomas well enough to know that he wasn't going to let anything happen to all those people at the singing. They were under his roof and they were his responsibility. And so was she. He was going to keep them all safe and if that meant his leg hurt or he got shot at again, he most likely didn't care. Why was it that the thing you admired most in others could also be the thing that drove you crazy about them?

She wanted to grab his arm and hold him back, but even with Thomas being wounded, she was no match for his strength. She watched as he slid the halter off the horse and handed it to her. He took the reins from her hands and with teeth clinched he swung himself up on the back of the horse. His face betrayed the pain that had to be rippling through him. He'd probably reopen the wound.

"Go back inside, Darcy. I'll be right back."

He clamped his legs around the huge gray and he galloped toward the forest's edge.

At the same moment, shrieks sounded from inside the barn and then there was a sound a bit like rolling thunder. Darcy had never heard that noise before, but instinctively she knew it was horses. A lot of horses, all moving together in a herd.

A large door where the gathering was taking place slid open and about ten of the horses came barreling out. They bucked and ran and whinnied and snorted until they'd all exited and then, like horses do, one of them stopped and so did the rest. The boys from the singing were already running after them with lead ropes.

Darcy glanced back at Thomas, who looked back at the commotion. Her heart raced wildly. Maybe he would come back now? The intruder was probably long gone anyway. But Thomas kept moving away from the stable.

Thomas heard and saw the commotion back at the stable, but he didn't stop. There were plenty of boys at the gathering who could tend to his horses. Darcy would be safe if she went back toward the others. And to keep them all protected, he knew he had to keep going.

He had easily closed more than half the distance between the runner and himself. But they were getting close to the highway now. If there was a car waiting, Thomas feared he might not make it in time to stop the intruder.

"Stop! You're trespassing!"

The runner looked back. Thomas saw his face, reflecting in the bright snow-lit night. It was not anyone he knew and yet his face seemed familiar.

Thomas saw the man's car parked at the edge of the woods. There was a creek several yards from the road and only one good place to cross. The man had not parked near enough to it to make his escape. Thomas clamped on to his mount and clicked his tongue against his cheek, urging the steady horse to increase speed and jump the creek. He'd forgotten the pain in his leg.

Thomas pulled up on the other side and cut the runner off before he reached the car. The man slipped and slid in the snow right under the horse's belly, but was not able to escape as Thomas jumped down and grabbed the man by the collar of his black coat.

The man stood and turned to him with his head dropped. It was a man he'd never met before, but he looked so much like an image he'd seen on Agent Ross's computer screen that Thomas knew that it had to be Wissenberg's son.

"Going somewhere?" he asked the man.

"This is not what it looks like. I promise," the man said. "I was trying to stop her. She's crazy."

"Who's crazy?" Thomas asked.

"My sister."

Darcy broke into high gear and arrived at top speed at the open barn, throwing her helmet aside. On her way, she passed a few able adolescents who had rushed forward to catch the loose horses. Most of the kids had backed up along the sides of the indoor paddock. One or two others had not been fortunate enough to get out of the way before the horses had run through. Darcy checked these kids first. A couple of scrapes and bruises, but thankfully no one had been seriously injured, mostly just frightened. Some of the grown-ups, including the Millers, had stayed on and were helping attend to the frightened kids.

Darcy scanned the room for Thomas's grandmother.

Nana Ruth stood back near the entrance to the main stable. She looked unharmed.

"Are you okay?" Darcy asked. "What happened?"

"I don't know," said Nana Ruth. "All of a sudden the door to the aisle was thrown open and ten or twelve horses came running through. It was madness."

"Did you see anyone suspicious inside the stable? Did any of the kids wander away from the group?"

"No," answered Nana Ruth. "I kept track of the children. Everyone was here and accounted for except for you and Thomas. Thankfully the kids had stopped singing and lined up close to the table for more food and hot chocolate. Otherwise there would have been many more injuries. Where is Thomas?" Nana's brows knitted together in a deep frown.

"He saw someone running into the woods. He went after them on the horse."

Nana whispered something under her breath that Darcy couldn't quite understand, but she knew it wasn't anything good.

"I'm going to go check the rest of the stable." Darcy turned away.

Nana grabbed her by the shoulder. "Take one of the boys with you. I don't think you should go in there alone."

Darcy scanned the large room for Amos. Nana was right. She shouldn't go into the stable alone. She was just so used to doing everything herself. Having people around that watched her back was a completely new experience for her.

She just hoped that the dangerous people who were after her wouldn't hurt any of these good people. If they did, she would never forgive herself.

Darcy spotted Amos helping some of the girls to the benches. She hastened toward him and asked for his help. Within a minute, they had passed through the great door and into the main aisle of the stable.

The horses that were still inside their stalls twitched their ears and showed the white in their eyes. They paced to and fro at the doors of their stalls. Their anxious calls of distress reverberated through the hollow barn.

A large whip had been thrown in the center of the aisle. Amos stopped and picked it up.

"I suppose this is how the intruder herded those horses through a closed door. It is a good thing the door lifts as well as slides, or it would have come down completely," said Amos. "That would have hurt even more people."

A *clippity-clop* sounded behind them. Darcy jumped, thinking someone had let out another horse. But when she turned to look back, she relaxed. Some of the teens were bringing in the horses that had escaped. The animals were restless and fearful, but the Amish teens were experienced and patient as they soothed them back into their proper homes.

"Everything looks fine," said Amos. "I think someone played a prank on us."

Darcy didn't believe that for a second. This was all because of the artwork and her and Jesse... Clearly, someone thought he still had them and was willing to do anything to get their hands on them.

Darcy shook her thoughts away. "There's two more rooms at the other end. I want to check those, too."

Amos followed her down the long aisle to the stable office. She was surprised to find the feed room door wide open and the lids off of all the food bins. The floor, too, had a thin layer of grains spread all over the floor.

"I'll clean this up," Amos said.

"Thank you, Amos. Do you think there's anything stolen from in here?"

"Sometimes people steal tack but I never heard of stealing horse feed," Amos said. "But I guess people are always surprising us."

Darcy nodded. "Do people play pranks like this often?"

"No, ma'am. But you know how *Englischer* kids can be."

Darcy forced a smile. She hadn't lied about being Amish, but she felt like she was lying by wearing their clothing. "I'm going to check the office. Be right back."

Darcy walked the remaining steps to Thomas's office. That was where he had told her he kept his tack and anything else of value. The office door was also open and clearly it had been forced as the bolt had ripped through the frame of the door and splintered the wood. Darcy peered inside just as someone dressed in all black came flying through the office doorway. He plowed her down and made his escape through the far doors.

Chapter Twenty

"Just give her the artwork," the man said to Thomas. "Or she's liable to dig up your whole community and she won't care who's in her way. And she especially won't care about Finlay's daughter. She knows the daughter has the key. And she knows you know where the daughter is."

Thomas squared up his shoulders. His mind was reeling. His leg was bleeding. His brain was trying to make sense of what this man was telling him. "You're Wissenberg's son?"

"I'm nobody," the man said. "A friend."

"You're on our side? Then why were you running away if you're here to warn us? Why should I trust you?"

"You should trust no one." With a sudden motion, the man pulled his arms together and took advantage of Thomas's momentary surprise to break free. He pushed Thomas backward. Thomas caught his heel on a root and fell back to the snowy ground.

Before Thomas could recover, the man raised his knee high to his chest and with a look of pure evil on his face rammed his boot down into Thomas's wound. Agony ripped through Thomas's whole body, crippling him for a good few seconds. By the time he stood again, the man was in his car on the other side of the road. The wheels spun and he revved his engine until the car sped away across the new fallen snow.

Thomas tried to read the license plate. But he could only make out that it was Canadian and started with the number six. Thomas looked back to the stable. He didn't know how much to believe of what the man had told him. He clearly had gotten Thomas to let his guard down so that he could get away. He hardly seemed trustworthy. On the other hand, Thomas didn't want to completely dismiss the possibility of there being a second intruder still threatening the safety of the folks at the stable. If the man was telling even a bit of the truth, it meant that Darcy's life was endangered over the key they had found. The key that wasn't even in the stables. But, of course, the intruders didn't know that.

Thomas looked for his horse. The animal had jogged several yards away from the scuffle, but now stood like a steed of war waiting for his rider to march back to battle. Thomas found a felled tree near the creek and used it to help him remount. It hurt to move his leg in any direction, but riding on a horse with four good legs would be a lot faster than a man walking on one with a gash in the side of it.

He clamped his teeth down and fought the pain. He should have listened to Darcy and gone back to the stable. He only hoped he wasn't too late and that his mistake wouldn't be the cause of injury to anyone else. Especially Darcy.

* * *

Darcy squealed as she went down flat on her back into the middle of the stable aisle. Amos raced out of the nearby feed room and saw the fleeing man in black.

"Are you hurt, miss?" he asked.

"I'm fine," she said.

"I'm going to get that kid," Amos said running after the man in black.

"Wait! No," Darcy grunted, trying to refill her lungs with air. But Amos leaped over her and chased after the intruder.

Darcy pulled herself up off the ground and followed behind. Amos was stopped at the large front doors to the barn. "He disappeared. I chased him out of the stable, but when I got here…nothing."

Darcy searched the ground. There should be footprints in the snow, right? But the ground revealed nothing but a confusion of boot prints going in every direction. There was nothing to glean from the snow.

"It's okay," Darcy said. "It probably wasn't wise to run after him anyway. But thank you for helping. You're a brave kid."

"You think we were in actual danger?" He turned to her with a look of surprise.

"The stampede was a massive diversion so that they could search Thomas's office," she said. "They didn't seem to care too much about hurting any of us. Yes, I would call that dangerous."

"But what could Thomas have in his office worth all of that?" Amos asked.

A key to a pile of stolen art worth ten million dollars, Darcy thought to herself.

"Nothing," she answered. "There is nothing in the world that could be worth that."

And it was the whole reason she knew what she had to do next…

Darcy and Nana sat on one side of the kitchen table, each having a cup of herbal tea as they hoped to calm their nerves. Elijah and Chief McClendon sat on the opposite side of the table sipping coffee. Thomas was back on his stool with his wounded leg propped up high. Abigail had cleaned the wound again and redressed it. This time she told him that he was confined to the house and should sit or lie down for at least the next twenty-four hours. She had given him a shot of antibiotics in the hip, which had hurt almost as bad as the cleansing. She'd tried to talk him in to a mild painkiller, but he had refused. He needed to keep his head clear.

He did, however, ask Amos to take care of his horses and the stable for the rest of the week.

McClendon took notes in his little electronic pad. He wrote down descriptions of the intruders and he took multiple accounts of the activities from various community members before all of the guests had scattered.

Most of them had left believing the whole affair had been the work of some rotten and thoughtless teens. But a few of the visitors had started connecting Jesse's beating, the fire and now the stampede with the possibility that something much more sinister was taking place. Thomas didn't know what the bishop had told those few inquisitive folks, but at this point everyone had gone home and Thomas knew that meant the others were away and safe.

"I should have canceled the singing after the fire," he said. "I didn't think the trouble would follow us here."

"What's done is done," said Nana as she pushed away from the table. "And *Gott* doesn't want us to go around living our lives in fear and regret. No one was seriously hurt. No broken bones. No trips to the hospital. That's all that matters. Now, I'm going to bed. I don't think I'll sleep a wink but I'm going to try. If you will all excuse me."

"Yes, ma'am," everyone said.

"Did you catch the model and color of the car?" McClendon asked.

"No, I didn't catch the make," Thomas said. "But it was a dark color. Maybe gray or blue. It had four doors. Looked new. Canadian plates—Ontario, I think. I only caught the first number. It was a six."

Thomas shifted his weight on the stool. McClendon typed in a few more notes. Everyone looked exhausted and weighed down.

"Can anyone think of anything else?" McClendon asked.

They all shook their heads. They'd been over everything. Every detail of his encounter in the woods and the escape of the intruder in his office.

"Then I will take Eli and Miss Simmons back to the Millers'. Let's call it a night," McClendon said. He looked at Elijah. "We can phone Agent Ross from the car and get him up to speed. I'm going to post a car here, Thomas. From the sounds of your conversation in the woods, these people will be back looking for the key since they didn't get it tonight."

Thomas had the strangest sinking feeling as the three of them said goodbye. He dismissed it as emotions born out of exhaustion and confusion and the pain ramming through his leg. He wanted to say a private good-night to Darcy. He wanted to finish the conversation they'd had under the stars. He wanted to go back to that moment when he'd held her hand on the reins and she'd shared her heart with him.

But he knew he couldn't. She wouldn't even look back at him as she left the house.

Thomas knew it was better that way. But that didn't matter. Knowing something is right doesn't always make it feel better. Sometimes knowing what is right was just sad. Thomas made his way slowly up the stairs and into his bedroom. He lay across the quilted covers, too lost in his thoughts to draw them back. He turned out his lantern and closed his eyes. But, like Nana, he knew he wouldn't be able to sleep.

Darcy sat quietly in the back of the chief's car, knowing exactly what she needed to do. She listened to Elijah speak to Agent Ross over the phone. She knew they were all doing everything they could to help. But it wasn't enough to stop the danger.

Her presence and this mess of her father's were putting others in harm's way. And Darcy was determined to put a stop to it.

Whether or not the attackers on her trail knew she was there dressed in Amish clothing was unclear. But it wasn't something she was going to bank others' lives on. If she left Willow Trace and made it obvious that she was back at her town house, then the focus of the hunt would resume there and she could know that these people were safe—that Thomas was safe. As they pulled into the Millers' drive, she realized she needed to make her move now.

"I'm going to leave," Darcy announced to Elijah and McClendon. "Please call a taxi for me."

"What?" McClendon said. "I don't think that's going to help anything. Where are you going to go?"

"Home."

"Alone? That's not safe."

"Am I free to go?" she asked.

"Well, of course you are," the chief said. "I just don't think it's advisable. You are safer here."

"Maybe I am. Maybe I'm not. But for sure everyone else is safer without me here."

Neither of them argued with that reasoning.

"I just need to go inside and change back into my own clothing. If you could call a taxi for me, I'd really appreciate it."

"Sure," McClendon said. "I'll call one now."

Darcy headed into the Millers' house to get her things. Elijah raced after her.

"Why are you doing this?" he asked.

She didn't answer. He knew why she was doing it. "Does Agent Ross have the letter and the key and the Bible that we found yesterday? And the box of photos?"

"Yes, he took all of it," Elijah said. "Well, except for the box the photos were in. Why?"

"I just want to keep with me something that belonged to my father," she said. "Could I have it?"

He nodded.

Darcy changed into her own things. She spread the frock she'd worn over the quilt-covered bed. She ran her fingers over the plain cotton fabric. She placed the black apron over the front and the prayer *kapp* at the collar. Heavy emotions welled inside her.

Her own clothing felt tight and restrictive against

her limbs. She said a quick goodbye to Hannah and to Bishop and Mrs. Miller. Elijah waited for her outside. McClendon had already left and the taxi had arrived. In his hands, Elijah was holding the beautiful wooden box that Jesse had made. He handed it to her. As she grasped it in her hands, she felt peace. She was doing the right thing by leaving.

She smiled at Elijah. "Take care of Thomas," she said.

"You're not coming back, are you?" he asked.

Darcy put her hand on his shoulder. Emotions swelled in her, rising so high that all her thoughts and words swam in them. She couldn't answer him except with her eyes. She climbed in the taxi and closed the door. She had one more goodbye to make. This one at the Lancaster General Hospital.

Then Darcy knew she would never be back to Willow Trace.

Chapter Twenty-One

Darcy sat next to Jesse in the ICU. She held his limp, cold hand in hers. The poor old man clung on to his life by a thread. She spoke softly to him. She doubted he could hear, but there were things to be said all the same.

"I don't know why you kept those paintings, Jesse. *Dad*. But I do know you must have had a reason. Thomas believes in you and, well, so do I.

"It's been a crazy few days finding out about the truth. About you and Mom. I understand why you and Grandma and Granddad made the decisions that you did after Mom was killed. And there's nothing to forgive. So you don't ever have to ask. You should know that I always loved you. Even when Grandma wanted me to be angry with you the way she was. I didn't know enough to understand what had happened, but now that I do, I know that you loved Mom. You did the right thing by testifying. And you did the right thing by writing to me."

Her eyes filled with tears. She wiped them away with her free hand. "I can't stay long. But I had to say goodbye. And don't worry. I'm going to make sure that

Wissenberg knows I've been to my house so that none of your friends will be in danger anymore. I will make Wissenberg think that I have the key and everything else he wants, even if that's not true, and then—then I'm going to disappear. They will know that I'm lost to them forever and with me, the hopes of ever finding the paintings. But I love you. I'm so, so glad you wrote to me. Wake up, Jesse. And know I love you."

Darcy wasn't sure but she thought she felt Jesse's hand tighten just ever so slightly around her fingers. "Thank you, Jesse. I'll be thinking of you."

Darcy stood. She bent over and kissed her father on the forehead. She had so much to thank him for. She would never forget her time here in Willow Trace. She would never forget the people and their kindness and their love for God. She would never forget her friendship with Thomas and how his quiet strength and faith had helped lead her to a budding search for her own peace. She knew she didn't fully understand God's love yet, but she had felt the power of its force in brief waves around her and she wanted more. Her heart was open and ready.

Wiping away one last straggling tear, Darcy headed for the door. She wasn't two steps outside Jesse's room when she came toe-to-toe with a familiar face.

"Agent Danvers." Darcy stopped fast as the tall agent was blocking the way. "What are you doing here?"

"I figured you'd be back to see him sooner or later," the woman said. She ran a hand over her blond spikes.

Darcy wasn't sure if she wanted to trust the US Marshals office. After all, they had completely failed Jesse. But Danvers was there and…well, she knew she didn't want to be alone in her town house. "I guess you read my mind."

"So you've finally come to your senses and decided to relocate?"

Darcy nodded.

"That is a wise, wise decision." A wide smile stretched across the agent's face, which seemed more filled with triumph than compassion.

Darcy looked back toward Jesse's room. Already, some of her newfound peace felt as if it were eroding. She didn't want to give him up, but she knew that she had to. She was doing the right thing for everyone. But if that were so, why did she feel so unsure?

Sleep would not come. Thomas sat up in his bed. His leg was throbbing and his mind raced with thoughts of Jesse and Darcy and the fire and everything else. He might as well get up and focus on something constructive.

He relit the lantern and grabbed his Bible. He looked up the two verses that Jesse had put in the letter. Exodus 38:9—*Next they made the courtyard. The south side was a hundred cubits long and had curtains of finely twisted linen.*

Thomas reached again to his side table. He picked up his journal and pencil. He turned to a clean page and started scribbling. *Three, eight, nine.* The reference numbers. But there was a number in the verse, as well.

He skipped a line, then wrote *one hundred.* But wait, he thought. It's not a just a hundred. It's a hundred cubits. In the footnote of the Bible, it stated that would be about one hundred fifty yards. Maybe the number he wanted was 150? But 389 what? And 150 what?

Then he wrote the verse from Numbers. Chapter seven. Verse seven. Seventy-seven. *He gave two carts and four oxen to the Gershonites, as their work required.* Two carts and four oxen. That could be six if he added the numbers or it could be twenty-four if he just wrote them side by side. But again twenty-four what?

Thomas scratched his head. *Not what,* he thought. *The question isn't what. The question is where.* Where the artwork was. Like he'd thought before. It's not a code. The verses provided an address. Some combination of these numbers provided a zip code or a street number or maybe even the postbox or bank number where the paintings were.

Then Thomas remembered what Darcy had said about the Bible being a part of the message. If the verses and the numbers were all that was needed then why had Jesse hidden the Bible, too? That only made sense. Thomas flipped back from one verse to the other. This wasn't Jesse's Bible, but it was the same edition. If something was important about the Bible, surely the intended message would be on the same pages as the two verses.

Thomas read the pages. He studied them. Something was there staring right at him, but what? Page numbers? Maybe. He scribbled those down, as well.

Thomas wrote the numbers several different ways. It was a lot of numbers. Too many for a zip code. Too many for a street address. But what other way could one locate something using numbers?

Coordinates. If he took the verse reference numbers and added the triple-digit page number to each of the verse reference numbers then… Thomas wondered if it was about what you needed to give a very precise longitude and latitude. He wasn't sure, but thought maybe a little time on a computer would help. Of course, he didn't have one. But Abigail did. He hated to wake her after all the help she'd been earlier at the singing, but this was important.

Thomas pushed himself off the bed and hobbled down the stairs and out to the stable, where he usually kept his phone. He was going to get this figured out.

Tonight.

Agent Danvers had been quiet as they walked out of the hospital. Darcy paid the cab driver who she had asked to wait. She took her things out of the backseat, then followed the agent to her truck and climbed in. The drive to her town house seemed interminably long. The snow had stopped and the main roads were completely clear, but still it seemed like they were moving at a snail's pace. Darcy had asked Agent Danvers what would happen when she relocated. What were all the people she knew going to be told? What would her design team think? Her boss? The US Marshal had not been too forthcoming with her responses. Something about it all being explained to her later.

Darcy knew she was doing the right thing. But she already missed Willow Trace. She missed all the friendly faces. She missed Thomas. She hadn't even been able to say goodbye.

Finally, they arrived at her town house. Darcy unlocked her car and took out the Bible that had belonged to Jesse—not the one he'd hidden away, but the worn one he'd obviously read regularly. In all the commotion of the last trip to her place, she had forgotten to take it to read to Jesse in the hospital. But she was glad she'd forgotten now, because she had it to read herself.

To learn more about God and also as a keepsake to remind her of Jesse and Thomas.

The first thing Darcy did when she got inside was turn on her phone. She wanted Wissenberg and whoever his little minions were to know that she had left Willow Trace. She got on her computer and answered several emails, too.

As she now rummaged through her town house, gathering the few things she wanted to take with her to her new life, Agent Danvers kept rushing her. In fact, the woman paced her living area, and was biting her nails and constantly talking on her phone in whispers. Darcy couldn't figure out what she was so nervous about. Darcy was the one who was giving up her life. Not Agent Danvers. Danvers was just doing her job. Shouldn't she be used to this sort of thing?

When Darcy emerged from her bedroom, she found Agent Danvers hovered over a huge mess on her coffee table. "What are you…?"

Darcy paused about halfway across the room. She could see what was spread out over the table. It was Jesse's box. The woman had completely disassembled it.

"What did you do that for?" Rage rushed through Darcy's veins.

"I knew there had to be more than one key," Danvers said. An evil smile spread over her lips. She reached down over the table and lifted up a small key.

Darcy stumbled back a step. Why would Agent Danvers be looking for a key?

"It's a place in Washington, DC," Abigail told Thomas over the phone.

His heart pounded. "This must be where the paintings are," he said.

"I don't know, Thomas," Abigail said. "It's some sort of restaurant and bar."

Thomas thought for a second. "Well, I may be off a little. I thought my Bible was the same edition as the one we found in Jesse's highboy. But it's possible that it's not—meaning the page numbers could be slightly different. We need to call Agent Ross."

"I don't have his number," Abigail said. "I'll have to call Elijah and I doubt he's going to answer his phone at this hour. In fact, I doubt he even has it in the house with him."

"You answered."

"My husband's an ER doctor. We always answer the phone," she said.

"Then we will just have to drive over there," Thomas said.

"*We?* Thomas, it's the middle of the night. This can wait till morning."

"I don't know, Abby," Thomas felt his pulse racing. He felt a sense of urgency that he couldn't explain. "I got this feeling that we need to take care of this tonight."

"Go back to bed, Thomas," she said. "I'm getting another call."

Thomas decided he would call Elijah himself, even though he knew Abigail was right. There was no way his friend had his phone on and inside the house. Eli's father, the bishop, tolerated phones for business and emergencies, but he wanted them out of the home whenever possible, which when you got right down to it was most of the time.

Elijah's line went to voice mail and Thomas left a detailed message explaining his theory about the location. He wanted to hitch up his buggy and ride over to the Millers'. He especially wanted to share what he'd discovered with Darcy. But Abigail was right. He knew that a buggy ride would be slow and painful with his leg hurting so much, and the Millers would hardly be happy to see him at this time of night. It could wait a few hours. It would have to.

Thomas pushed himself up and started to go back to the house, when he heard his own phone ringing. Maybe Elijah had kept his phone nearby and had heard the message? It wouldn't have surprised him with all the excitement that they'd had the past few days if Elijah wanted it close in case of another emergency.

But when he looked down at the phone, it wasn't Elijah's number calling. It was Abigail. He answered.

"Change your mind?"

"No, I didn't change my mind," Abigail said. "That was Blake on the other line. He called to tell me that Jesse woke up."

Chapter Twenty-Two

Abigail did come to pick up Thomas and the two of them hurried to the Millers'. But not so much to tell Elijah about the coordinates, as to tell Darcy that her father had woken up. Jesse was going to live. What a blessing!

The coordinates didn't even matter anymore. Now that Jesse was awake and alive, he could tell them everything. This was all going to be over. Darcy would be safe.

"I'm glad I have a key," Abigail said, as she exited the car and skipped up to the front porch. Thomas stayed in the car to rest his leg.

Abigail let herself in and disappeared into the dark house. About three minutes later she reemerged not with Darcy, but with a dress and apron in her hands.

"She's gone," Abigail said. "The bed's made and my dress was laying right across it."

Thomas felt the worst sinking sensation travel from his head to his gut. He opened the car door and started to climb out. "Where's Elijah?"

"I'll go get him," Abigail said. "Hannah is going to kill me for waking them up."

"And I'm going to kill Elijah for letting Darcy escape," he said. Of course, he didn't mean it. Elijah couldn't keep her there if she'd wanted to leave. He was just so upset. Hurt. Why would she leave? How could she leave? Without even saying goodbye...

"You're not really a US Marshal, are you?" Darcy felt nauseous, as if she could faint.

"Just now figuring that out?" Danvers snapped.

"Then who are you?"

"What's it to you?" Danvers said. "You'd be dead already if I didn't need you to open the mailbox."

"Mailbox? You know where to use the key?"

"You don't?"

"No."

"You left us all the clues," Danvers said. "The ones your dear old dad left for you."

"But you don't have them. An agent at the FBI has them," Darcy said. "And you don't have the key, either. That key only works on the box. The one you just broke into a thousand pieces."

"I have friends in the FBI," she said smugly. "Friends who work in Cryptography. I couldn't get my hands on the key. It was held in a different department. But I got the address and I bought myself some time before that Agent Ross who you got involved will find out about it. And as far as your key goes...well, you're right. One of the keys works on the box. But you and your handsome farmer friend didn't look hard enough. Your father was too paranoid to have just one key in one hiding place. There was another one. And I found it."

Darcy had to admit the key did look just like the

one they found in the highboy. "How did you know to look in the box?"

"You and your friend were pretty loud at the cottage."

"That was you?" Darcy said. "You shot Thomas?"

"Yes, but I missed the fatal shot I was aiming for and I really don't like it when I miss."

Darcy looked around her home. Could she run? Could she make it to her car? Maybe she could cut through the back and escape down the alley. If she could get her phone, she could call 911. But she'd left it back in her bedroom.

"I need to get something," Darcy said, turning toward the bedroom.

Danvers quickly pulled a pistol from her phony US Marshals coat. "I don't think so. I think you're going to be sticking right next to me until the post office facility opens up at eight o'clock tomorrow morning. Now, let's go. We got a little driving to do."

"The coordinates point to a mailing facility in northern Virginia," said Elijah after hanging up the phone with Agent Ross.

"Not a restaurant," Thomas said.

"No, you didn't have the right Bible. The one Jesse left has slightly different page numbers, so that shifted the exact location slightly. Anyway, Ross is going to drive down there right now. He said it would take about three hours."

"What about Darcy?" Thomas asked.

"No one can get a hold of her. She's not answering her phone."

"Anybody call the US Marshals?"

"You think she went with Danvers?"

"I hope not. But maybe she thought it was the only way to stay safe?" Thomas rubbed his scraggly beard with his hand. "What about the taxi driver? You said she left in a taxi. Can he tell us where he took her?"

"Worth a try."

Elijah lifted his phone and within a couple of minutes, he was speaking with the driver. Thomas could hear his friend using every means of persuasion that he could to get the driver to talk to him. Finally, he clicked off. "She went to the hospital. Stayed about fifteen minutes then came out, paid the fare and left with a woman with short, spiky blond hair."

Thomas took off his hat and twisted it in his hands. What were they going to do?

"I'll call Agent Ross. I don't think Agent Danvers would take a call from us, but she wouldn't be able to ignore another federal agent."

"It's worth a try," Thomas said, trying to slow his pounding heart.

"And relax," Eli said. "I'm sure it's not too late. It's only been a few hours. We'll get her back with her dad in no time."

Elijah turned away with his phone again. Thomas hoped his friend was right. He hoped they weren't too late to stop Darcy from making the biggest mistake of her life. He wished there was something else he could do…besides just rely on Elijah's connections. But he was thankful they had them.

Elijah's eyes met Thomas and his friend dropped the phone to his side. "There's no Agent Danvers working in the US Marshals."

* * *

Agent Danvers held the gun at Darcy's chest and Darcy froze. She didn't even dare breathe. She couldn't believe she'd been so stupid to think that it was normal that Agent Danvers was hovering around her father's hospital bed waiting for her to show up. She couldn't believe that none of them had suspected the so-called agent earlier back at the hospital, when she acted so nervous and over important. No wonder she seemed so callous and flippant about relocation. She wasn't even an agent. She was a criminal and she'd sat in on a meeting with the Lancaster chief of police without anyone suspecting.

Suddenly, there was a loud knock at the door.

"Our escorts are here," Danvers announced. The fake agent pressed Darcy toward the front door. Darcy opened it to find two huge men standing there.

"Miss Simmons," Danvers said, "meet my two brothers. They've been kind enough to volunteer to escort us to Virginia. I wouldn't have even worried about it if it weren't for that meddlesome farmer and his friend. But I have a feeling they may come looking for my truck and me, which is why we're going to take your car. At least, part of the way."

Darcy studied the two men. She remembered Thomas's description of the guy in the woods that he'd caught. Thomas had said he looked like a young version of Wissenberg. Well, so did these two guys. In fact they looked so much alike they could be twins, and they strongly resembled the man she suspected to be their father. Now that she was looking for it, she realized Danvers looked like him, too. Especially if she didn't have the fake blond hair, but the smoother darker hair of her brothers.

"Well, they're my half brothers," she added. "Different mother."

Wissenberg's family. How nice of them to all work together, she thought.

Danvers took a set of keys from one of the men. "Go get her ID and car keys."

One of the men disappeared into her home while Danvers pushed Darcy through the front door, gun at her back, and led her to the passenger side of her red car.

"You didn't think I'd let you drive, did you?"

Danvers handcuffed Darcy to the passenger door. Apparently, she hadn't bothered to lock it that night she'd left with Thomas and Elijah. She truly had been in a state of shock. She wished she had left the Bible in the backseat. The one that belonged to Jesse. It would have helped to calm her nerves. But still she remembered the words of Bishop Miller. She was a child of God. He would take care of her. And she believed it.

God, I know I don't know You too well. But I'm trusting You'll help get me out of this. If You can.

And Thomas always said that anything was possible, *if it's God's will.*

Danvers walked around to the driver side. One of her half brothers came running out with her clutch bag. He handed it to Danvers, who clawed out her keys and threw the bag at Darcy's feet.

Her clutch. Darcy's heartbeat quickened. She didn't expect that God could answer her prayer so fast. But He had. He had given her hope.

Yes, the clutch had her ID in it. It had her car keys in it. It also had her phone in it. Unless they'd been smart enough to take it out. She hoped they hadn't been. She hoped the guy was as stupid as he looked. And she hoped that the phone was still tucked away in its little zippered compartment.

"We will be a few cars back," the man said. And off they all went. Danvers drove frantically through her little town and then even faster once she got to the highway. Darcy felt bile and adrenaline roiling through her. She was nauseous. What did they need her for?

"So where are we going?" Darcy asked.

"South," she said.

"I can see that. Anyway, why do you need me?"

"Only you or Jesse can get to the postal box. Even with the key, it's in a secured area. Anyone allowed access has to have ID."

"What are you going to with me afterward?"

"Take you for a little swim," Danvers said.

"So is your name Wissenberg, too?"

"Anyone tell you you ask too many questions?"

Darcy took that as her cue to fall silent, though her thoughts kept racing. She just wanted to get her hands on her phone and get help. But would she have a chance before this madwoman ended her life?

Thomas thought he had felt every sort of emotion there was, but what he experienced now he had no words for. It was more than panic. More than rage. It was some sort of combustible power inside him that he knew folding his hat over in his hands would never soothe away.

"We have to do something," Thomas said.

"Agent Ross is sending a car for us," Elijah said. "He's going to have us meet him at the heliport. It's the only way we can catch them. They have a huge head start on us."

"They're going to let us go with them?" Thomas knew that had to be completely due to Elijah's friendship with Agent Ross.

Elijah nodded. "Agent Ross said any man smart enough to figure out that address without any cryptography training is welcome on his team anytime. Anyway, he needs you."

Thomas gave his friend a doubtful look. "We're pretty sure Danvers has the address. But we don't think she has the key. One of us will have to have a trade-off of Darcy for the key."

"And what if they do have a key? What if they don't need us?"

"Pray that they do," Elijah said.

Chapter Twenty-Three

Agent Danvers pulled off the interstate and followed a winding single-lane road for about three miles. Darcy was growing more and more worried. This was not how she'd imagined the drive to the secure box. It was much too rural. She'd held out some hope that if they were in a busy area, she might be able to give her captors the slip, or at least call out for help. But out here, no one would hear her.

They passed a gas station and a cluster of old motels. One had a diner in the front of it named Mickey's. Danvers pulled into the parking lot.

"Are we stopping to eat?" Darcy asked.

"No."

"Good. Because it doesn't look very good." Darcy's sarcasm was just a weak outlet for her fear.

"Shut up." Danvers pulled Darcy's red compact car in next to a brand-new luxury sedan—a Mercedes that was sleek, black and loaded. "I'm going to move you to this other car. And I'm going to make a pit stop."

Danvers reached over and released her handcuff. "Don't run. My brothers are right beside us."

She wasn't kidding. The giant twins were pulling in just on the other side of the Mercedes. Darcy reached for her clutch. She got out and walked to the other car. One of the brothers casually got out of his car and waved to her like they were old friends.

"Susan, it's so crazy running in to you here."

Susan? What was he talking about?

"Let me get the door for you," he said. "Oh, look. I think you dropped something."

Click!

Darcy realized he had just come over to lock her in the car, and that the faux casual chitchat was his way of making their interaction look natural in case anyone in the diner was watching. This time she was handcuffed to the seat. Not her hands but her ankle. He shut the door in her face. "So good seeing you."

Danvers was busy grabbing a bag from her brothers' backseat. Then she disappeared into the diner.

Stay calm, Darcy told herself. She reached into the clutch and felt around the side pocket. Her heart leaped with joy. The phone was there. She pulled it out, careful not to look down at what she was doing. She didn't want to alert the twins to her discovery and what she hoped would be her rescue.

Thomas could feel his phone buzzing in the seat beside him. He hated that he would have to let go of the armrest to see who was calling. He knew holding on to the armrest gave him a false sense of security, but it was nice to have the assurance all the same.

He was buckled tightly into a seat on a small helicopter. Agent Ross was across from him, as was Elijah. They were on a quick path to Alexandria, Virginia, and to a secure and private lockbox facility located at the exact coordinates that Jesse had cleverly hidden within the confines of a letter and a Bible.

The helicopter ride—the first he'd ever taken—was noisy and unsettling to his stomach. But he couldn't say he didn't find it intriguing. He imagined being this high up was a little like seeing the world through God's eyes. Some of it was so beautiful. But some of it not. Most of what they could see now was nothing but highways everywhere, a concrete jungle he'd once heard someone call it.

Thomas picked up his phone and tried to ignore the ground and sky that flashed by him as he read the display. It was Darcy. He couldn't believe it.

"She texted," Thomas yelled to Agent Ross. "She wrote, 'It's Danvers. With her now. Please help.'"

He held the phone over for Ross to look at. Ross took the phone in his hands. "Hold on while I get a lock on her location."

Ross spoke over some sort of radio system that only he could hear. "My team is locating her. They've also got an ID on this Danvers. I asked the hospital to send over the security tapes from the other day when you all met in the conference room. Since Darcy is in such immediate danger, I want to find out as much as we can about what we are dealing with. The facial recognition came up fast. The woman's name is Kelsey Moon. She's the illegitimate daughter of Wissenberg and Lenore Moon. She changed her name to Danvers so that no one would associate her with her mother or father since they'd both been in prison. When she turned eighteen, she joined the army. She served a term in Afghanistan as a ranger, but was dishonorably discharged for stealing documents from an officer's computer. She's a trained killer. And we think she's teamed up with her twin half brothers on this venture to steal back this stolen art. The license plate you saw last night could very well belong to Remy Wissenberg, who we found lives in Ontario under the name of Rossen. It seems all three of the children changed their name to slow or divert anyone from discovering connections they had to their father and—in Danvers's case—her mother, too. But all the while they stayed in touch. The other twin moved to Europe. We were able to trace the computer-generated calls to his location in Lublin, Poland, which is the birthplace of Wissenberg's father."

"Nice family," Elijah said.

Ross held up a hand as more information was coming through. Then he yelled something to the pilot and the chopper changed directions sharply.

"Okay. We're heading in. Five minutes to destination. We're going to get her."

Thomas grabbed at his stomach, as the aircraft pitched and swooped. But the rest of him had hope. They were going to find Darcy. And get her away from this killer.

Darcy spent one second too long getting her phone back into the zippered part of her purse. Danvers caught her red-handed.

"Idiot!" Danvers yelled, only she looked nothing like the Agent Danvers from before. She'd changed out of the monochromatic pantsuit and replaced it with a stylish pair of black dress slacks and a sexy blue sweater, which clung to her thin body like a wetsuit. The spiky blond hair was gone, revealing her true, long, flaxen locks.

She grabbed the phone from Darcy and threw it

into the street. Then she got into the driver's seat. She reached into her bag and pulled out her gun. With the gun in one hand and the other hand steering wheel, they pulled out of Mickey's parking lot and back onto the one-lane highway.

"Thomas, this is going to be okay," Elijah said. "Darcy is going to be fine."

Agent Ross smiled as he tucked a weapon away in a holster under his arm. "He's right. We've got her location and we are one minute to touch down at that diner. We may not even have to use the key as bait. This will be a total ambush if Darcy has been able to conceal her phone from her."

Thomas hoped—no, he prayed—that Ross was right. He could let Darcy go back to her *Englisch* life if that's what made her happy, but he couldn't lose her like this. That he just couldn't live with.

The chopper passed over a patch of forest, then a river and another patch of forest. They began to descend through an opening in the trees. Thomas saw a group of buildings and a highway running through the middle.

"There's her car!" Thomas saw the small red compact in the lot on the other side of the street.

"He's gonna set down here," Ross shouted. "More space."

The pilot was busy maneuvering the helicopter. He leveled it out, then they went down almost like they were connected to a rope and bucket in a well. Thomas kept his eyes on the car. Was it empty?

"I don't see anyone," he said. "Maybe they went inside."

"What's that on the ground next to the sports car?"

"It's her phone," Ross answered. "That's what the GPS tells us."

The chopper landed. People from the diner began to come out and see what all the noise was about. Ross hopped out of the chopper and ran toward Darcy's car. He was shaking his head. He walked toward the crowd of people at the door and flashed his badge. A second later he was sprinting back to the chopper. He jumped back in and waved his hand in a circle. They lifted up into the air again. Ross took his seat.

"They are already gone. We need to get to that post office." Ross clenched his teeth, his face tight. So much for the ambush.

"Put this on." Danvers handed Darcy a long black winter coat, a pair of sunglasses and a white knit ski cap. Darcy did as she said and about two minutes later they pulled into the mailing facility located on Moses Road. The strange message at the beginning of Jesse's letter didn't seem so cryptic anymore. It seemed Moses had been guarding the paintings all along, just like the letter had said.

Danvers had her pistol on Darcy's back as they walked inside. The facility was one of the bigger nationwide shipping companies that boxed things for individuals or companies. Only this one was private and offered a second layer of security for their box rentals.

She had done plenty of business with places like this working for Winnefords. It was sometimes faster than the regular postal service. In the back of the store was the counter where their staff packed, weighed and labeled shipments. In the front of the store were hundreds of PO boxes that people rented, instead of receiving mail at their homes or offices. And to the side was a private locked chamber, where you could secure valuables without going to a bank. Darcy imagined it was frequented by some pretty shady customers.

Danvers directed Darcy to the checkout desk. "Hand him your ID and tell him you want to open box twenty-four. Here's the key."

Twenty-four. Two and four. That had been a part of the verses, too. Jesse had left every needed clue in his letter. She just hoped that Thomas got her text and that Agent Ross knew where to come. She prayed. Because if they didn't get there soon, her life was going to be over.

Danvers pressed the key into her open hand. "And don't try anything. Even if you get away from me, my brothers are watching."

Darcy did as Danvers said. She placed her key on the counter and showed the man her ID. She couldn't believe it when the man typed some information into her computer, then smiled.

"Hello, Miss Simmons. It's been a long time since you've been to your box. But you are still paid up through next year."

"I'd like to have access today, please."

"Of course." The attendant came out from the cashier stand and escorted them to the private chamber of rental boxes. He pressed a code in the keypad and the electronic door slid open.

"You have five minutes to exit," the attendant said and then turned back to the line at the cashier stand.

Darcy looked around the giant mailing facility. Danvers wasn't going to try anything here. There were too many people and too many cameras. Still, the phony agent kept the concealed weapon at her back and edged her into the chamber, where there were rows and rows and walls and walls of boxes.

Darcy knew each one of the walls would have a box 24. They'd have to hurry if they wanted to try them all in five minutes.

She moved forward toward the first row of boxes, but Danvers steered her roughly in another direction. "It's this set of boxes."

It was numbered 150. "I thought the other verse had the number *one hundred* in it?"

Danvers pushed her forward. "So you *did* understand the message."

That realization seemed to make Danvers nervous. She had been pushy before but now she seemed in a downright panic. "Give me the key back," she growled, ripping it from Darcy's hands.

She pulled Darcy along with her to box 24 of aisle 150. She inserted the key and slid out a large cylinder. It was made of a unique type of wood and it was locked. Now what?

Apparently, Danvers didn't care about this step. She looked triumphant as she shoved the huge piece at Darcy.

"Carry it out to the car," Danvers ordered her. "Time to go."

Darcy lugged the huge wooden case in her arms through the mailing store. It was now or never—she had to get away.

But Danvers still had one hand around her elbow and the other pointing a gun into her side. If Darcy tried to escape, it would be too easy for Danvers to put a bullet in her. But Darcy was hoping that Danvers would hesitate to shoot her in such a public place. It was her only chance. As soon as she got to the front, she'd make a run for it. She didn't care if the brothers were there. Really, what did she have to lose?

When she got to the front doors, she stopped. "My hands are kind of full. Can you get it?"

Danvers gave her a little snarl as she stepped forward to open the heavy glass door for her. Darcy put her foot out in front of Danvers's ankle, tripping her and throwing her slightly off balance. As she stumbled forward into the opening door, Darcy threw the heavy cylinder container onto her back. Danvers went down. Darcy stepped over her and ran as fast as she could into the parking lot.

Chapter Twenty-Four

Before the chopper landed, Ross handed bulletproof vests to both Elijah and Thomas. They donned them, but refused to carry weapons. Thomas didn't even want to wear the vest. The only armor he needed was the Lord's protection. But Elijah gave him a look that said he'd better comply.

The helicopter landed in the far corner of the parking lot of the mailing facility, which it shared with some other not so prosperous businesses. It was a good hundred yards from the front of the store. Ross, Elijah and the two other agents and pilot ran across the asphalt at lightning speed. Thomas moved as fast as he could. With his injured leg, he could not keep up with Elijah or the trained agents. He also heard sirens wailing not so far away. More help was on the way. He just hoped they'd made it in time. He hoped Danvers was here with Darcy. Maybe they still needed the key.

Lord, let us get there in time to help Darcy.

Thomas had prayed over and over. But he feared they would be too late. About thirty seconds after they landed, a large black SUV with its siren blaring pulled into the lot. Another FBI team. It parked much closer to the front of the store. Four men exited. They all carried rifles and wore bulletproof armor.

The few customers that meandered through the lot hurried to move away.

Thomas followed at a distance toward the center of the parking lot.

They were here. Danvers and those twins and Darcy. He could sense it in the air like an evil wind. Ross and his team had not been too late. But where were they? Everything seemed quiet—a little too quiet. No way all of them were inside.

Thomas stood still for a second, just scanning the lot. He spotted movement on the ground between the cars.

"Darcy!"

But then a car engine started behind him. He turned just in time to see a black sedan moving at him at full speed. It was the twins.

"Thomas!" Darcy stood up from between two nearby cars. He looked toward her voice.

"Get down! Get down!" Ross's voice echoed across the parking lot.

Thomas dove between two cars just in time before the black sedan raced across the lane where he'd just stood. Shots rang out through the parking facility. Glass broke. Tires screeched. More shots fired. People in the periphery let out squeals and shouts of fear.

Thomas breathed heavily. He looked under the cars to the left and the right. Finally, he saw her. He tuned out all the chaos around them and then he ran hunched down low to where she hid between the cars.

"Darcy." He knelt down and hugged her to him. She held on to him, burying her head into his chest. "It's okay. You're okay now. It's all over." He stroked her hair. It hung down loose around her shoulders like it had the first day he'd met her. "Thanks to *Gott* this is all over."

She hugged him tighter. Thomas's senses were filled with her presence. It was over. And he was happy that she was safe.

"Danvers," Darcy said. "She's getting away with the paintings."

"Where?" Thomas said.

Darcy looked around the lot to where Danvers had parked the black Mercedes, just in time to see her slipping into the car with the stolen goods. "There!"

Ross must have been watching them because within seconds, the agent was after Danvers and his team closed in on her. A couple of blown tires later and the whole younger generation of Wissenbergs were in handcuffs.

"All clear!" Ross yelled across the lot. His men had Danvers and the twins apprehended. Darcy couldn't believe it was all over. Thomas had walked her back to a second SUV, which had come to take them home. One of the FBI team had put a blanket around her shoulders and brought her a bottle of water. The others were running damage control in and around the store. A news crew had arrived and was filming in the distance. Agent Ross was escorting Danvers to a police squad car. The helicopter had flown off while an EMS squad had arrived on the scene. It was just like something out of a movie, Darcy thought. One where the good guys actually win.

She sat down inside the vehicle. She still shook and

her heart pounded. But she knew it was over. This time it was really over. Another of the team placed the cylinder box from the mailbox at her feet on the floor of the SUV.

"Do you know how to open it?" the man asked.

She shook her head.

"Well, it stays here for now. Keep an eye on it." He winked at them and raced off again to finish questioning people and taking statements.

Darcy looked at the case. The lock was a simple three-digit combination. She ran her hands over the lock. "You think Jesse made this?"

"You can ask him yourself," Thomas said.

"What?" She turned to him, eyes wide.

"Jesse woke up. He's going to be okay," Thomas said. "Blake said he's very weak but that he expects over time Jesse will make a full recovery."

Darcy squealed with delight. She threw her arms around Thomas. How wonderful! All her prayers were coming true.

And Thomas was beside her and that felt good. She knew God had saved her once again. From this day forward she would never live her life the same.

She smiled up at Thomas. "Thank you for coming today. For all you've done, Thomas. You've changed my life."

"Me?" he said.

"Well, yes, you," she said. "Your faith is so strong. And seeing it in you made me want it for myself."

"Then I guess we can thank Jesse for inviting us both over at the same time so that we could meet that day," he said. His grin was beautiful. Everything about him was beautiful. Even his beard, she'd learn to like.

She looked down again at the lock again. "Do you think the combination was in the letter?"

"We can try it." Thomas said. He called out all the three-number combinations that he remembered. Darcy tried each combination accordingly, but the lock remained firmly closed.

"You know, Jesse had my name on the account here," she told him. "That's the only reason Danvers needed me. She found a second key in the wooden box from the well, and her spies in the FBI broke the code from the letter for her, but only an account holder with photo ID would be allowed in the vault."

"I wondered how she was able to open it. We hoped she still needed the key, and would be willing to trade it for you. If she hadn't needed you to get into the vault… I'm glad you're still in one piece."

"Not as glad as I am. But how did she find Jesse?"

"She didn't. Wissenberg did. Remember how Ross said that someone from the US Marshals visited him in prison?"

She nodded.

"Well, Ross's team finally got a name with the face in the video surveillance. It was an older man. Maybe someone that knew Wissenberg before he went to jail. Anyway, he was paid a large sum of money after the third visit to Wissenberg and then he disappeared."

"Do they think he was killed?"

Thomas shrugged. "I don't know, but I'm guessing Danvers got that jacket she was wearing from someone."

Darcy shivered. She pulled the blanket around herself and closed her fingers around it. Her hand brushed the locket. She thought of Jesse. She couldn't wait to see him. She couldn't wait to go back to Willow Trace. She couldn't wait to...

"The locket," she said. "The combination. Of course, it's the date on the locket. Try ten-four. One-zero-four."

He reached down and rolled the combination lock to one-zero-four. It clicked and fell open. Inside was a thick file and about twenty rolled-up scrolls. No wonder it was so heavy.

Thomas pulled out the file and one of the paintings. "What's this?"

They spread the folder and its contents between them. It was a file on Wissenberg. There were pictures of him with different people. And an article about the car crash that her mother had died in. "I think this may connect Wissenberg to my mother's car crash."

"We'll give it to Agent Ross. He'll know what to do with it." Thomas put it aside and unfurled the painting. It was one of the ones in the photos they found in the box.

"It's beautiful," Thomas said.

She looked over at him and they both laughed. "I thought the Amish don't really like art?"

"Well, it's not a necessity so we don't own any. But it sure is beautiful."

"I see you already opened the box." Ross hopped into the vehicle. He lifted the paintings and the files out of the box and secured them in the back of the SUV. Elijah climbed into the front passenger seat. "I know a little Amish wife I just can't wait to get back home to," he said.

"And those paintings will finally go where they belong," Ross said. "To their owners."

"The names on the back of the photos?" Darcy asked.

"Yep, every single one of them," Ross said. "One of our agents just had a quick chat with your father in the hospital. Mostly just to inform him of the seizure of his stolen property."

Darcy was suddenly horrified. "Will he go to jail?"

Elijah smiled. "No. The statute of limitations has well passed, even on this small fortune. Anyway, he has a great defense."

"Really?" Thomas asked. "And what is that?"

"He did it to protect you," Ross said to Darcy.

"What? How would that protect me?"

"Wissenberg knew he kept them. Some of these were paintings he had wanted very badly. And your father told him that he'd give them to him as soon as he got out of jail as long as he didn't harm you," Ross said. "But with two life sentences, I don't think he was ever counting on Wissenberg getting out of jail."

"So why the photos and keeping track of the actual owners?"

"He planned to give the paintings back to them, once Wissenberg passed."

"Or have me do it if Wissenberg outlived him," Darcy said. Thomas had been right all along. Jesse had had reasons. Good reasons. And now they were headed back to see him. She couldn't wait. She could go home now.

But Darcy frowned. Somehow going back to her town house and a life working at Winnefords didn't seem appealing to her in the least.

Thomas sat back in his seat, his eyes falling to the file of pictures and documents they found.

"There was this in the cylinder, too." He passed the folder forward to Elijah. A letter slipped from inside.

Elijah picked it up and handed it to Darcy. "This is to you."

Darcy slowly opened the letter from her father. Thomas watched as her eyes filled with tears.

"Good grief." She wiped her eyes. "I'm like a fountain."

"You had a rough week." Thomas reached over and held her hand. It would be his last chance, but he couldn't mourn that right now. He was too grateful to have the chance at all. He'd been so afraid they would be too late. He was so thankful they weren't.

She squeezed his hand. "It's so sweet. It's just a letter saying that he loves me. And that if I have this letter, then he is gone and he misses me. He tells me that my name was Daria. Daria Rachel Finlay."

"It's a beautiful name. Do you want to be called Daria?"

"No. I'm Darcy now. Can't change that. But maybe one day if I have a daughter…"

Thomas looked away. He didn't want to think about her getting married and having a daughter with someone else. He couldn't have her and he didn't want anyone else to, either. He hated himself for the selfish, possessive feelings he had. He should want her to be happy, even if it meant leaving him behind. And he knew she'd be leaving. She wasn't Amish. He'd simply have to get over his feelings. Just like he had with Mary.

"He wrote more," she said. "Do you want to hear?"

"*Ja*, if you want to share."

"He wrote that he loved me more than anything except God Himself. And that every day he would pray for me to know the love and peace that he'd found in Willow Trace."

Thomas felt his teeth clench. "It must have been a hard way to live, knowing that you were out there and he couldn't see you. Couldn't see you grow up. Couldn't hold you. Couldn't give you his love and protection."

"But no one except for my father knew his burden," Elijah said. "He hid it well. To protect you."

"What will happen to Jesse? Where will he go? His house burned down," Darcy asked. "He'll need someone to take care of him."

"We will rebuild his cottage," Thomas said. "There's already been some talk of starting on it as soon as we get the materials in. And he'll live with me in the interim." Thomas smiled. This way he'd get to see Darcy at least a few times. He knew she would visit her father while he was recuperating.

"But what if I want him to live with me?" Darcy said. "What if I want to take care of him? I'm his daughter."

"You're not Amish," Thomas said. "He took vows. He's not going to go back to the *Englisch*."

"Then I guess I will have to look into becoming Amish."

Epilogue

The following September

Darcy had done it. Just like her father before her. She'd left her education, her high-powered job and her town house behind. She'd taken care of Jesse and they'd moved together back into the cottage, rebuilt by the Willow Trace community.

It had all come slowly. At first, she'd just attended Sunday meetings. Then she'd started to learn the songs. She loved the songs. Then she'd learned the Bible, and prayer had become part of her daily life. And Jesse had guided her along. Encouraged her. Loved her. How could she have given up on that?

Darcy had started a sewing business, which she ran from the cottage, performing alterations for both *Englischers* and Amish. Her reputation for perfection and speed had her with an overflow within a few months. So, she expanded to have a turn-around desk at a store in Lancaster, where folks could drop off and pick up items.

In addition, word had gotten out—thanks to Nana

Ruth—that Darcy could sew wedding dresses. So now, instead of just making them for Winnefords like she used to do, she made them for brides all over Lancaster County. Of course, she didn't make dresses for the Amish—Amish women made their own wedding dresses. But since the *Englischers* didn't, she loved making them for many women in and around the Lancaster area who wanted a simple, elegant gown but couldn't afford the haute couture prices of the department stores.

There were some in the Ordnung who disapproved of her business, just as they had of her father's furniture, but times were different now. Most of the Amish were turning from farming to alternate livelihoods in order to survive in today's economy. And really there was no difference in her making a fancy wedding dress than it was for an Amish carpenter to make fancy custom cabinets for an *Englisch* client.

In any case, Darcy shared any extra profit with the community, as Thomas did. And she also had started a mission, where she invited any women who wanted to come to the cottage on Saturday nights and sew with the extra materials that she had left over from the dresses. Working together, they made clothes for the poor. Darcy was pretty sure a few of the older single ladies came to see her father as well as help the poor. But she didn't blame them. He was charming and sweet and everything she'd ever wanted in a father. She could never regret the decision to settle in Willow Trace and become part of his life—especially when it had brought her so many ongoing rewards in her faith and in fellowship with her community.

And all of this had led her to today. Today was a very

special day for Darcy. Today was the day she would be baptized in the Amish faith and she would take her vows, just like her father. Everyone would be there— Jesse, Nana, Thomas, Abigail, Blake, Hannah and Elijah. She was shaking both from nerves and from the overflow of joy in her heart. She had baked three apple pies, as there would be a large supper after the service.

Jesse was out hitching his mare to the buggy. She just needed to load up the pies. She saw Jesse through the kitchen window out in the field calling in the horse. Every horse reminded her of that star-filled night with Thomas on the back of the gray plow horse. She'd thought then that Thomas had romantic feelings for her. But since she'd moved to Willow Trace, Thomas had been nothing but a good neighbor.

He was around at Sunday church, barn raisings and the rebuilding of Jesse's cottage. But she probably spent more time with Nana than Thomas. Nana invited Jesse and her regularly to lunch at Nolt cottage and occasionally brought them jars of jam as an excuse to come over and chat. But not Thomas.

Thomas had been different since her decision to stay in Willow Trace. Kind as always. Helpful. But he'd never tried to kiss her again. He'd never asked her to dinner or to go on a buggy ride. She'd once asked Hannah and Abigail if he had another girlfriend. They'd laughed at her and called her silly. But she wondered sometimes, now that she loved Thomas so dearly, did he love her back? Did he ever love her as more than a friend? She had thought so once, but now she was no longer sure.

She dreamed of the one kiss they'd shared. It seemed so long ago. She longed to be in his arms again, but after today, she had vowed to herself, she would move on and stop thinking of him in that way. It wasn't healthy. Anyway, starting today, she would truly become Amish. She could court and she could marry. And if Thomas wasn't the one for her, then God might have someone else, and if not, she was okay with just being Darcy, the Amish seamstress, and living out her life with her father.

Darcy scooped the three pies onto a tray and carried them out to the buggy. Quite a change from her zippy old red sports car. Cars and department stores seemed like a distant memory to her. Sometimes when her friends from work would visit, she would feel a bit nostalgic for her past. But deep down, she knew to have the peace she felt now, she would make this decision a million times over. God had called her to where she was and she was glad to be there. It wasn't for Thomas and it wasn't for Jesse. She did this for God.

Today was about a love that she'd never known before—a love her father had brought to her by getting her to Willow Trace. It was all part of God's design.

Darcy looked across into the north paddock, as she headed toward the buggy. She saw Thomas's horse, King, there in the paddock. Why? Thomas only used King for his own riding when he wasn't using a buggy. And Thomas should have been hitching up his own buggy right that minute to come to her baptism. Did this mean he was not coming? She pushed back a sad feeling of disappointment and hurried on to her buggy.

"A big day for you." Thomas's voice sounded behind her and her heart nearly leaped from her chest.

She stopped and turned around, almost dropping the tray of pies. "Oh, Thomas. You scared me half to death. What are you doing here?"

"Let me help you with those." He reached down and swept the tray from her hands. Their fingers brushed against one another and she hated herself for noticing and liking the way it felt.

"Thanks. I was just taking them to the buggy."

"You should bring a change of clothes, too. Miller's pond is pretty cold. That's where the all the baptisms take place. I was baptized there myself." He took the pies to the buggy and said hello to Jesse, who excused himself into the house. Darcy didn't know which one of them to follow. She chose Thomas.

"You came all the way here to tell me that? Are you not going?"

He walked back to her. His smile was erased from his face, which gave Darcy the strangest, most awful feeling in her gut. And that's when she noticed.

"You shaved. I thought you weren't supposed to shave after you got married. What in the world? That's downright scandalous!"

"You're right. No one shaves after being married." He stopped right in front of her, looking more serious than she liked. He reached up and ran a hand over his smooth chin. It made him look five years younger. But as strange as the beard had seemed to her at first, he now looked silly without it. She could not possibly imagine what would cause him to do something so drastic.

Then a thought came into her head, making her nauseous. He was leaving. Thomas was leaving the Ordnung. Why else would he do such a thing?

"Thomas, what have you done?" She was almost in tears.

Looking confused by her reaction, he tilted his head

to the side. "I shaved my beard. I thought you hated my beard?"

"Well, I—I guess I got used to it. Has Nana seen you? What are you trying to do? Put her in her grave?"

Thomas smiled again. "Darcy, slow down. Listen to me. I'm trying to tell you why."

She couldn't breathe. This was it. He was leaving. Why? What had made him decide to do such a thing? She couldn't look at him.

"So, I think you've noticed that I haven't come around much since…well, in months."

She covered her face with her hands to her forehead. Why was he doing this today of all days?

"Well, maybe you did not notice." He shrugged. "But I stayed away because I was waiting to say something to you."

No. No. She didn't want him to tell her that he was leaving. Not today. Not any day. He couldn't leave. She loved him. And she just realized at that moment how very much. She turned away, head down, her hands twisting nervously in front of her.

"Darcy, I can't do this if you turn away. Will you look at me, please?" He reach down and stilled her hands. She turned toward him and lifted her eyes. He smiled down at her and held on tighter to her hands.

"There. That's better."

"I still can't believe you shaved your beard."

"Well…I did it for you. For us. For next month. Did you see how much celery Nana has planted?"

"Celery?" She was about to have a nervous breakdown over his announcement and he was talking about how much celery Nana had planted?

He leaned down and touched his lips to hers. So soft.

So sweet. He tasted like apples, just like he had after the fire. He lifted their hands, and then untangled them so that he could touch her face and draw her closer.

"Yes, celery," he whispered, drawing her body into his. "Everyone plants celery when someone in the family is getting married." He kissed her again. "Well, usually it's the bride's family, but Nana was just stepping in for you and Jesse."

"Thomas, I have no idea what you're talking about."

He tried to kiss her again, but she pulled her head back. "Thomas, seriously. Stop. What are you talking about? Celery? And weddings? And you still haven't told me why you shaved."

"Ja." He kissed her again. "I'm getting to that part." He cleared his throat. "I shaved because it is time—past time—for me to put my first marriage with Mary behind me. I held on to the beard all these years because I was not ready to be a single man again and risk my heart. But you changed all of that." He got down on one knee before her.

"Miss Darcy Simmons, I love you and have for a very long time—so I'm hoping very much that you will agree to be my wife. What do you say?"

She was crying now and nodding. But mostly crying tears of joy. Tears she didn't know how she could ever stop. "I love you, too. Yes, Thomas, yes. Of course, I will marry you."

"Good." He stood, and kissed her again, hard and long, until they were both breathless. "God forgive me, I have wanted to do that since the minute I saw you with your little purse standing on that porch over there."

"Why didn't you?"

"Because I wanted to do it for the rest of my life and

at the time, that didn't seem possible. Once you made the decision to come here and live with your father, I could hardly hold myself back... But you still had to decide whether or not to be baptized, and I thought that a lifetime with you might be worth waiting for." He kissed her again. "You don't know how hard it has been staying away from you."

"Please don't ever do it again." She laughed.

"I won't. That I can promise you. And I'll grow my beard back. But this beard is for you. For us."

"Sounds perfect." She put her hands on each of his bare cheeks. "So, now tell me, when were you planning for us to eat all of this celery that Nana has grown?"

He smiled and picked her up into his arms, holding her close. "Well, you tell me... How fast can you make a wedding dress?"

"Pretty fast, Mr. Nolt. Pretty fast."

"*Gutt*. I was counting on that."

* * * * *

If you enjoyed this story, don't miss Kit Wilkinson's other stories of danger and love in Amish country

PLAIN SECRETS
DANGER IN AMISH COUNTRY
"RETURN TO WILLOW TRACE"
LANCASTER COUNTY TARGET

Find these and other great reads
at www.LoveInspired.com

WE HOPE YOU ENJOYED THESE

LOVE INSPIRED®

AND

LOVE INSPIRED® SUSPENSE BOOKS.

Whether you prefer heartwarming contemporary romance or heart-pounding suspense, Love Inspired® books has it all!

Look for 6 new titles available every month from both Love Inspired® and Love Inspired® Suspense.

Love Inspired®

www.LoveInspired.com